WILLIAM SHAKESPEARE

TWELFTH NIGHT

The complete play illustrated by John H. Howard

Published by the Can of Worms Press

cartoon *Shakespeare*

TWELFTH NIGHT
Published by Can of Worms Press 2005

Can of Worms Enterprises Ltd
1 Sutherland Walk
London SE17 3EF, UK

Tel: +44 (0)207 708 2942
Email: info@canofwormspress.co.uk
Website: www.canofwormspress.co.uk
        www.cartoonshakespeare.com

ISBN: 1-904104-09-6
Copyright © Oval Projects Ltd 1985
Copyright © Can of Worms Enterprises Ltd 2005

British Library Cataloguing in Publication Data
A catalogue record for this book is available from the British
Library.

Edited by David Gibson
Lettering by Steve Craddock and June Sinclair
Cover design by Alison Eddy on behalf of
Can of Worms Design Group

Printed and bound in Hong Kong and Great Britain

THE STORY

Count **Orsino,** the ruler of an imaginary country called Illyria, is madly in love with the Countess **Olivia.** But Olivia is in mourning for her brother and will have nothing to do with Orsino. Olivia has to put up with **Sir Toby Belch,** her uncle, and **Feste,** the court jester she inherited from her father. Sir Toby is busy encouraging his wealthy friend **Sir Andrew Aguecheek** to court Olivia. Sir Toby and Sir Andrew spend a good deal of time getting drunk together with Sir Andrew paying for the drinks.

Into this story comes **Viola.** She has been washed up on the shores of Illyria after a shipwreck. She believes her identical twin brother, **Sebastian,** has been drowned. Viola decides to dress up as a boy and enter the service of Orsino. She takes the name Cesario, and becomes Orsino's page. The Count is very taken with the new 'boy' and sends Cesario to woo Olivia on his behalf. The plan backfires when Olivia falls for Cesario.

Malvolio, who runs Olivia's household, disapproves of Sir Toby, Sir Andrew, and **Maria,** Olivia's maid. To get their own back they arrange for Malvolio to think that Olivia is in love with him. While strolling in the garden Malvolio finds a letter, apparently from Olivia, but in fact forged by Maria. He carefully follows the weird instructions given in the letter. Olivia finds Malvolio's behaviour so strange that she believes he is mad and asks Sir Toby to look after him. Instead Sir Toby and the others lock up Malvolio and torment him.

Sir Andrew discovers Olivia's passion for Cesario, and announces he is going to give up all hope of her. Sir Toby and **Fabian** convince him she is only flirting with Cesario to make him jealous. They incite him to challenge Cesario to a duel. Neither Sir Andrew nor Viola, as Cesario, are keen to fight and try hard to avoid each other.

In the meantime, the lost twin, **Sebastian,** has turned up in Illyria. He is convinced that Viola was lost in the shipwreck. With him is **Antonio,** the ship's captain who rescued him. Sebastian wants to go sight-seeing but Antonio, who is a wanted man in Illyria, has to keep out of the way. They part having agreed to meet later at their hotel. Antonio then bumps into Viola. Mistaking her for Sebastian he saves her from the fight with Sir Andrew. But he is recognised by the police and arrested.

Sebastian runs into Sir Toby and Sir Andrew. They mistake him for Cesario and try to pick a fight with him. Olivia interrupts them, and assuming Sebastian to be Cesario, she invites him home. Never having seen this woman in his life, Sebastian is surprised, but accepts anyway. They are later secretly married.

Orsino has grown tired of the lack of progress he is making with Olivia and arrives at her mansion with his entourage, including Viola. Olivia reveals to Orsino that she and Cesario are married. Viola, as Cesario, denies it. Sir Toby and Sir Andrew appear, wounded from another fight with Sebastian. Sebastian himself joins the assembled company and comes face to face with Viola. The identity puzzle is solved.

Olivia is not at all put out at having married the wrong person, and Orsino quickly accepts that Cesario is in fact Viola, and proposes to her. Sir Toby and Maria, flushed with the success of having made a fool of Malvolio, have also wed. Malvolio is finally released. He is told about the joke that has been played on him and is not amused.

Everybody goes off to celebrate their good fortune, except Malvolio who is left out in the cold. Feste, also alone, laments in a song how silly everything and everyone is.

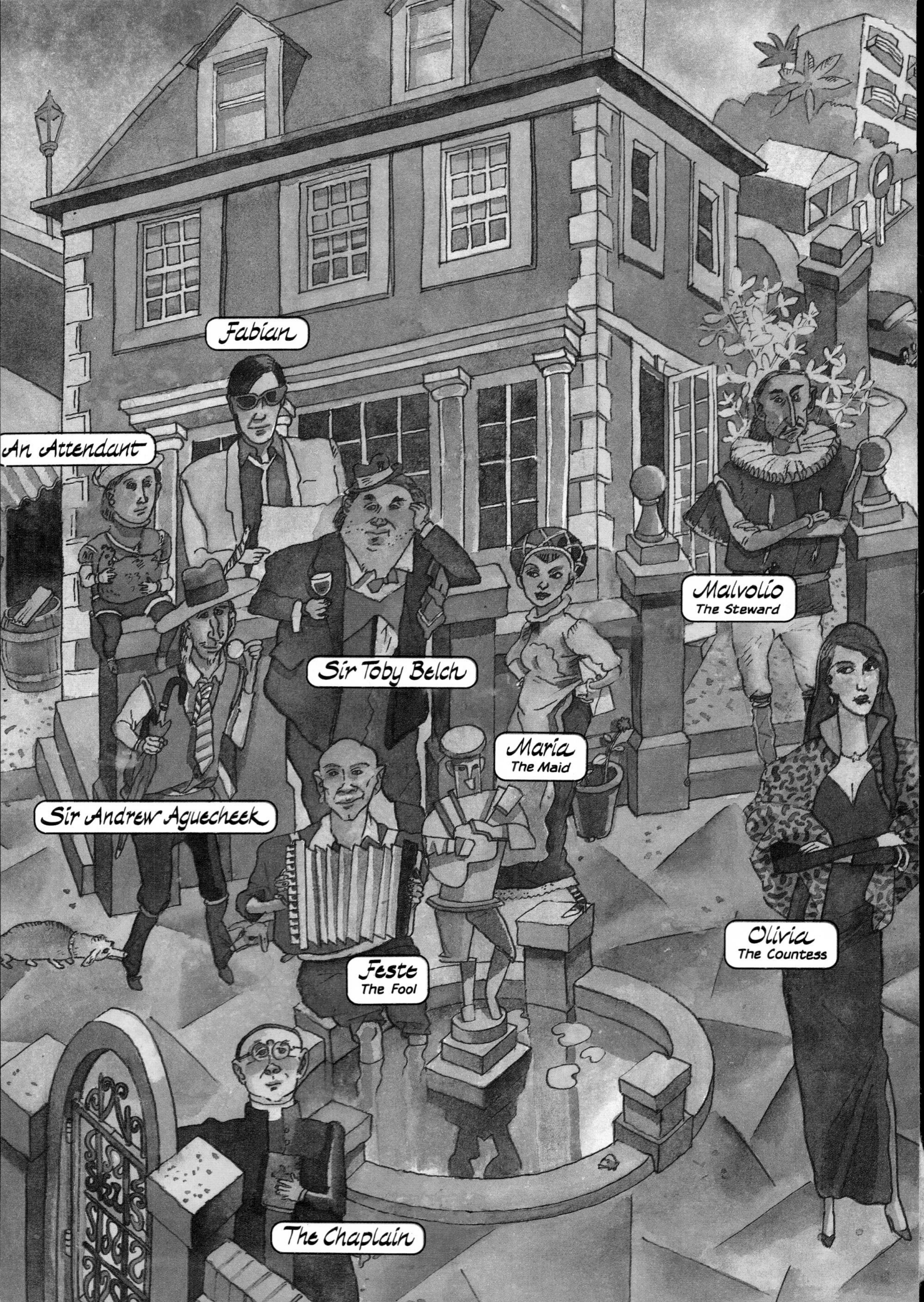
Fabian
An Attendant
Malvolio
The Steward
Sir Toby Belch
Maria
The Maid
Sir Andrew Aguecheek
Olivia
The Countess
Feste
The Fool
The Chaplain

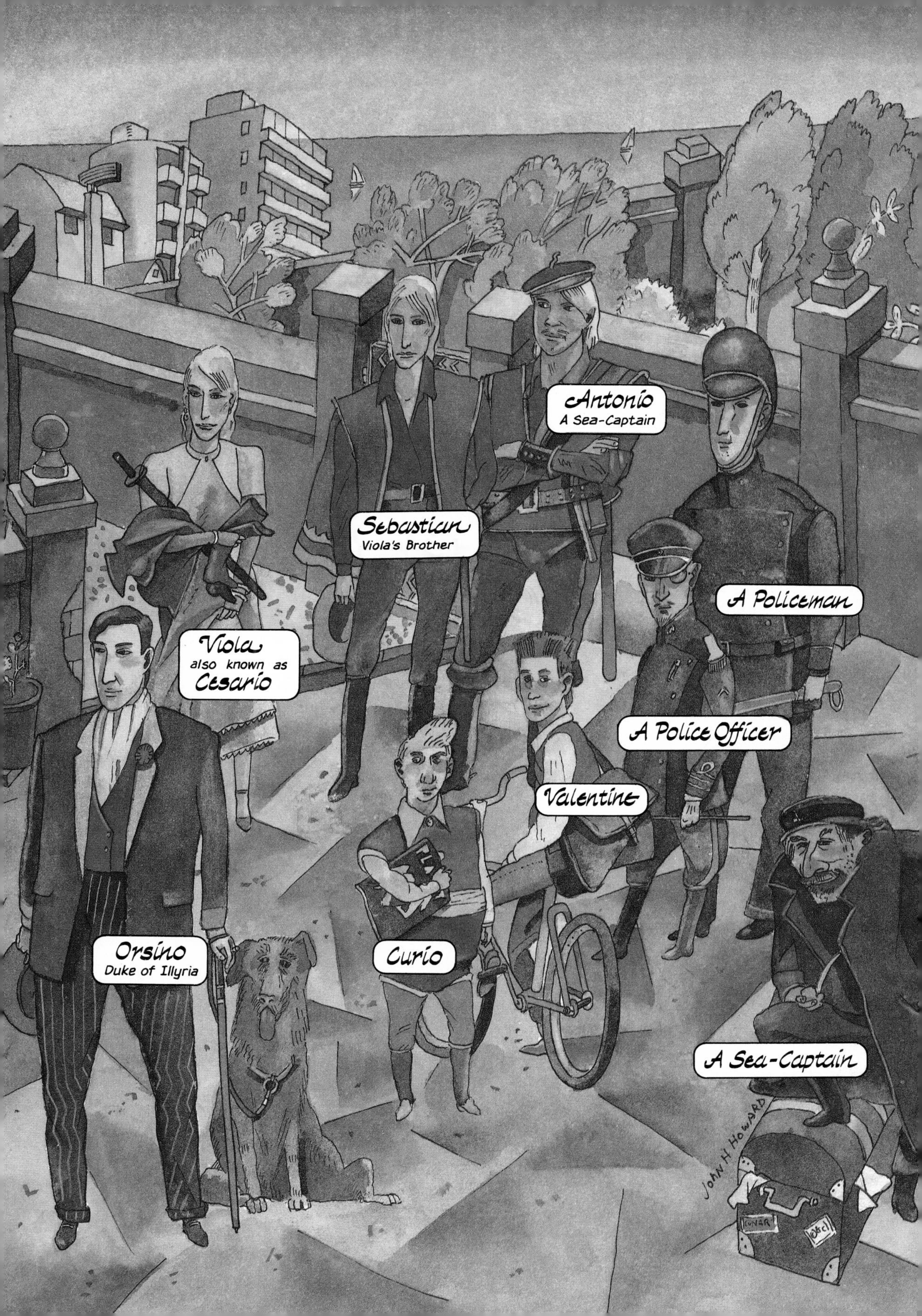
Antonio
A Sea-Captain
Sebastian
Viola's Brother
A Policeman
Viola
also known as
Cesario
A Police Officer
Valentine
Orsino
Duke of Illyria
Curio
A Sea-Captain
JOHN H HOWARD

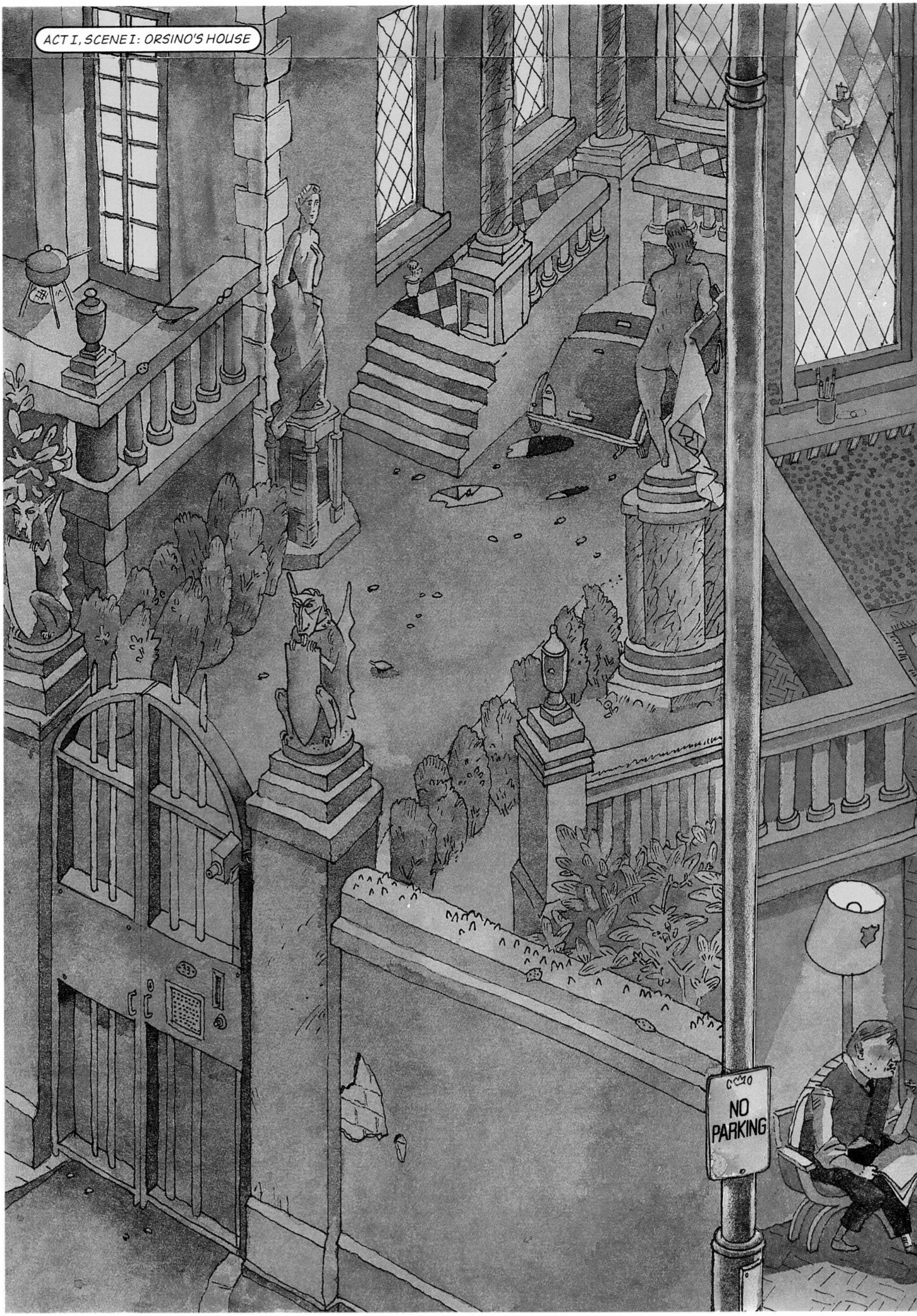
ACT I, SCENE I: ORSINO'S HOUSE
NO PARKING

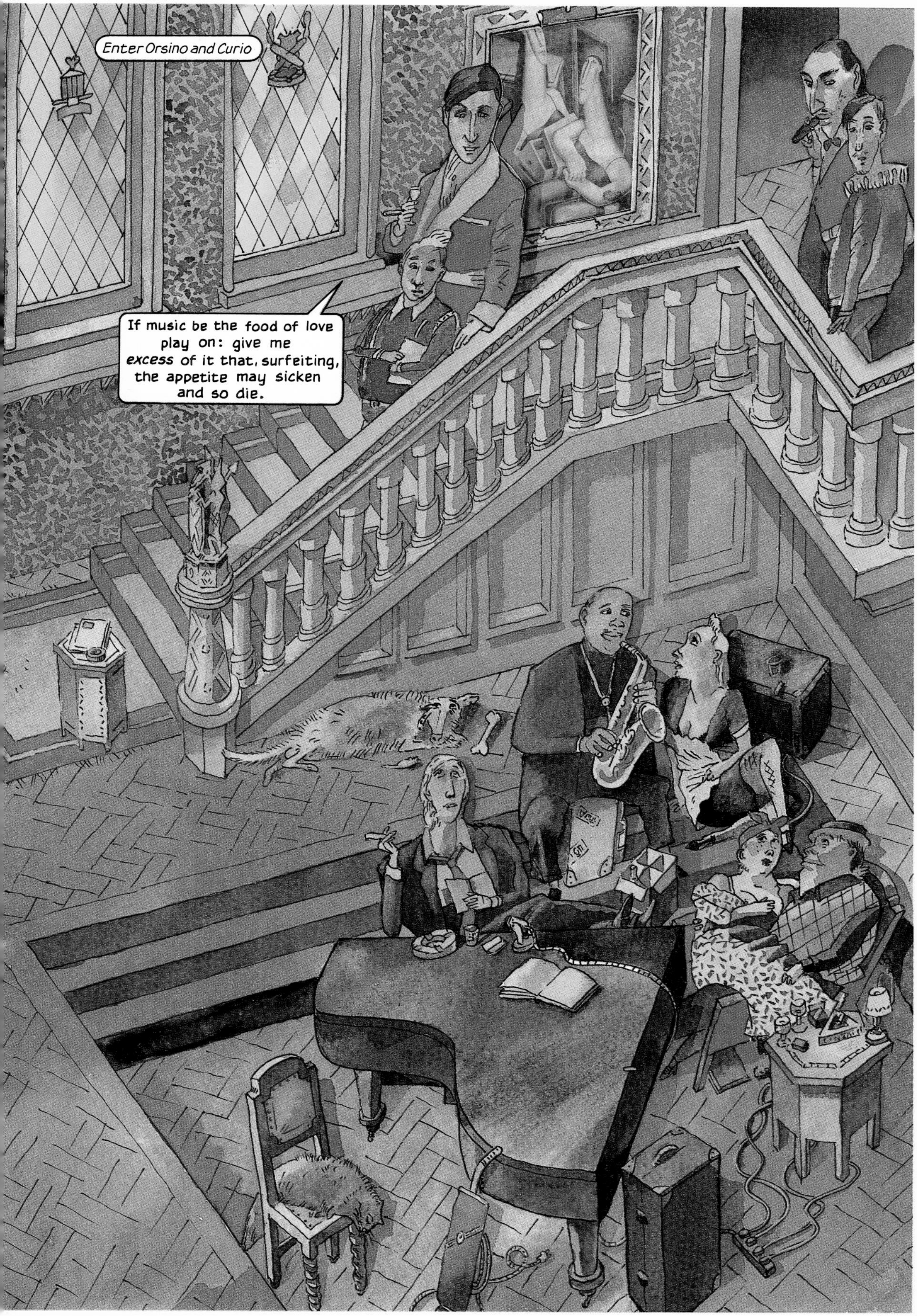
Enter Orsino and Curio
If music be the food of love play on: give me *excess* of it that, surfeiting, the appetite may sicken and so die.

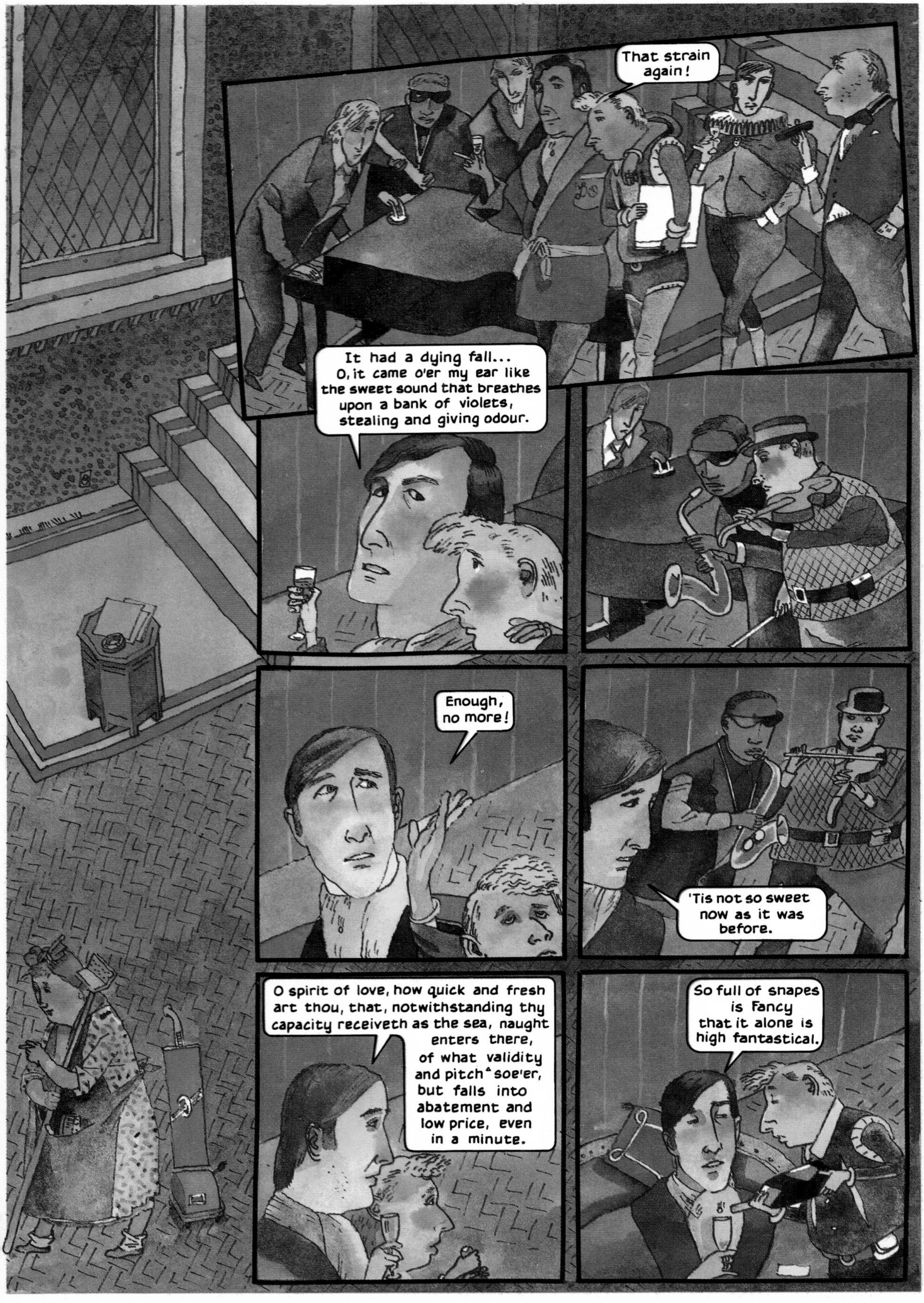
That strain again!
It had a dying fall... O, it came o'er my ear like the sweet sound that breathes upon a bank of violets, stealing and giving odour.
Enough, no more!
'Tis not so sweet now as it was before.
O spirit of love, how quick and fresh art thou, that, notwithstanding thy capacity receiveth as the sea, naught enters there, of what validity and pitch[a] soe'er, but falls into abatement and low price, even in a minute.
So full of snapes is Fancy that it alone is high fantastical.

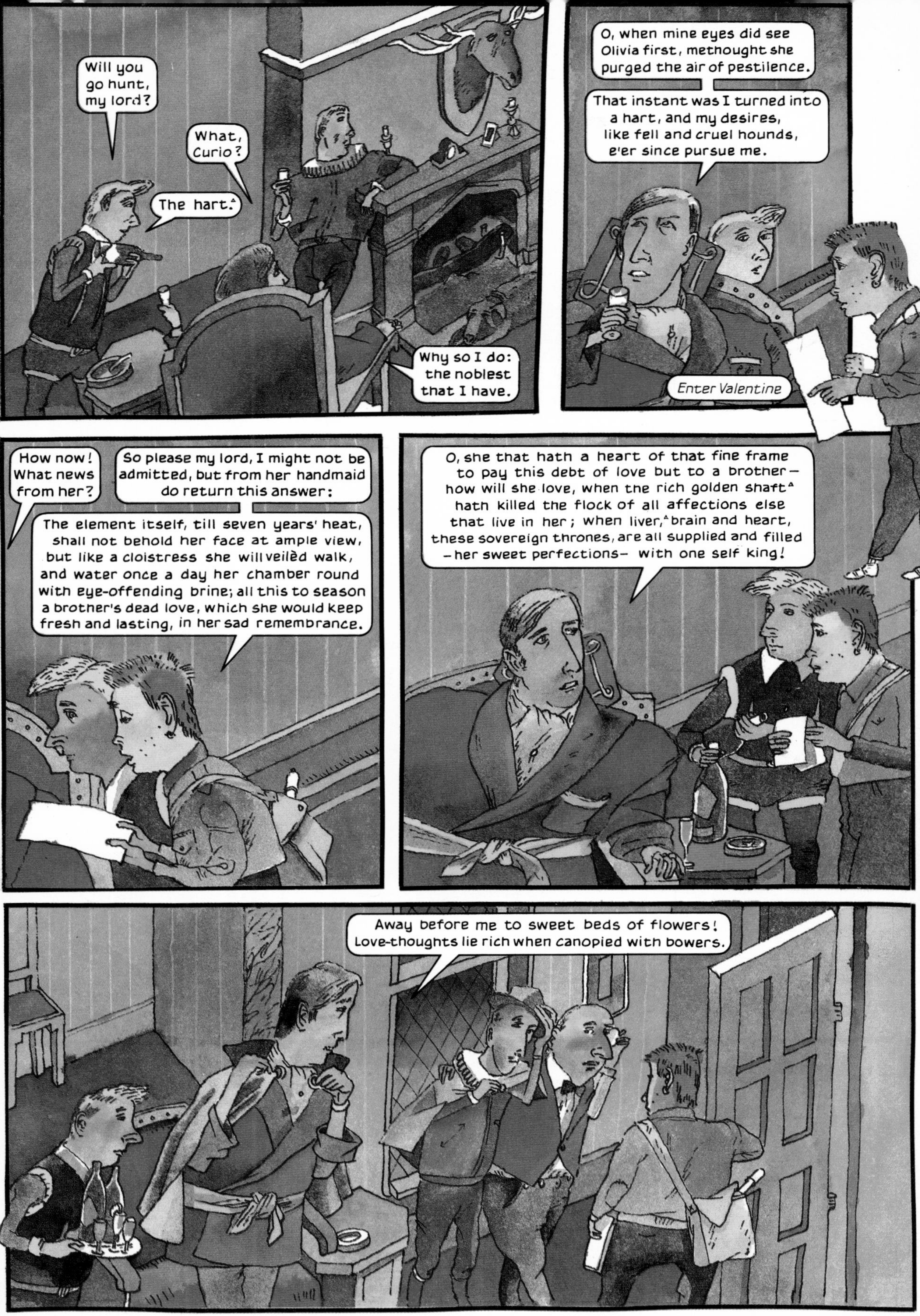

Will you go hunt, my lord?
What, Curio?
The hart.^
Why so I do: the noblest that I have.
O, when mine eyes did see Olivia first, methought she purged the air of pestilence.
That instant was I turned into a hart, and my desires, like fell and cruel hounds, e'er since pursue me.
Enter Valentine
How now! What news from her?
So please my lord, I might not be admitted, but from her handmaid do return this answer:
The element itself, till seven years' heat, shall not behold her face at ample view, but like a cloistress she will veilèd walk, and water once a day her chamber round with eye-offending brine; all this to season a brother's dead love, which she would keep fresh and lasting, in her sad remembrance.
O, she that hath a heart of that fine frame to pay this debt of love but to a brother — how will she love, when the rich golden shaft^ hath killed the flock of all affections else that live in her; when liver,^ brain and heart, these sovereign thrones, are all supplied and filled — her sweet perfections — with one self king!
Away before me to sweet beds of flowers! Love-thoughts lie rich when canopied with bowers.

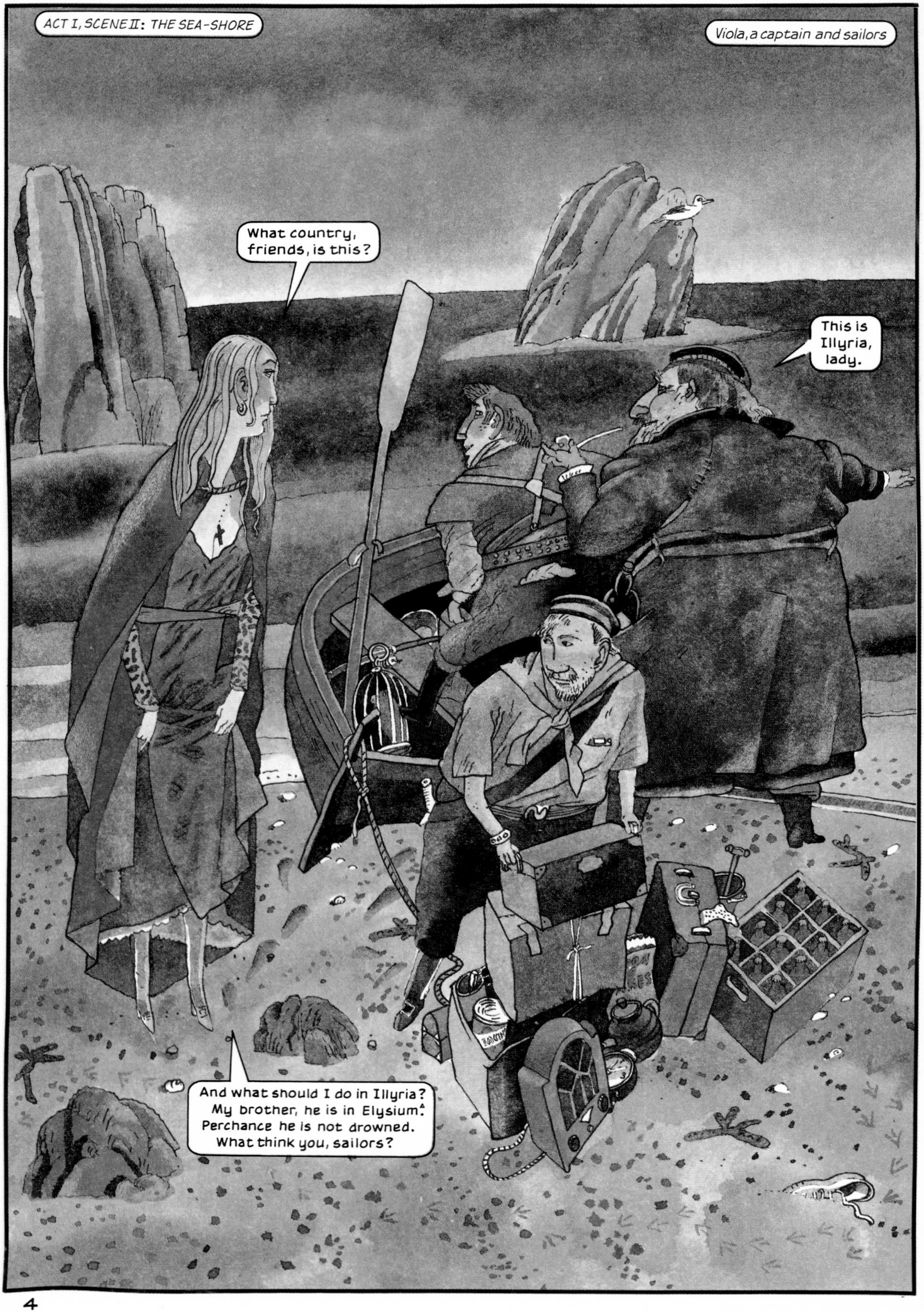

ACT I, SCENE II: THE SEA-SHORE
Viola, a captain and sailors
What country, friends, is this?
This is Illyria, lady.
And what should I do in Illyria? My brother, he is in Elysium. Perchance he is not drowned. What think you, sailors?

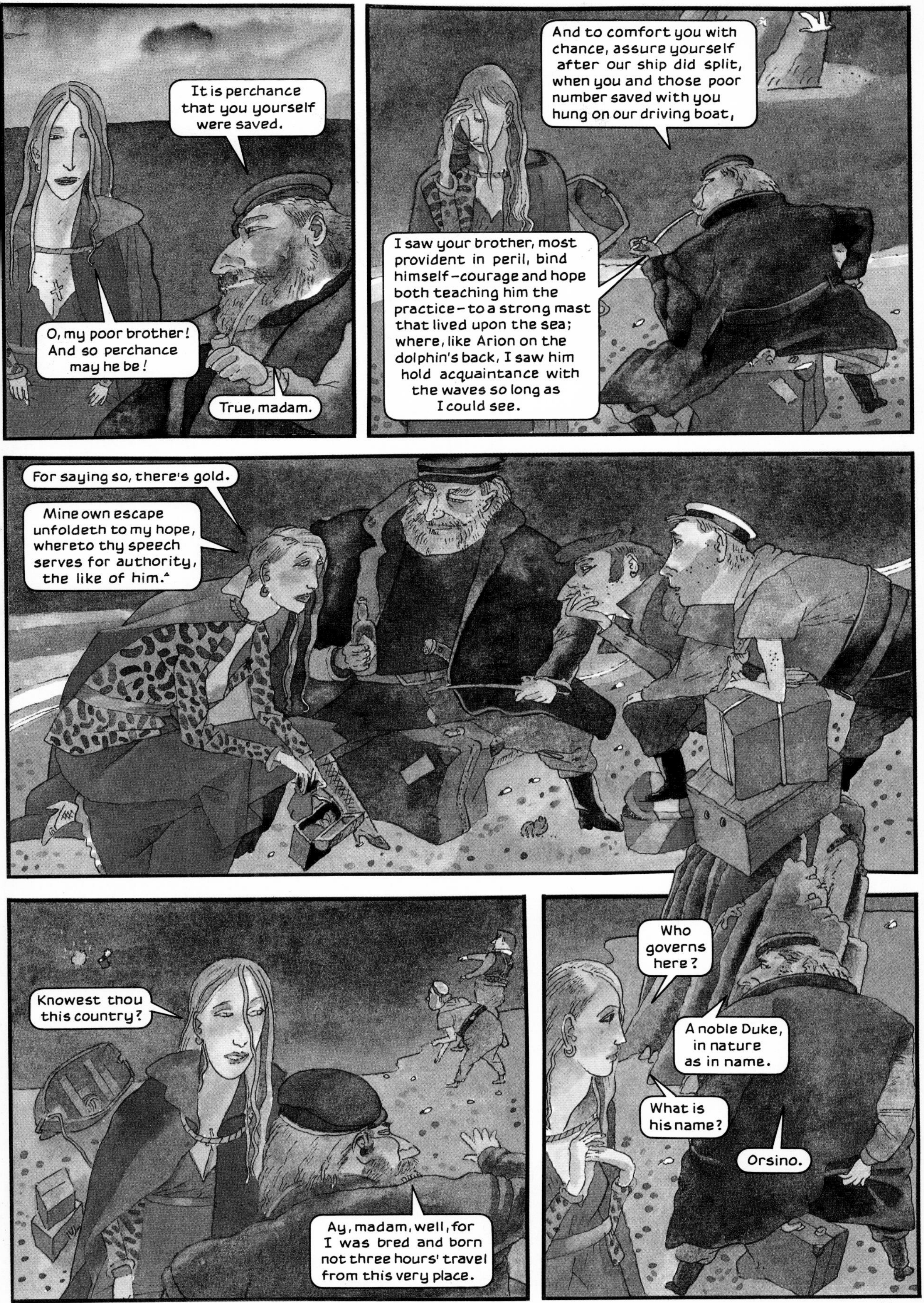

It is perchance that you yourself were saved.
O, my poor brother! And so perchance may he be!
True, madam.
And to comfort you with chance, assure yourself after our ship did split, when you and those poor number saved with you hung on our driving boat,
I saw your brother, most provident in peril, bind himself–courage and hope both teaching him the practice–to a strong mast that lived upon the sea; where, like Arion on the dolphin's back, I saw him hold acquaintance with the waves so long as I could see.
For saying so, there's gold.
Mine own escape unfoldeth to my hope, whereto thy speech serves for authority, the like of him.
Knowest thou this country?
Ay, madam, well, for I was bred and born not three hours' travel from this very place.
Who governs here?
A noble Duke, in nature as in name.
What is his name?
Orsino.

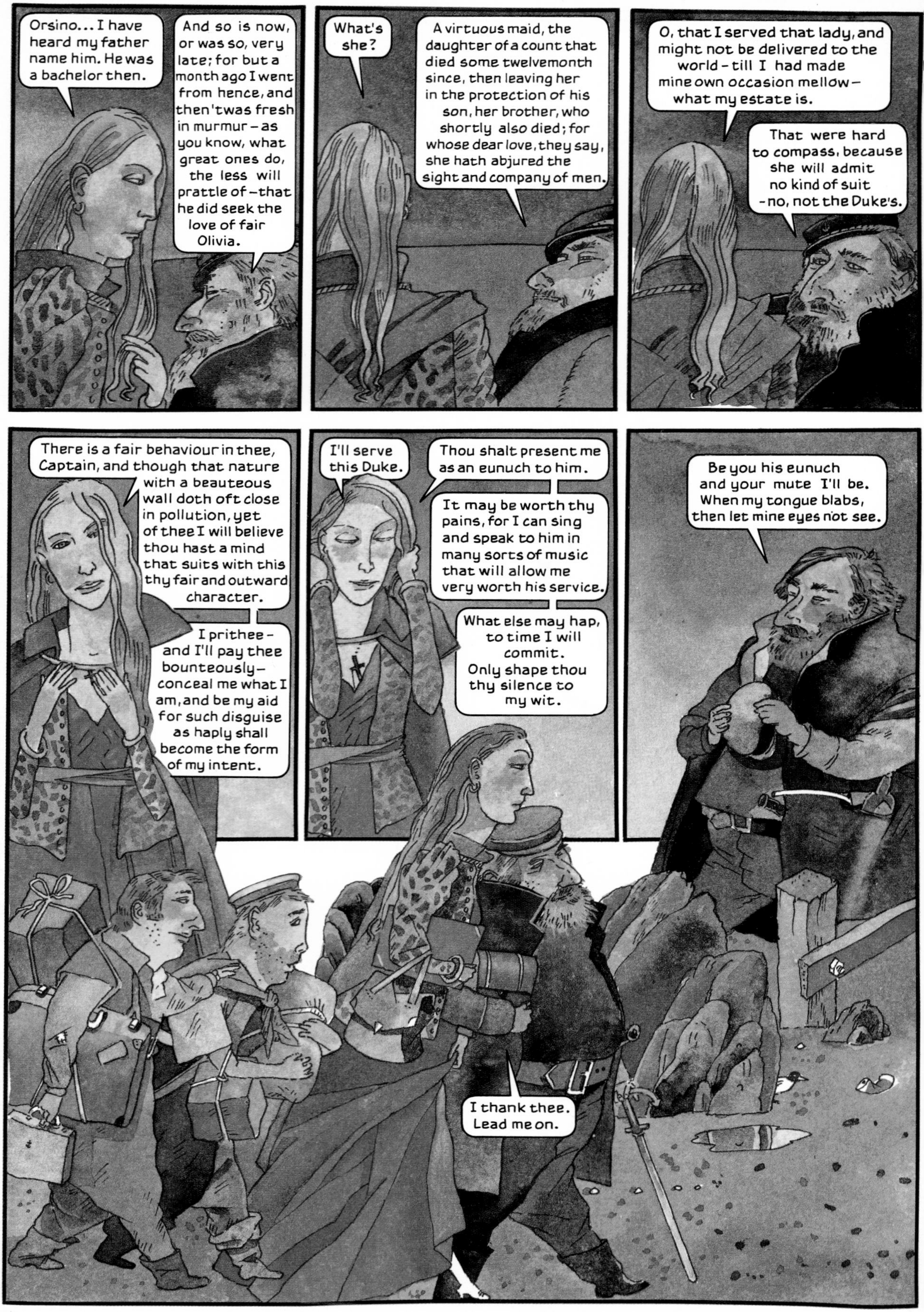

Orsino... I have heard my father name him. He was a bachelor then.
And so is now, or was so, very late; for but a month ago I went from hence, and then'twas fresh in murmur – as you know, what great ones do, the less will prattle of – that he did seek the love of fair Olivia.
What's she?
A virtuous maid, the daughter of a count that died some twelvemonth since, then leaving her in the protection of his son, her brother, who shortly also died; for whose dear love, they say, she hath abjured the sight and company of men.
O, that I served that lady, and might not be delivered to the world – till I had made mine own occasion mellow – what my estate is.
That were hard to compass, because she will admit no kind of suit – no, not the Duke's.
There is a fair behaviour in thee, Captain, and though that nature with a beauteous wall doth oft close in pollution, yet of thee I will believe thou hast a mind that suits with this thy fair and outward character.
I prithee – and I'll pay thee bounteously – conceal me what I am, and be my aid for such disguise as haply shall become the form of my intent.
I'll serve this Duke.
Thou shalt present me as an eunuch to him.
It may be worth thy pains, for I can sing and speak to him in many sorts of music that will allow me very worth his service.
What else may hap, to time I will commit.
Only shape thou thy silence to my wit.
Be you his eunuch and your mute I'll be.
When my tongue blabs, then let mine eyes not see.
I thank thee.
Lead me on.

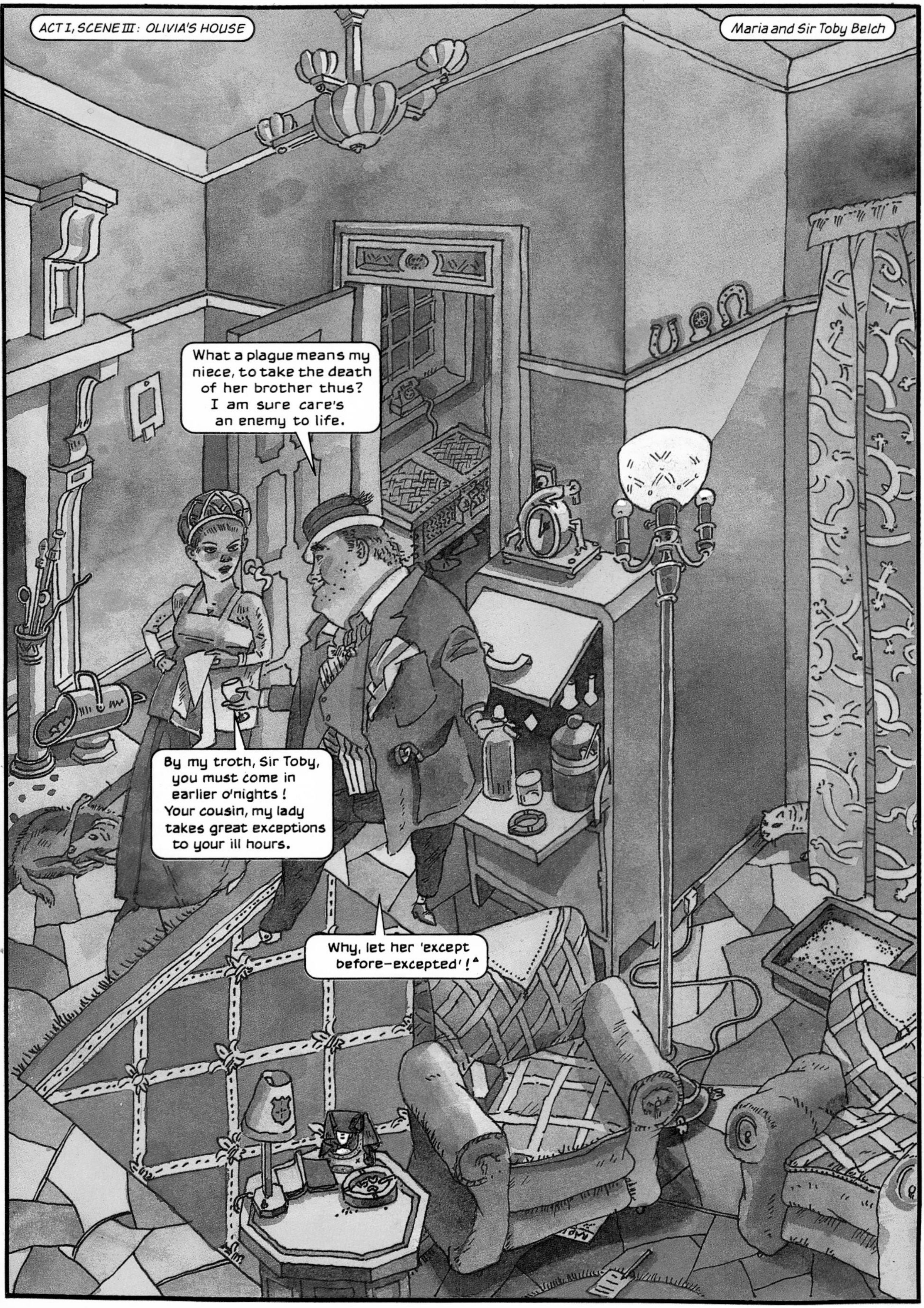
ACT I, SCENE III: OLIVIA'S HOUSE
Maria and Sir Toby Belch
What a plague means my niece, to take the death of her brother thus? I am sure care's an enemy to life.
By my troth, Sir Toby, you must come in earlier o'nights! Your cousin, my lady takes great exceptions to your ill hours.
Why, let her 'except before-excepted'!▲

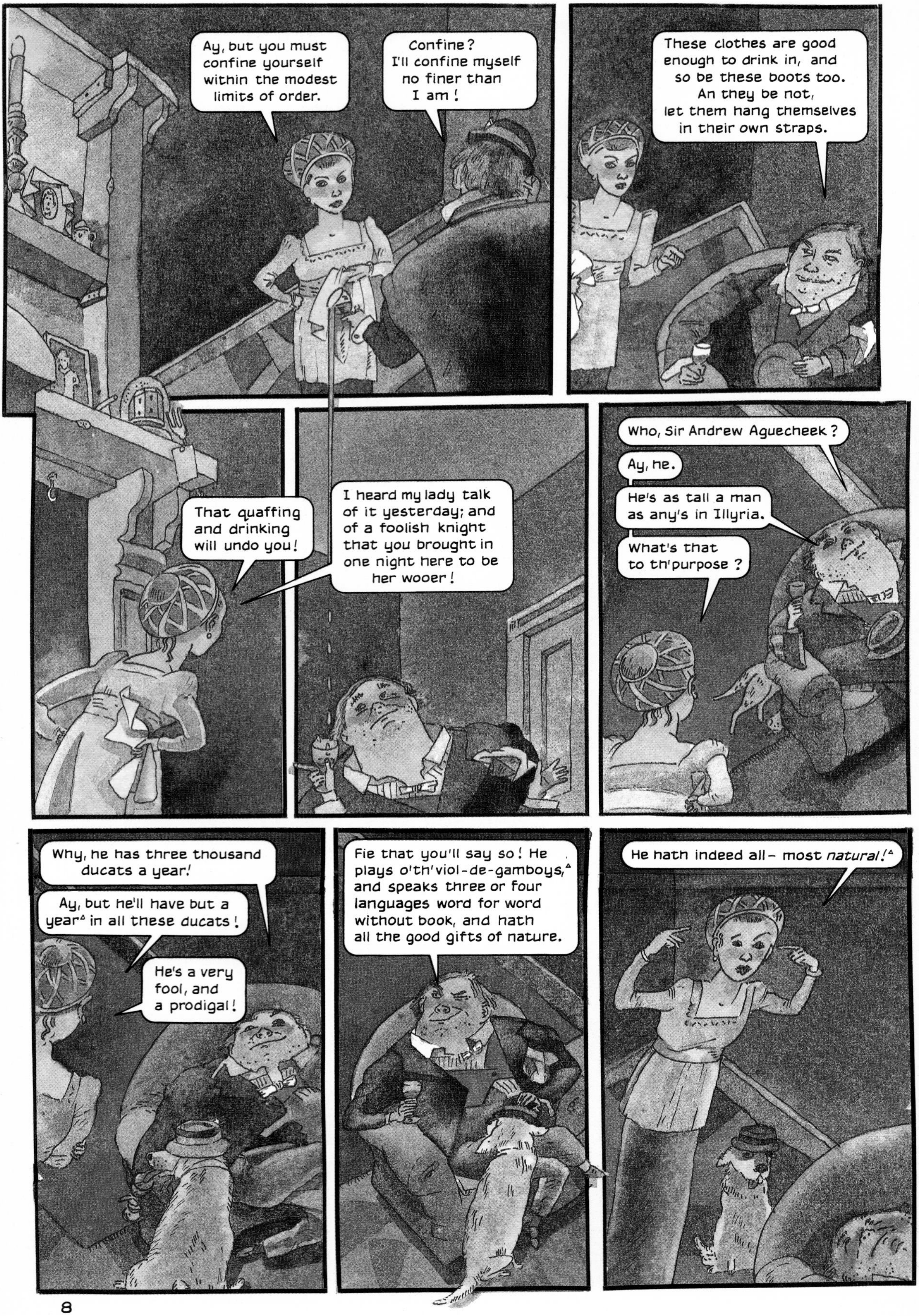

Ay, but you must confine yourself within the modest limits of order.
Confine? I'll confine myself no finer than I am!
These clothes are good enough to drink in, and so be these boots too. An they be not, let them hang themselves in their own straps.
That quaffing and drinking will undo you!
I heard my lady talk of it yesterday; and of a foolish knight that you brought in one night here to be her wooer!
Who, Sir Andrew Aguecheek?
Ay, he.
He's as tall a man as any's in Illyria.
What's that to th'purpose?
Why, he has three thousand ducats a year!
Ay, but he'll have but a year[Δ] in all these ducats!
He's a very fool, and a prodigal!
Fie that you'll say so! He plays o'th'viol-de-gamboys,[Δ] and speaks three or four languages word for word without book, and hath all the good gifts of nature.
He hath indeed all- most *natural*![Δ]

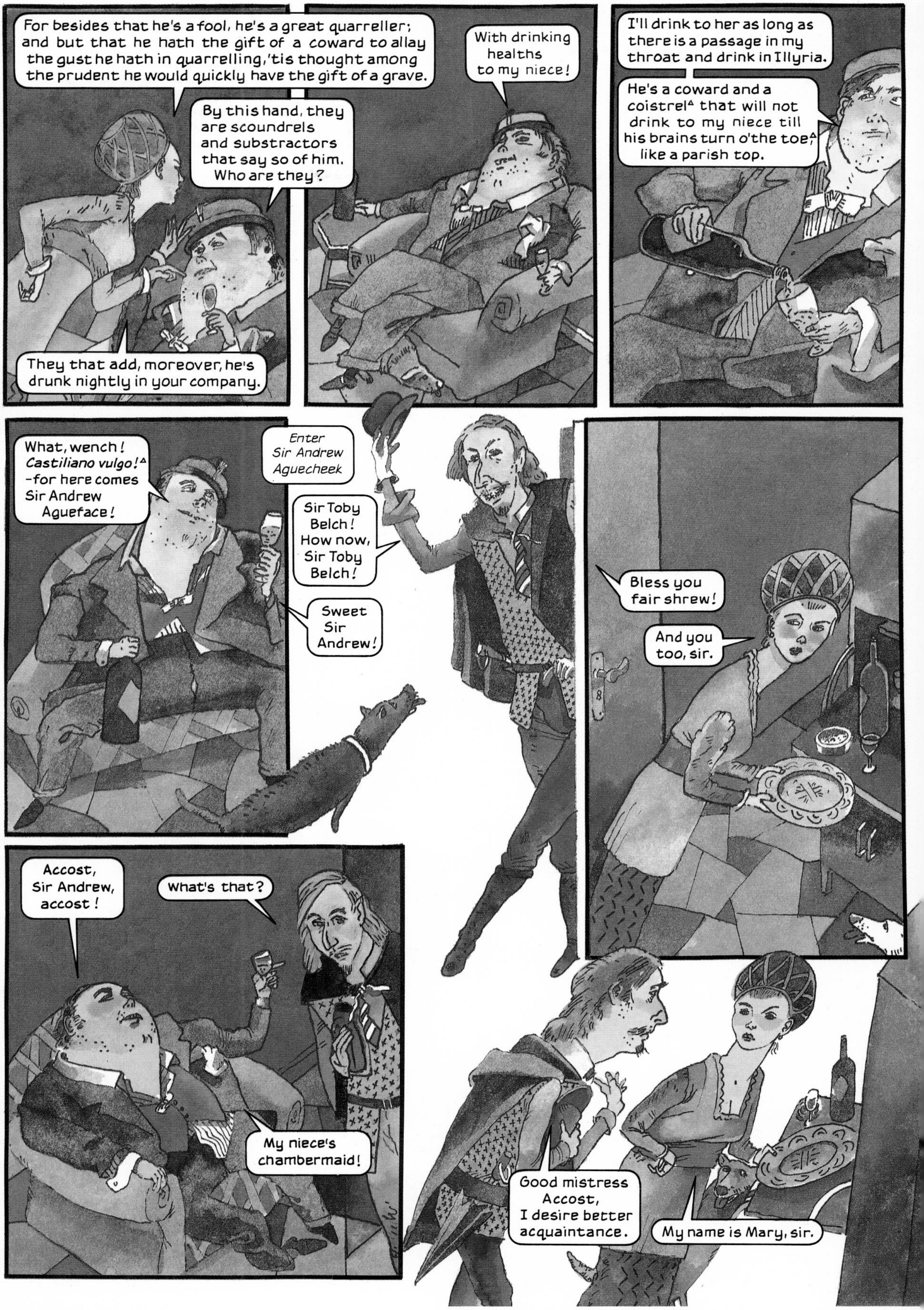

For besides that he's a fool, he's a great quarreller; and but that he hath the gift of a coward to allay the gust he hath in quarrelling, 'tis thought among the prudent he would quickly have the gift of a grave.
By this hand, they are scoundrels and substractors that say so of him. Who are they?
They that add, moreover, he's drunk nightly in your company.
With drinking healths to my niece!
I'll drink to her as long as there is a passage in my throat and drink in Illyria.
He's a coward and a coistrel^ that will not drink to my niece till his brains turn o'the toe,^ like a parish top.
What, wench! Castiliano vulgo!^ -for here comes Sir Andrew Agueface!
Enter Sir Andrew Aguecheek
Sir Toby Belch! How now, Sir Toby Belch!
Sweet Sir Andrew!
Bless you fair shrew!
And you too, sir.
Accost, Sir Andrew, accost!
What's that?
My niece's chambermaid!
Good mistress Accost, I desire better acquaintance.
My name is Mary, sir.

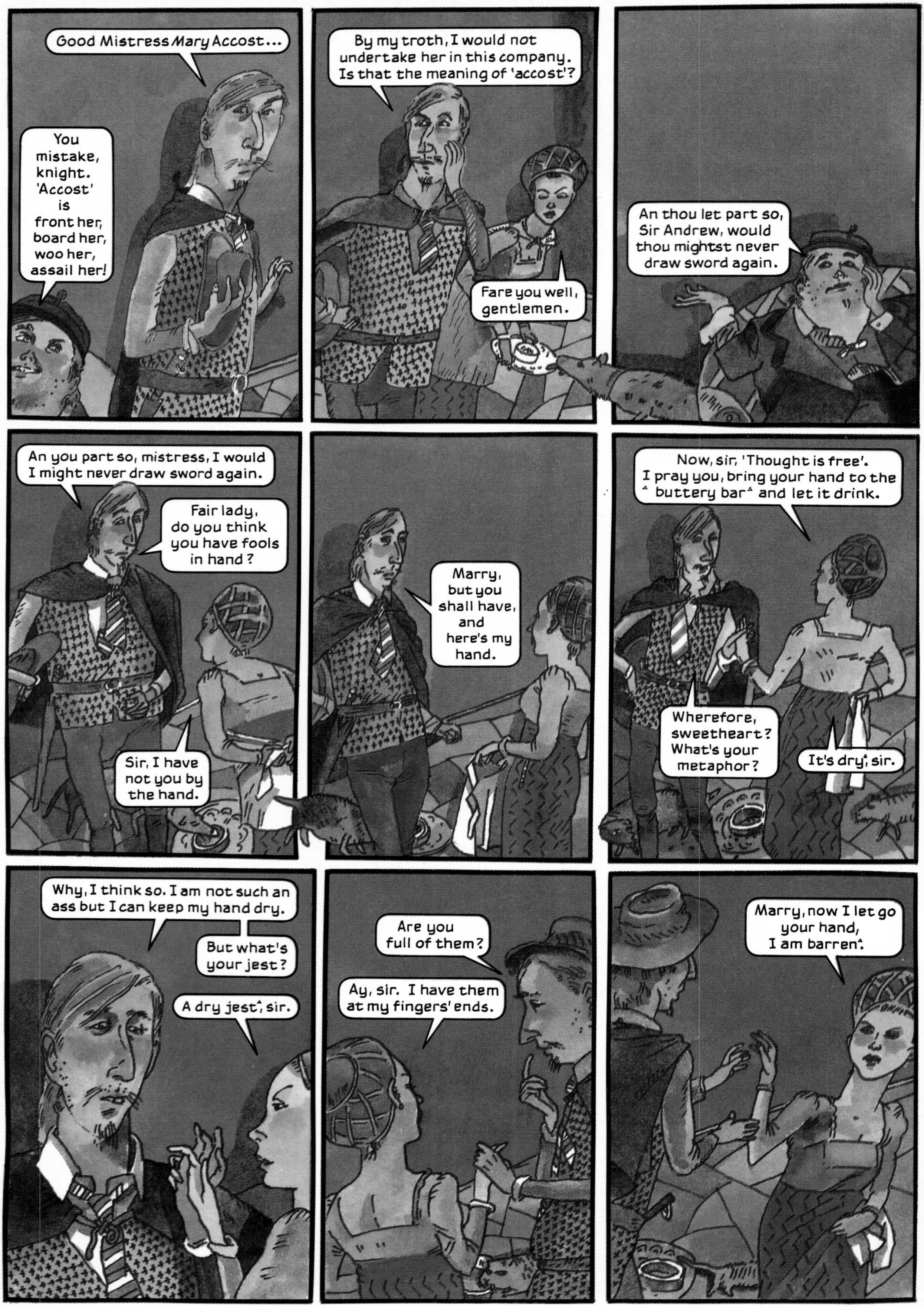

Good Mistress Mary Accost...
You mistake, knight. 'Accost' is front her, board her, woo her, assail her!
By my troth, I would not undertake her in this company. Is that the meaning of 'accost'?
Fare you well, gentlemen.
An thou let part so, Sir Andrew, would thou mightst never draw sword again.
An you part so, mistress, I would I might never draw sword again.
Fair lady, do you think you have fools in hand?
Sir, I have not you by the hand.
Marry, but you shall have, and here's my hand.
Now, sir, 'Thought is free'. I pray you, bring your hand to the buttery bar and let it drink.
Wherefore, sweetheart? What's your metaphor?
It's dry, sir.
Why, I think so. I am not such an ass but I can keep my hand dry.
But what's your jest?
A dry jest, sir.
Are you full of them?
Ay, sir. I have them at my fingers' ends.
Marry, now I let go your hand, I am barren.

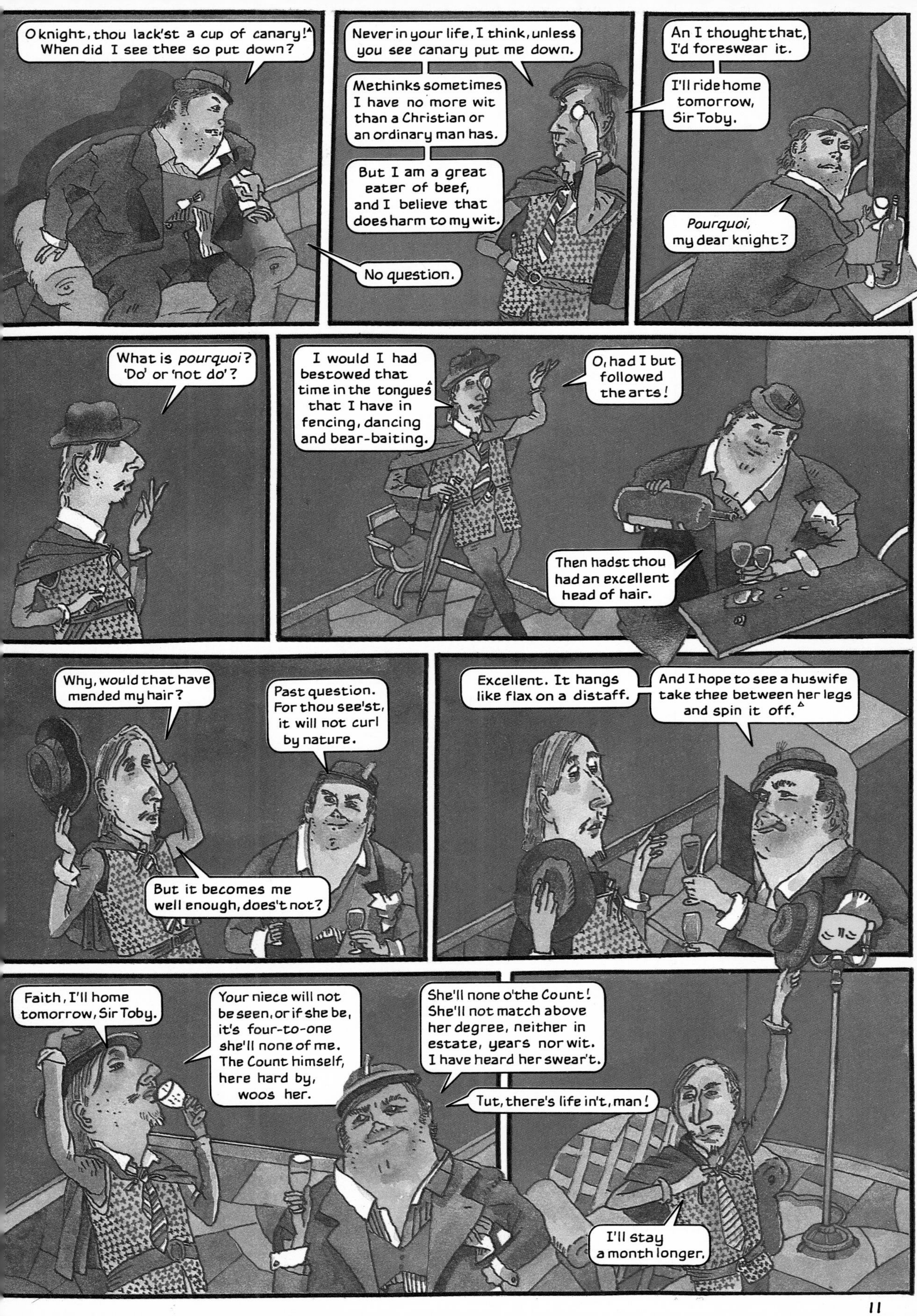

O knight, thou lack'st a cup of canary! When did I see thee so put down?
Never in your life, I think, unless you see canary put me down.
Methinks sometimes I have no more wit than a Christian or an ordinary man has.
But I am a great eater of beef, and I believe that does harm to my wit.
No question.
An I thought that, I'd foreswear it.
I'll ride home tomorrow, Sir Toby.
Pourquoi, my dear knight?
What is *pourquoi*? 'Do' or 'not do'?
I would I had bestowed that time in the tongues that I have in fencing, dancing and bear-baiting.
O, had I but followed the arts!
Then hadst thou had an excellent head of hair.
Why, would that have mended my hair?
Past question. For thou see'st, it will not curl by nature.
But it becomes me well enough, does't not?
Excellent. It hangs like flax on a distaff.
And I hope to see a huswife take thee between her legs and spin it off.
Faith, I'll home tomorrow, Sir Toby.
Your niece will not be seen, or if she be, it's four-to-one she'll none of me. The Count himself, here hard by, woos her.
She'll none o'the Count! She'll not match above her degree, neither in estate, years nor wit. I have heard her swear't.
Tut, there's life in't, man!
I'll stay a month longer.

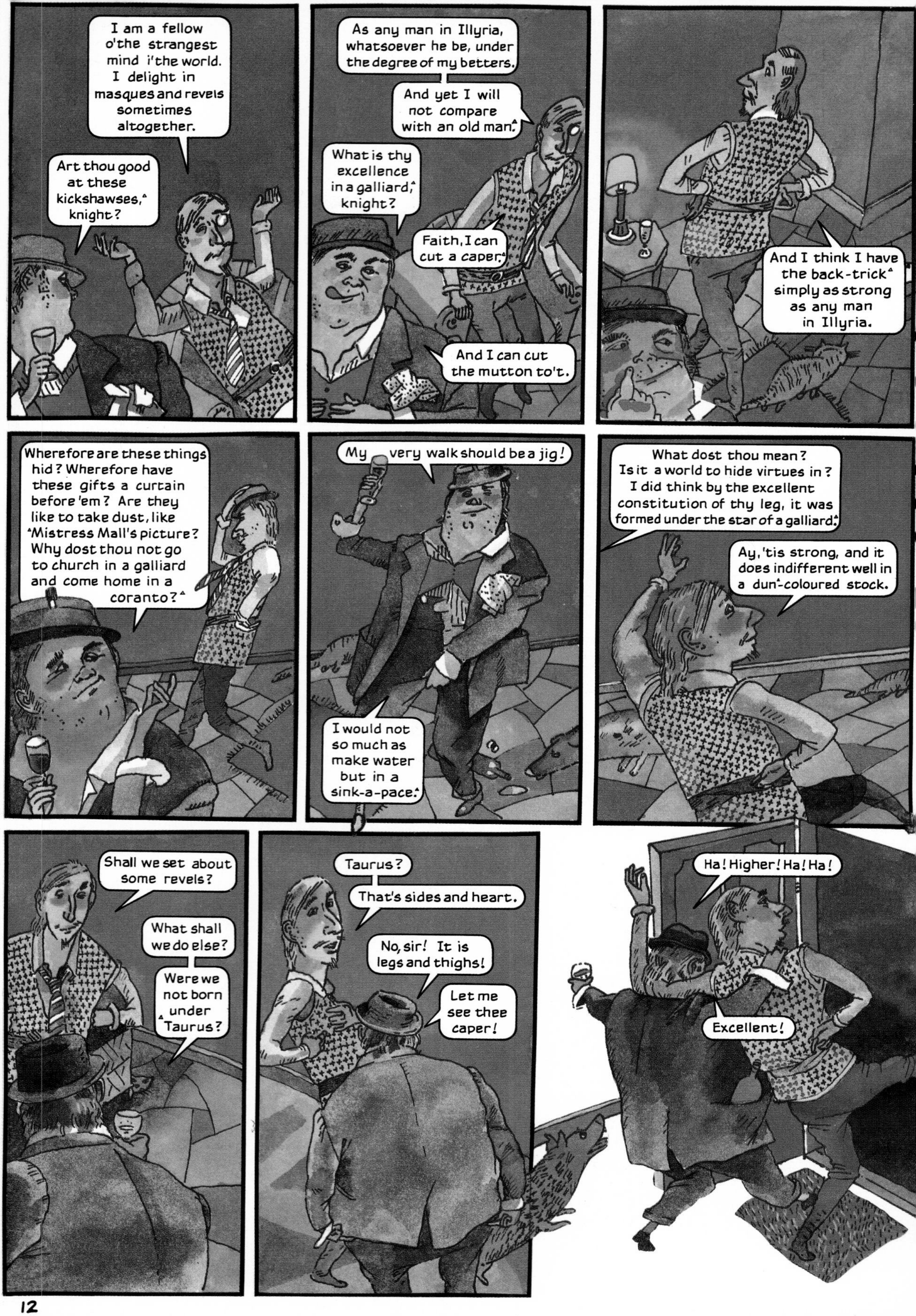

I am a fellow o'the strangest mind i'the world. I delight in masques and revels sometimes altogether.
Art thou good at these kickshawses, knight?
As any man in Illyria, whatsoever he be, under the degree of my betters.
And yet I will not compare with an old man.
What is thy excellence in a galliard, knight?
Faith, I can cut a caper.
And I can cut the mutton to't.
And I think I have the back-trick simply as strong as any man in Illyria.
Wherefore are these things hid? Wherefore have these gifts a curtain before 'em? Are they like to take dust, like Mistress Mall's picture? Why dost thou not go to church in a galliard and come home in a coranto?
My very walk should be a jig!
I would not so much as make water but in a sink-a-pace.
What dost thou mean? Is it a world to hide virtues in? I did think by the excellent constitution of thy leg, it was formed under the star of a galliard.
Ay, 'tis strong, and it does indifferent well in a dun-coloured stock.
Shall we set about some revels?
What shall we do else?
Were we not born under Taurus?
Taurus?
That's sides and heart.
No, sir! It is legs and thighs!
Let me see thee caper!
Ha! Higher! Ha! Ha!
Excellent!

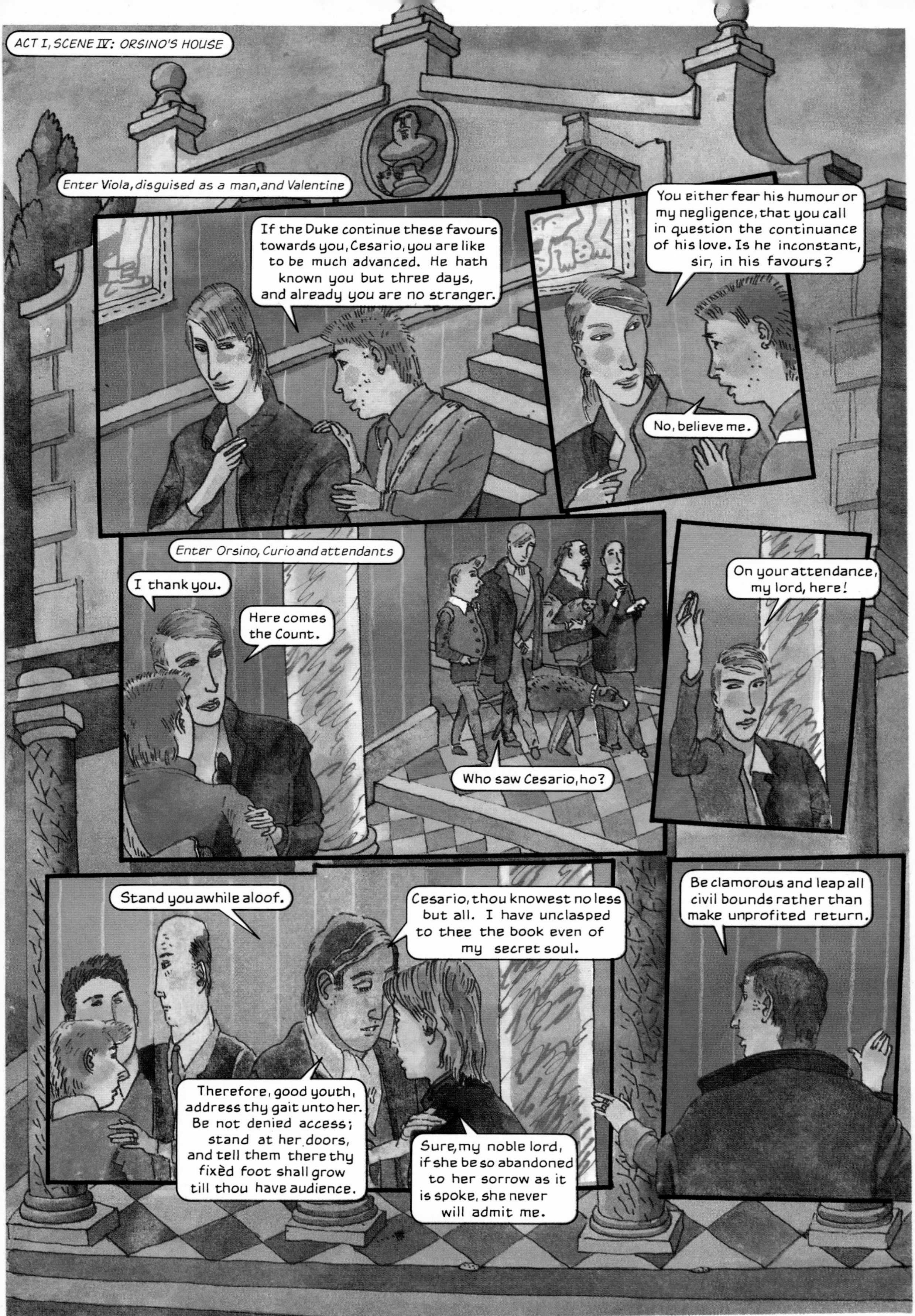
ACT I, SCENE IV: ORSINO'S HOUSE
Enter Viola, disguised as a man, and Valentine
If the Duke continue these favours towards you, Cesario, you are like to be much advanced. He hath known you but three days, and already you are no stranger.
You either fear his humour or my negligence, that you call in question the continuance of his love. Is he inconstant, sir, in his favours?
No, believe me.
Enter Orsino, Curio and attendants
I thank you.
Here comes the Count.
Who saw Cesario, ho?
On your attendance, my lord, here!
Stand you awhile aloof.
Cesario, thou knowest no less but all. I have unclasped to thee the book even of my secret soul.
Therefore, good youth, address thy gait unto her. Be not denied access; stand at her doors, and tell them there thy fixèd foot shall grow till thou have audience.
Sure, my noble lord, if she be so abandoned to her sorrow as it is spoke, she never will admit me.
Be clamorous and leap all civil bounds rather than make unprofited return.

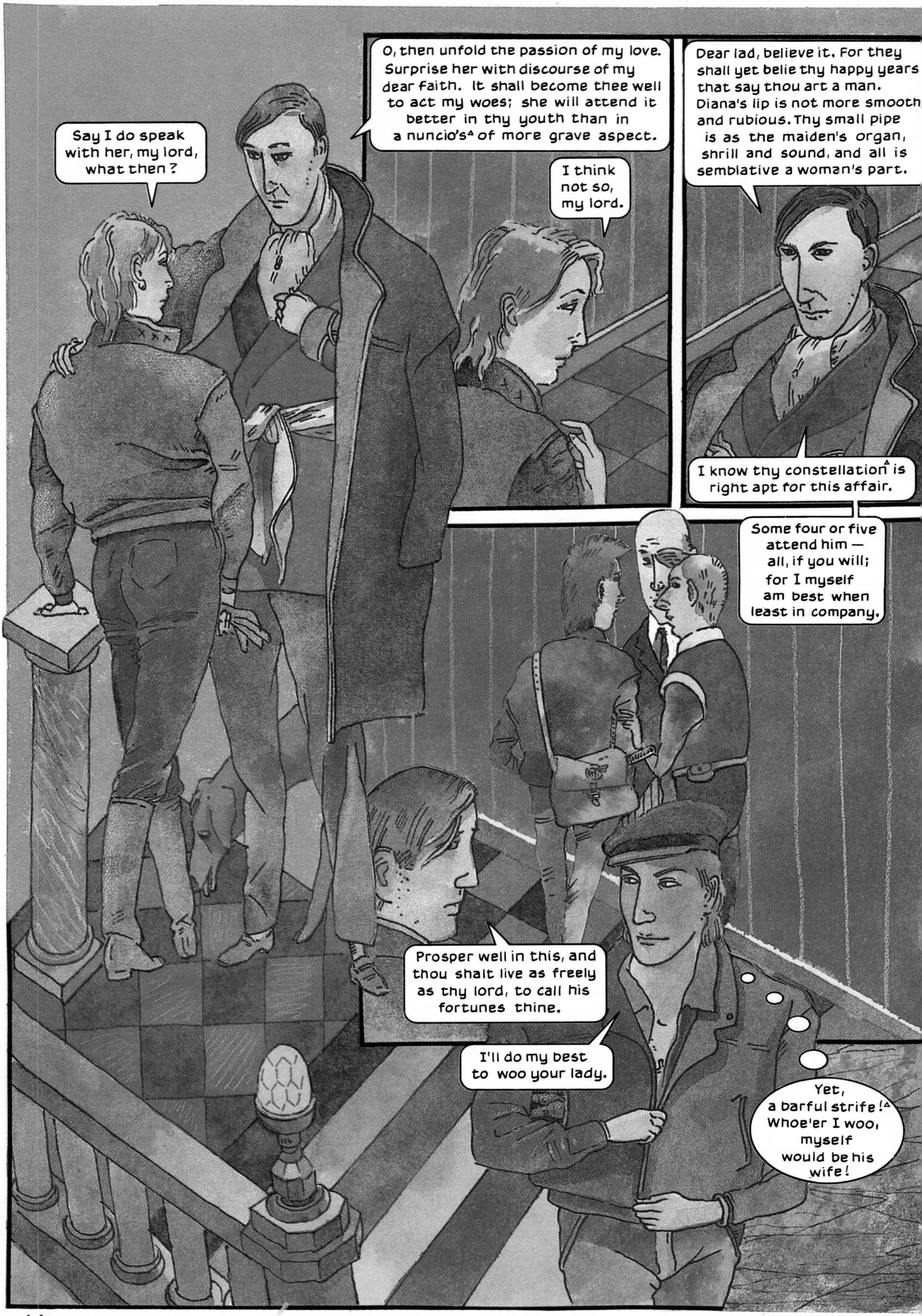

Say I do speak with her, my lord, what then?
O, then unfold the passion of my love. Surprise her with discourse of my dear faith. It shall become thee well to act my woes; she will attend it better in thy youth than in a nuncio's^ of more grave aspect.
I think not so, my lord.
Dear lad, believe it. For they shall yet belie thy happy years that say thou art a man. Diana's lip is not more smooth and rubious. Thy small pipe is as the maiden's organ, shrill and sound, and all is semblative a woman's part.
I know thy constellation^ is right apt for this affair.
Some four or five attend him — all, if you will; for I myself am best when least in company.
Prosper well in this, and thou shalt live as freely as thy lord, to call his fortunes thine.
I'll do my best to woo your lady.
Yet, a barful strife!^ Whoe'er I woo, myself would be his wife!

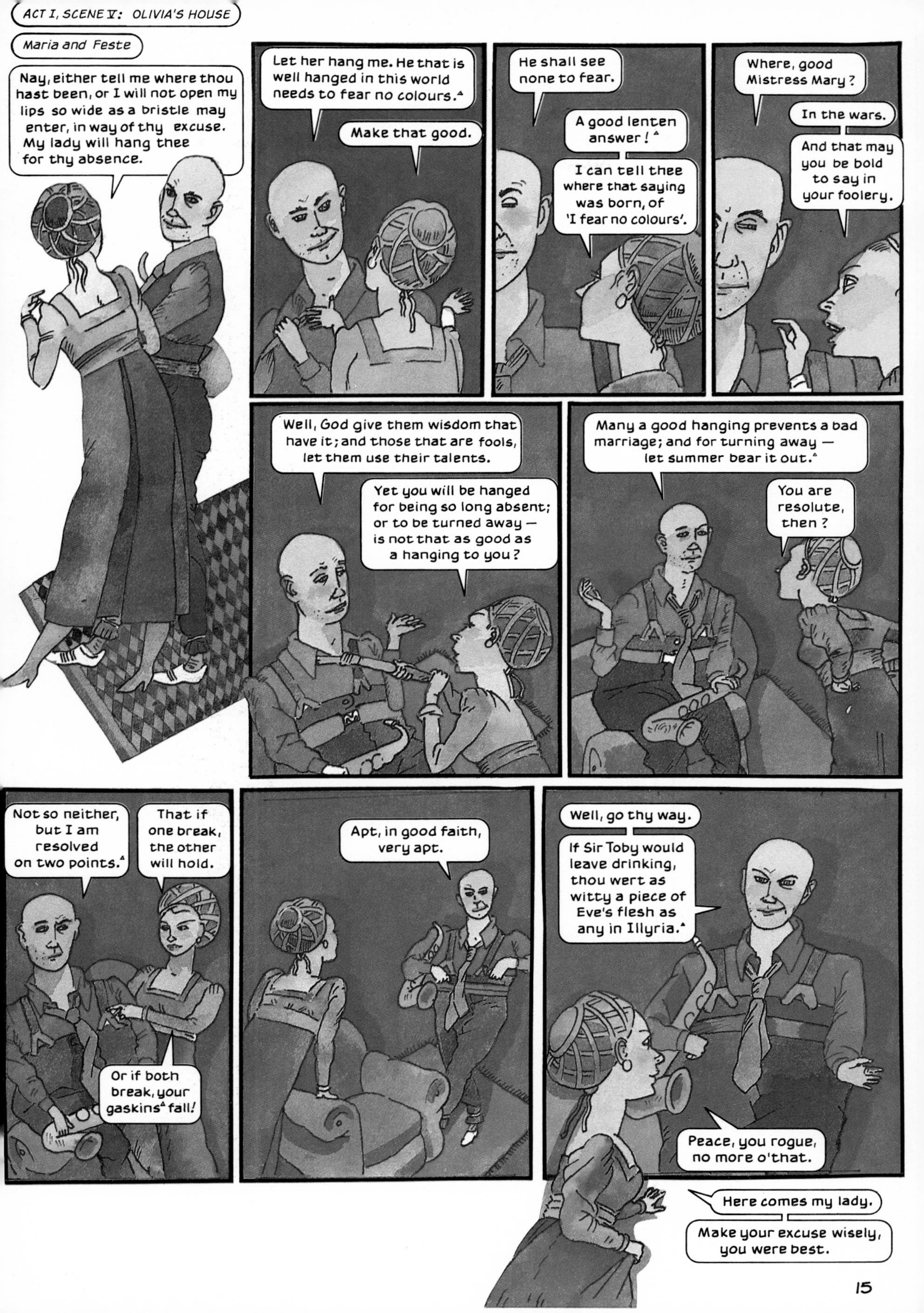
ACT I, SCENE V: OLIVIA'S HOUSE
Maria and Feste
Nay, either tell me where thou hast been, or I will not open my lips so wide as a bristle may enter, in way of thy excuse. My lady will hang thee for thy absence.
Let her hang me. He that is well hanged in this world needs to fear no colours.
Make that good.
He shall see none to fear.
A good lenten answer!
I can tell thee where that saying was born, of 'I fear no colours'.
Where, good Mistress Mary?
In the wars.
And that may you be bold to say in your foolery.
Well, God give them wisdom that have it; and those that are fools, let them use their talents.
Yet you will be hanged for being so long absent; or to be turned away — is not that as good as a hanging to you?
Many a good hanging prevents a bad marriage; and for turning away — let summer bear it out.
You are resolute, then?
Not so neither, but I am resolved on two points.
That if one break, the other will hold.
Or if both break, your gaskins fall!
Apt, in good faith, very apt.
Well, go thy way.
If Sir Toby would leave drinking, thou wert as witty a piece of Eve's flesh as any in Illyria.
Peace, you rogue, no more o'that.
Here comes my lady.
Make your excuse wisely, you were best.

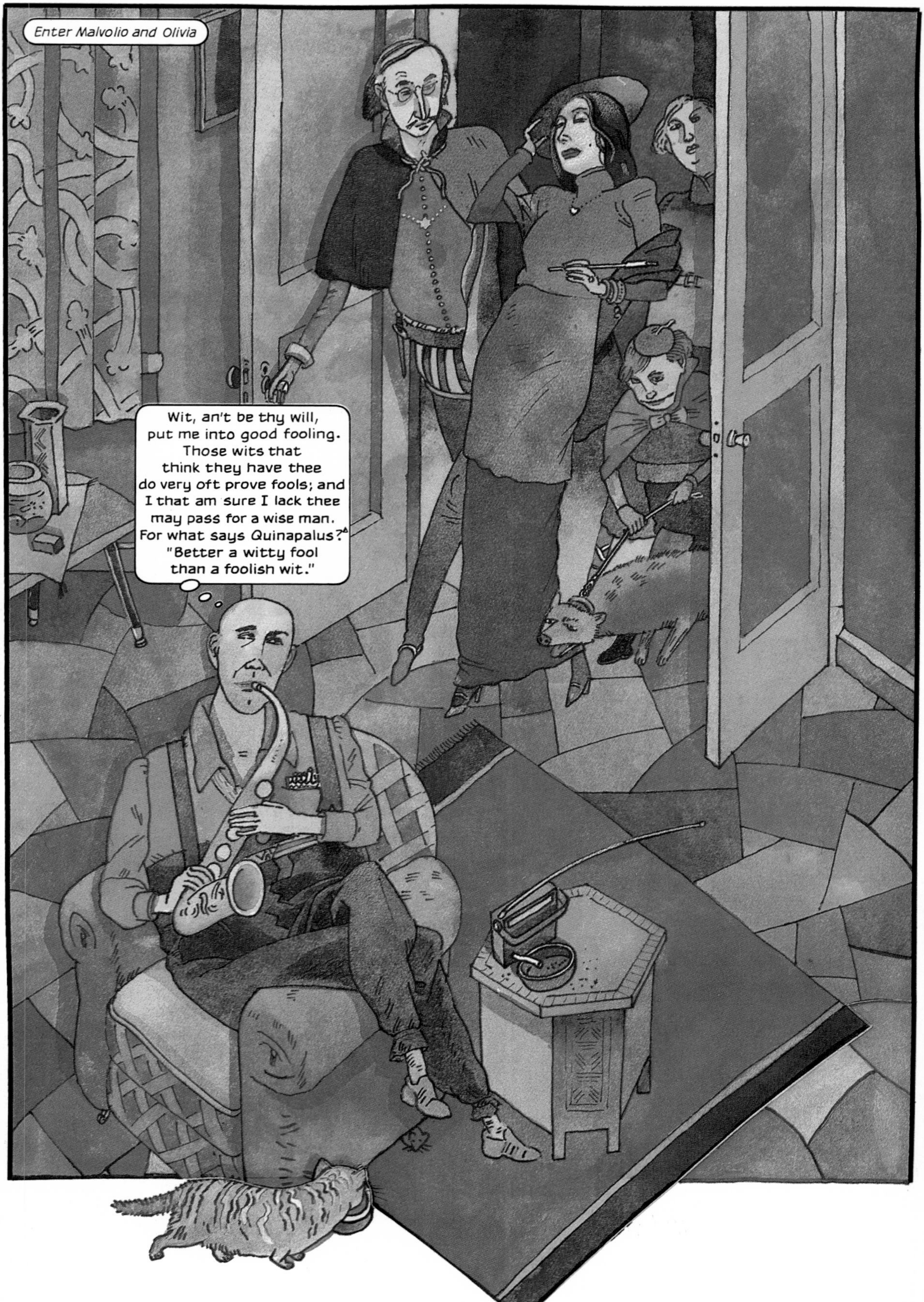
Enter Malvolio and Olivia
Wit, an't be thy will, put me into good fooling. Those wits that think they have thee do very oft prove fools; and I that am sure I lack thee may pass for a wise man. For what says Quinapalus?[a] "Better a witty fool than a foolish wit."

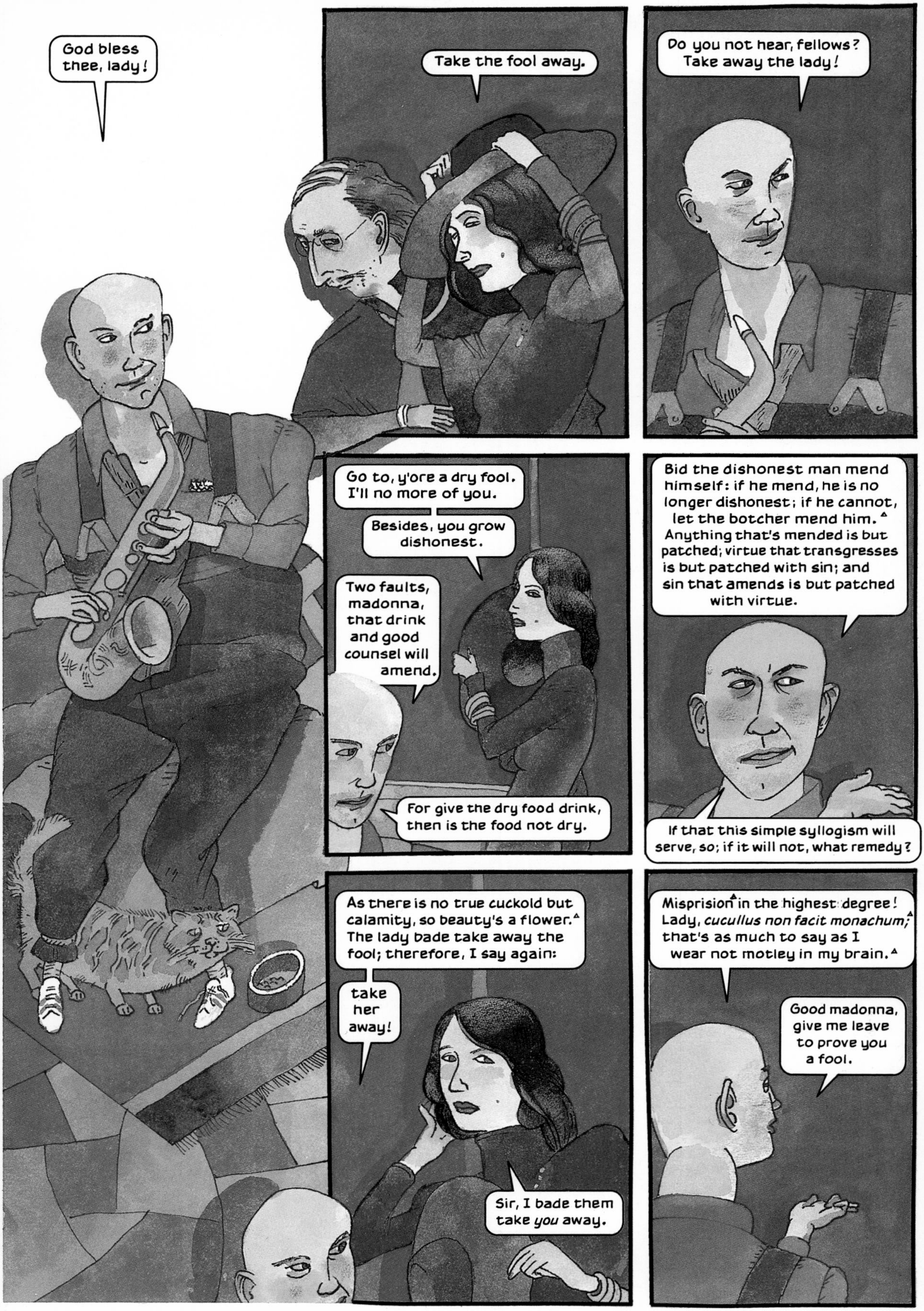
God bless thee, lady!
Take the fool away.
Do you not hear, fellows? Take away the lady!
Go to, y'ore a dry fool. I'll no more of you.
Besides, you grow dishonest.
Two faults, madonna, that drink and good counsel will amend.
For give the dry food drink, then is the food not dry.
Bid the dishonest man mend himself: if he mend, he is no longer dishonest; if he cannot, let the botcher mend him.
Anything that's mended is but patched; virtue that transgresses is but patched with sin; and sin that amends is but patched with virtue.
If that this simple syllogism will serve, so; if it will not, what remedy?
As there is no true cuckold but calamity, so beauty's a flower.
The lady bade take away the fool; therefore, I say again:
take her away!
Sir, I bade them take *you* away.
Misprision in the highest degree! Lady, *cucullus non facit monachum*; that's as much to say as I wear not motley in my brain.
Good madonna, give me leave to prove you a fool.

Can you do it?

Dexteriously, good madonna.

Make your proof.

I must catechize you for it, madonna. Good my mouse of virtue, answer me.

Well, sir, for want of other idleness, I'll bide your proof.

Good madonna, why mourn'st thou?

Good fool, for my brother's death.

I think his soul is in hell, madonna.

I know his soul is in heaven, fool.

The more fool, madonna, to mourn your brother's soul, being in heaven.

Take away the fool, gentlemen!

What think you of this fool, Malvolio? Doth he not mend?▲

Yes, and shall do, till the pangs of death shake him.

Infirmity, that decays the wise, doth ever make the better fool.

God send you, sir, a speedy infirmity, for the better increasing your folly.

Sir Toby will be sworn that I am no fox,▲ but he will not pass his word for twopence that you are no fool.

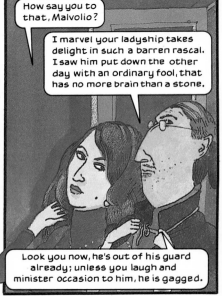

How say you to that, Malvolio?

I marvel your ladyship takes delight in such a barren rascal. I saw him put down the other day with an ordinary fool, that has no more brain than a stone.

Look you now, he's out of his guard already; unless you laugh and minister occasion to him, he is gagged.

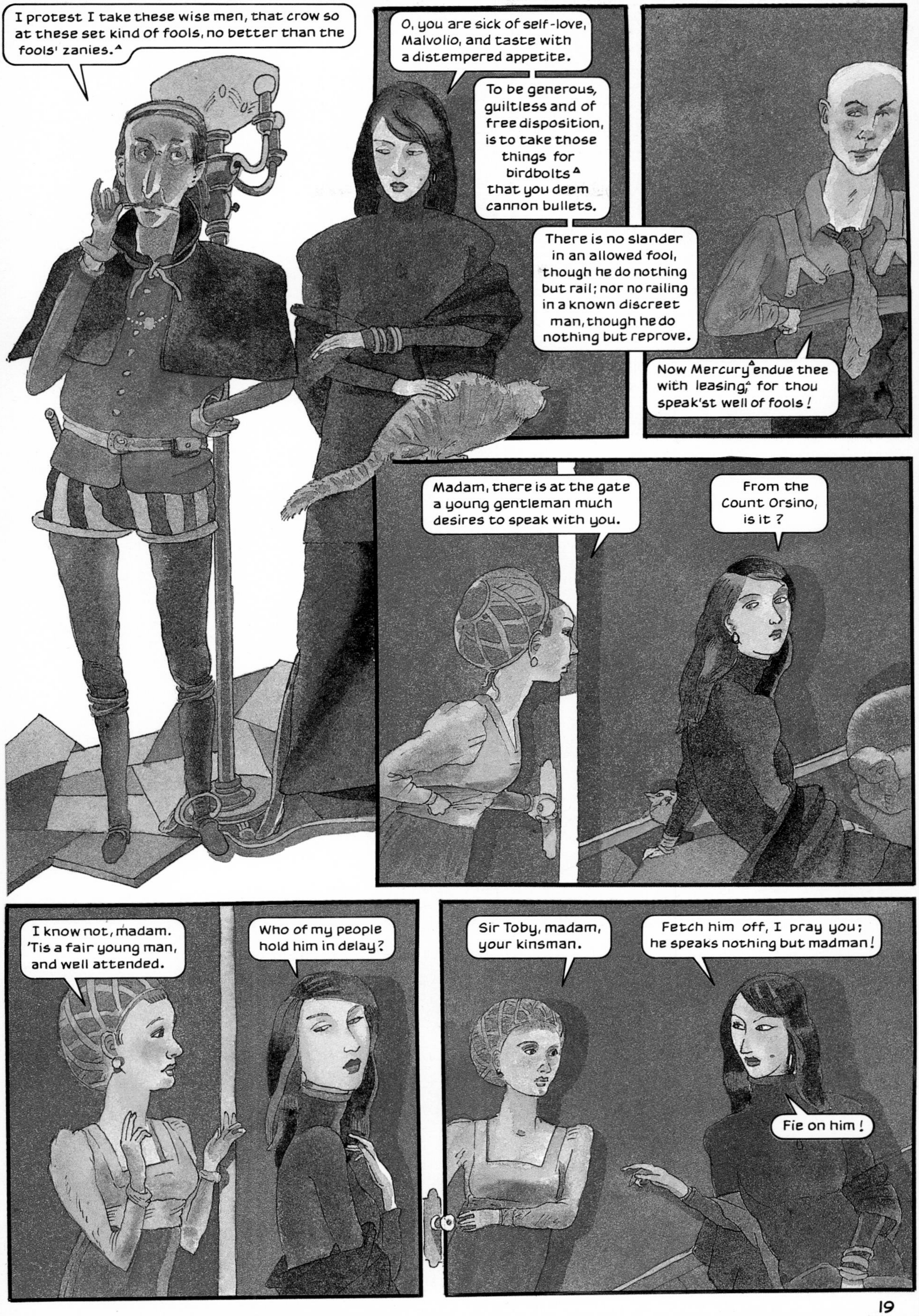
I protest I take these wise men, that crow so at these set kind of fools, no better than the fools' zanies.
O, you are sick of self-love, Malvolio, and taste with a distempered appetite.
To be generous, guiltless and of free disposition, is to take those things for birdbolts that you deem cannon bullets.
There is no slander in an allowed fool, though he do nothing but rail; nor no railing in a known discreet man, though he do nothing but reprove.
Now Mercury endue thee with leasing, for thou speak'st well of fools!
Madam, there is at the gate a young gentleman much desires to speak with you.
From the Count Orsino, is it?
I know not, madam. 'Tis a fair young man, and well attended.
Who of my people hold him in delay?
Sir Toby, madam, your kinsman.
Fetch him off, I pray you; he speaks nothing but madman!
Fie on him!

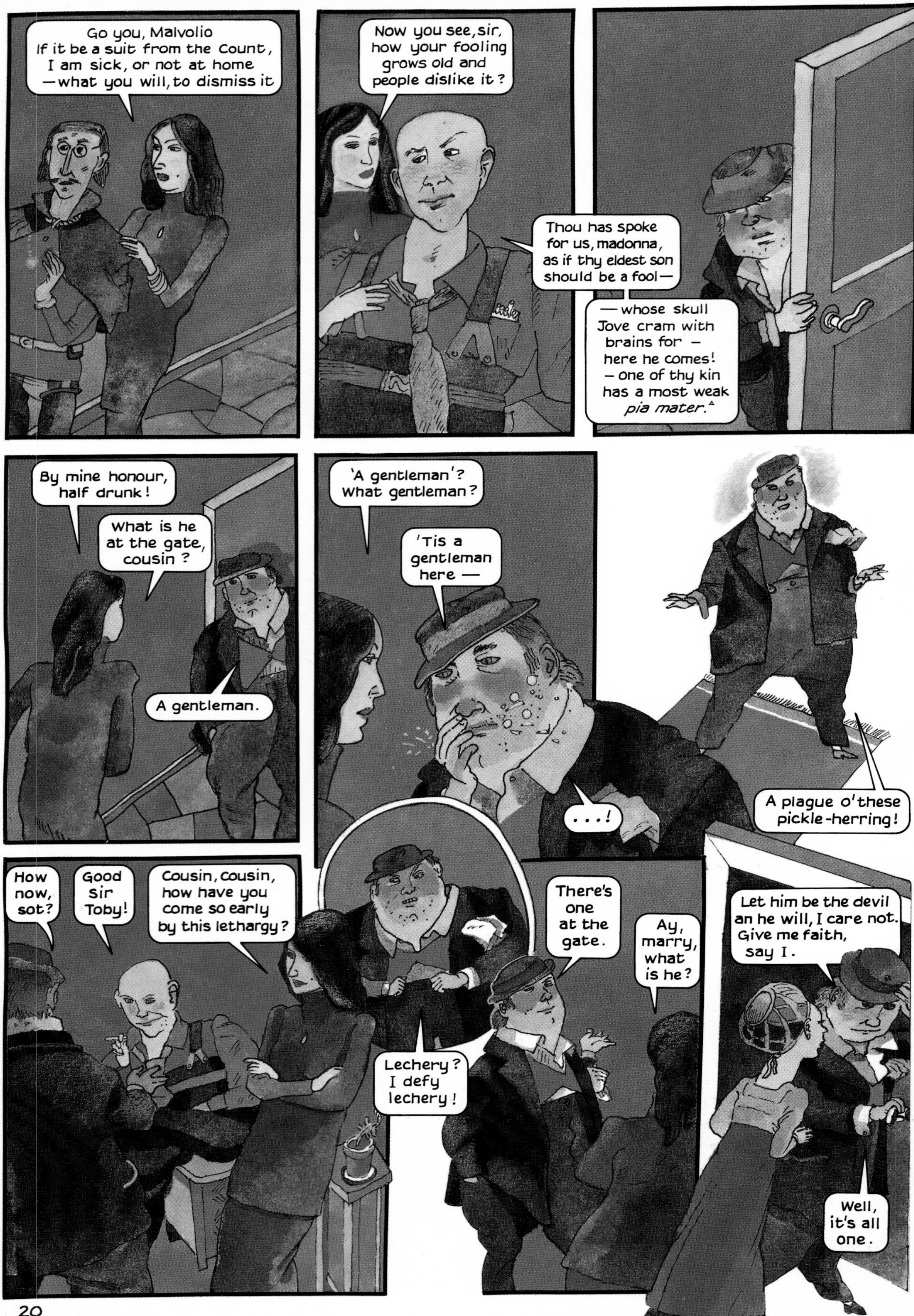

Go you, Malvolio If it be a suit from the Count, I am sick, or not at home —what you will, to dismiss it
Now you see, sir, how your fooling grows old and people dislike it?
Thou has spoke for us, madonna, as if thy eldest son should be a fool—
—whose skull Jove cram with brains for — here he comes! – one of thy kin has a most weak *pia mater*.
By mine honour, half drunk!
What is he at the gate, cousin?
A gentleman.
'A gentleman'? What gentleman?
'Tis a gentleman here —
. . . !
A plague o'these pickle-herring!
How now, sot?
Good Sir Toby!
Cousin, cousin, how have you come so early by this lethargy?
Lechery? I defy lechery!
There's one at the gate.
Ay, marry, what is he?
Let him be the devil an he will, I care not. Give me faith, say I.
Well, it's all one.

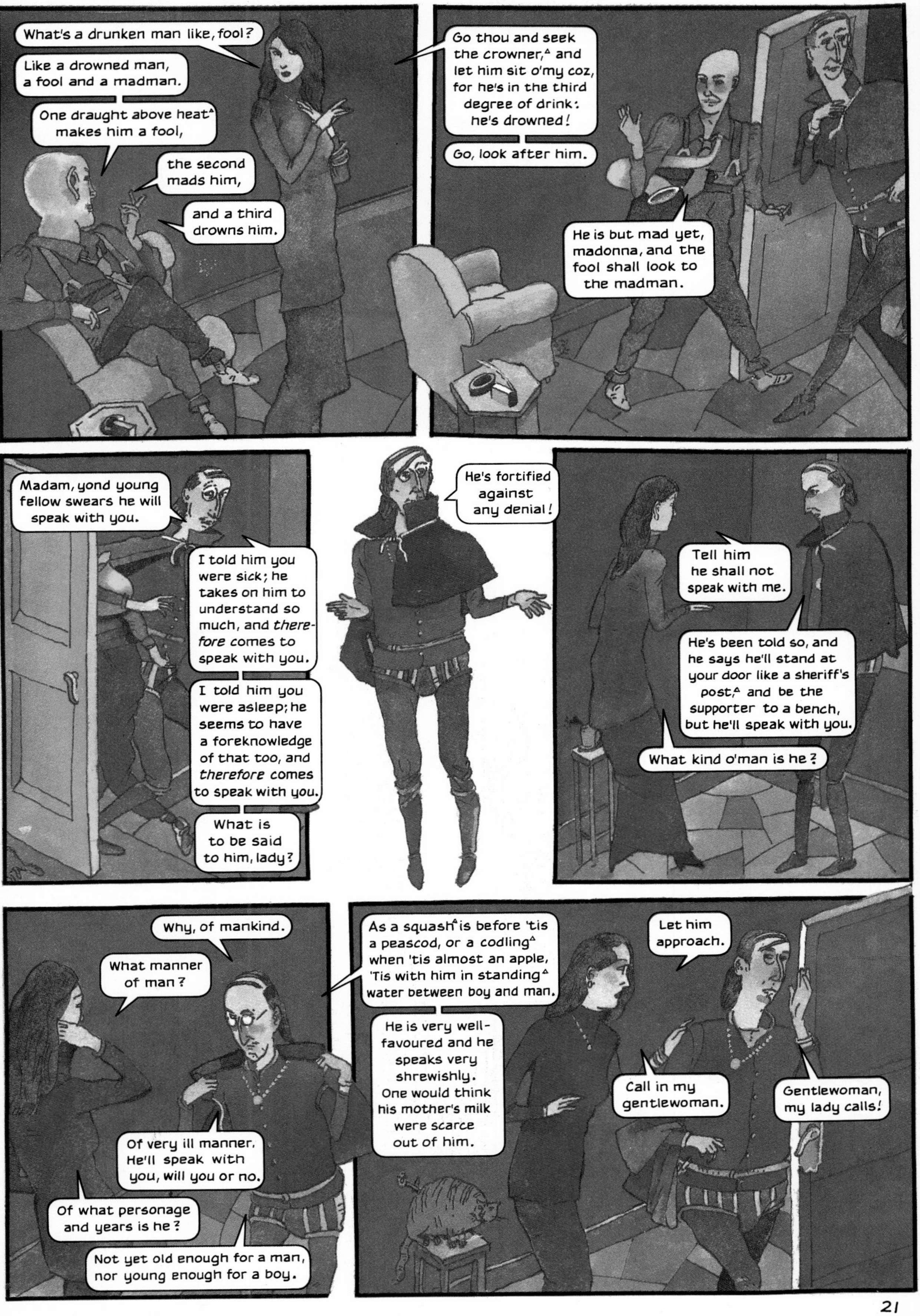

What's a drunken man like, fool?
Like a drowned man, a fool and a madman.
One draught above heat makes him a fool,
the second mads him,
and a third drowns him.
Go thou and seek the crowner, and let him sit o'my coz, for he's in the third degree of drink: he's drowned!
Go, look after him.
He is but mad yet, madonna, and the fool shall look to the madman.
Madam, yond young fellow swears he will speak with you.
I told him you were sick; he takes on him to understand so much, and therefore comes to speak with you.
I told him you were asleep; he seems to have a foreknowledge of that too, and therefore comes to speak with you.
What is to be said to him, lady?
He's fortified against any denial!
Tell him he shall not speak with me.
He's been told so, and he says he'll stand at your door like a sheriff's post, and be the supporter to a bench, but he'll speak with you.
What kind o'man is he?
Why, of mankind.
What manner of man?
Of very ill manner. He'll speak with you, will you or no.
Of what personage and years is he?
Not yet old enough for a man, nor young enough for a boy.
As a squash is before 'tis a peascod, or a codling when 'tis almost an apple, 'Tis with him in standing water between boy and man.
He is very well-favoured and he speaks very shrewishly. One would think his mother's milk were scarce out of him.
Let him approach.
Call in my gentlewoman.
Gentlewoman, my lady calls!

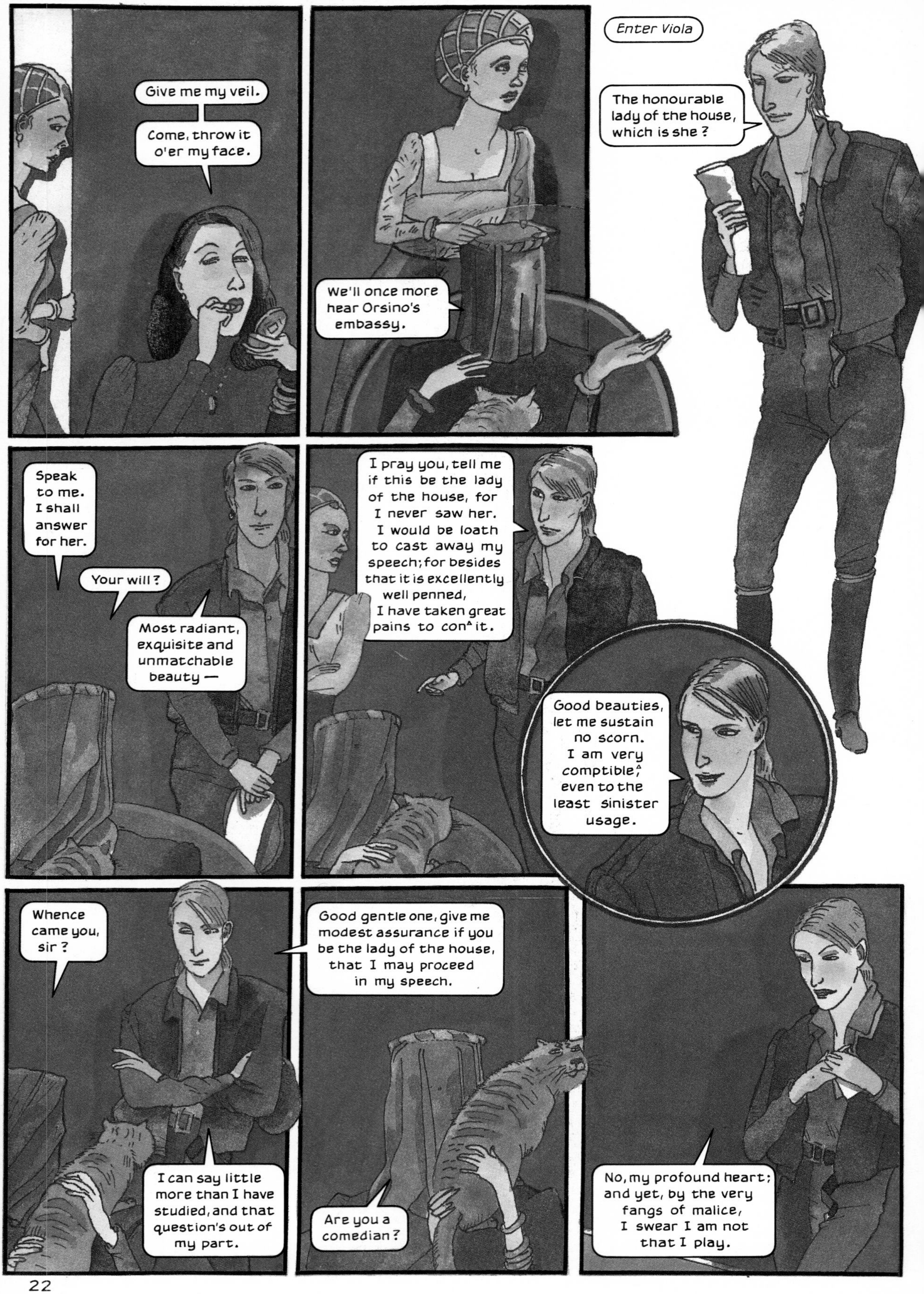
Give me my veil.
Come, throw it o'er my face.
We'll once more hear Orsino's embassy.
Enter Viola
The honourable lady of the house, which is she?
Speak to me. I shall answer for her.
Your will?
Most radiant, exquisite and unmatchable beauty —
I pray you, tell me if this be the lady of the house, for I never saw her. I would be loath to cast away my speech; for besides that it is excellently well penned, I have taken great pains to con it.
Good beauties, let me sustain no scorn. I am very comptible, even to the least sinister usage.
Whence came you, sir?
I can say little more than I have studied, and that question's out of my part.
Good gentle one, give me modest assurance if you be the lady of the house, that I may proceed in my speech.
Are you a comedian?
No, my profound heart; and yet, by the very fangs of malice, I swear I am not that I play.

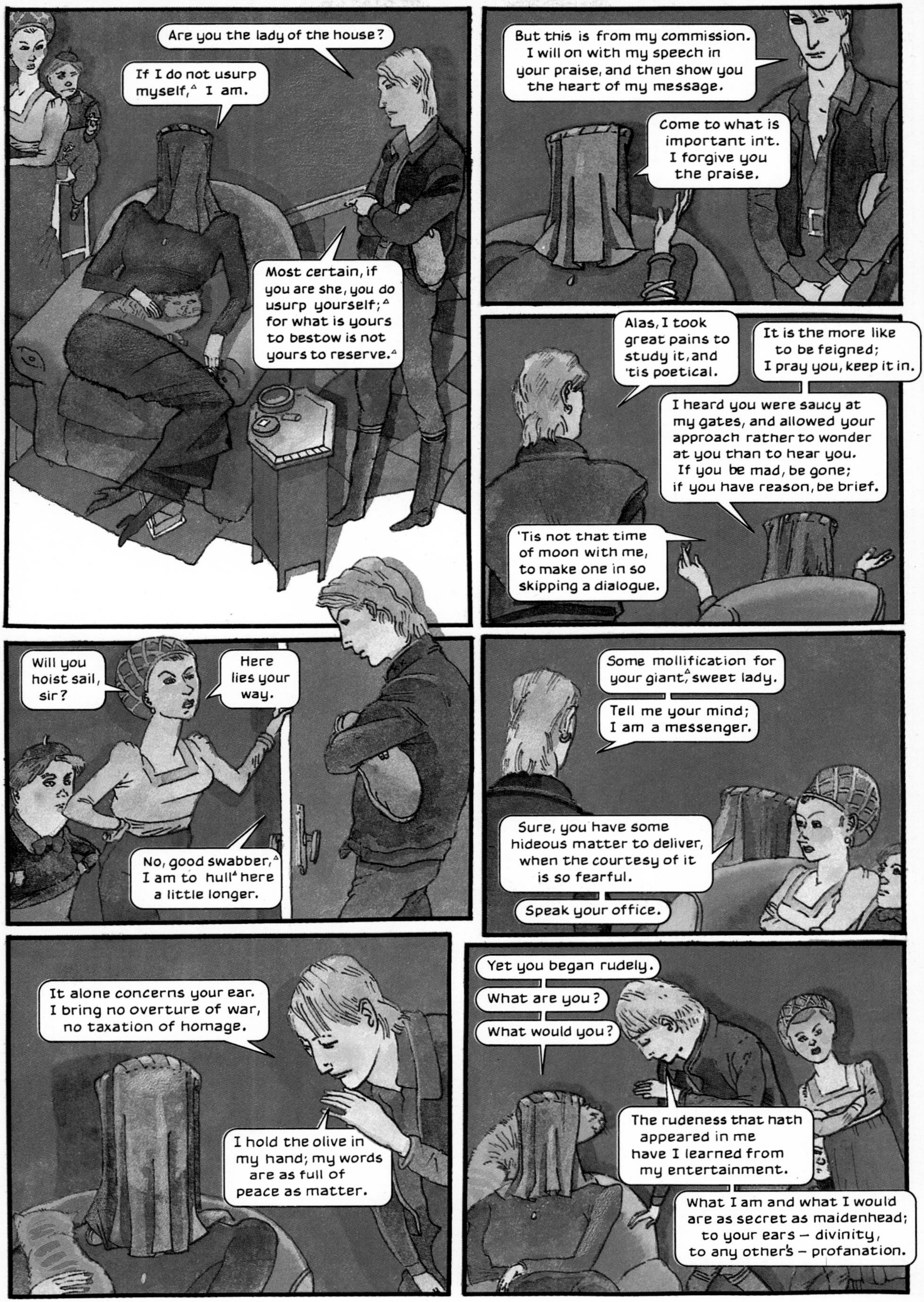

Are you the lady of the house?
If I do not usurp myself,△ I am.
Most certain, if you are she, you do usurp yourself;△ for what is yours to bestow is not yours to reserve.△
But this is from my commission. I will on with my speech in your praise, and then show you the heart of my message.
Come to what is important in't. I forgive you the praise.
Alas, I took great pains to study it, and 'tis poetical.
It is the more like to be feigned; I pray you, keep it in.
I heard you were saucy at my gates, and allowed your approach rather to wonder at you than to hear you. If you be mad, be gone; if you have reason, be brief.
'Tis not that time of moon with me, to make one in so skipping a dialogue.
Will you hoist sail, sir?
Here lies your way.
No, good swabber,△ I am to hull△ here a little longer.
Some mollification for your giant,△ sweet lady.
Tell me your mind; I am a messenger.
Sure, you have some hideous matter to deliver, when the courtesy of it is so fearful.
Speak your office.
It alone concerns your ear. I bring no overture of war, no taxation of homage.
I hold the olive in my hand; my words are as full of peace as matter.
Yet you began rudely.
What are you?
What would you?
The rudeness that hath appeared in me have I learned from my entertainment.
What I am and what I would are as secret as maidenhead; to your ears – divinity, to any other's – profanation.

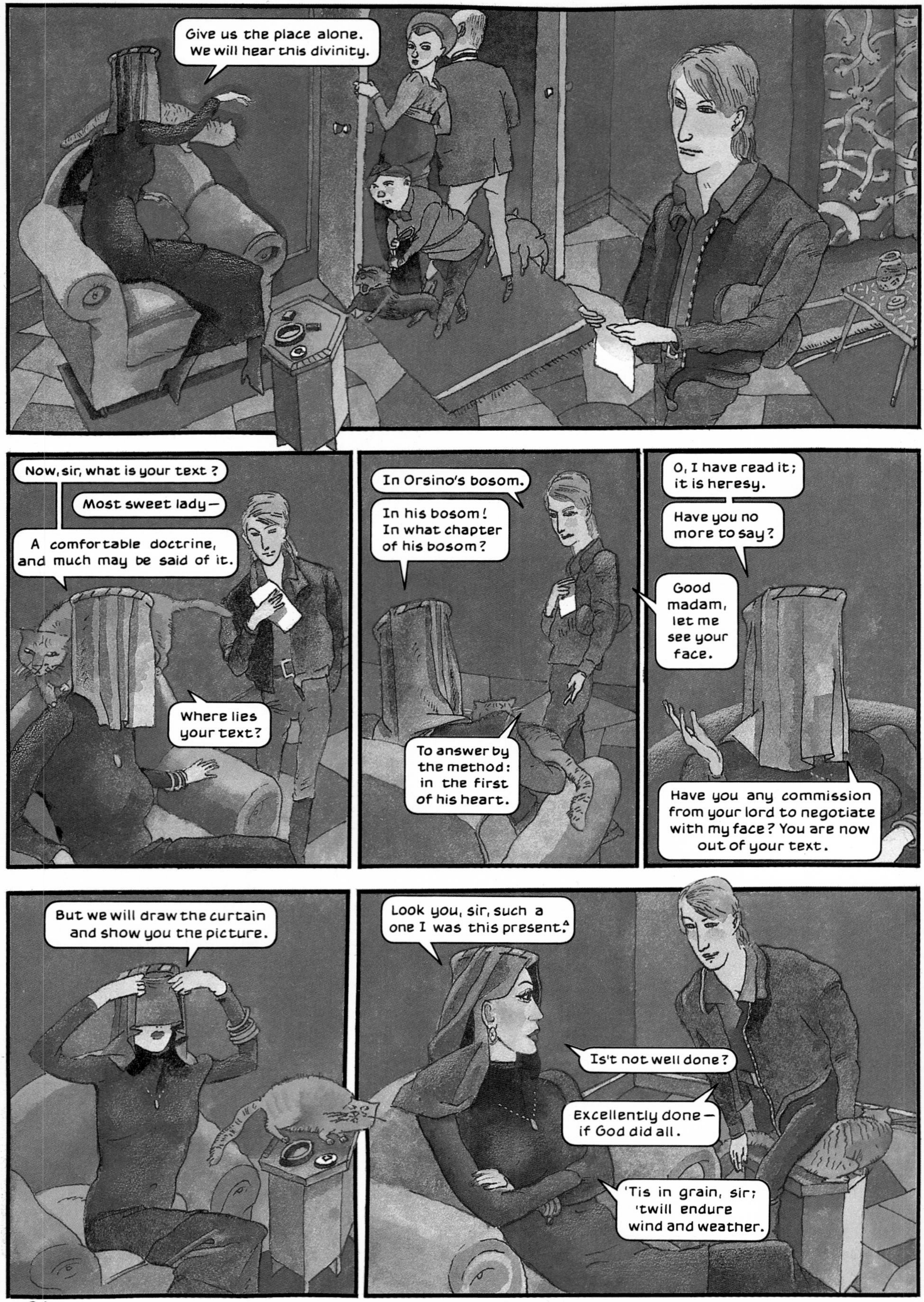

Give us the place alone. We will hear this divinity.
Now, sir, what is your text?
Most sweet lady—
A comfortable doctrine, and much may be said of it.
Where lies your text?
In Orsino's bosom.
In his bosom! In what chapter of his bosom?
To answer by the method: in the first of his heart.
O, I have read it; it is heresy.
Have you no more to say?
Good madam, let me see your face.
Have you any commission from your lord to negotiate with my face? You are now out of your text.
But we will draw the curtain and show you the picture.
Look you, sir, such a one I was this present.^
Is't not well done?
Excellently done— if God did all.
'Tis in grain, sir; 'twill endure wind and weather.

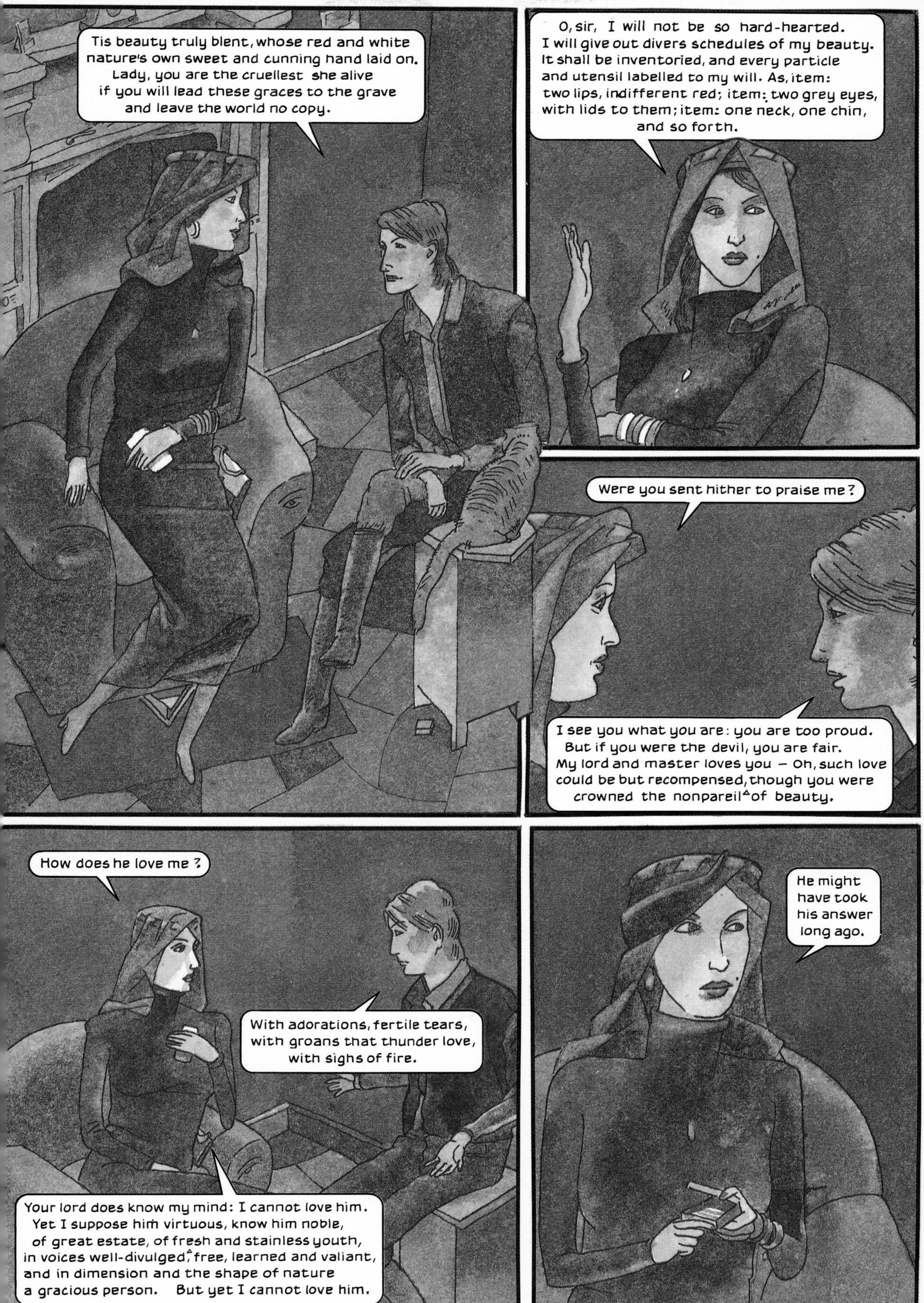

Tis beauty truly blent, whose red and white nature's own sweet and cunning hand laid on. Lady, you are the cruellest she alive if you will lead these graces to the grave and leave the world no copy.
O, sir, I will not be so hard-hearted. I will give out divers schedules of my beauty. It shall be inventoried, and every particle and utensil labelled to my will. As, item: two lips, indifferent red; item: two grey eyes, with lids to them; item: one neck, one chin, and so forth.
Were you sent hither to praise me?
I see you what you are: you are too proud. But if you were the devil, you are fair. My lord and master loves you – Oh, such love could be but recompensed, though you were crowned the nonpareil^ of beauty.
How does he love me?
With adorations, fertile tears, with groans that thunder love, with sighs of fire.
Your lord does know my mind: I cannot love him. Yet I suppose him virtuous, know him noble, of great estate, of fresh and stainless youth, in voices well-divulged^, free, learned and valiant, and in dimension and the shape of nature a gracious person. But yet I cannot love him.
He might have took his answer long ago.

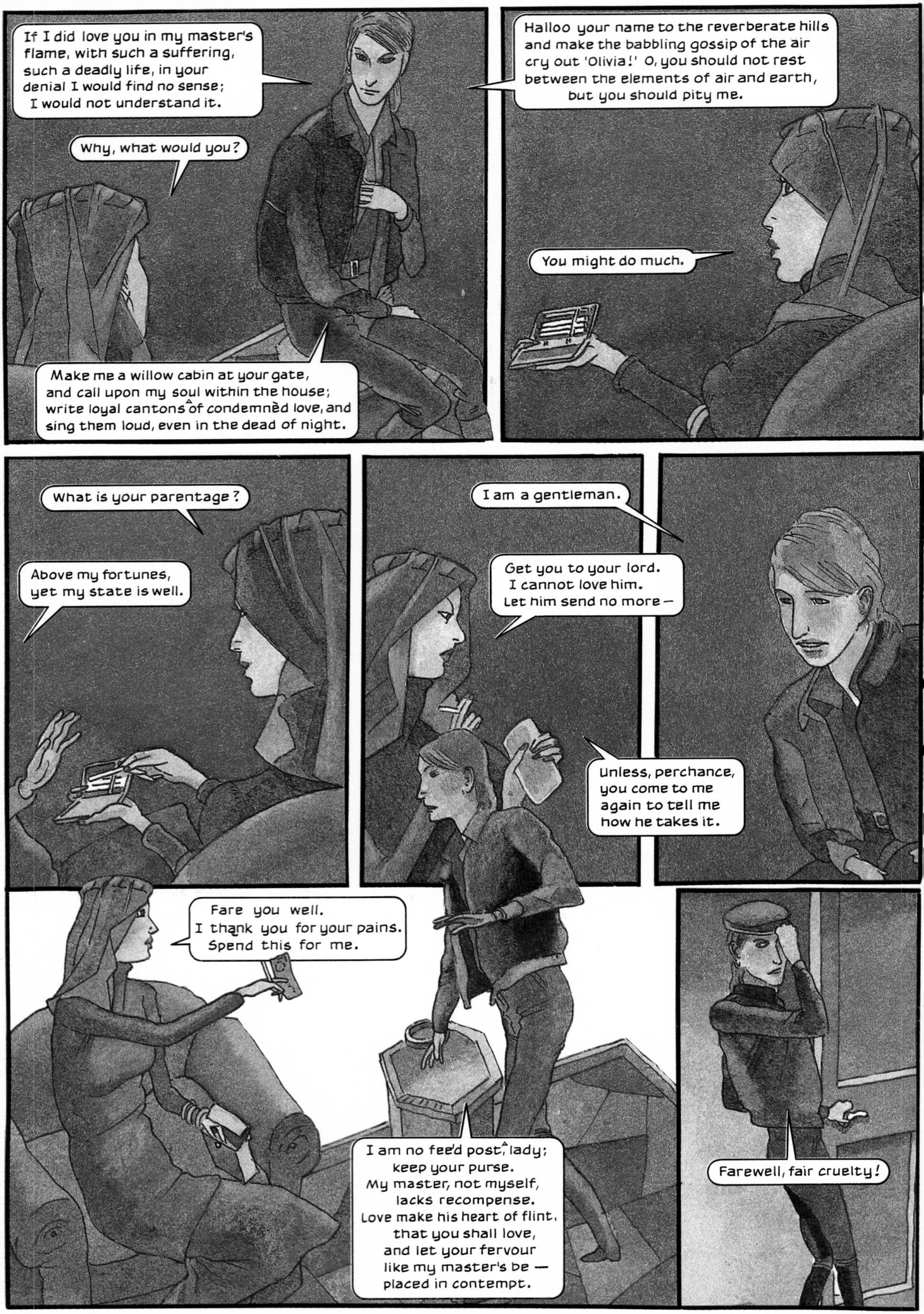
If I did love you in my master's flame, with such a suffering, such a deadly life, in your denial I would find no sense; I would not understand it.
Why, what would you?
Make me a willow cabin at your gate, and call upon my soul within the house; write loyal cantons of condemnèd love, and sing them loud, even in the dead of night.
Halloo your name to the reverberate hills and make the babbling gossip of the air cry out 'Olivia!' O, you should not rest between the elements of air and earth, but you should pity me.
You might do much.
What is your parentage?
Above my fortunes, yet my state is well.
I am a gentleman.
Get you to your lord. I cannot love him. Let him send no more —
Unless, perchance, you come to me again to tell me how he takes it.
Fare you well. I thank you for your pains. Spend this for me.
I am no fee'd post, lady; keep your purse. My master, not myself, lacks recompense. Love make his heart of flint, that you shall love, and let your fervour like my master's be — placed in contempt.
Farewell, fair cruelty!

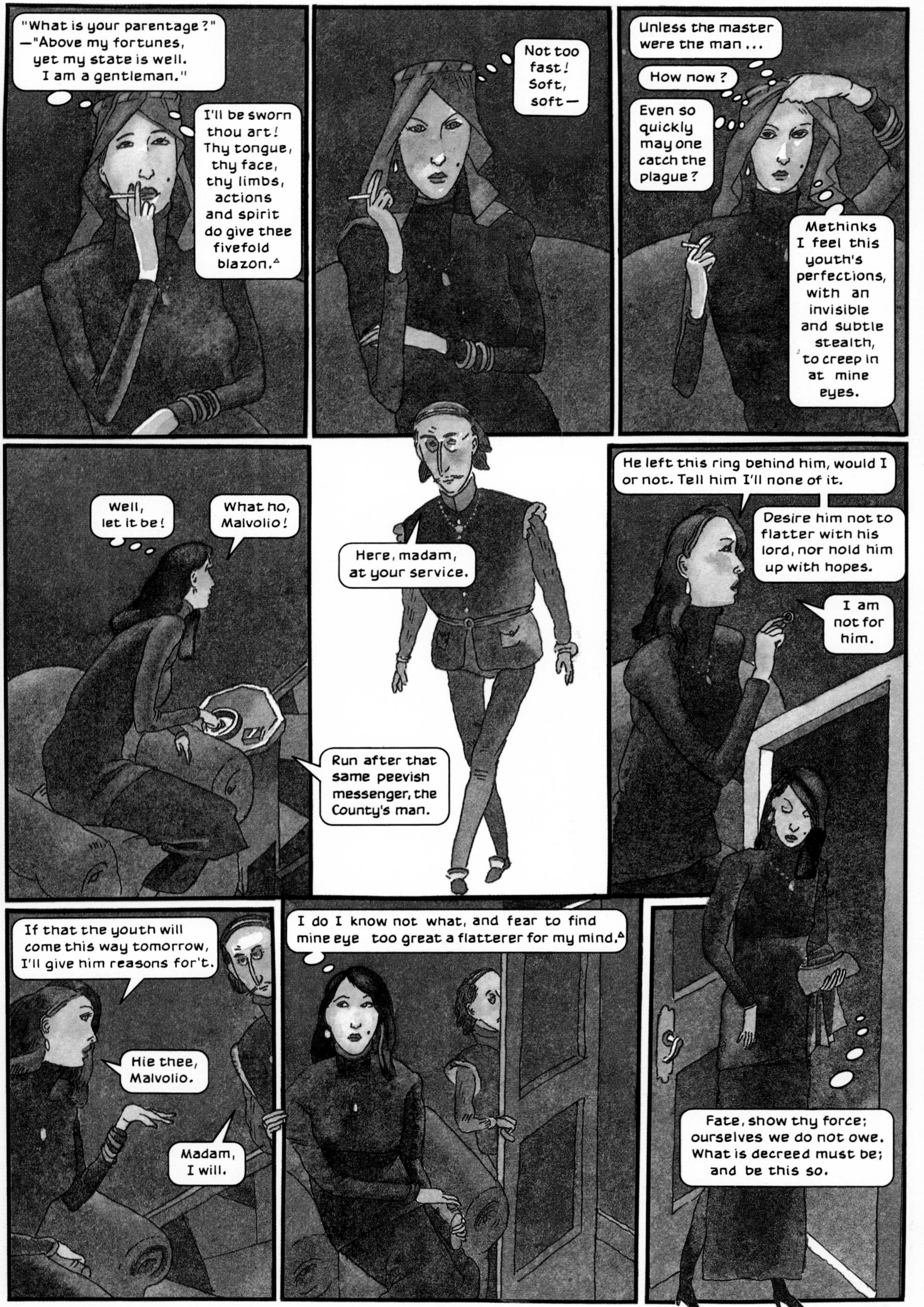
"What is your parentage?" —"Above my fortunes, yet my state is well. I am a gentleman."
I'll be sworn thou art! Thy tongue, thy face, thy limbs, actions and spirit do give thee fivefold blazon.△
Not too fast! Soft, soft—
Unless the master were the man...
How now?
Even so quickly may one catch the plague?
Methinks I feel this youth's perfections, with an invisible and subtle stealth, to creep in at mine eyes.
Well, let it be!
What ho, Malvolio!
Here, madam, at your service.
Run after that same peevish messenger, the County's man.
He left this ring behind him, would I or not. Tell him I'll none of it.
Desire him not to flatter with his lord, nor hold him up with hopes.
I am not for him.
If that the youth will come this way tomorrow, I'll give him reasons for't.
Hie thee, Malvolio.
Madam, I will.
I do I know not what, and fear to find mine eye too great a flatterer for my mind.△
Fate, show thy force; ourselves we do not owe. What is decreed must be; and be this so.

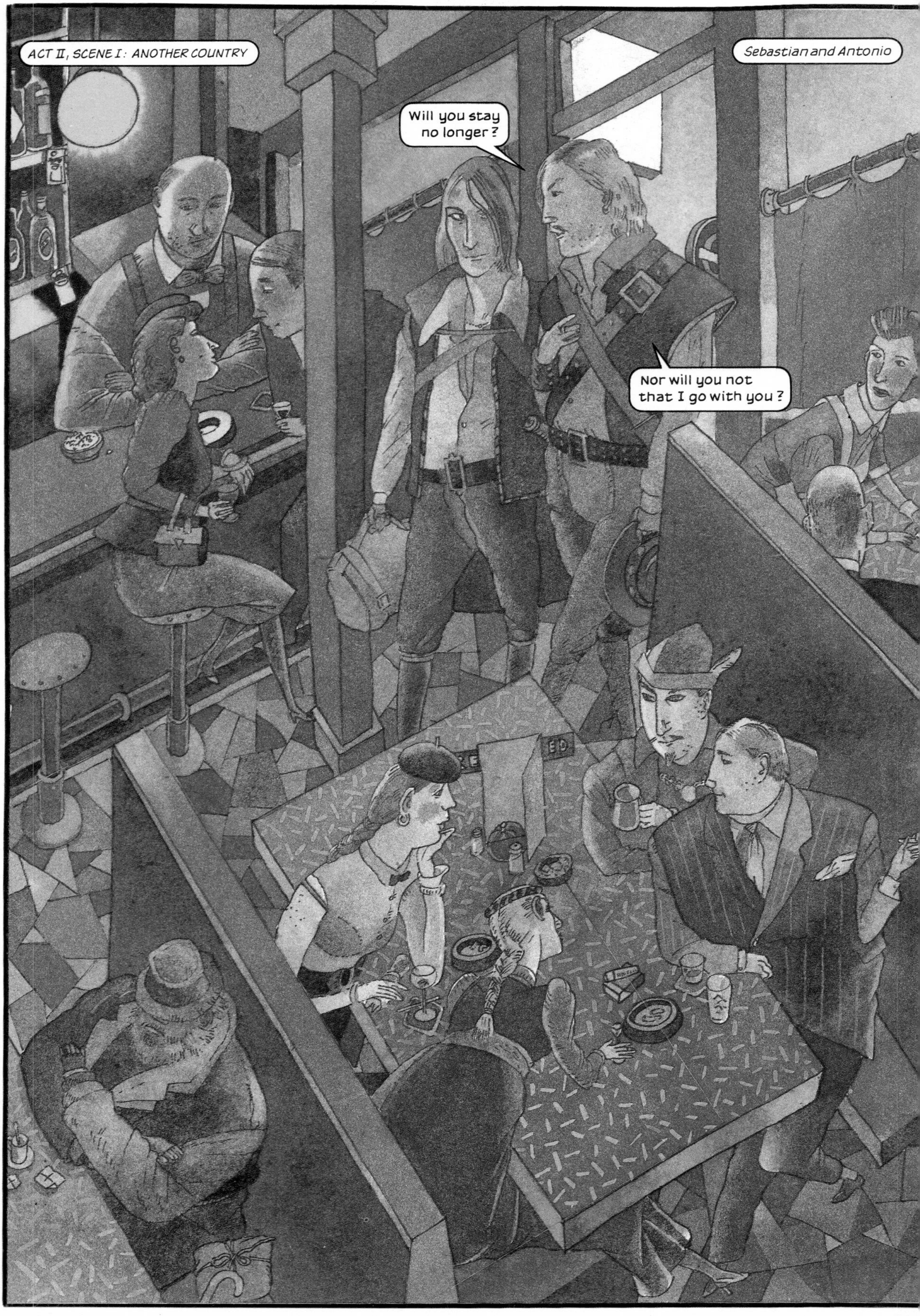
ACT II, SCENE I: ANOTHER COUNTRY
Sebastian and Antonio
Will you stay no longer?
Nor will you not that I go with you?

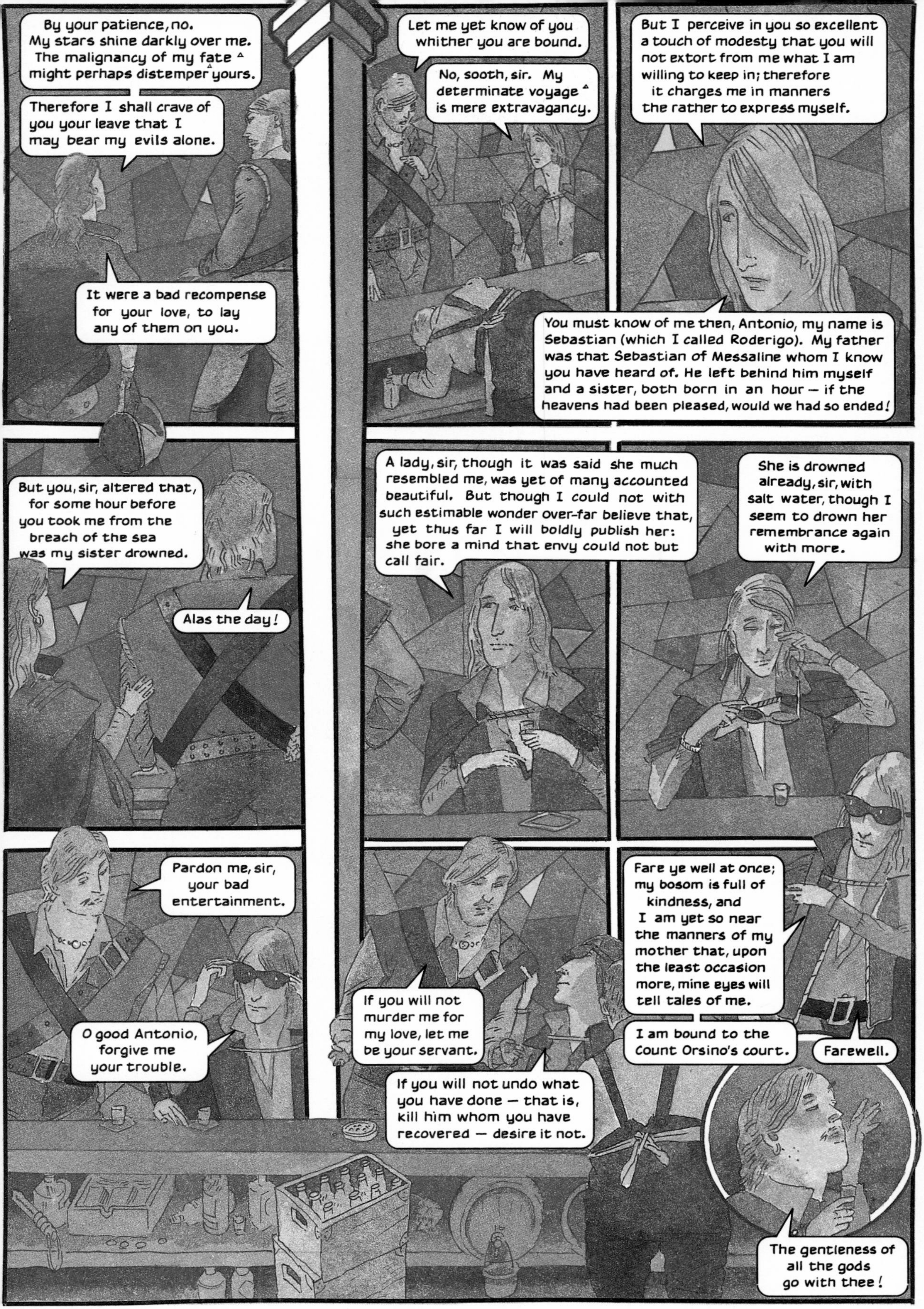

By your patience, no. My stars shine darkly over me. The malignancy of my fate might perhaps distemper yours.
Therefore I shall crave of you your leave that I may bear my evils alone.
It were a bad recompense for your love, to lay any of them on you.
Let me yet know of you whither you are bound.
No, sooth, sir. My determinate voyage is mere extravagancy.
But I perceive in you so excellent a touch of modesty that you will not extort from me what I am willing to keep in; therefore it charges me in manners the rather to express myself.
You must know of me then, Antonio, my name is Sebastian (which I called Roderigo). My father was that Sebastian of Messaline whom I know you have heard of. He left behind him myself and a sister, both born in an hour – if the heavens had been pleased, would we had so ended!
But you, sir, altered that, for some hour before you took me from the breach of the sea was my sister drowned.
Alas the day!
A lady, sir, though it was said she much resembled me, was yet of many accounted beautiful. But though I could not with such estimable wonder over-far believe that, yet thus far I will boldly publish her: she bore a mind that envy could not but call fair.
She is drowned already, sir, with salt water, though I seem to drown her remembrance again with more.
Pardon me, sir, your bad entertainment.
O good Antonio, forgive me your trouble.
If you will not murder me for my love, let me be your servant.
If you will not undo what you have done – that is, kill him whom you have recovered – desire it not.
Fare ye well at once; my bosom is full of kindness, and I am yet so near the manners of my mother that, upon the least occasion more, mine eyes will tell tales of me.
I am bound to the Count Orsino's court.
Farewell.
The gentleness of all the gods go with thee!

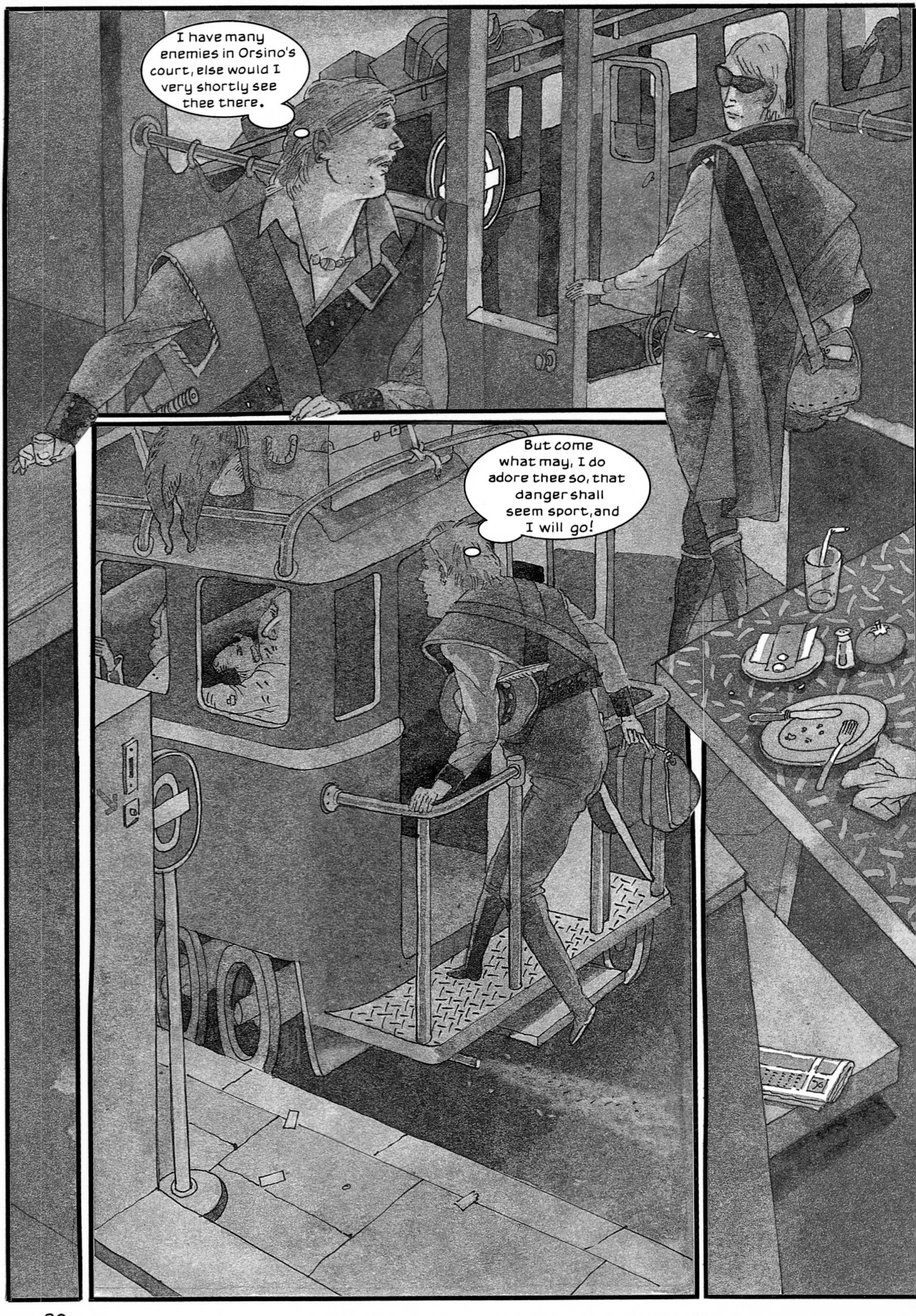
I have many enemies in Orsino's court, else would I very shortly see thee there.
But come what may, I do adore thee so, that danger shall seem sport, and I will go!

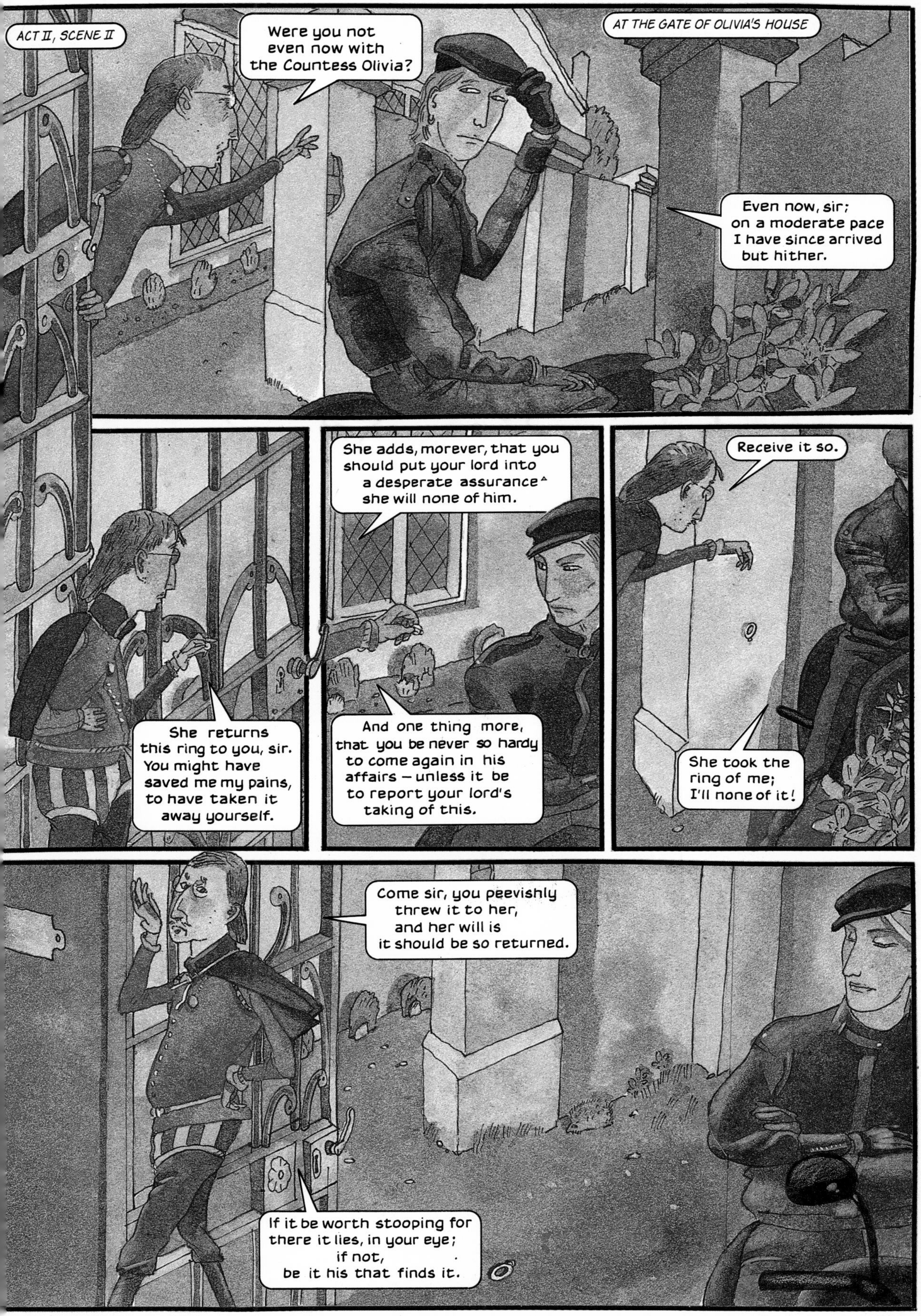

ACT II, SCENE II
Were you not even now with the Countess Olivia?
AT THE GATE OF OLIVIA'S HOUSE
Even now, sir; on a moderate pace I have since arrived but hither.
She returns this ring to you, sir. You might have saved me my pains, to have taken it away yourself.
She adds, morever, that you should put your lord into a desperate assurance she will none of him.
And one thing more, that you be never so hardy to come again in his affairs – unless it be to report your lord's taking of this.
Receive it so.
She took the ring of me; I'll none of it!
Come sir, you peevishly threw it to her, and her will is it should be so returned.
If it be worth stooping for there it lies, in your eye; if not, be it his that finds it.

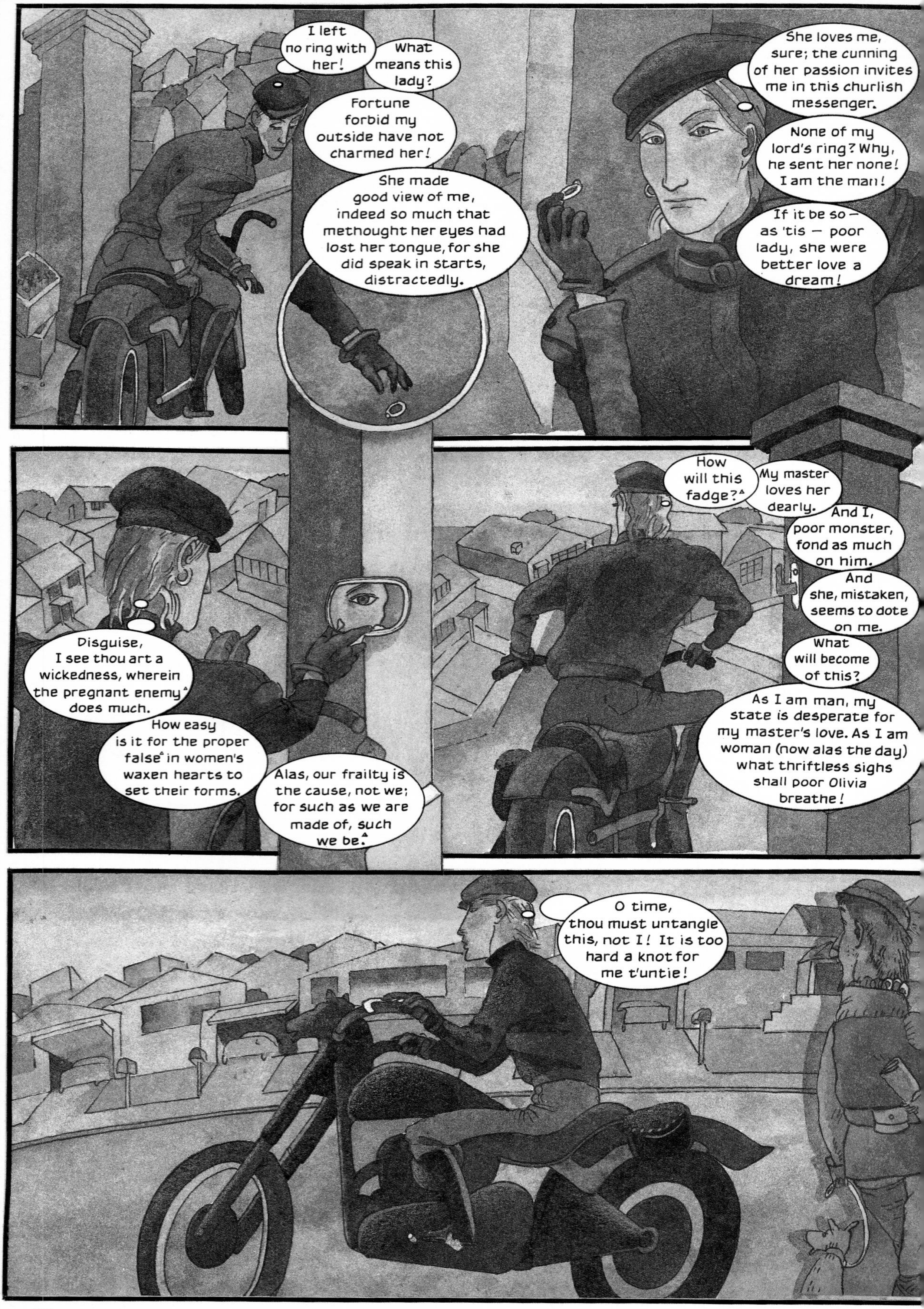

I left no ring with her!
What means this lady?
Fortune forbid my outside have not charmed her!
She made good view of me, indeed so much that methought her eyes had lost her tongue, for she did speak in starts, distractedly.
She loves me, sure; the cunning of her passion invites me in this churlish messenger.
None of my lord's ring? Why, he sent her none! I am the man!
If it be so — as 'tis — poor lady, she were better love a dream!
Disguise, I see thou art a wickedness, wherein the pregnant enemy^ does much.
How easy is it for the proper false^ in women's waxen hearts to set their forms.
Alas, our frailty is the cause, not we; for such as we are made of, such we be.^
How will this fadge?^
My master loves her dearly.
And I, poor monster, fond as much on him.
And she, mistaken, seems to dote on me.
What will become of this?
As I am man, my state is desperate for my master's love. As I am woman (now alas the day) what thriftless sighs shall poor Olivia breathe!
O time, thou must untangle this, not I! It is too hard a knot for me t'untie!

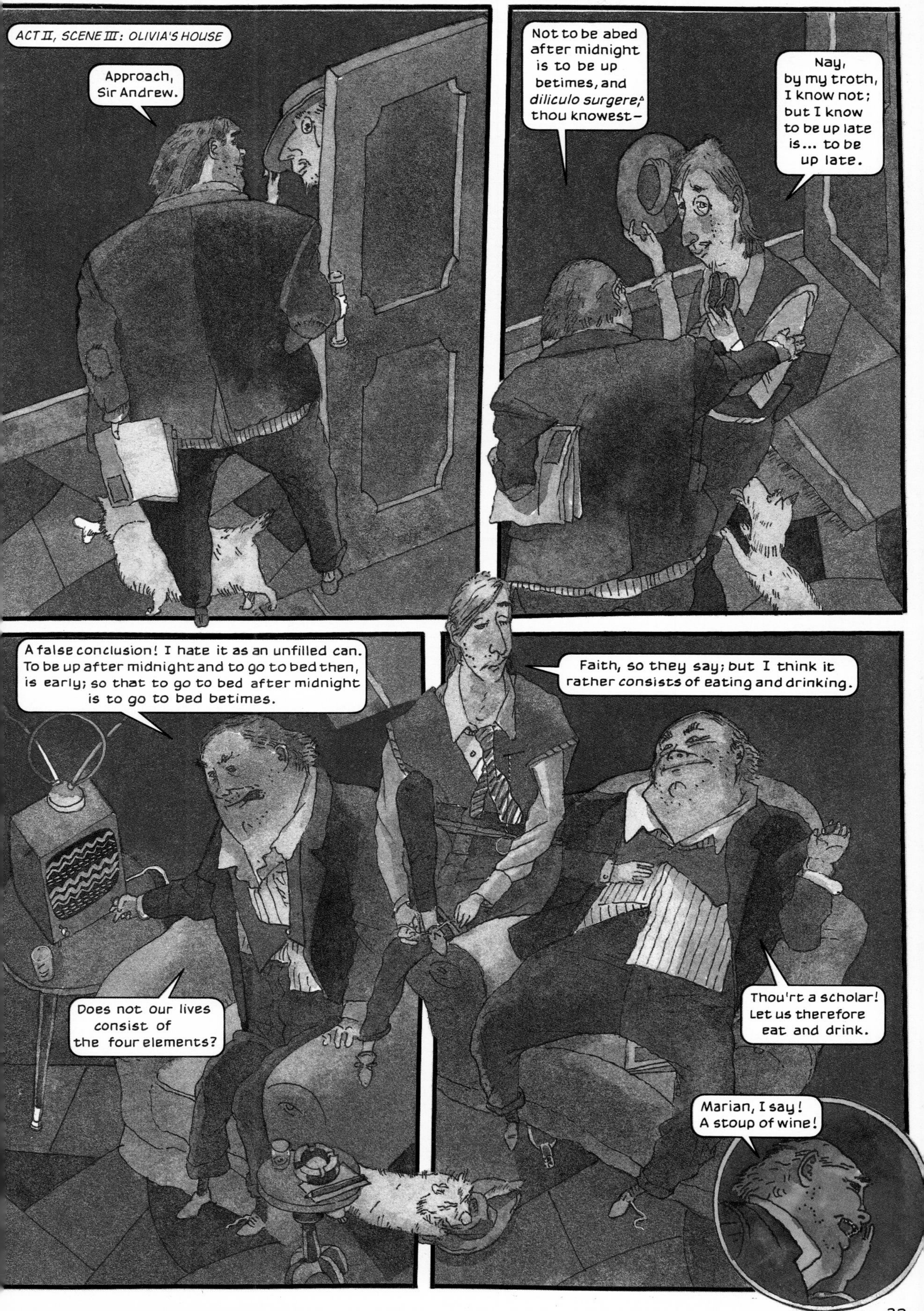
ACT II, SCENE III: OLIVIA'S HOUSE
Approach, Sir Andrew.
Not to be abed after midnight is to be up betimes, and *diliculo surgere,*[A] thou knowest–
Nay, by my troth, I know not; but I know to be up late is... to be up late.
A false conclusion! I hate it as an unfilled can. To be up after midnight and to go to bed then, is early; so that to go to bed after midnight is to go to bed betimes.
Does not our lives consist of the four elements?
Faith, so they say; but I think it rather *consists* of eating and drinking.
Thou'rt a scholar! Let us therefore eat and drink.
Marian, I say! A stoup of wine!

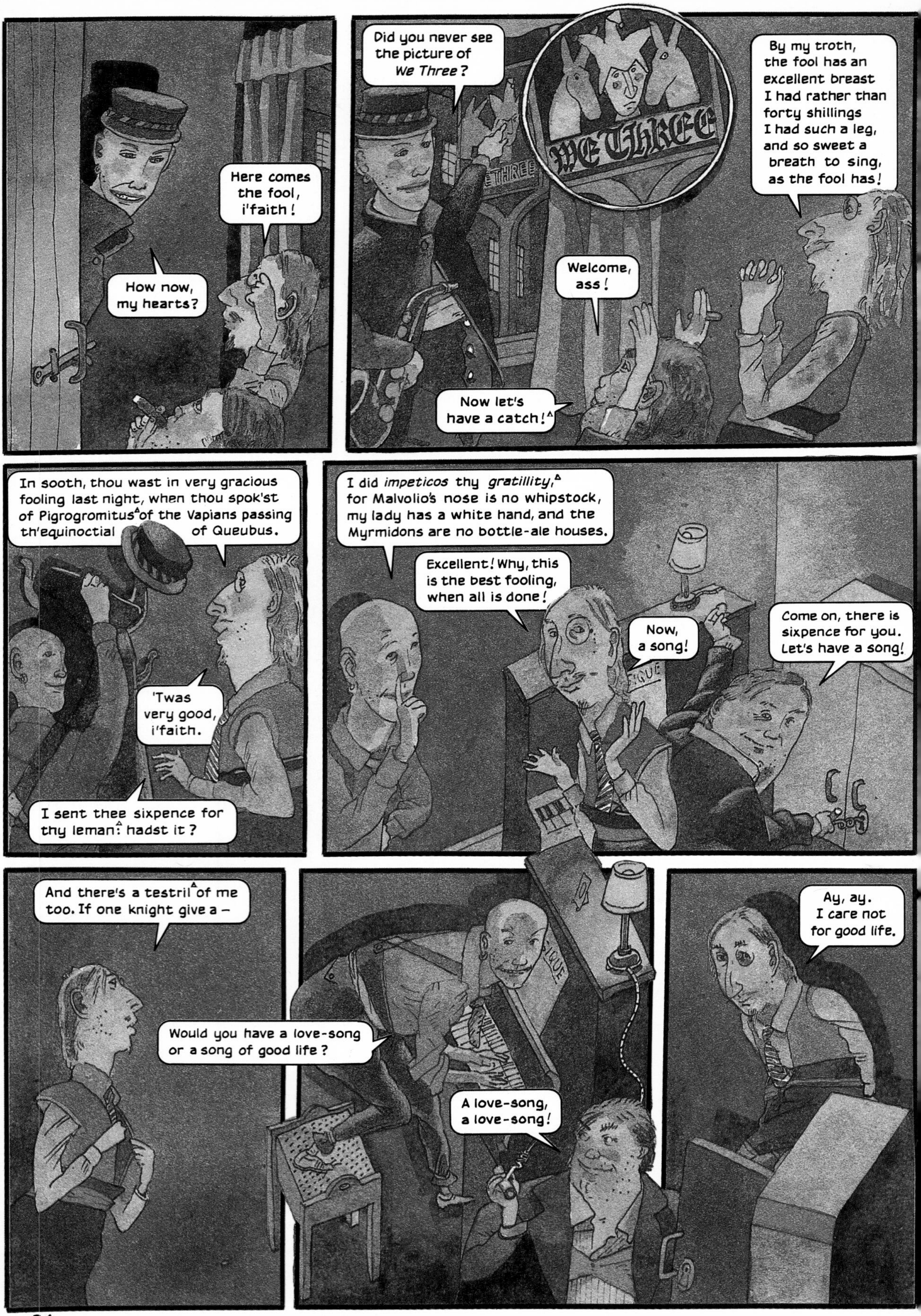
Here comes the fool, i'faith!
How now, my hearts?
Did you never see the picture of *We Three*?
WE THREE
By my troth, the fool has an excellent breast I had rather than forty shillings I had such a leg, and so sweet a breath to sing, as the fool has!
Welcome, ass!
Now let's have a catch!
In sooth, thou wast in very gracious fooling last night, when thou spok'st of Pigrogromitus of the Vapians passing th'equinoctial of Queubus.
'Twas very good, i'faith.
I sent thee sixpence for thy leman: hadst it?
I did *impeticos* thy *gratillity*, for Malvolio's nose is no whipstock, my lady has a white hand, and the Myrmidons are no bottle-ale houses.
Excellent! Why, this is the best fooling, when all is done!
Now, a song!
Come on, there is sixpence for you. Let's have a song!
And there's a testril of me too. If one knight give a –
Would you have a love-song or a song of good life?
A love-song, a love-song!
Ay, ay. I care not for good life.

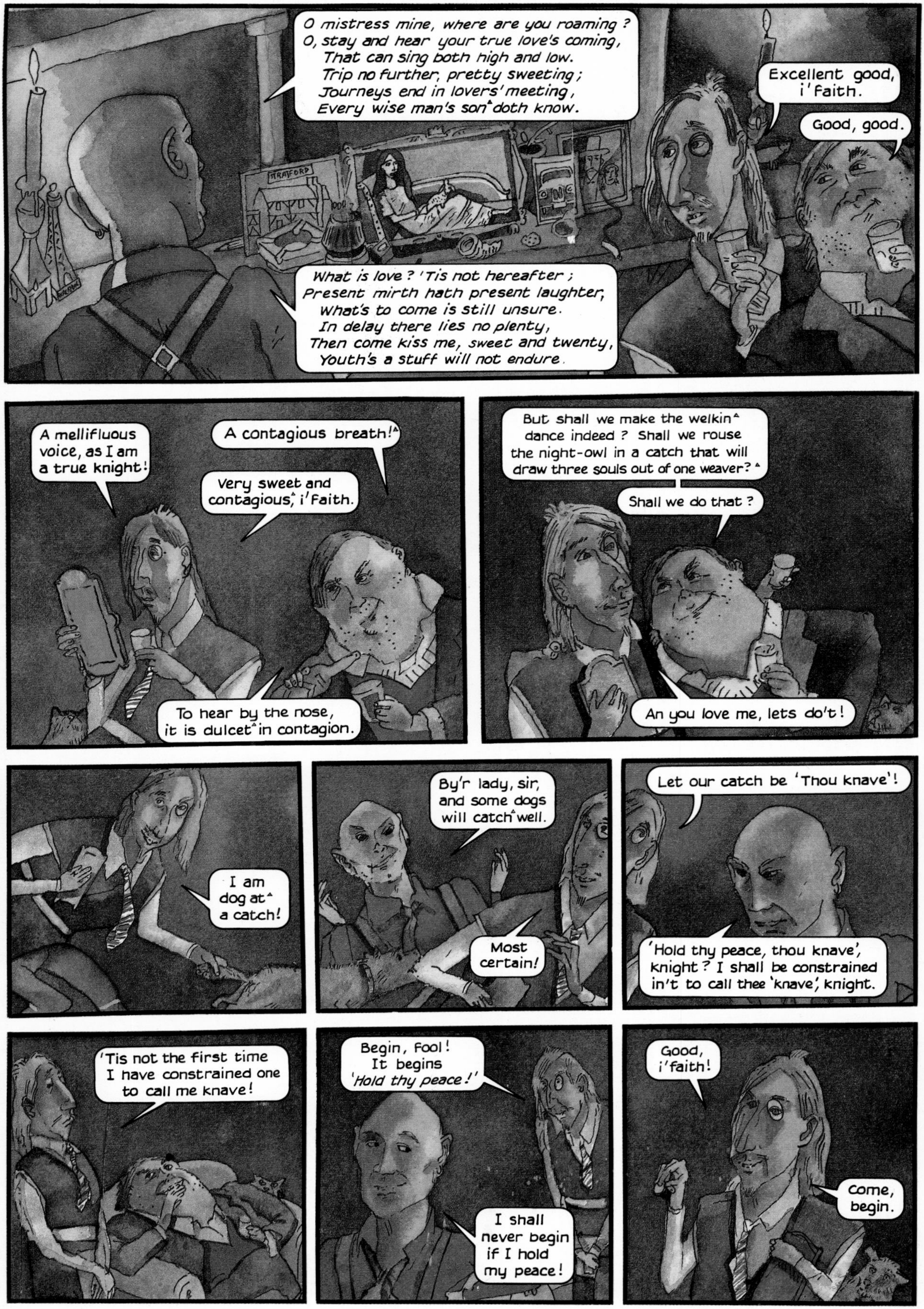

O mistress mine, where are you roaming? O, stay and hear your true love's coming, That can sing both high and low. Trip no further, pretty sweeting; Journeys end in lovers' meeting, Every wise man's son doth know.
Excellent good, i'faith.
Good, good.
What is love? 'Tis not hereafter; Present mirth hath present laughter, What's to come is still unsure. In delay there lies no plenty, Then come kiss me, sweet and twenty, Youth's a stuff will not endure.
A mellifluous voice, as I am a true knight!
A contagious breath!
Very sweet and contagious, i'faith.
To hear by the nose, it is dulcet in contagion.
But shall we make the welkin dance indeed? Shall we rouse the night-owl in a catch that will draw three souls out of one weaver?
Shall we do that?
An you love me, lets do't!
I am dog at a catch!
By'r lady, sir, and some dogs will catch well.
Most certain!
Let our catch be 'Thou knave'!
'Hold thy peace, thou knave', knight? I shall be constrained in't to call thee 'knave', knight.
'Tis not the first time I have constrained one to call me knave!
Begin, Fool! It begins 'Hold thy peace!'
I shall never begin if I hold my peace!
Good, i'faith!
Come, begin.

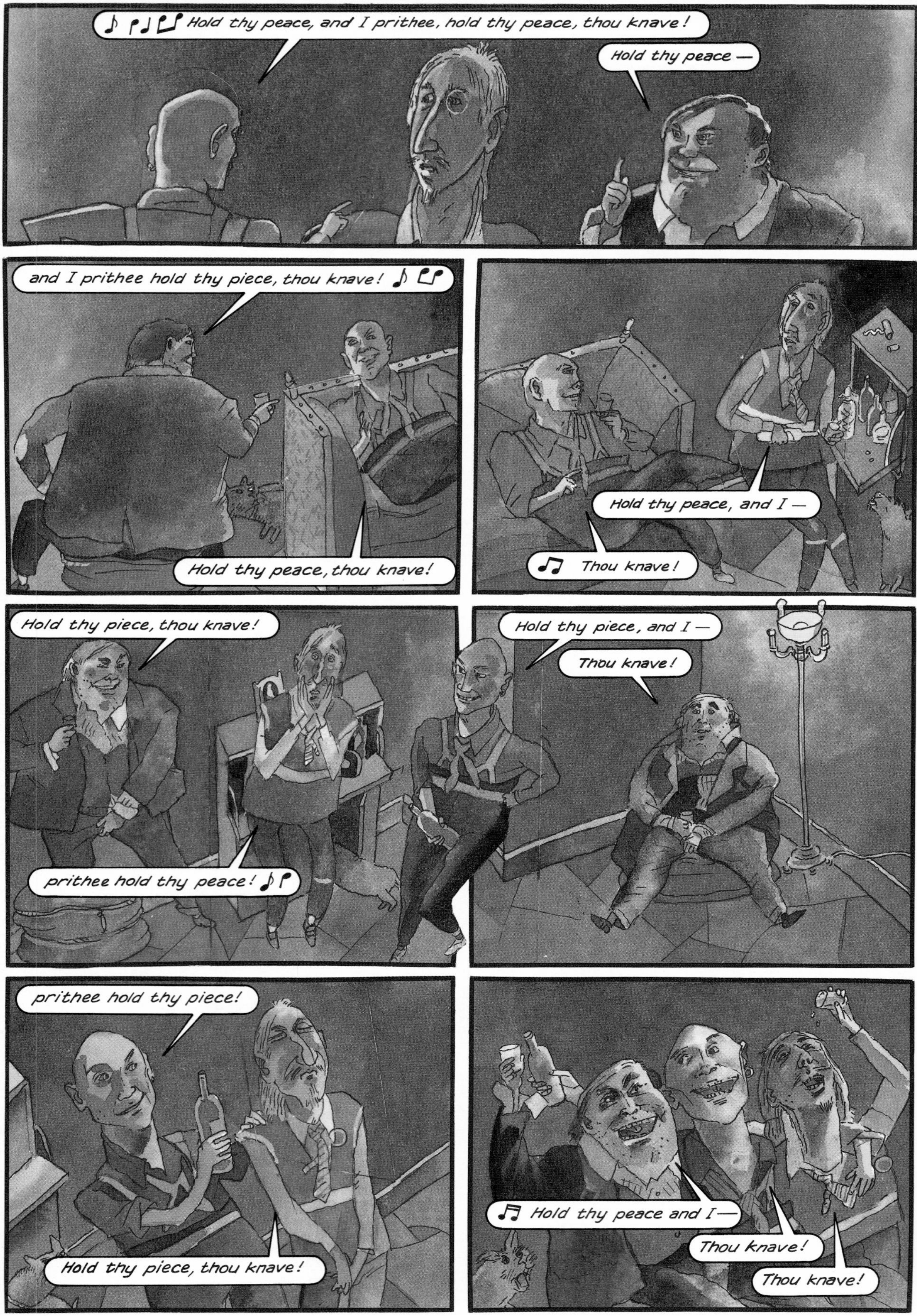
Hold thy peace, and I prithee, hold thy peace, thou knave!
Hold thy peace —
and I prithee hold thy piece, thou knave!
Hold thy peace, thou knave!
Hold thy peace, and I —
Thou knave!
Hold thy piece, thou knave!
prithee hold thy peace!
Hold thy piece, and I —
Thou knave!
prithee hold thy piece!
Hold thy piece, thou knave!
Hold thy peace and I —
Thou knave!
Thou knave!

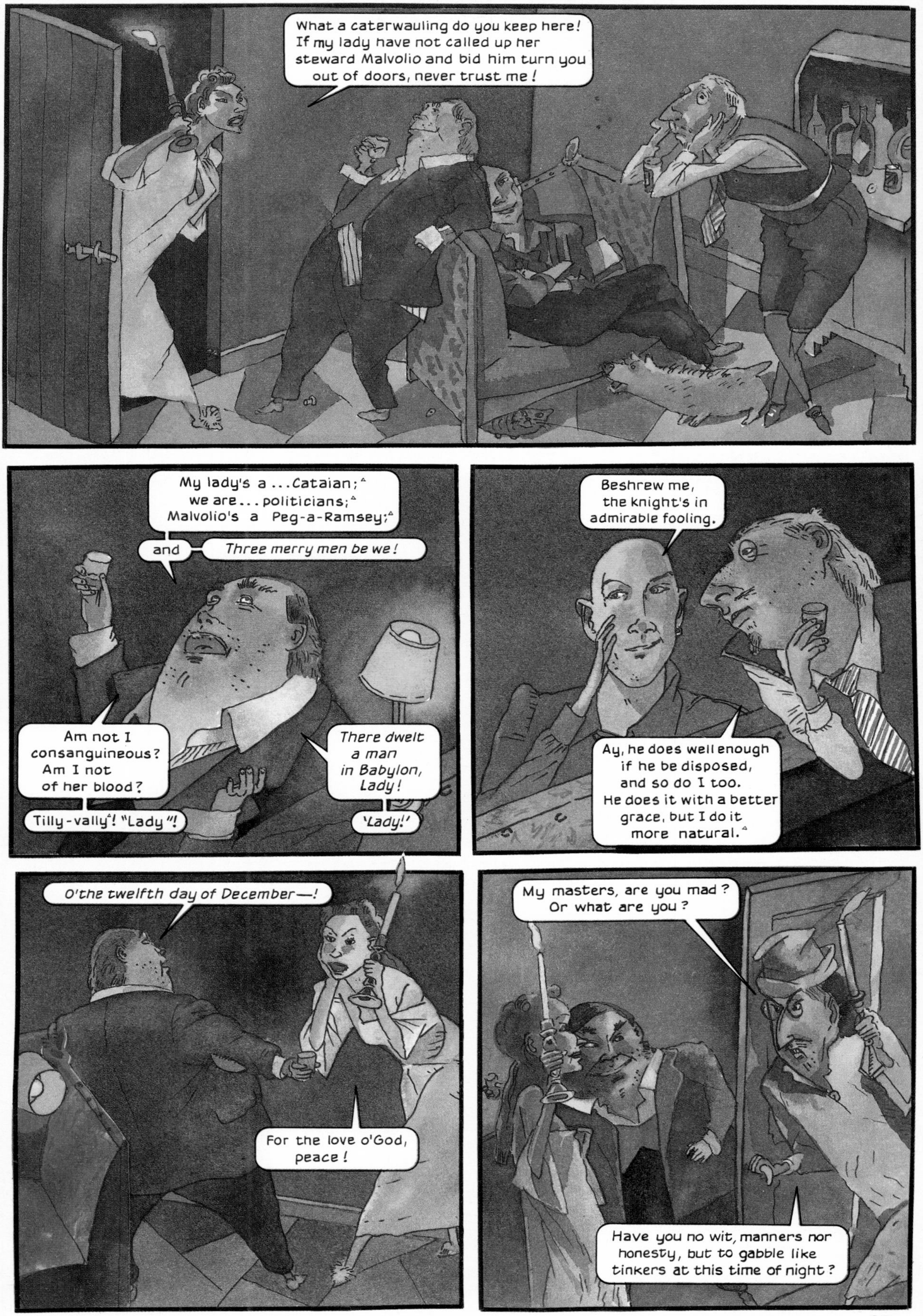
What a caterwauling do you keep here! If my lady have not called up her steward Malvolio and bid him turn you out of doors, never trust me!
My lady's a ...Cataian; we are... politicians; Malvolio's a Peg-a-Ramsey;
and
Three merry men be we!
Am not I consanguineous? Am I not of her blood?
Tilly-vally! "Lady"!
There dwelt a man in Babylon, Lady!
'Lady!'
Beshrew me, the knight's in admirable fooling.
Ay, he does well enough if he be disposed, and so do I too. He does it with a better grace, but I do it more natural.
O'the twelfth day of December—!
For the love o'God, peace!
My masters, are you mad? Or what are you?
Have you no wit, manners nor honesty, but to gabble like tinkers at this time of night?

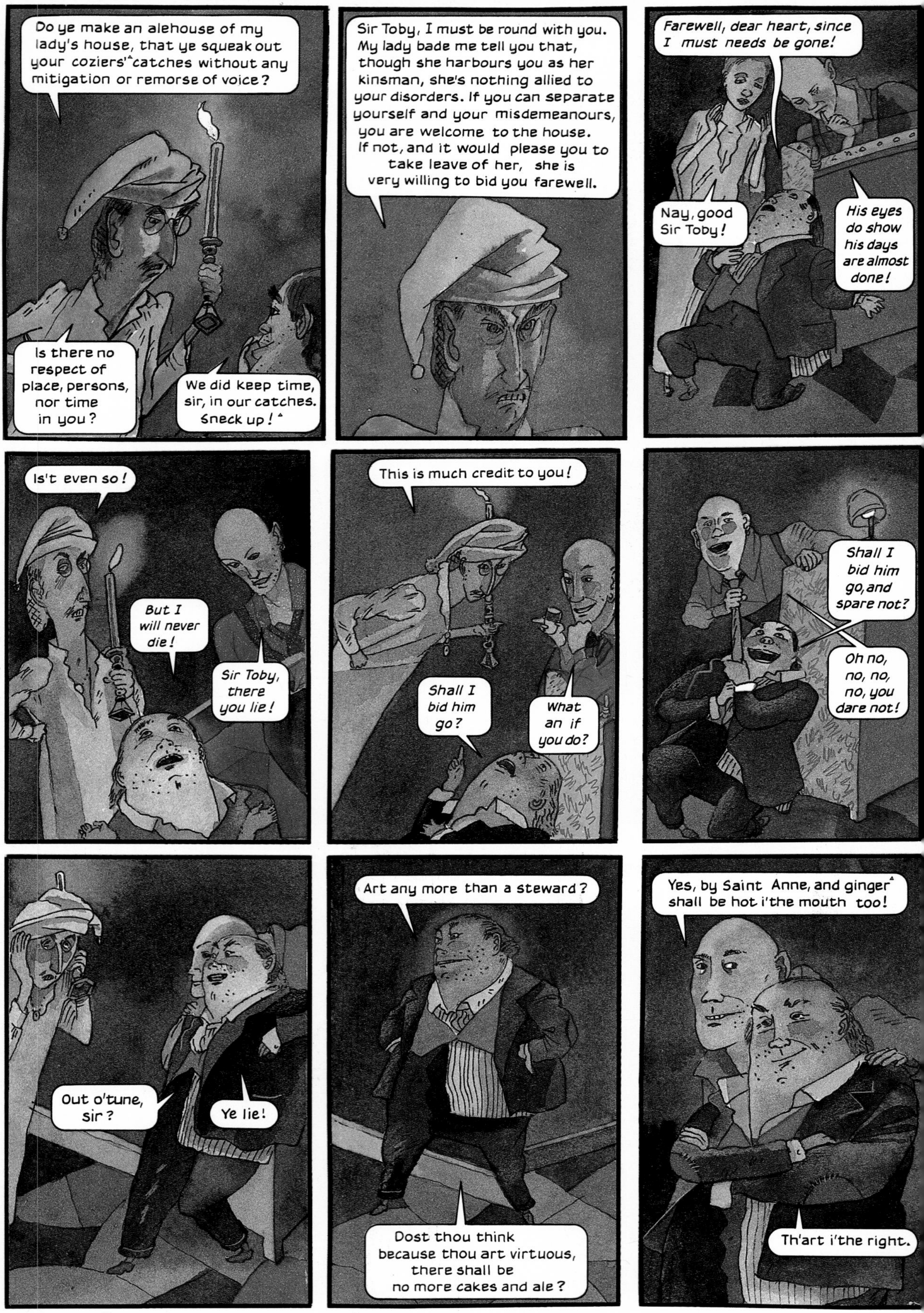
Do ye make an alehouse of my lady's house, that ye squeak out your coziers'^ catches without any mitigation or remorse of voice?
Is there no respect of place, persons, nor time in you?
We did keep time, sir, in our catches. Sneck up!^
Sir Toby, I must be round with you. My lady bade me tell you that, though she harbours you as her kinsman, she's nothing allied to your disorders. If you can separate yourself and your misdemeanours, you are welcome to the house. If not, and it would please you to take leave of her, she is very willing to bid you farewell.
Farewell, dear heart, since I must needs be gone!
Nay, good Sir Toby!
His eyes do show his days are almost done!
Is't even so!
But I will never die!
Sir Toby, there you lie!
This is much credit to you!
Shall I bid him go?
What an if you do?
Shall I bid him go, and spare not?
Oh no, no, no, no, you dare not!
Out o'tune, sir?
Ye lie!
Art any more than a steward?
Dost thou think because thou art virtuous, there shall be no more cakes and ale?
Yes, by Saint Anne, and ginger^ shall be hot i'the mouth too!
Th'art i'the right.

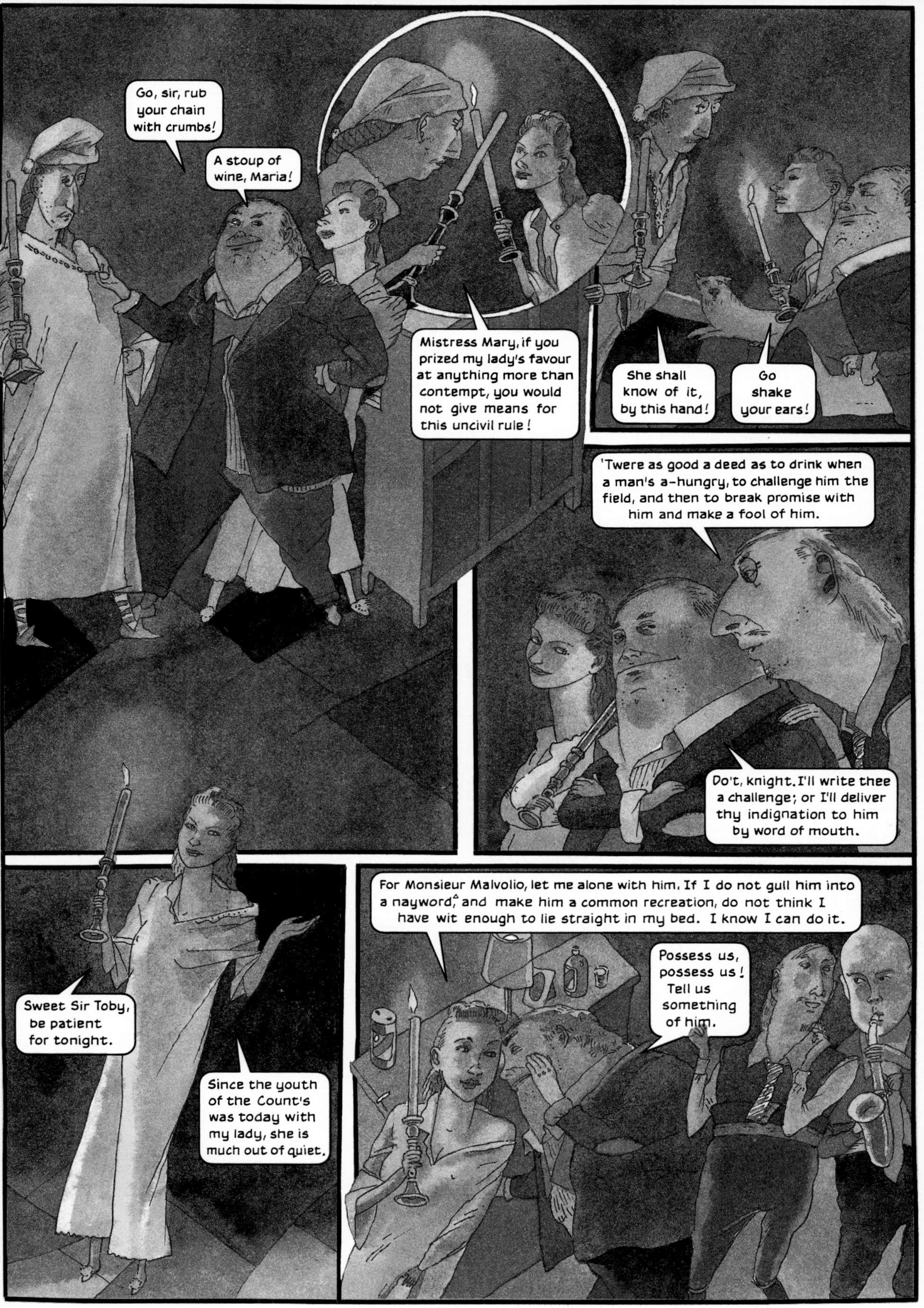
Go, sir, rub your chain with crumbs!
A stoup of wine, Maria!
Mistress Mary, if you prized my lady's favour at anything more than contempt, you would not give means for this uncivil rule!
She shall know of it, by this hand!
Go shake your ears!
'Twere as good a deed as to drink when a man's a-hungry, to challenge him the field, and then to break promise with him and make a fool of him.
Do't, knight. I'll write thee a challenge; or I'll deliver thy indignation to him by word of mouth.
Sweet Sir Toby, be patient for tonight.
Since the youth of the Count's was today with my lady, she is much out of quiet.
For Monsieur Malvolio, let me alone with him. If I do not gull him into a nayword,^ and make him a common recreation, do not think I have wit enough to lie straight in my bed. I know I can do it.
Possess us, possess us! Tell us something of him.

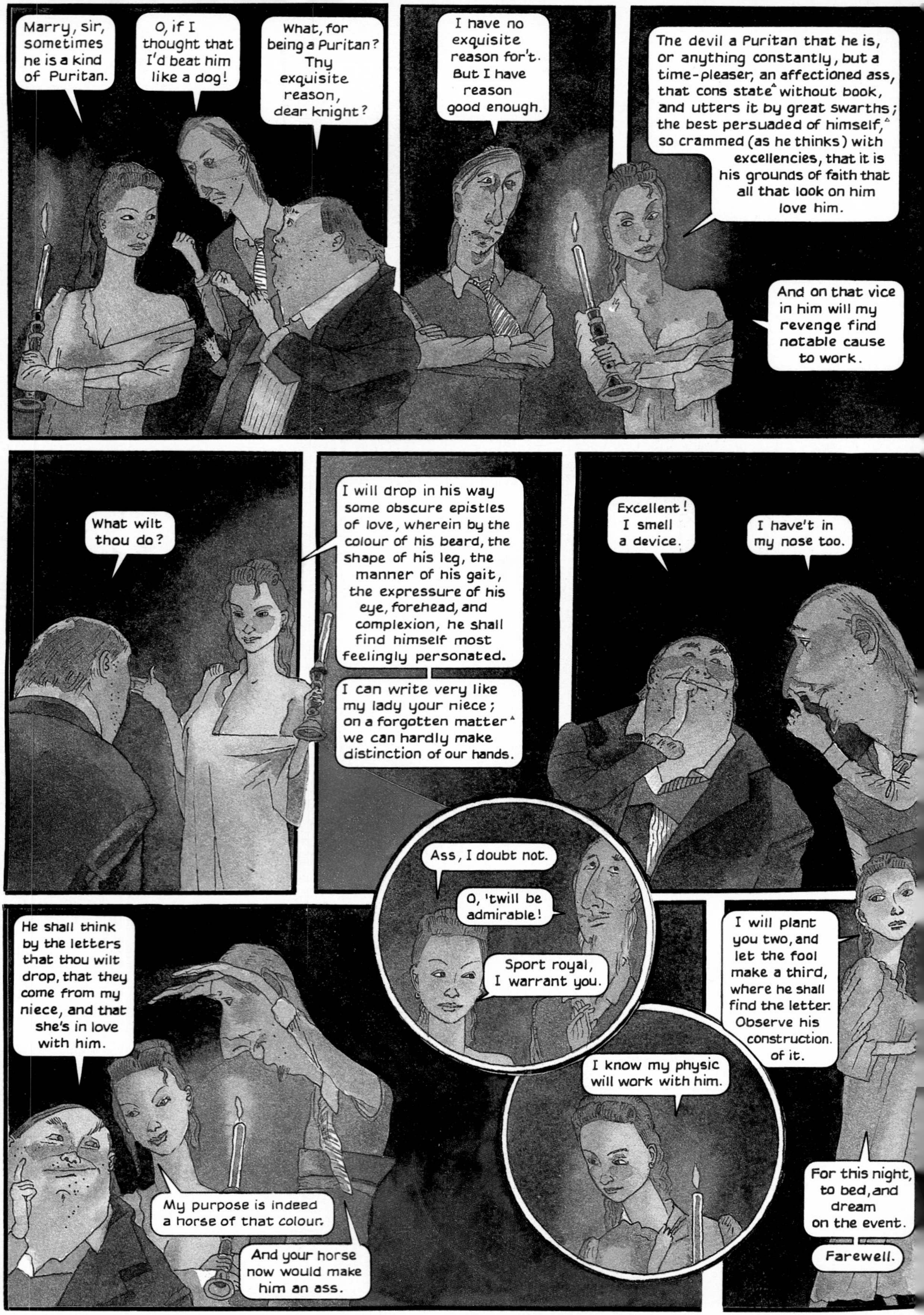
Marry, sir, sometimes he is a kind of Puritan.
O, if I thought that I'd beat him like a dog!
What, for being a Puritan? Thy exquisite reason, dear knight?
I have no exquisite reason for't. But I have reason good enough.
The devil a Puritan that he is, or anything constantly, but a time-pleaser, an affectioned ass, that cons state without book, and utters it by great swarths; the best persuaded of himself, so crammed (as he thinks) with excellencies, that it is his grounds of faith that all that look on him love him.
And on that vice in him will my revenge find notable cause to work.
What wilt thou do?
I will drop in his way some obscure epistles of love, wherein by the colour of his beard, the shape of his leg, the manner of his gait, the expressure of his eye, forehead, and complexion, he shall find himself most feelingly personated.
I can write very like my lady your niece; on a forgotten matter we can hardly make distinction of our hands.
Excellent! I smell a device.
I have't in my nose too.
He shall think by the letters that thou wilt drop, that they come from my niece, and that she's in love with him.
My purpose is indeed a horse of that colour.
And your horse now would make him an ass.
Ass, I doubt not.
O, 'twill be admirable!
Sport royal, I warrant you.
I know my physic will work with him.
I will plant you two, and let the fool make a third, where he shall find the letter. Observe his construction of it.
For this night, to bed, and dream on the event.
Farewell.

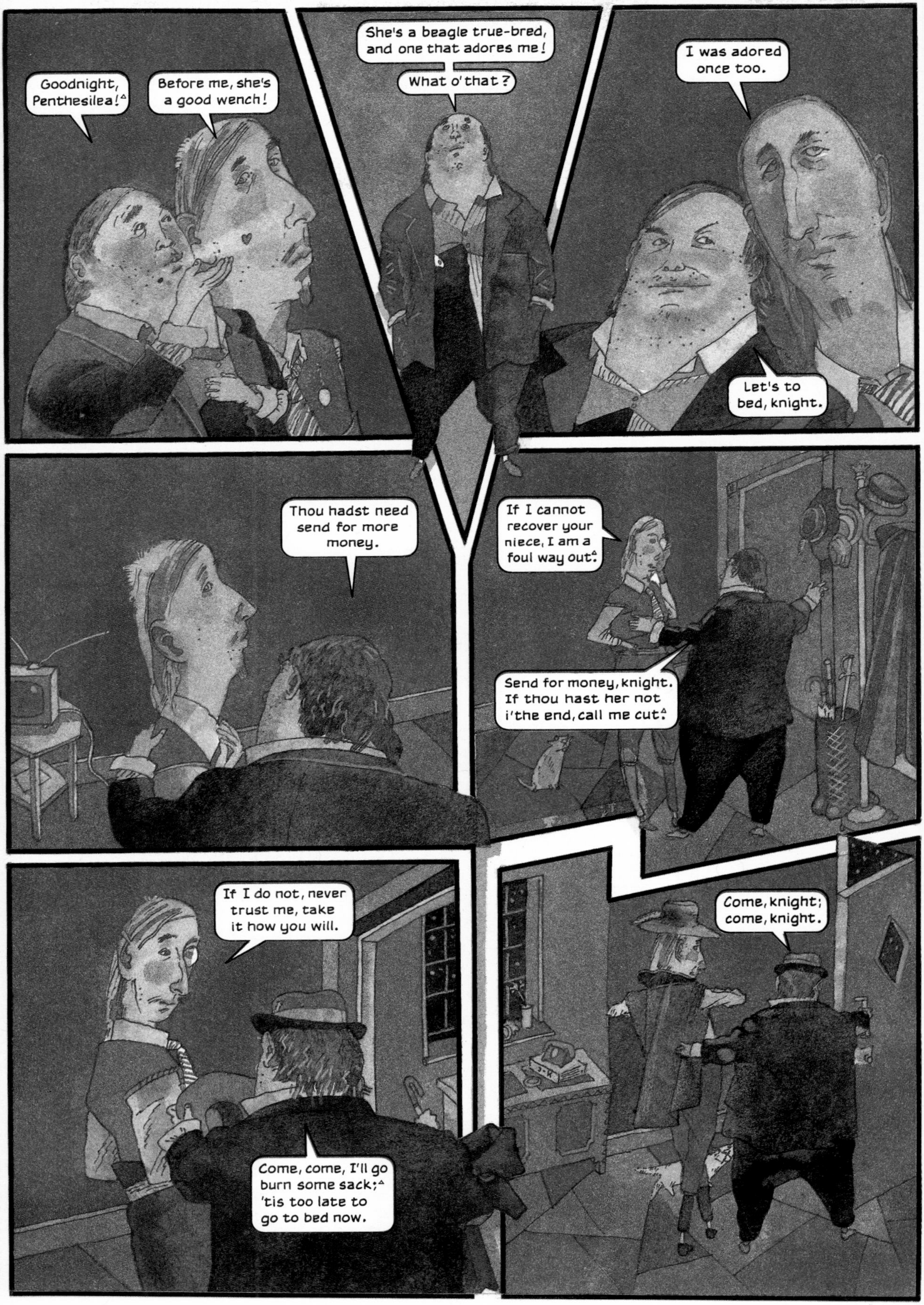

Goodnight, Penthesilea!△
Before me, she's a good wench!
She's a beagle true-bred, and one that adores me!
What o'that?
I was adored once too.
Let's to bed, knight.
Thou hadst need send for more money.
If I cannot recover your niece, I am a foul way out△.
Send for money, knight. If thou hast her not i'the end, call me cut△.
If I do not, never trust me, take it how you will.
Come, come, I'll go burn some sack;△ 'tis too late to go to bed now.
Come, knight; come, knight.

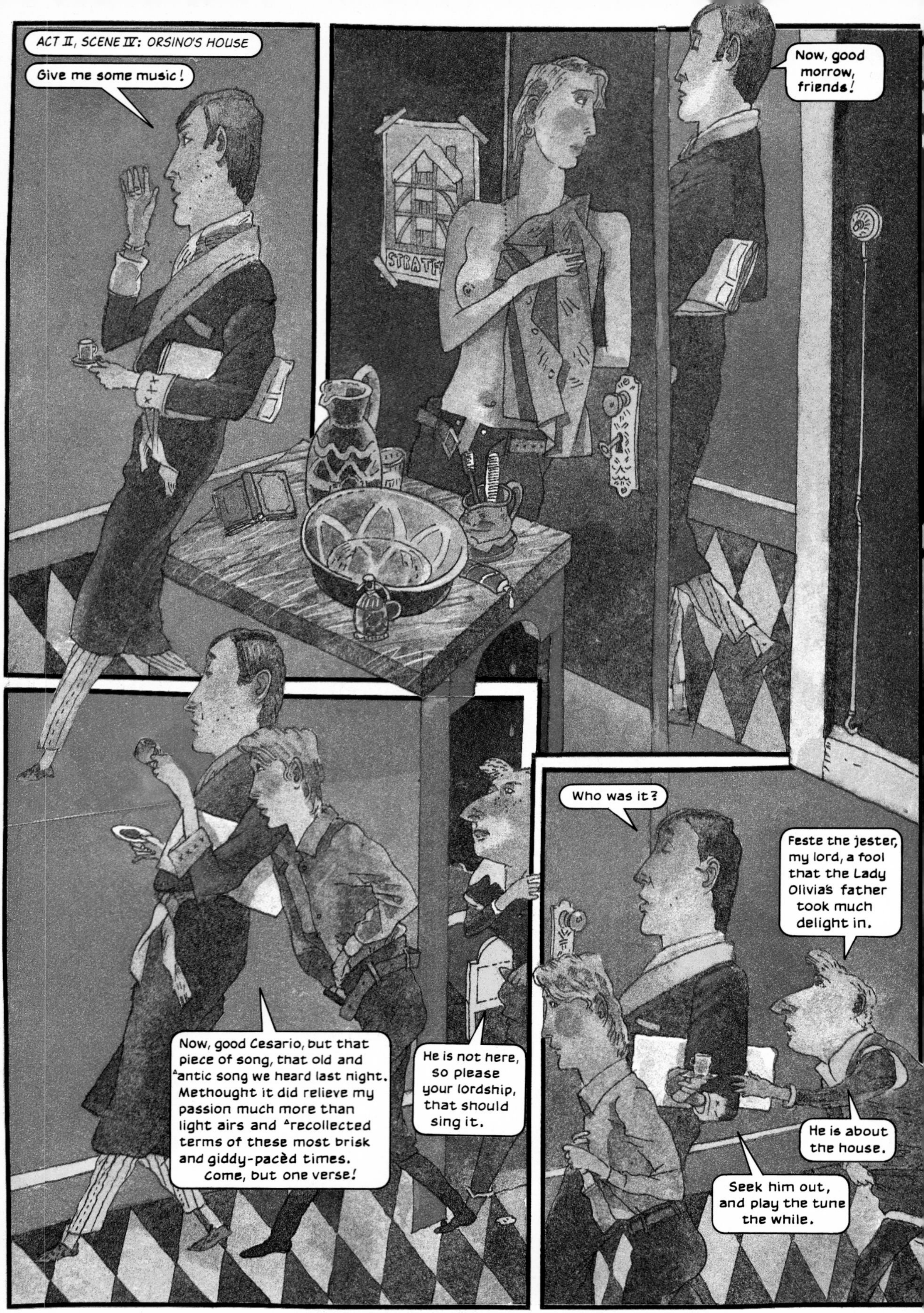
ACT II, SCENE IV: ORSINO'S HOUSE
Give me some music!
Now, good morrow, friends!
Now, good Cesario, but that piece of song, that old and ^antic song we heard last night. Methought it did relieve my passion much more than light airs and ^recollected terms of these most brisk and giddy-pacèd times. Come, but one verse!
He is not here, so please your lordship, that should sing it.
Who was it?
Feste the jester, my lord, a fool that the Lady Olivia's father took much delight in.
He is about the house.
Seek him out, and play the tune the while.

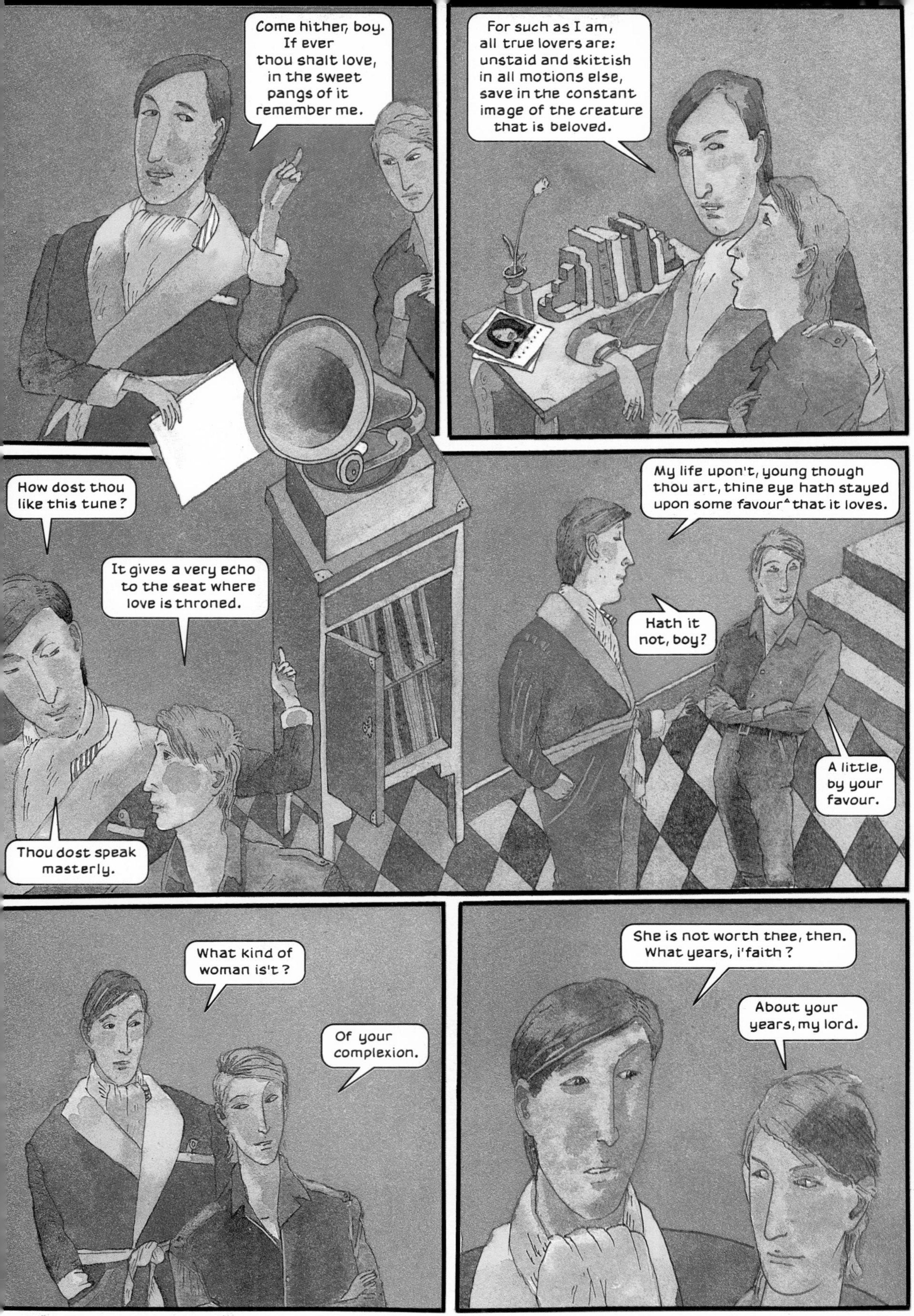

Come hither, boy. If ever thou shalt love, in the sweet pangs of it remember me.
For such as I am, all true lovers are: unstaid and skittish in all motions else, save in the constant image of the creature that is beloved.
How dost thou like this tune?
It gives a very echo to the seat where love is throned.
Thou dost speak masterly.
My life upon't, young though thou art, thine eye hath stayed upon some favour^ that it loves.
Hath it not, boy?
A little, by your favour.
What kind of woman is't?
Of your complexion.
She is not worth thee, then. What years, i'faith?
About your years, my lord.

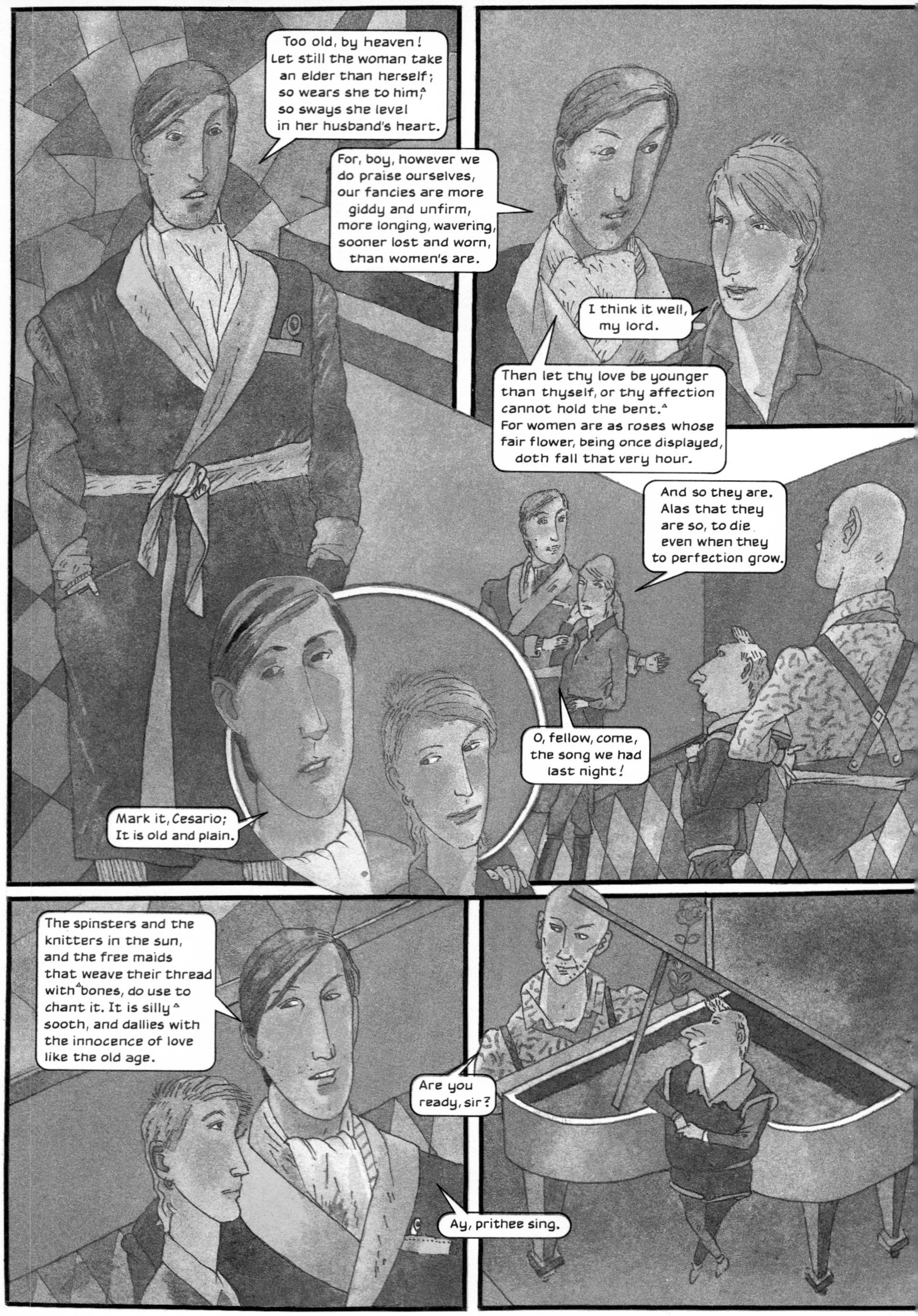

Too old, by heaven! Let still the woman take an elder than herself; so wears she to him, so sways she level in her husband's heart.
For, boy, however we do praise ourselves, our fancies are more giddy and unfirm, more longing, wavering, sooner lost and worn, than women's are.
I think it well, my lord.
Then let thy love be younger than thyself, or thy affection cannot hold the bent. For women are as roses whose fair flower, being once displayed, doth fall that very hour.
And so they are. Alas that they are so, to die even when they to perfection grow.
O, fellow, come, the song we had last night!
Mark it, Cesario; It is old and plain.
The spinsters and the knitters in the sun, and the free maids that weave their thread with bones, do use to chant it. It is silly sooth, and dallies with the innocence of love like the old age.
Are you ready, sir?
Ay, prithee sing.

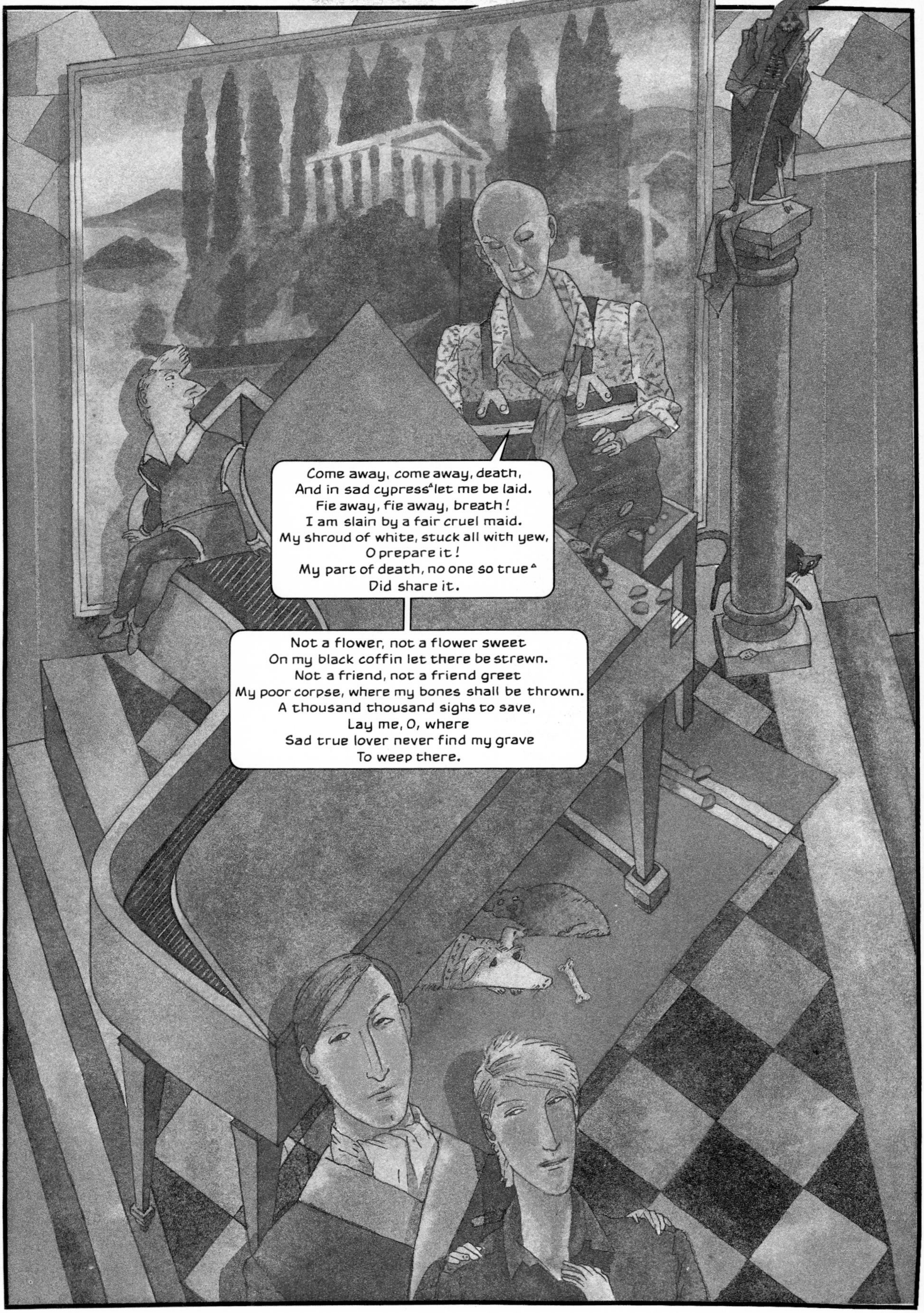
Come away, come away, death,
And in sad cypress let me be laid.
Fie away, fie away, breath!
I am slain by a fair cruel maid.
My shroud of white, stuck all with yew,
O prepare it!
My part of death, no one so true
Did share it.
Not a flower, not a flower sweet
On my black coffin let there be strewn.
Not a friend, not a friend greet
My poor corpse, where my bones shall be thrown.
A thousand thousand sighs to save,
Lay me, O, where
Sad true lover never find my grave
To weep there.

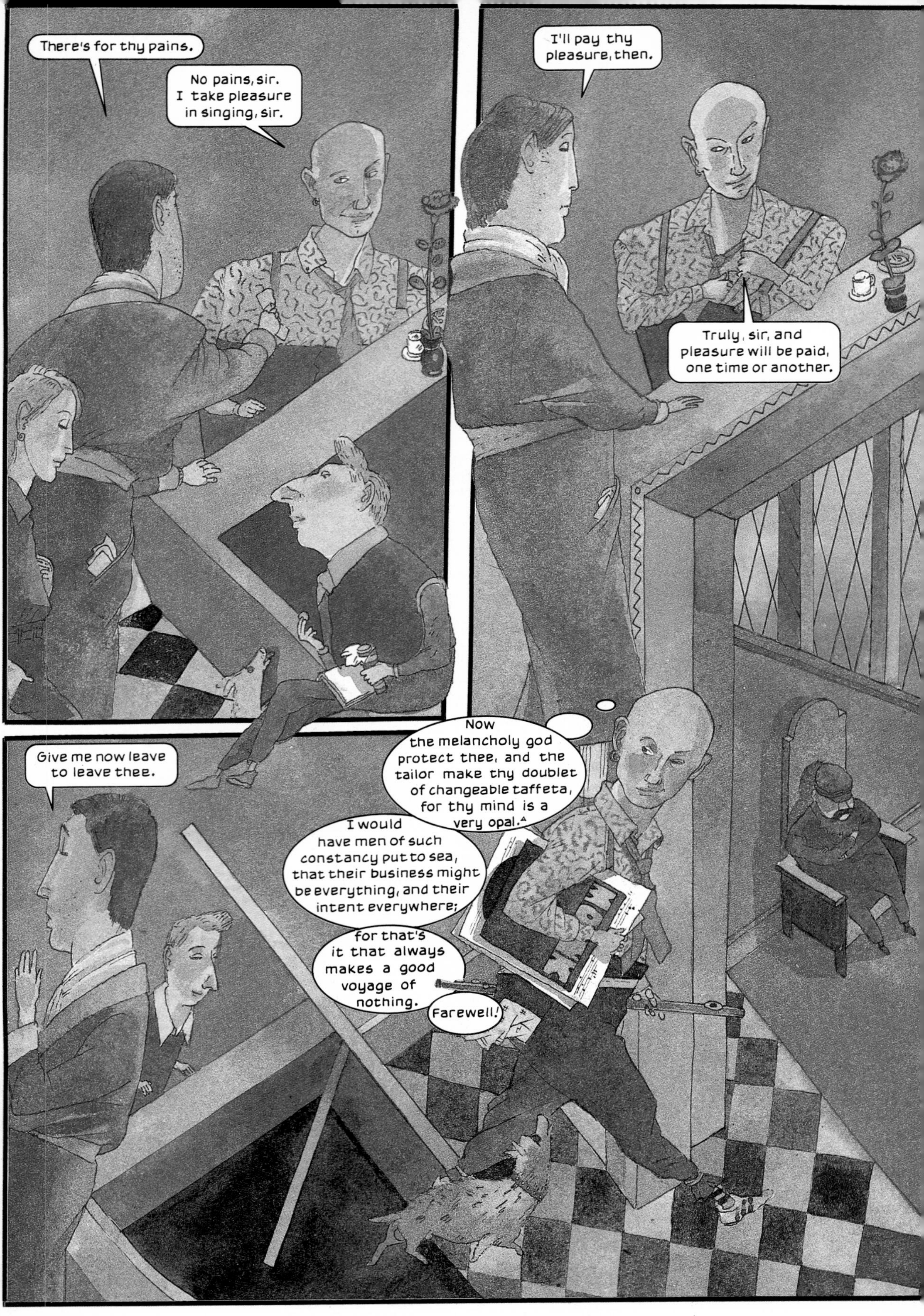

There's for thy pains.
No pains, sir. I take pleasure in singing, sir.
I'll pay thy pleasure, then.
Truly, sir, and pleasure will be paid, one time or another.
Give me now leave to leave thee.
Now the melancholy god protect thee, and the tailor make thy doublet of changeable taffeta, for thy mind is a very opal.^
I would have men of such constancy put to sea, that their business might be everything, and their intent everywhere;
for that's it that always makes a good voyage of nothing.
Farewell!

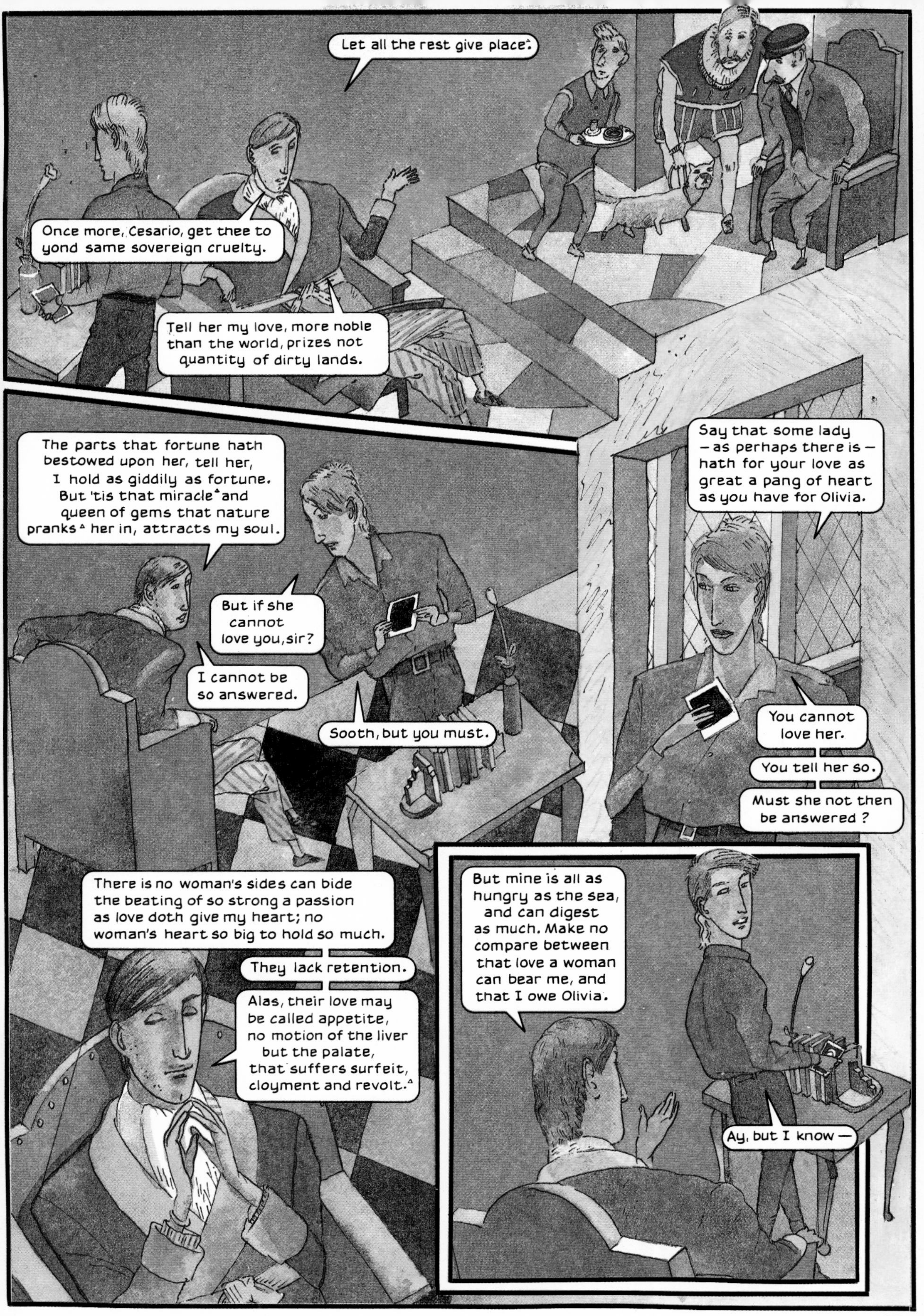

Let all the rest give place.
Once more, Cesario, get thee to yond same sovereign cruelty.
Tell her my love, more noble than the world, prizes not quantity of dirty lands.
The parts that fortune hath bestowed upon her, tell her, I hold as giddily as fortune. But 'tis that miracle and queen of gems that nature pranks her in, attracts my soul.
But if she cannot love you, sir?
I cannot be so answered.
Sooth, but you must.
Say that some lady — as perhaps there is — hath for your love as great a pang of heart as you have for Olivia.
You cannot love her.
You tell her so.
Must she not then be answered?
There is no woman's sides can bide the beating of so strong a passion as love doth give my heart; no woman's heart so big to hold so much.
They lack retention.
Alas, their love may be called appetite, no motion of the liver but the palate, that suffers surfeit, cloyment and revolt.
But mine is all as hungry as the sea, and can digest as much. Make no compare between that love a woman can bear me, and that I owe Olivia.
Ay, but I know —

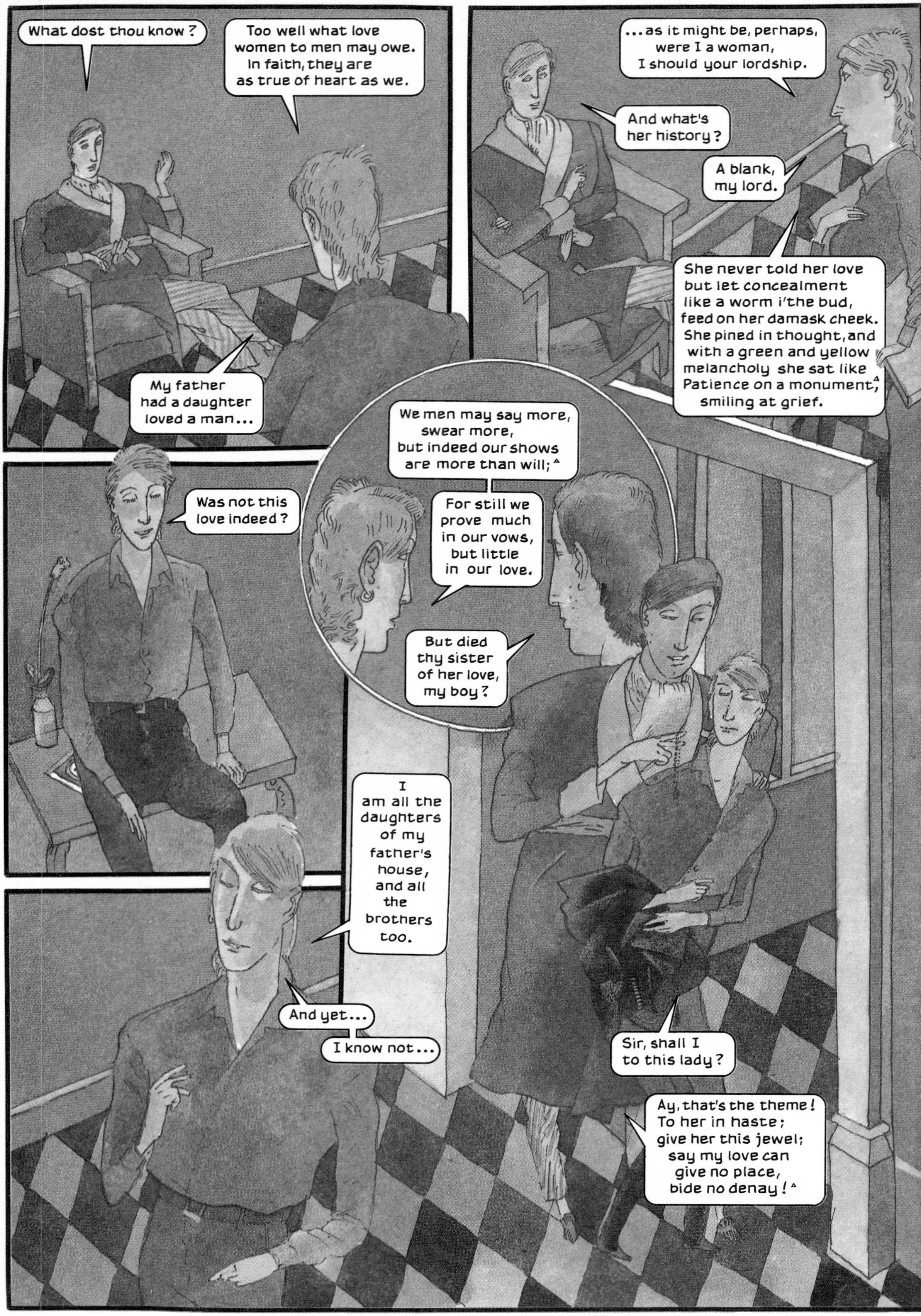
What dost thou know?
Too well what love women to men may owe. In faith, they are as true of heart as we.
My father had a daughter loved a man...
...as it might be, perhaps, were I a woman, I should your lordship.
And what's her history?
A blank, my lord.
She never told her love but let concealment like a worm i'the bud, feed on her damask cheek. She pined in thought, and with a green and yellow melancholy she sat like Patience on a monument, smiling at grief.
Was not this love indeed?
We men may say more, swear more, but indeed our shows are more than will;
For still we prove much in our vows, but little in our love.
But died thy sister of her love, my boy?
I am all the daughters of my father's house, and all the brothers too.
And yet...
I know not...
Sir, shall I to this lady?
Ay, that's the theme! To her in haste; give her this jewel; say my love can give no place, bide no denay!

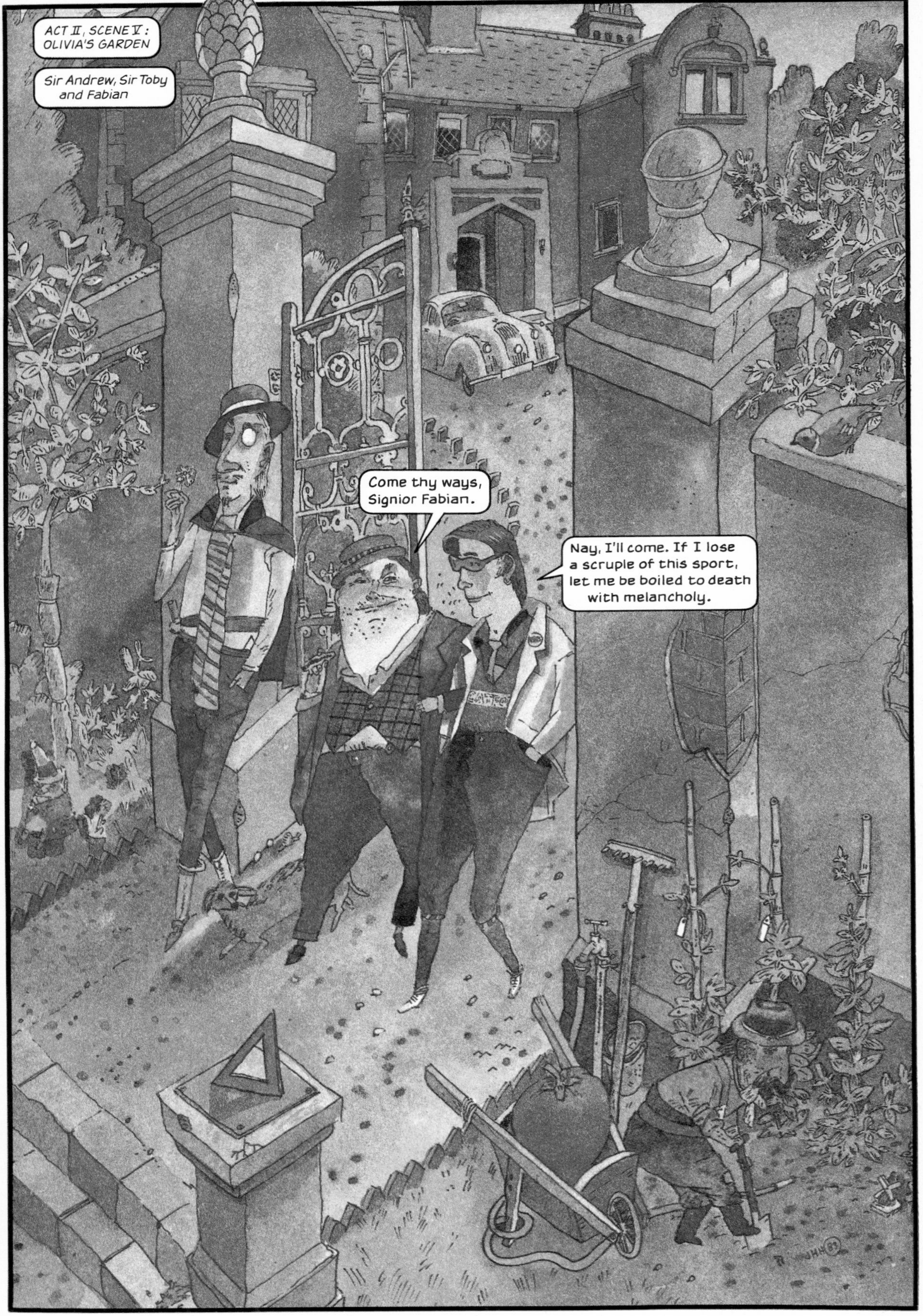

ACT II, SCENE V:
OLIVIA'S GARDEN
Sir Andrew, Sir Toby and Fabian
Come thy ways, Signior Fabian.
Nay, I'll come. If I lose a scruple of this sport, let me be boiled to death with melancholy.

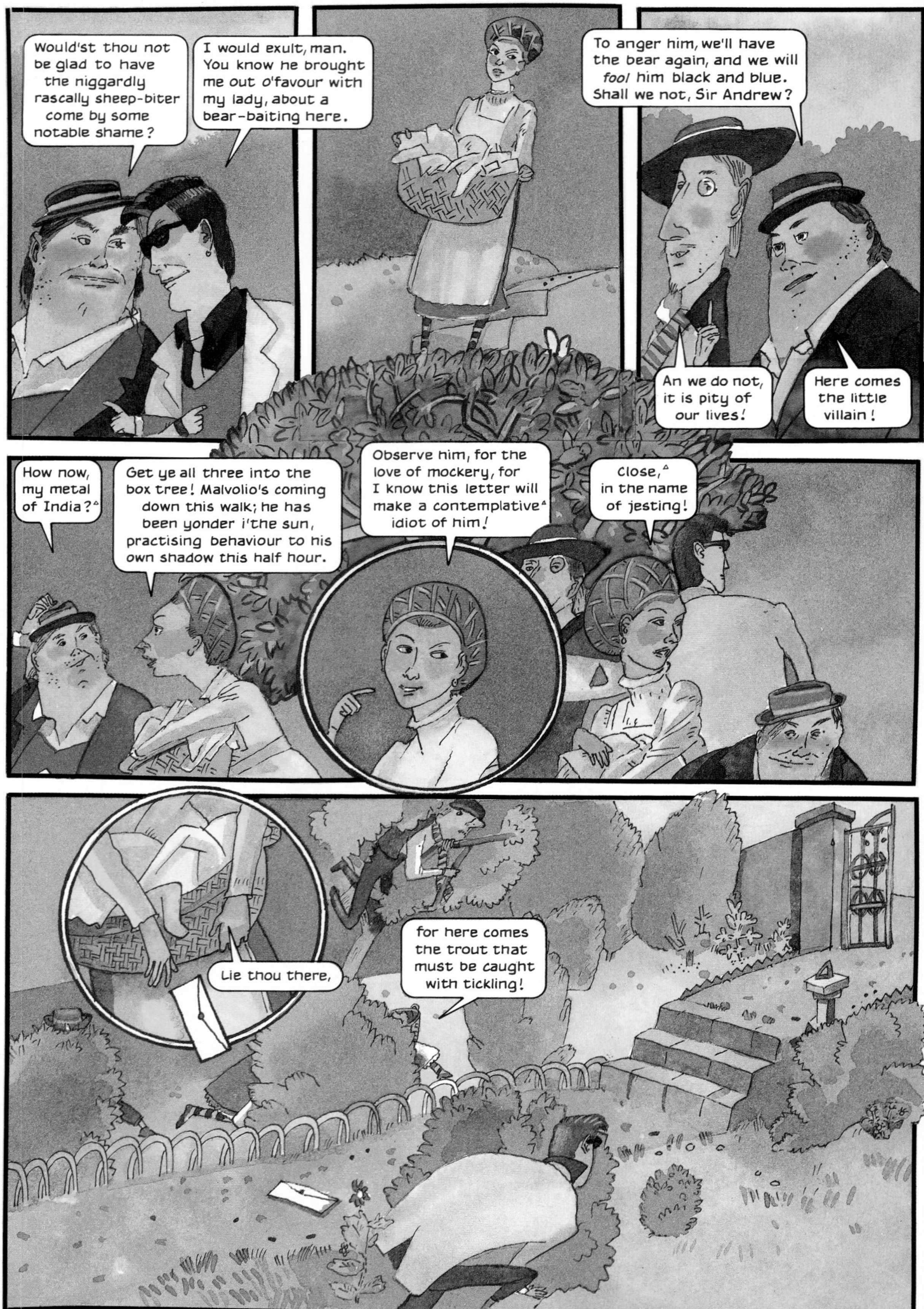
Would'st thou not be glad to have the niggardly rascally sheep-biter come by some notable shame?
I would exult, man. You know he brought me out o'favour with my lady, about a bear-baiting here.
To anger him, we'll have the bear again, and we will *fool* him black and blue. Shall we not, Sir Andrew?
An we do not, it is pity of our lives!
Here comes the little villain!
How now, my metal of India?
Get ye all three into the box tree! Malvolio's coming down this walk; he has been yonder i'the sun, practising behaviour to his own shadow this half hour.
Observe him, for the love of mockery, for I know this letter will make a contemplative idiot of him!
Close, in the name of jesting!
Lie thou there,
for here comes the trout that must be caught with tickling!

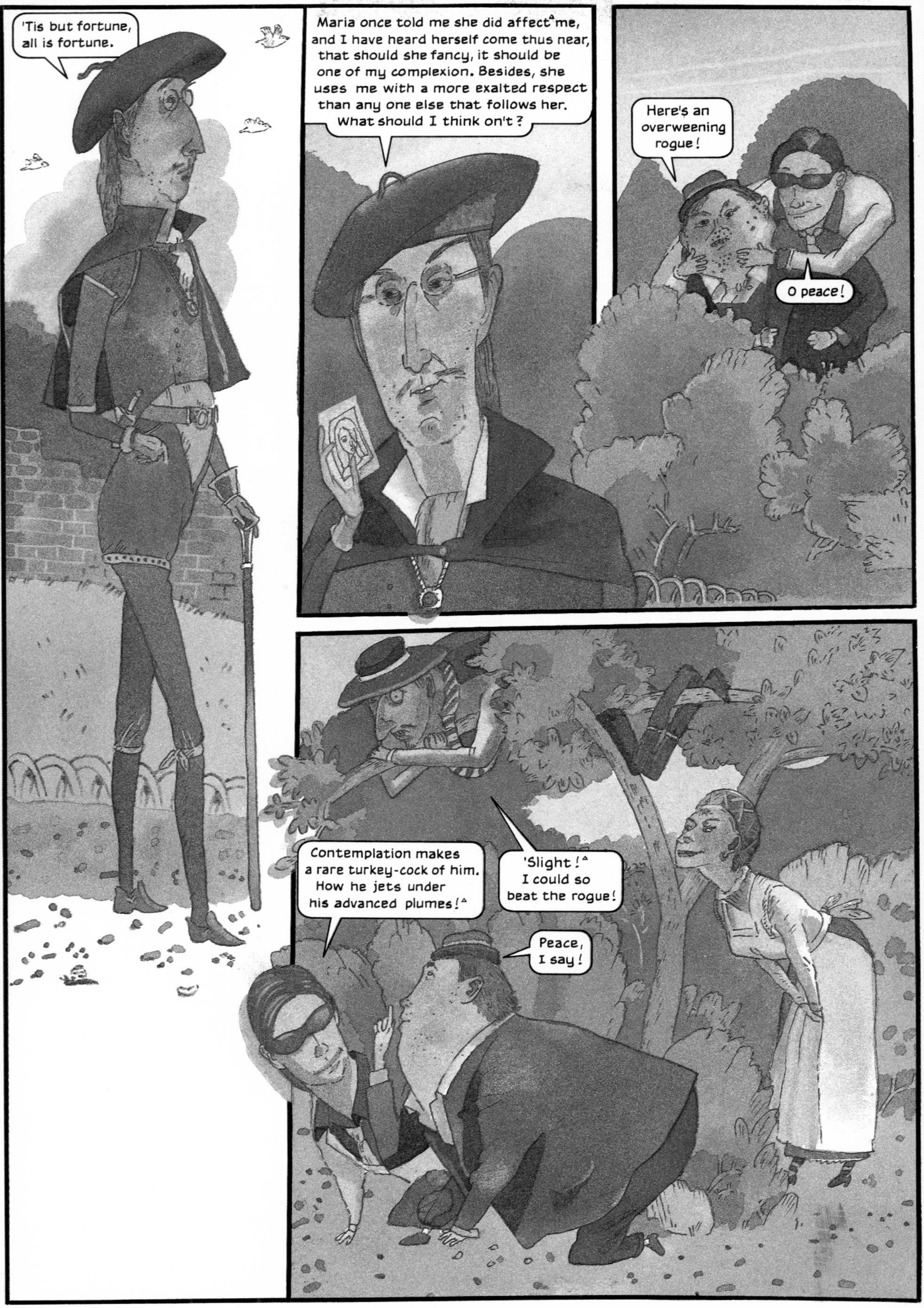
'Tis but fortune, all is fortune.
Maria once told me she did affect me, and I have heard herself come thus near, that should she fancy, it should be one of my complexion. Besides, she uses me with a more exalted respect than any one else that follows her. What should I think on't?
Here's an overweening rogue!
O peace!
Contemplation makes a rare turkey-cock of him. How he jets under his advanced plumes!
'Slight! I could so beat the rogue!
Peace, I say!

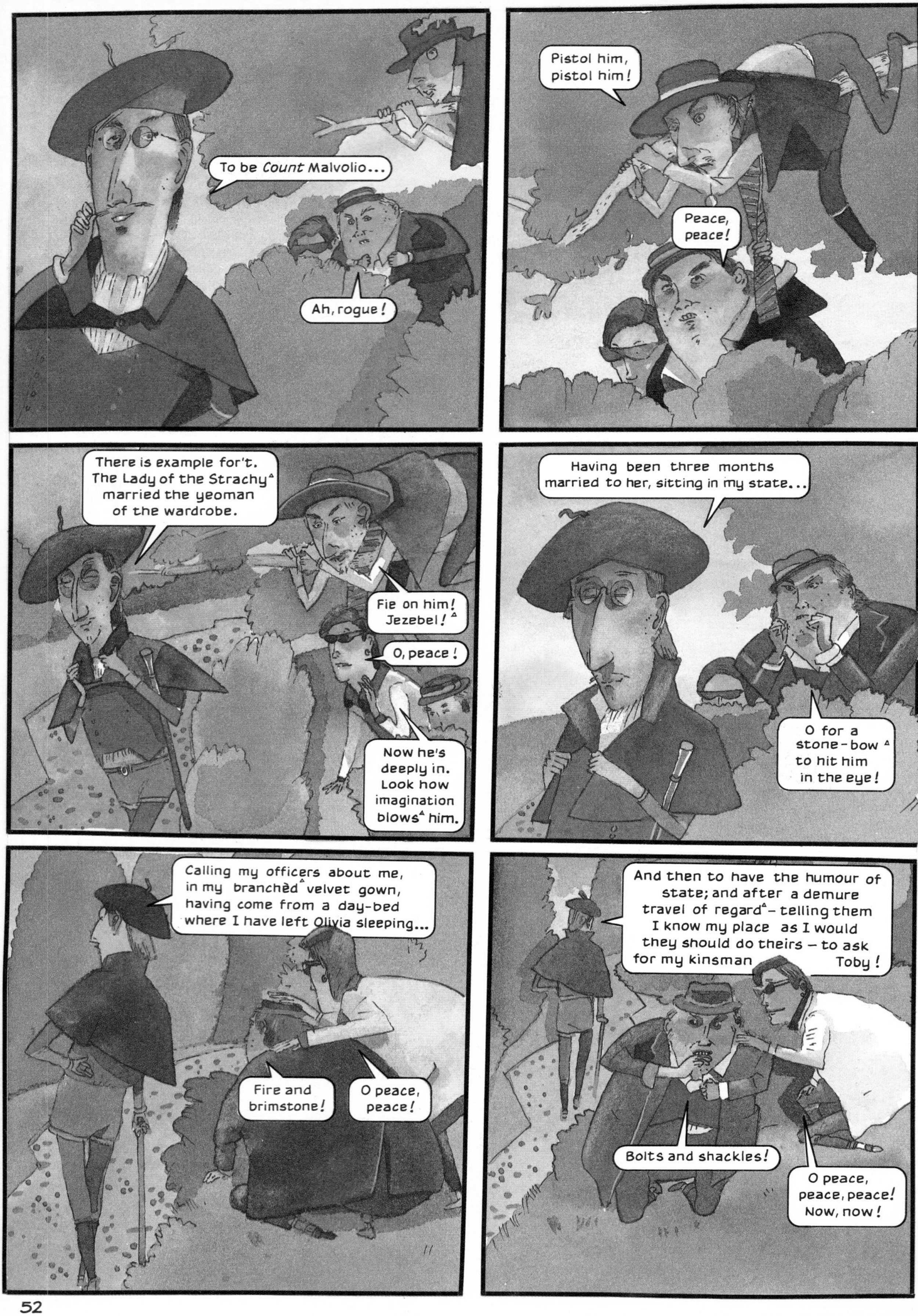
To be *Count* Malvolio...
Ah, rogue!
Pistol him, pistol him!
Peace, peace!
There is example for't. The Lady of the Strachy married the yeoman of the wardrobe.
Fie on him! Jezebel!
O, peace!
Now he's deeply in. Look how imagination blows him.
Having been three months married to her, sitting in my state...
O for a stone-bow to hit him in the eye!
Calling my officers about me, in my branched velvet gown, having come from a day-bed where I have left Olivia sleeping...
Fire and brimstone!
O peace, peace!
And then to have the humour of state; and after a demure travel of regard – telling them I know my place as I would they should do theirs – to ask for my kinsman Toby!
Bolts and shackles!
O peace, peace, peace! Now, now!

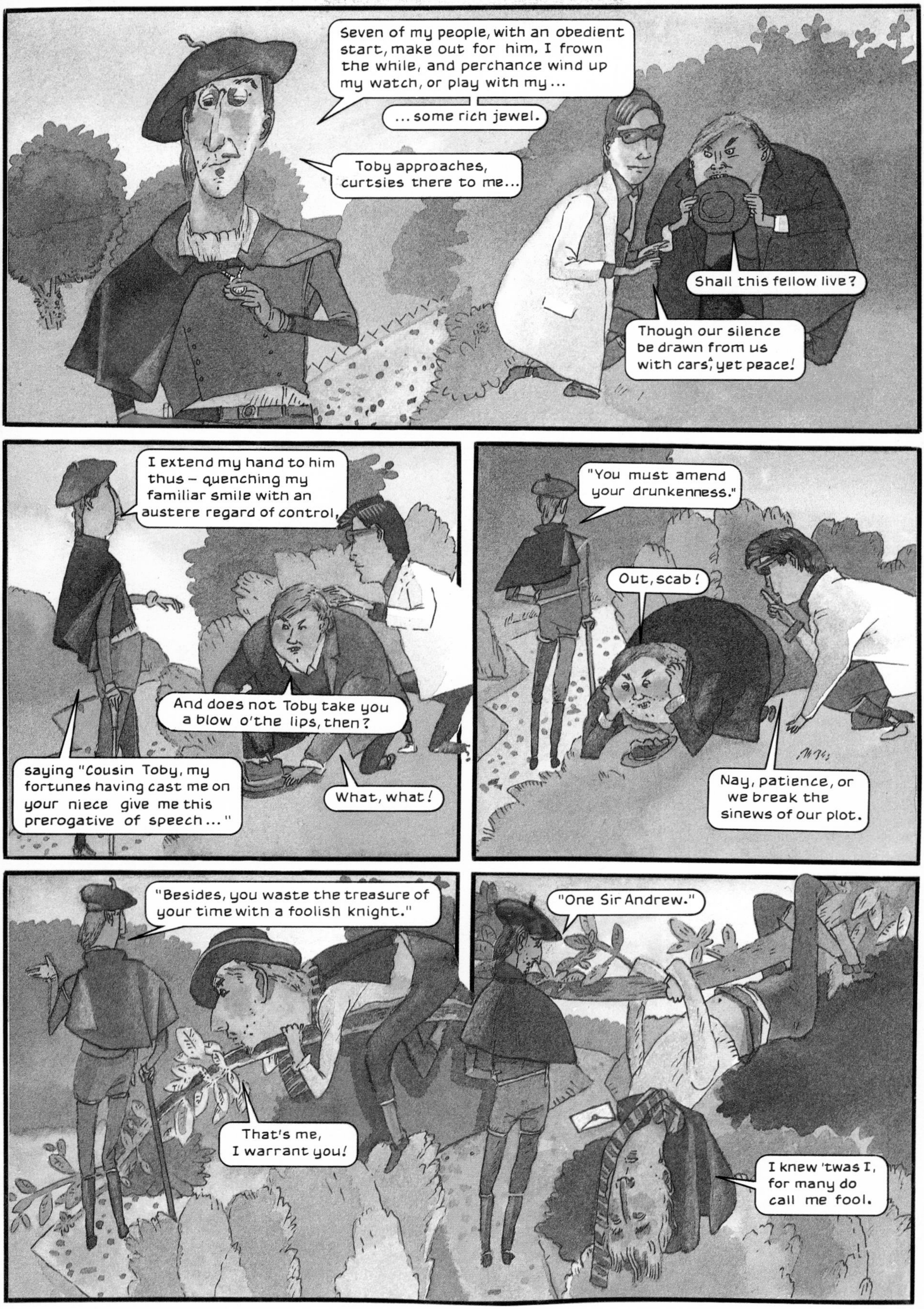
Seven of my people, with an obedient start, make out for him, I frown the while, and perchance wind up my watch, or play with my...
...some rich jewel.
Toby approaches, curtsies there to me...
Shall this fellow live?
Though our silence be drawn from us with cars, yet peace!
I extend my hand to him thus – quenching my familiar smile with an austere regard of control,
saying "Cousin Toby, my fortunes having cast me on your niece give me this prerogative of speech..."
And does not Toby take you a blow o'the lips, then?
What, what!
"You must amend your drunkenness."
Out, scab!
Nay, patience, or we break the sinews of our plot.
"Besides, you waste the treasure of your time with a foolish knight."
That's me, I warrant you!
"One Sir Andrew."
I knew 'twas I, for many do call me fool.

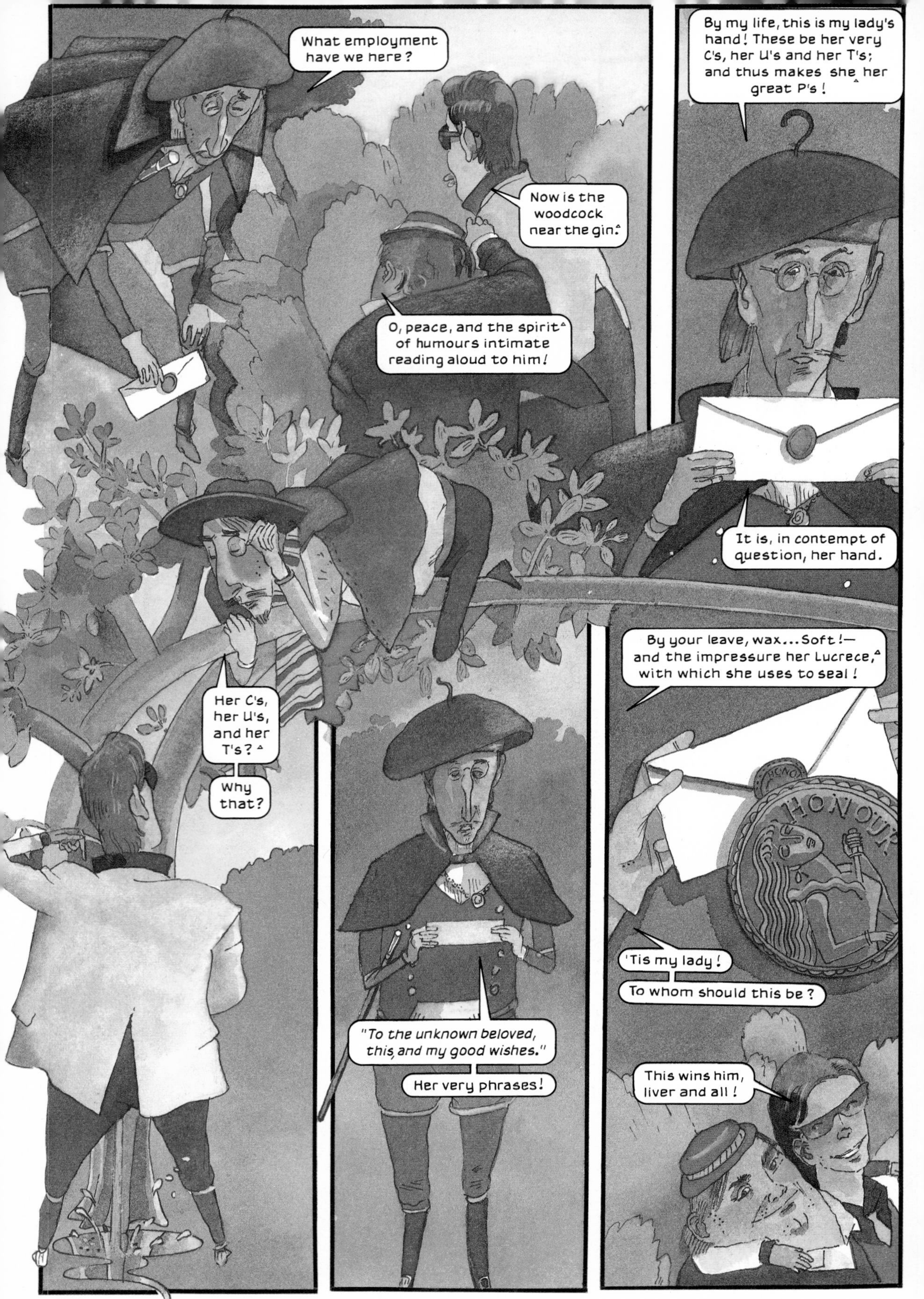
What employment have we here?
Now is the woodcock near the gin.
O, peace, and the spirit of humours intimate reading aloud to him!
By my life, this is my lady's hand! These be her very C's, her U's and her T's; and thus makes she her great P's!
It is, in contempt of question, her hand.
Her C's, her U's, and her T's?
Why that?
"To the unknown beloved, this, and my good wishes."
Her very phrases!
By your leave, wax... Soft!— and the impressure her Lucrece, with which she uses to seal!
HONOUR
'Tis my lady!
To whom should this be?
This wins him, liver and all!

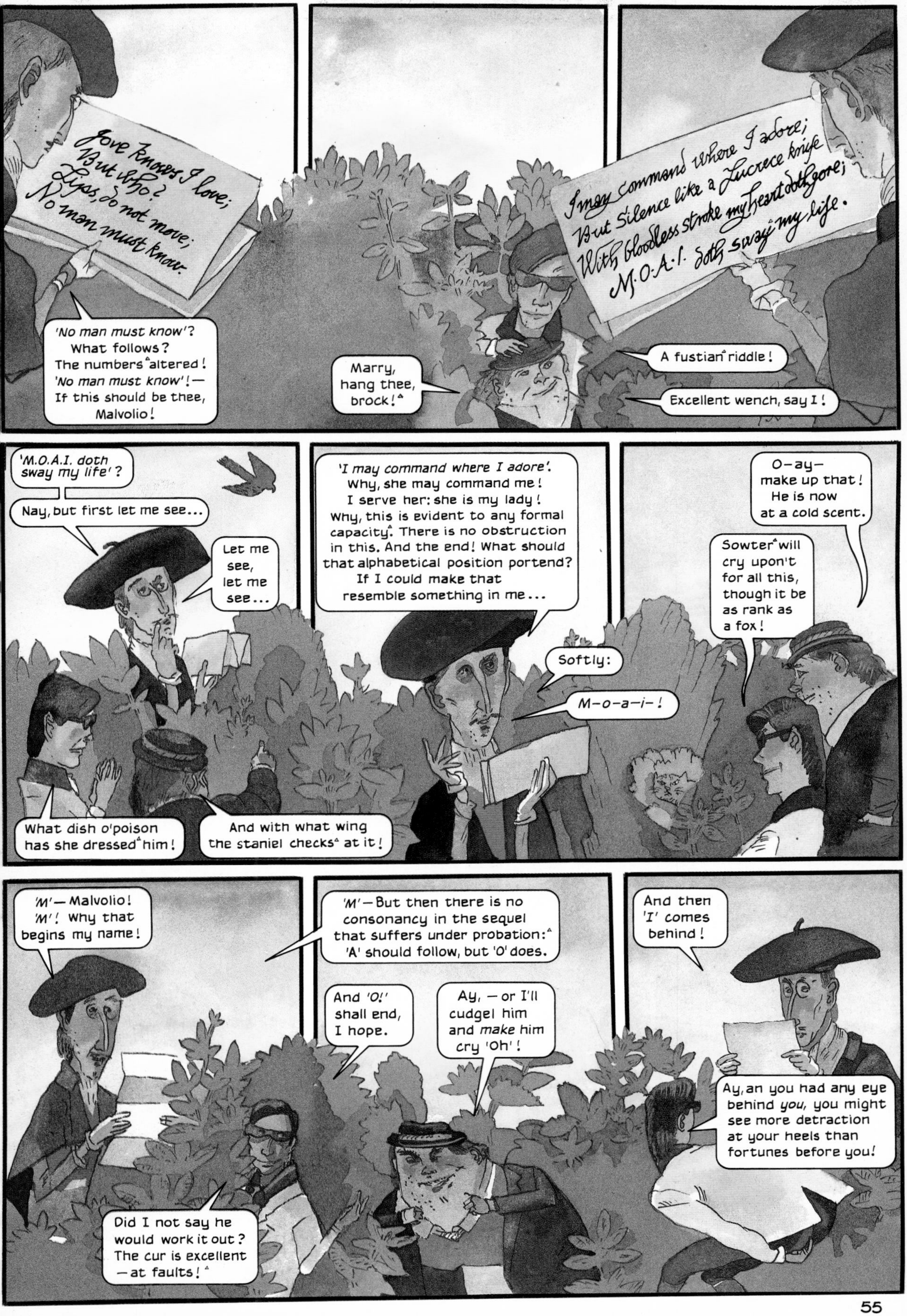

Jove knows I love;
But who?
Lips, do not move;
No man must know.
'No man must know'? What follows? The numbers altered! 'No man must know'!— If this should be thee, Malvolio!
Marry, hang thee, brock!
I may command where I adore;
But Silence like a Lucrece knife
With bloodless stroke my heart doth gore;
M.O.A.I. doth sway my life.
A fustian riddle!
Excellent wench, say I!
'M.O.A.I. doth sway my life'?
Nay, but first let me see...
Let me see, let me see...
What dish o'poison has she dressed him!
And with what wing the staniel checks at it!
'I may command where I adore'. Why, she may command me! I serve her: she is my lady! Why, this is evident to any formal capacity. There is no obstruction in this. And the end! What should that alphabetical position portend? If I could make that resemble something in me...
Softly:
M-o-a-i-!
O-ay— make up that! He is now at a cold scent.
Sowter will cry upon't for all this, though it be as rank as a fox!
'M'—Malvolio! 'M'! Why that begins my name!
'M'—But then there is no consonancy in the sequel that suffers under probation: 'A' should follow, but 'O' does.
And 'O!' shall end, I hope.
Ay, —or I'll cudgel him and make him cry 'Oh'!
Did I not say he would work it out? The cur is excellent —at faults!
And then 'I' comes behind!
Ay, an you had any eye behind you, you might see more detraction at your heels than fortunes before you!

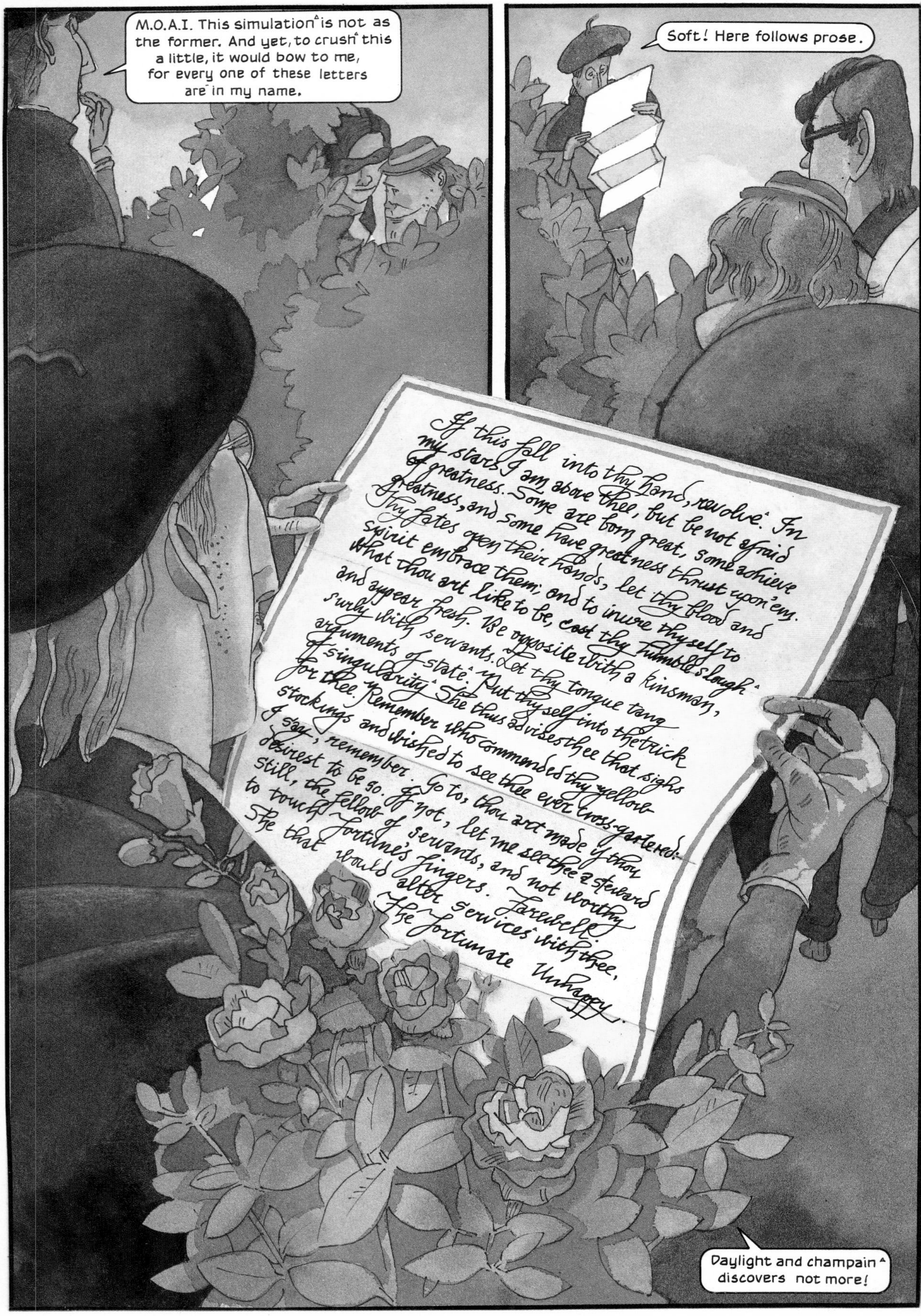
M.O.A.I. This simulation is not as the former. And yet, to crush this a little, it would bow to me, for every one of these letters are in my name.
Soft! Here follows prose.
If this fall into thy hand, revolve. In
my stars I am above thee, but be not afraid
of greatness. Some are born great, some achieve
greatness, and some have greatness thrust upon 'em.
Thy fates open their hands, let thy blood and
spirit embrace them; and to inure thyself to
what thou art like to be, cast thy humble slough
and appear fresh. Be opposite with a kinsman,
surly with servants. Let thy tongue tang
arguments of state. Put thyself into the trick
of singularity. She thus advises thee that sighs
for thee. Remember who commended thy yellow
stockings and wished to see thee ever cross-gartered.
I say, remember. Go to, thou art made if thou
desirest to be so. If not, let me see thee a steward
still, the fellow of servants, and not worthy
to touch Fortune's fingers. Farewell.
She that would alter services with thee,
The Fortunate Unhappy.
Daylight and champain discovers not more!

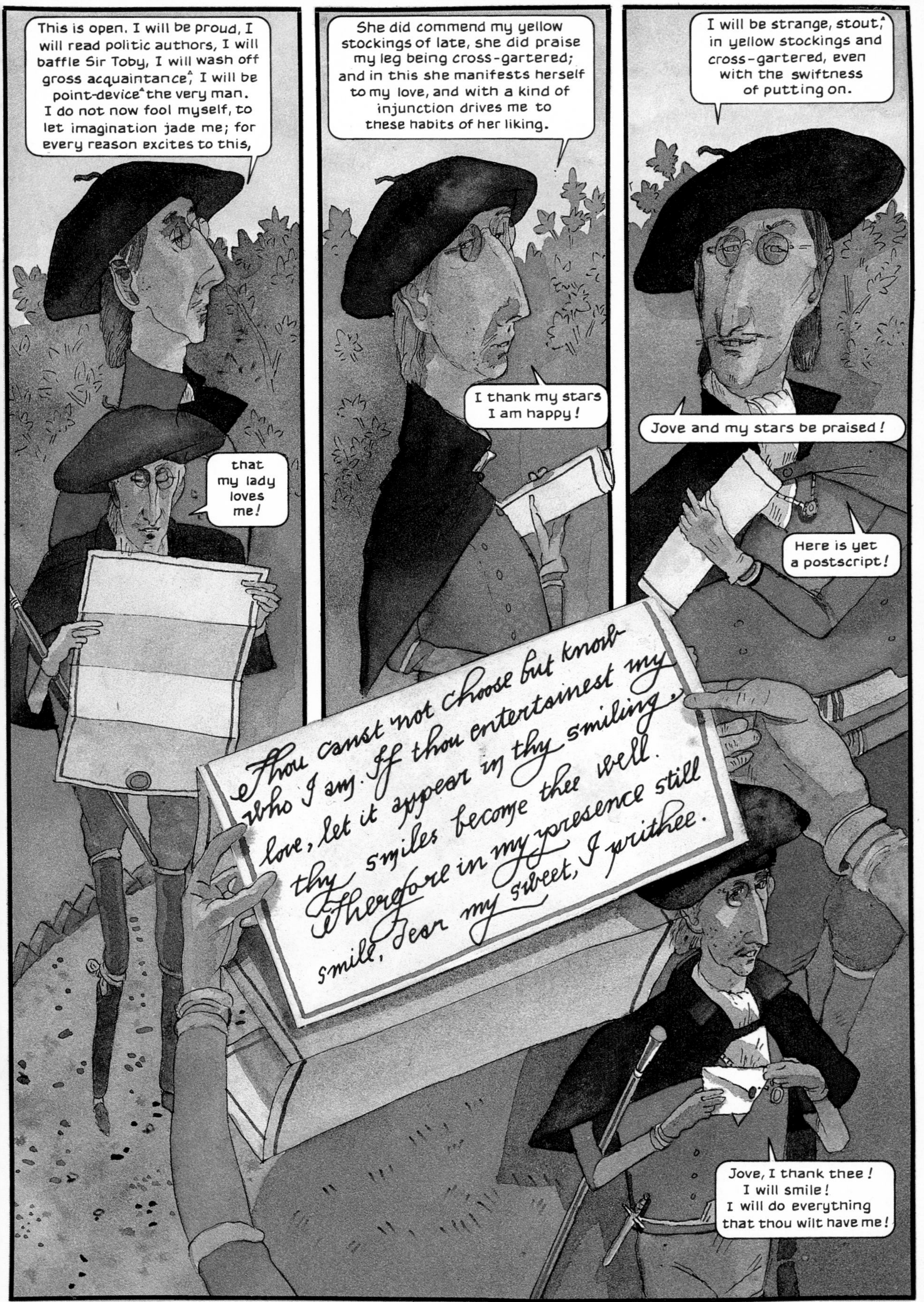

This is open. I will be proud, I will read politic authors, I will baffle Sir Toby, I will wash off gross acquaintance, I will be point-device the very man. I do not now fool myself, to let imagination jade me; for every reason excites to this,
that my lady loves me!
She did commend my yellow stockings of late, she did praise my leg being cross-gartered; and in this she manifests herself to my love, and with a kind of injunction drives me to these habits of her liking.
I thank my stars I am happy!
I will be strange, stout, in yellow stockings and cross-gartered, even with the swiftness of putting on.
Jove and my stars be praised!
Here is yet a postscript!
Thou canst not choose but know who I am. If thou entertainest my love, let it appear in thy smiling; thy smiles become thee well. Therefore in my presence still smile, dear my sweet, I prithee.
Jove, I thank thee! I will smile! I will do everything that thou wilt have me!

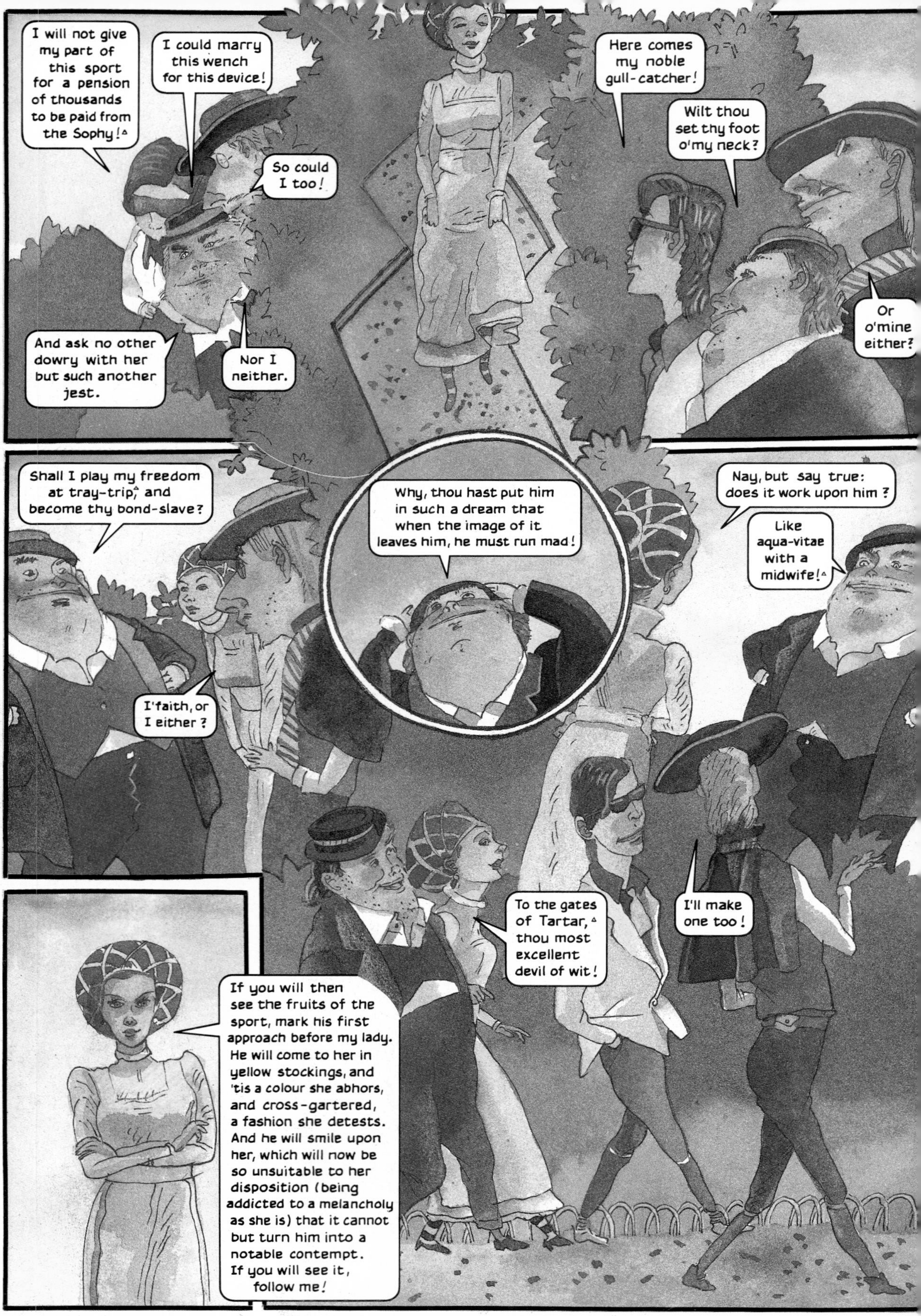
I will not give my part of this sport for a pension of thousands to be paid from the Sophy!
I could marry this wench for this device!
So could I too!
And ask no other dowry with her but such another jest.
Nor I neither.
Here comes my noble gull-catcher!
Wilt thou set thy foot o'my neck?
Or o'mine either?
Shall I play my freedom at tray-trip, and become thy bond-slave?
I'faith, or I either?
Why, thou hast put him in such a dream that when the image of it leaves him, he must run mad!
Nay, but say true: does it work upon him?
Like aqua-vitae with a midwife!
To the gates of Tartar, thou most excellent devil of wit!
I'll make one too!
If you will then see the fruits of the sport, mark his first approach before my lady. He will come to her in yellow stockings, and 'tis a colour she abhors, and cross-gartered, a fashion she detests. And he will smile upon her, which will now be so unsuitable to her disposition (being addicted to a melancholy as she is) that it cannot but turn him into a notable contempt. If you will see it, follow me!

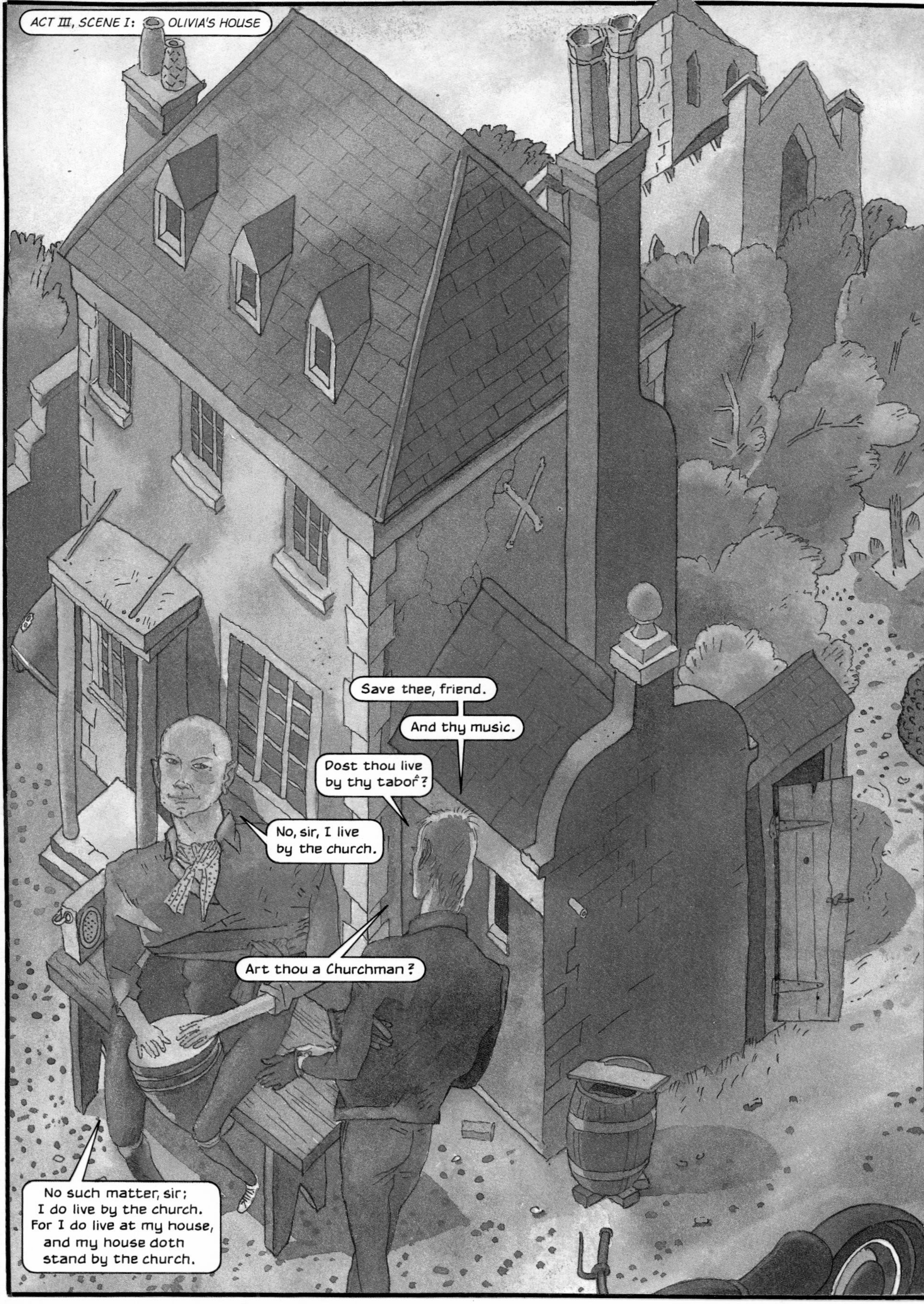

ACT III, SCENE I: OLIVIA'S HOUSE
Save thee, friend.
And thy music.
Dost thou live by thy tabor?
No, sir, I live by the church.
Art thou a Churchman?
No such matter, sir; I do live by the church. For I do live at my house, and my house doth stand by the church.

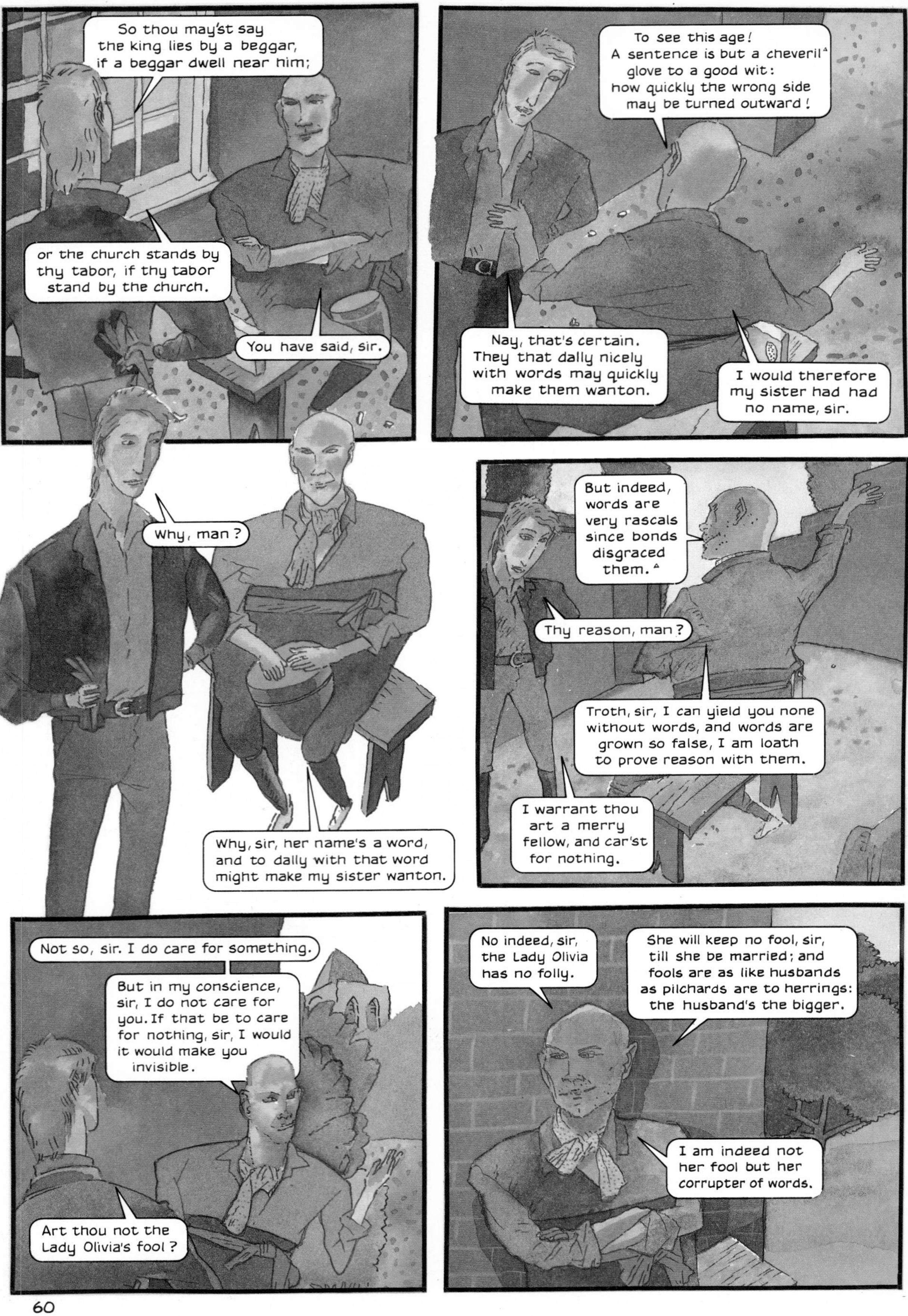
So thou may'st say the king lies by a beggar, if a beggar dwell near him;
or the church stands by thy tabor, if thy tabor stand by the church.
You have said, sir.
To see this age! A sentence is but a cheveril glove to a good wit: how quickly the wrong side may be turned outward!
Nay, that's certain. They that dally nicely with words may quickly make them wanton.
I would therefore my sister had had no name, sir.
Why, man?
Why, sir, her name's a word, and to dally with that word might make my sister wanton.
But indeed, words are very rascals since bonds disgraced them.
Thy reason, man?
Troth, sir, I can yield you none without words, and words are grown so false, I am loath to prove reason with them.
I warrant thou art a merry fellow, and car'st for nothing.
Not so, sir. I do care for something.
But in my conscience, sir, I do not care for you. If that be to care for nothing, sir, I would it would make you invisible.
Art thou not the Lady Olivia's fool?
No indeed, sir, the Lady Olivia has no folly.
She will keep no fool, sir, till she be married; and fools are as like husbands as pilchards are to herrings: the husband's the bigger.
I am indeed not her fool but her corrupter of words.

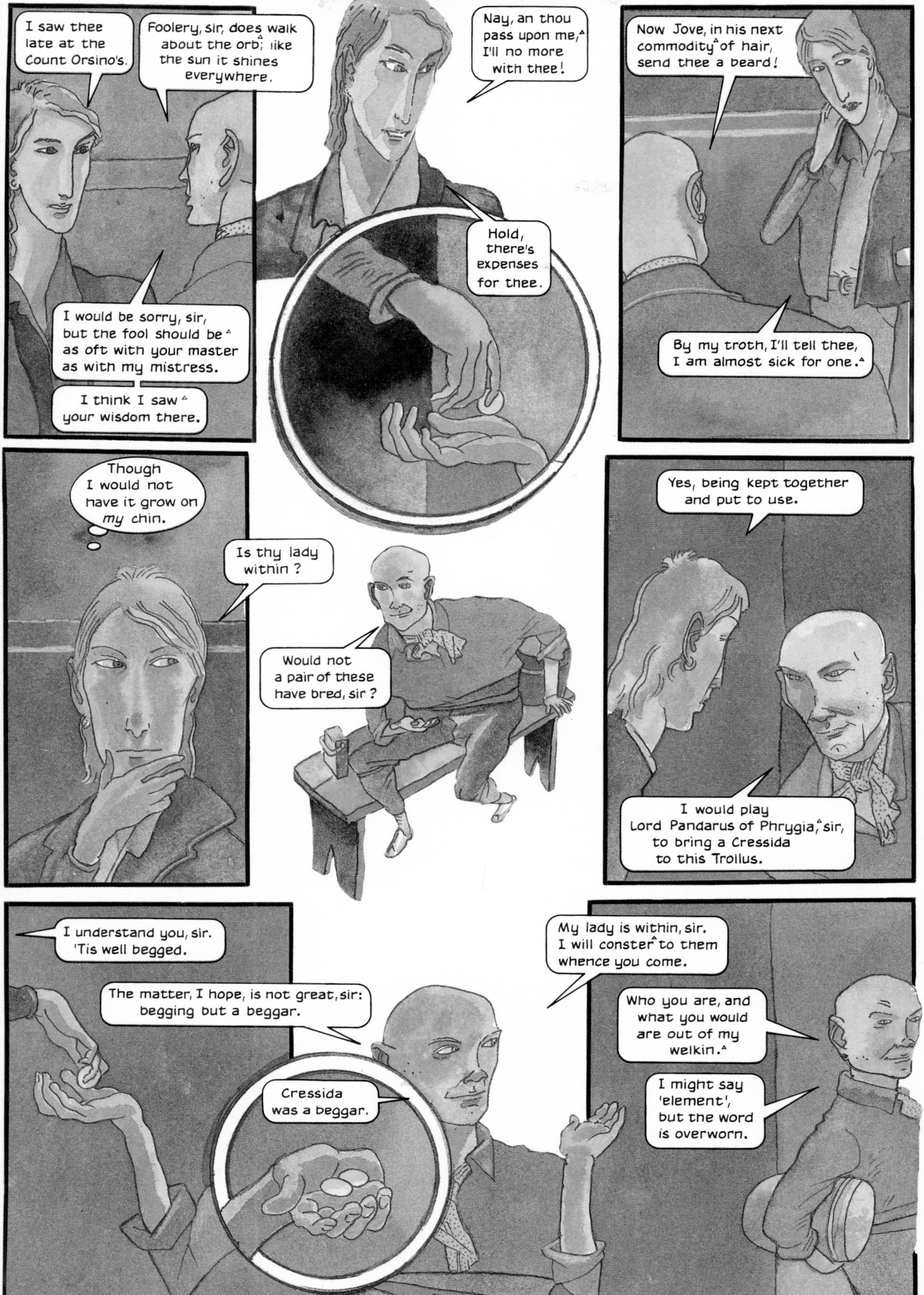
I saw thee late at the Count Orsino's.
Foolery, sir, does walk about the orb; like the sun it shines everywhere.
I would be sorry, sir, but the fool should be as oft with your master as with my mistress.
I think I saw your wisdom there.
Nay, an thou pass upon me, I'll no more with thee!
Hold, there's expenses for thee.
Now Jove, in his next commodity of hair, send thee a beard!
By my troth, I'll tell thee, I am almost sick for one.
Though I would not have it grow on *my* chin.
Is thy lady within?
Would not a pair of these have bred, sir?
Yes, being kept together and put to use.
I would play Lord Pandarus of Phrygia, sir, to bring a Cressida to this Troilus.
I understand you, sir. 'Tis well begged.
The matter, I hope, is not great, sir: begging but a beggar.
Cressida was a beggar.
My lady is within, sir. I will conster to them whence you come.
Who you are, and what you would are out of my welkin.
I might say 'element', but the word is overworn.

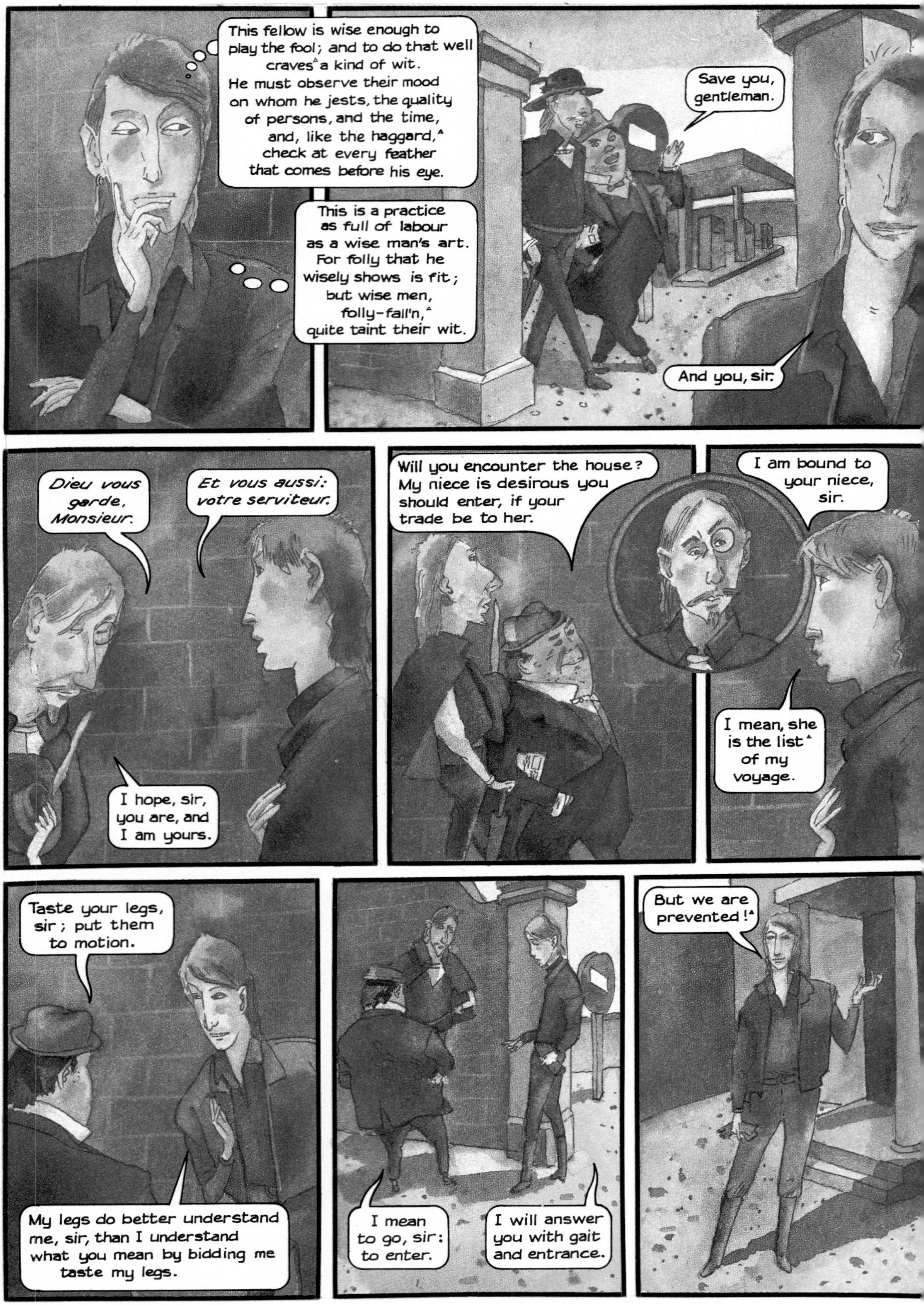
This fellow is wise enough to play the fool; and to do that well craves^ a kind of wit.
He must observe their mood on whom he jests, the quality of persons, and the time, and, like the haggard,^ check at every feather that comes before his eye.
This is a practice as full of labour as a wise man's art. For folly that he wisely shows is fit; but wise men, folly-fall'n,^ quite taint their wit.
Save you, gentleman.
And you, sir.
Dieu vous garde, Monsieur.
Et vous aussi: votre serviteur.
I hope, sir, you are, and I am yours.
Will you encounter the house? My niece is desirous you should enter, if your trade be to her.
I am bound to your niece, sir.
I mean, she is the list^ of my voyage.
Taste your legs, sir; put them to motion.
My legs do better understand me, sir, than I understand what you mean by bidding me taste my legs.
I mean to go, sir: to enter.
I will answer you with gait and entrance.
But we are prevented!^

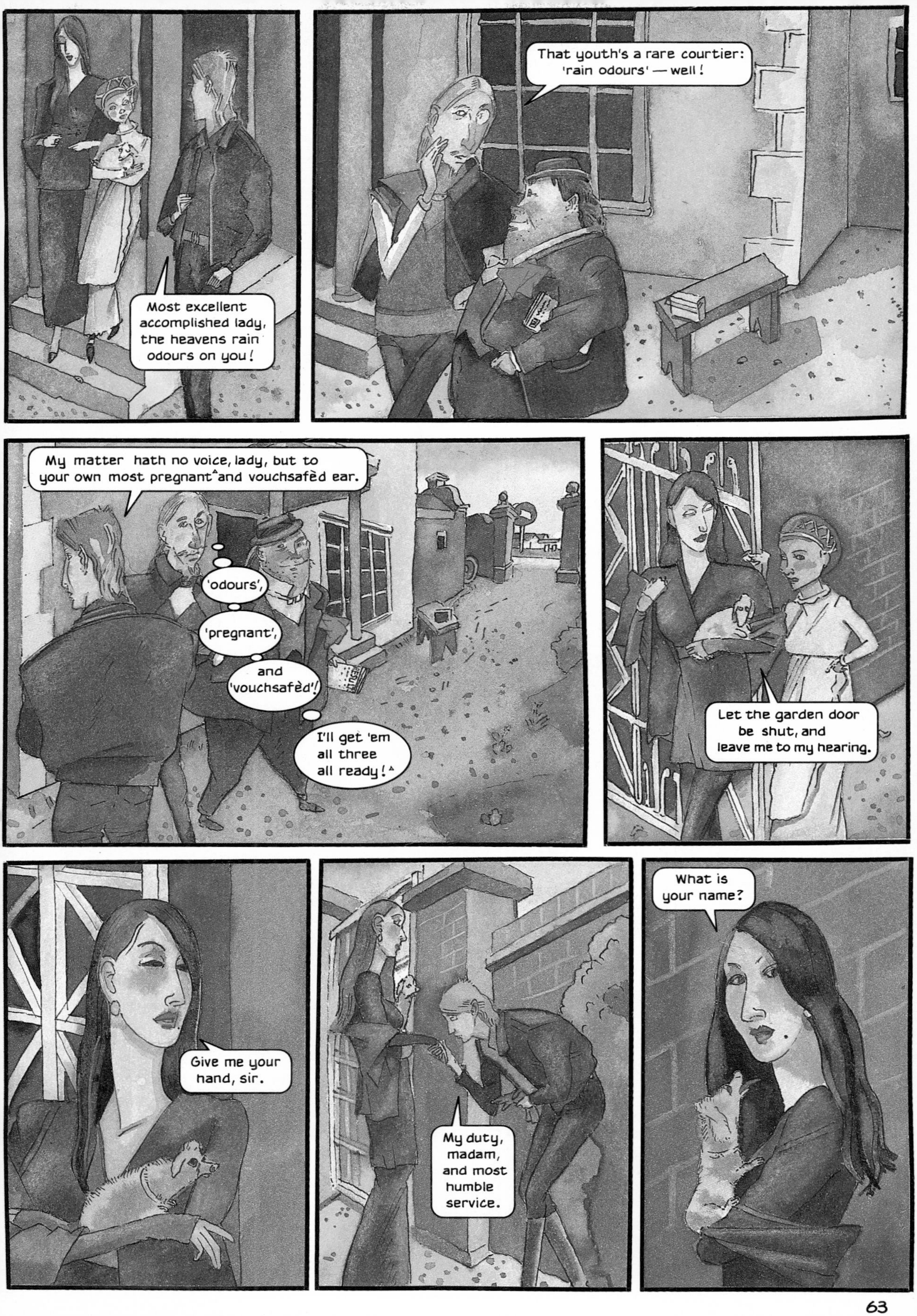
Most excellent accomplished lady, the heavens rain odours on you!
That youth's a rare courtier: 'rain odours' — well!
My matter hath no voice, lady, but to your own most pregnant and vouchsafèd ear.
'odours',
'pregnant',
and 'vouchsafèd'!
I'll get 'em all three all ready!
Let the garden door be shut, and leave me to my hearing.
Give me your hand, sir.
My duty, madam, and most humble service.
What is your name?

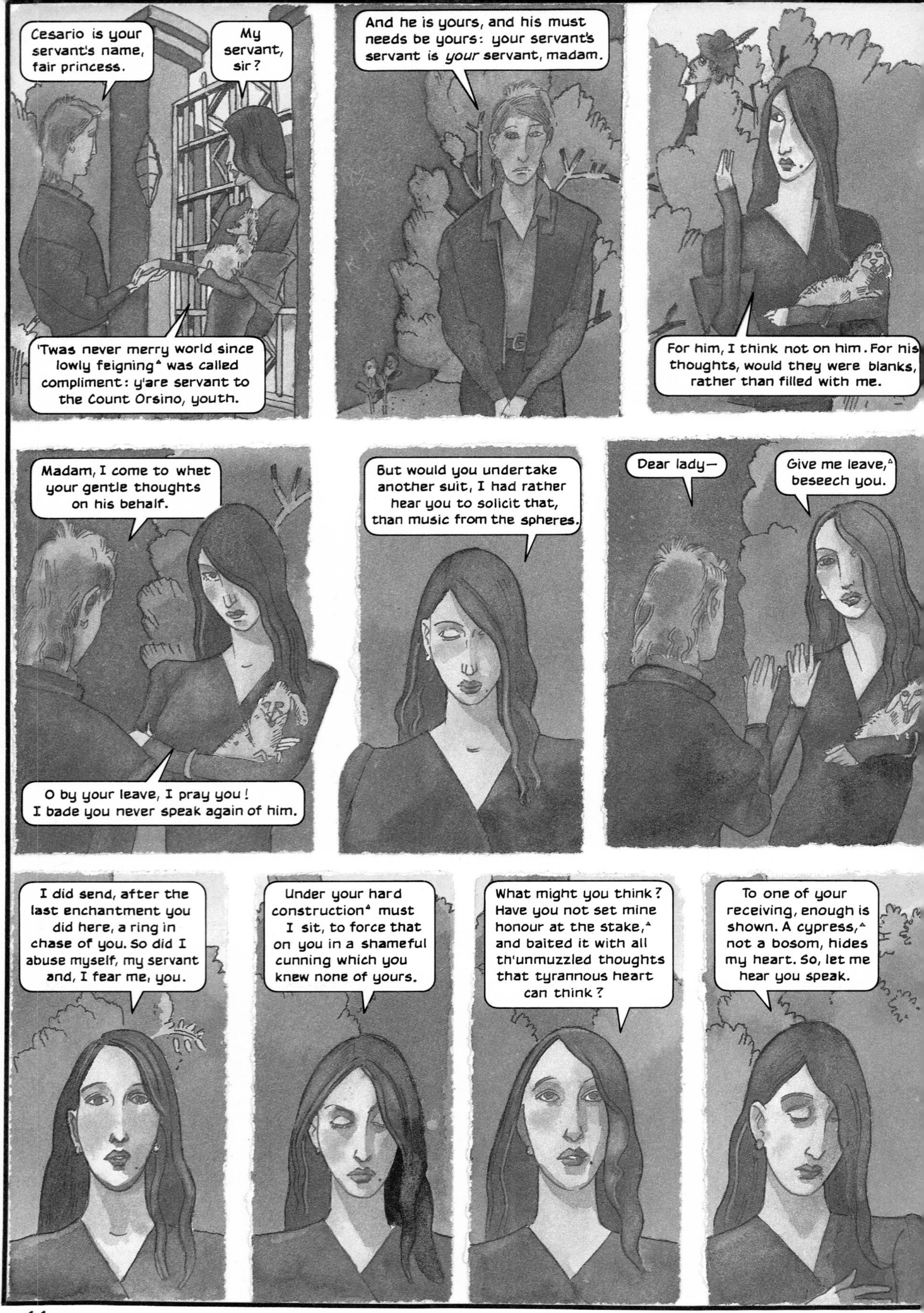

Cesario is your servant's name, fair princess.
My servant, sir?
'Twas never merry world since lowly feigning[a] was called compliment: y'are servant to the Count Orsino, youth.
And he is yours, and his must needs be yours: your servant's servant is *your* servant, madam.
For him, I think not on him. For his thoughts, would they were blanks, rather than filled with me.
Madam, I come to whet your gentle thoughts on his behalf.
O by your leave, I pray you! I bade you never speak again of him.
But would you undertake another suit, I had rather hear you to solicit that, than music from the spheres.
Dear lady—
Give me leave,[a] beseech you.
I did send, after the last enchantment you did here, a ring in chase of you. So did I abuse myself, my servant and, I fear me, you.
Under your hard construction[a] must I sit, to force that on you in a shameful cunning which you knew none of yours.
What might you think? Have you not set mine honour at the stake,[a] and baited it with all th'unmuzzled thoughts that tyrannous heart can think?
To one of your receiving, enough is shown. A cypress,[a] not a bosom, hides my heart. So, let me hear you speak.

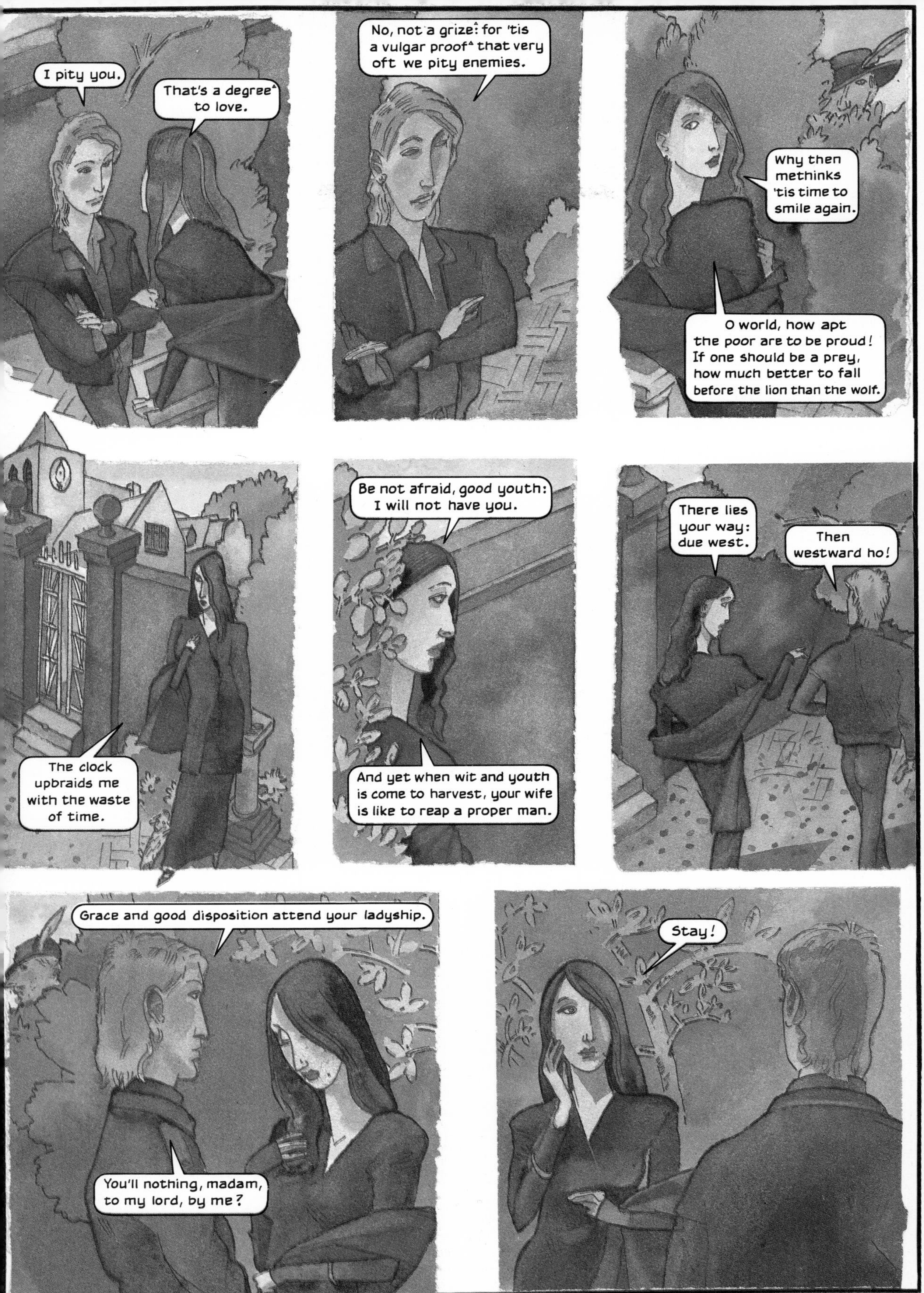
I pity you.
That's a degree to love.
No, not a grize: for 'tis a vulgar proof that very oft we pity enemies.
Why then methinks 'tis time to smile again.
O world, how apt the poor are to be proud! If one should be a prey, how much better to fall before the lion than the wolf.
The clock upbraids me with the waste of time.
Be not afraid, good youth: I will not have you.
And yet when wit and youth is come to harvest, your wife is like to reap a proper man.
There lies your way: due west.
Then westward ho!
Grace and good disposition attend your ladyship.
You'll nothing, madam, to my lord, by me?
Stay!

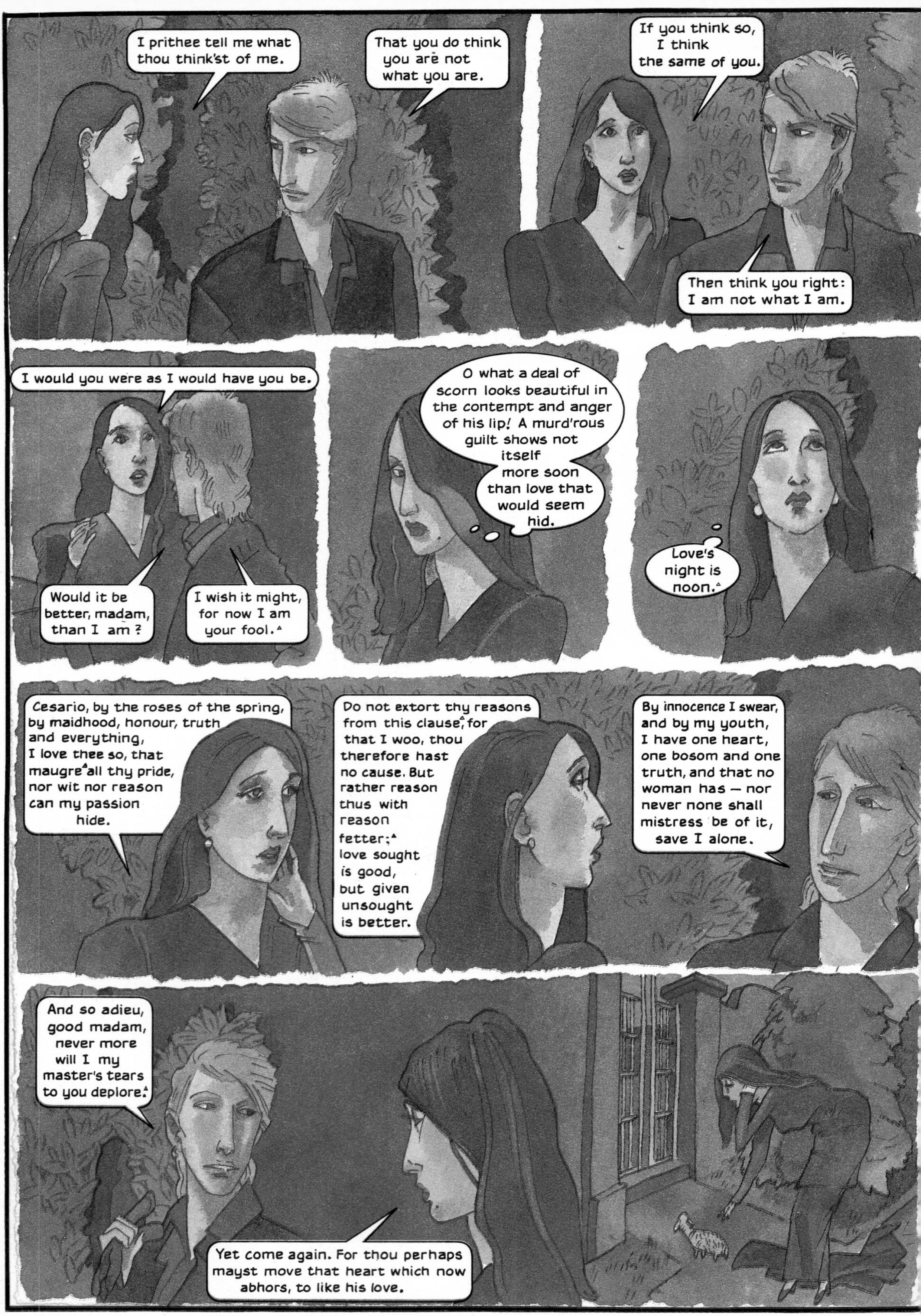
I prithee tell me what thou think'st of me.
That you do think you are not what you are.
If you think so, I think the same of you.
Then think you right: I am not what I am.
I would you were as I would have you be.
Would it be better, madam, than I am?
I wish it might, for now I am your fool.
O what a deal of scorn looks beautiful in the contempt and anger of his lip! A murd'rous guilt shows not itself more soon than love that would seem hid.
Love's night is noon.
Cesario, by the roses of the spring, by maidhood, honour, truth and everything, I love thee so, that maugre all thy pride, nor wit nor reason can my passion hide.
Do not extort thy reasons from this clause, for that I woo, thou therefore hast no cause. But rather reason thus with reason fetter; love sought is good, but given unsought is better.
By innocence I swear, and by my youth, I have one heart, one bosom and one truth, and that no woman has — nor never none shall mistress be of it, save I alone.
And so adieu, good madam, never more will I my master's tears to you deplore.
Yet come again. For thou perhaps mayst move that heart which now abhors, to like his love.

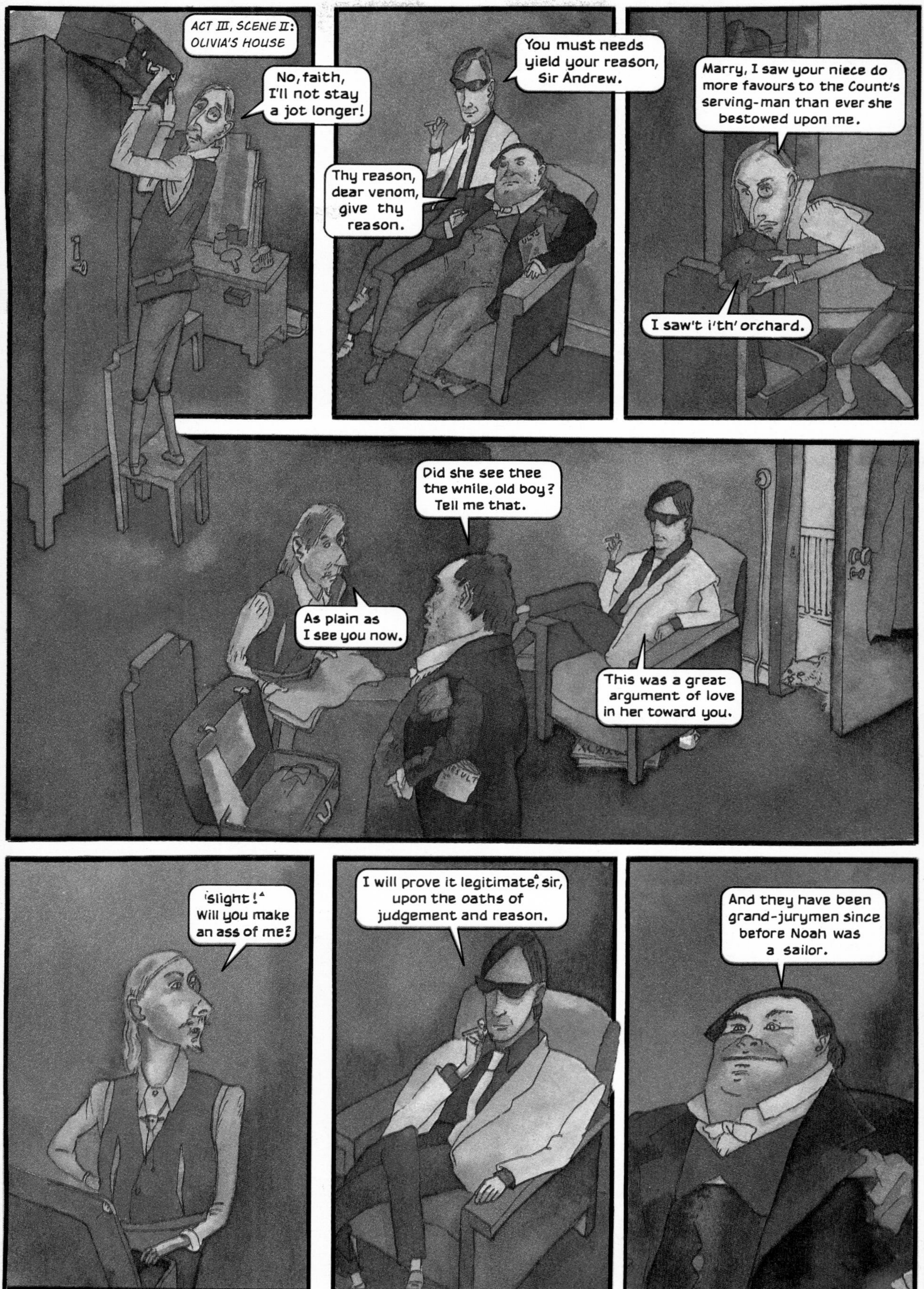

ACT III, SCENE II: OLIVIA'S HOUSE
No, faith, I'll not stay a jot longer!
You must needs yield your reason, Sir Andrew.
Thy reason, dear venom, give thy reason.
Marry, I saw your niece do more favours to the Count's serving-man than ever she bestowed upon me.
I saw't i'th' orchard.
Did she see thee the while, old boy? Tell me that.
As plain as I see you now.
This was a great argument of love in her toward you.
'slight!△ Will you make an ass of me?
I will prove it legitimate△, sir, upon the oaths of judgement and reason.
And they have been grand-jurymen since before Noah was a sailor.

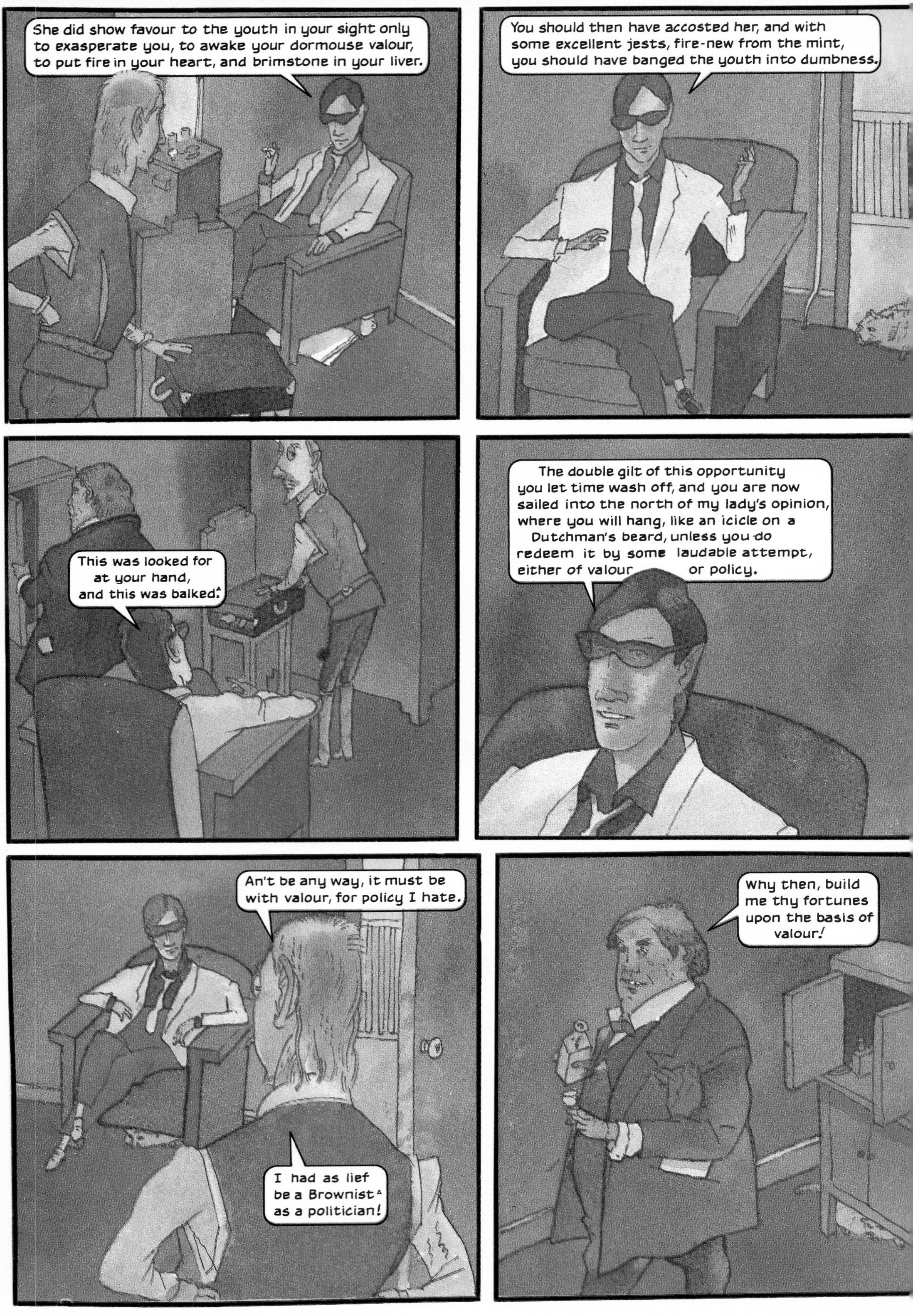
She did show favour to the youth in your sight only to exasperate you, to awake your dormouse valour, to put fire in your heart, and brimstone in your liver.
You should then have accosted her, and with some excellent jests, fire-new from the mint, you should have banged the youth into dumbness.
This was looked for at your hand, and this was balked.
The double gilt of this opportunity you let time wash off, and you are now sailed into the north of my lady's opinion, where you will hang, like an icicle on a Dutchman's beard, unless you do redeem it by some laudable attempt, either of valour or policy.
An't be any way, it must be with valour, for policy I hate.
I had as lief be a Brownist as a politician!
Why then, build me thy fortunes upon the basis of valour!

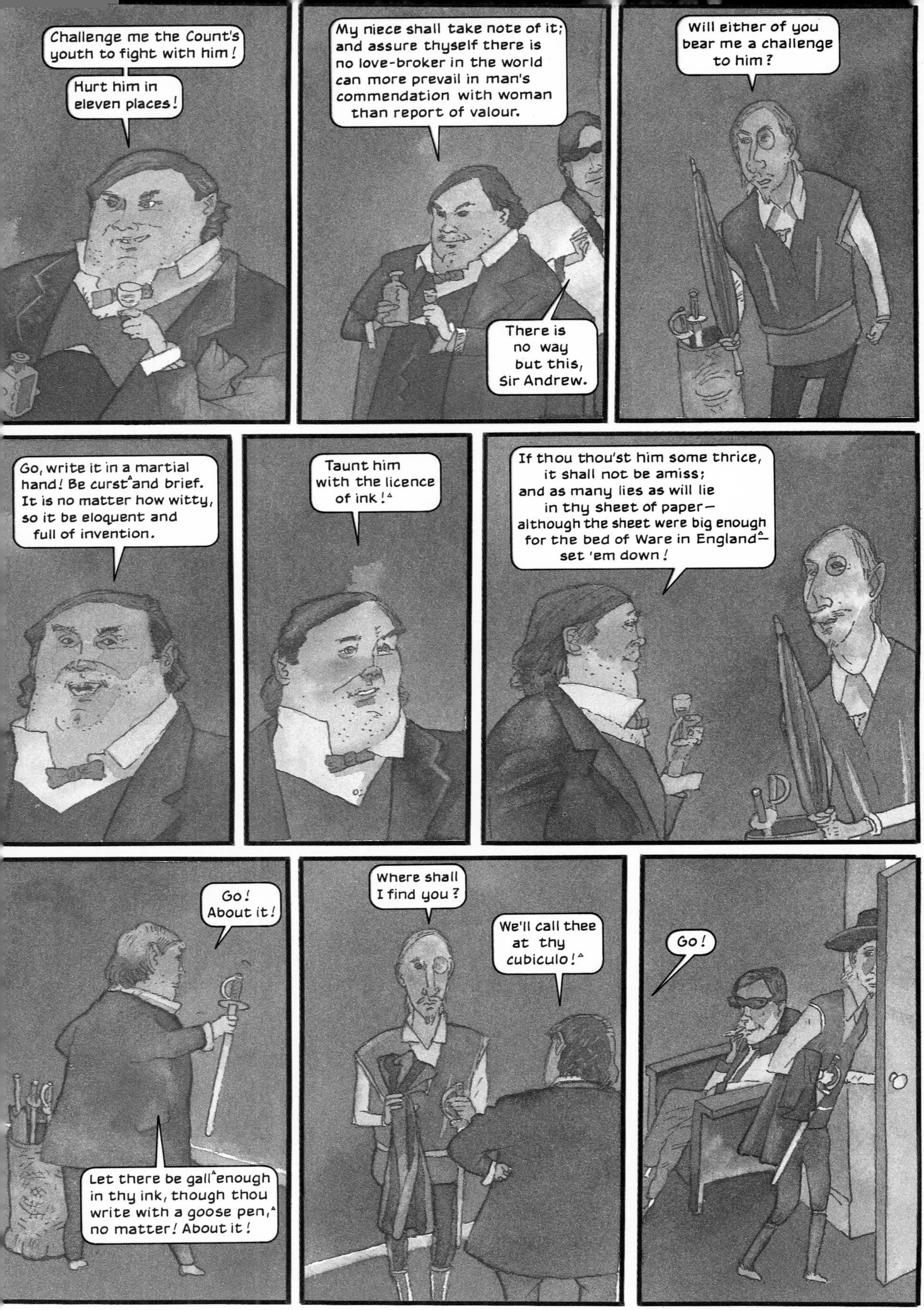
Challenge me the Count's youth to fight with him!
Hurt him in eleven places!
My niece shall take note of it; and assure thyself there is no love-broker in the world can more prevail in man's commendation with woman than report of valour.
There is no way but this, Sir Andrew.
Will either of you bear me a challenge to him?
Go, write it in a martial hand! Be curst and brief. It is no matter how witty, so it be eloquent and full of invention.
Taunt him with the licence of ink!
If thou thou'st him some thrice, it shall not be amiss; and as many lies as will lie in thy sheet of paper— although the sheet were big enough for the bed of Ware in England— set 'em down!
Go! About it!
Let there be gall enough in thy ink, though thou write with a goose pen, no matter! About it!
Where shall I find you?
We'll call thee at thy cubiculo!
Go!

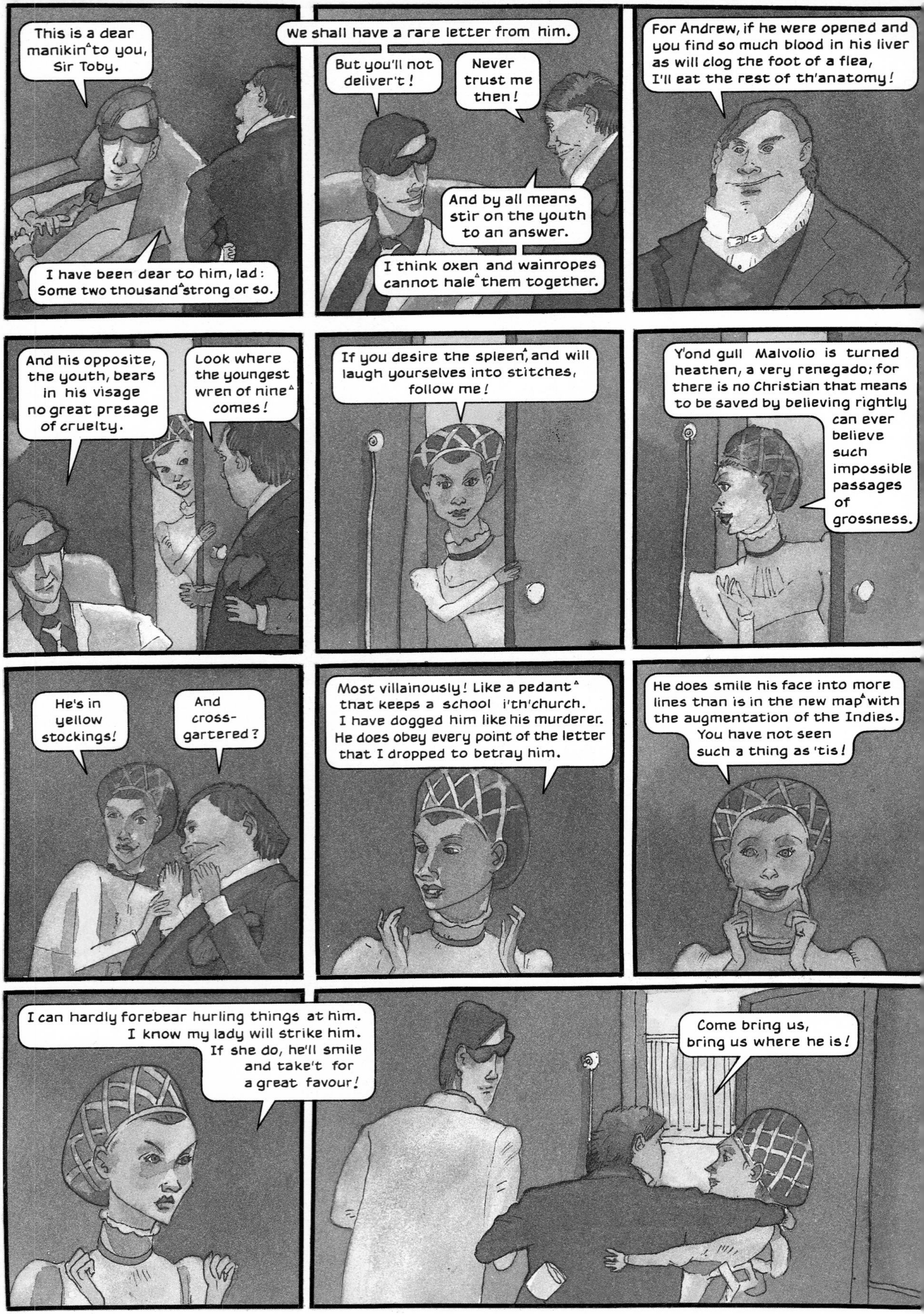
This is a dear manikin to you, Sir Toby.
I have been dear to him, lad: Some two thousand strong or so.
We shall have a rare letter from him.
But you'll not deliver't!
Never trust me then!
And by all means stir on the youth to an answer.
I think oxen and wainropes cannot hale them together.
For Andrew, if he were opened and you find so much blood in his liver as will clog the foot of a flea, I'll eat the rest of th'anatomy!
And his opposite, the youth, bears in his visage no great presage of cruelty.
Look where the youngest wren of nine comes!
If you desire the spleen, and will laugh yourselves into stitches, follow me!
Y'ond gull Malvolio is turned heathen, a very renegado; for there is no Christian that means to be saved by believing rightly can ever believe such impossible passages of grossness.
He's in yellow stockings!
And cross-gartered?
Most villainously! Like a pedant that keeps a school i'th'church. I have dogged him like his murderer. He does obey every point of the letter that I dropped to betray him.
He does smile his face into more lines than is in the new map with the augmentation of the Indies. You have not seen such a thing as 'tis!
I can hardly forebear hurling things at him. I know my lady will strike him. If she do, he'll smile and take't for a great favour!
Come bring us, bring us where he is!

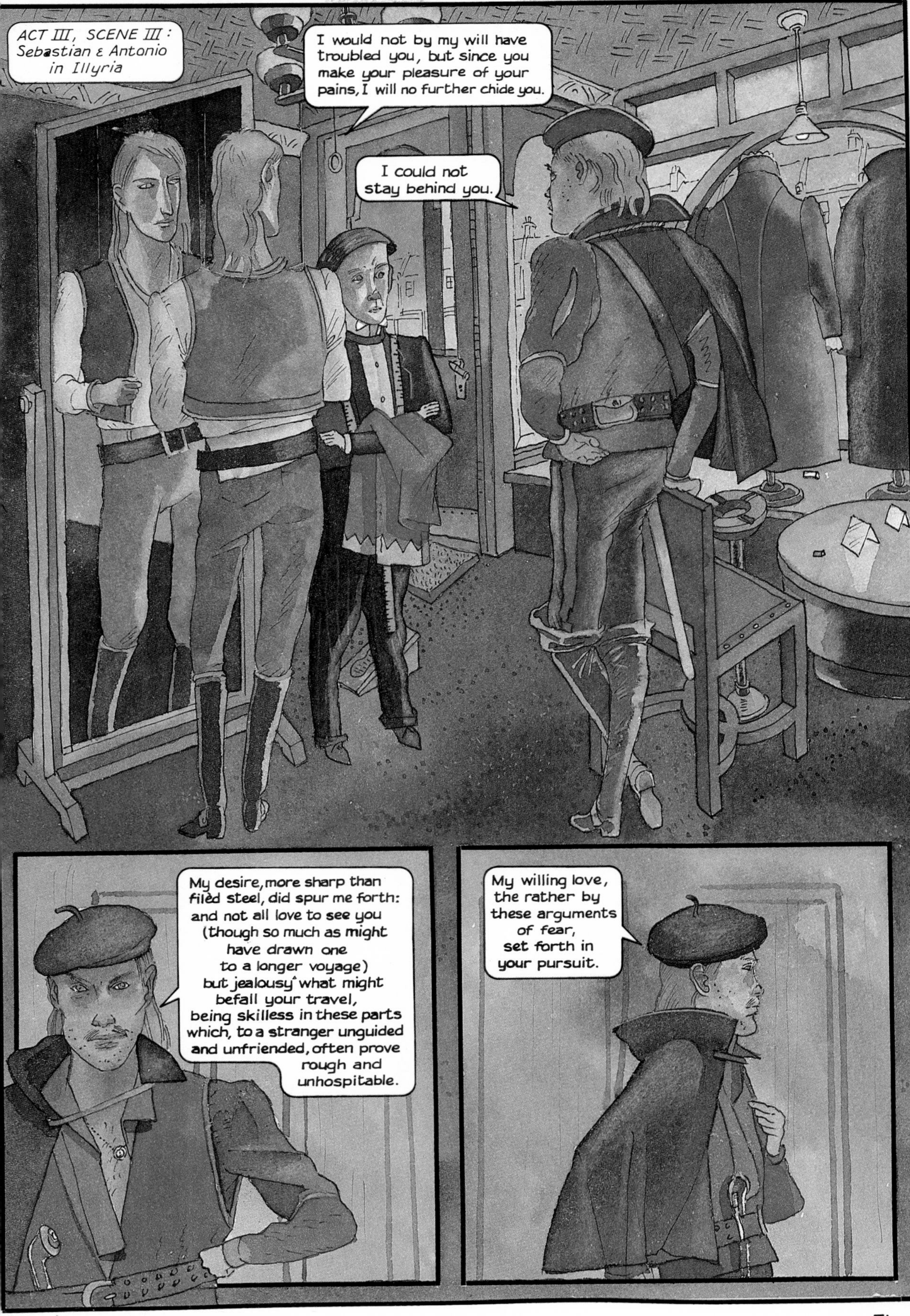

ACT III, SCENE III: Sebastian & Antonio in Illyria
I would not by my will have troubled you, but since you make your pleasure of your pains, I will no further chide you.
I could not stay behind you.
My desire, more sharp than filèd steel, did spur me forth: and not all love to see you (though so much as might have drawn one to a longer voyage) but jealousy what might befall your travel, being skilless in these parts which, to a stranger unguided and unfriended, often prove rough and unhospitable.
My willing love, the rather by these arguments of fear, set forth in your pursuit.

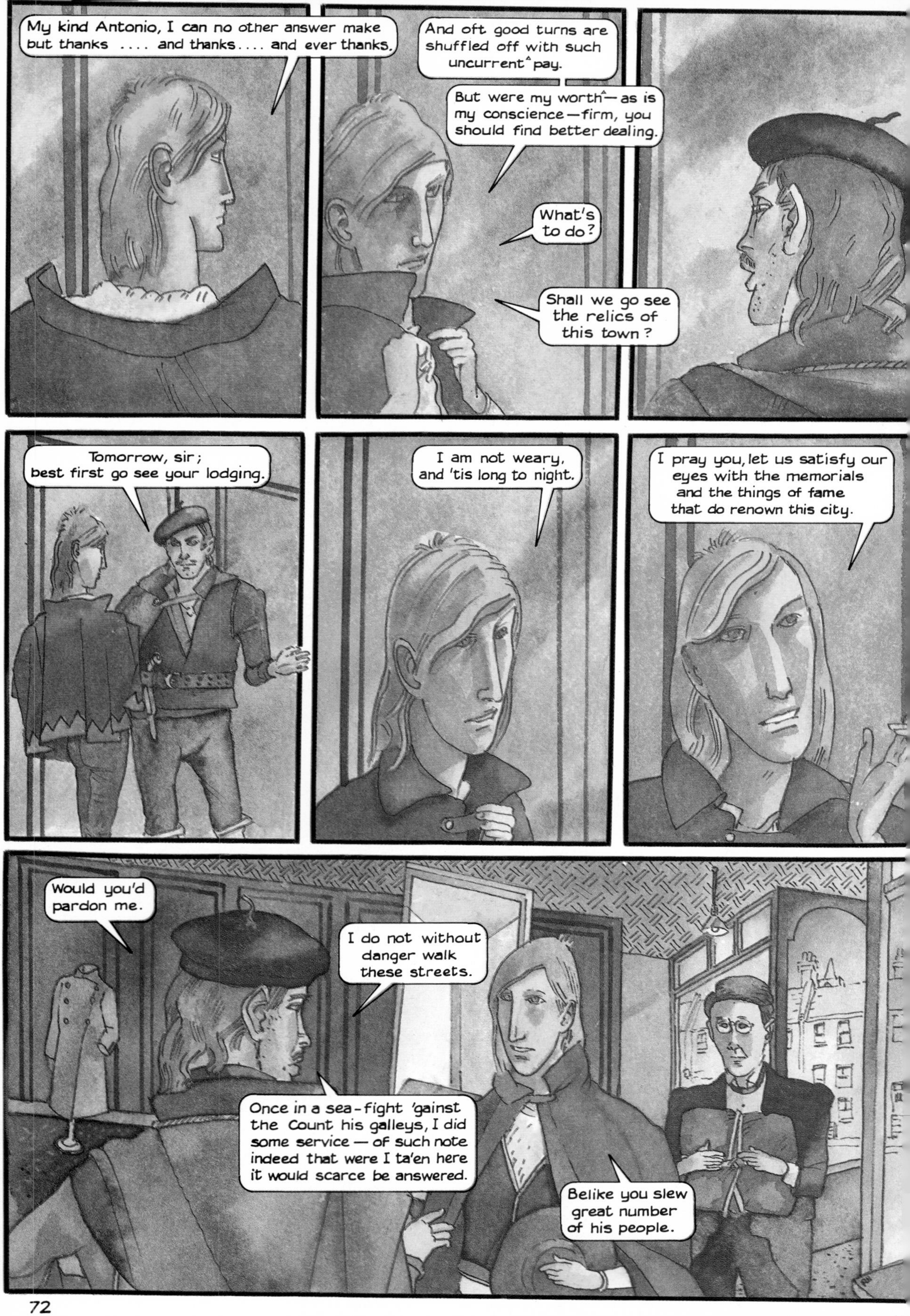
My kind Antonio, I can no other answer make but thanks .... and thanks.... and ever thanks.
And oft good turns are shuffled off with such uncurrent^ pay.
But were my worth^— as is my conscience—firm, you should find better dealing.
What's to do?
Shall we go see the relics of this town?
Tomorrow, sir; best first go see your lodging.
I am not weary, and 'tis long to night.
I pray you, let us satisfy our eyes with the memorials and the things of fame that do renown this city.
Would you'd pardon me.
I do not without danger walk these streets.
Once in a sea-fight 'gainst the Count his galleys, I did some service — of such note indeed that were I ta'en here it would scarce be answered.
Belike you slew great number of his people.

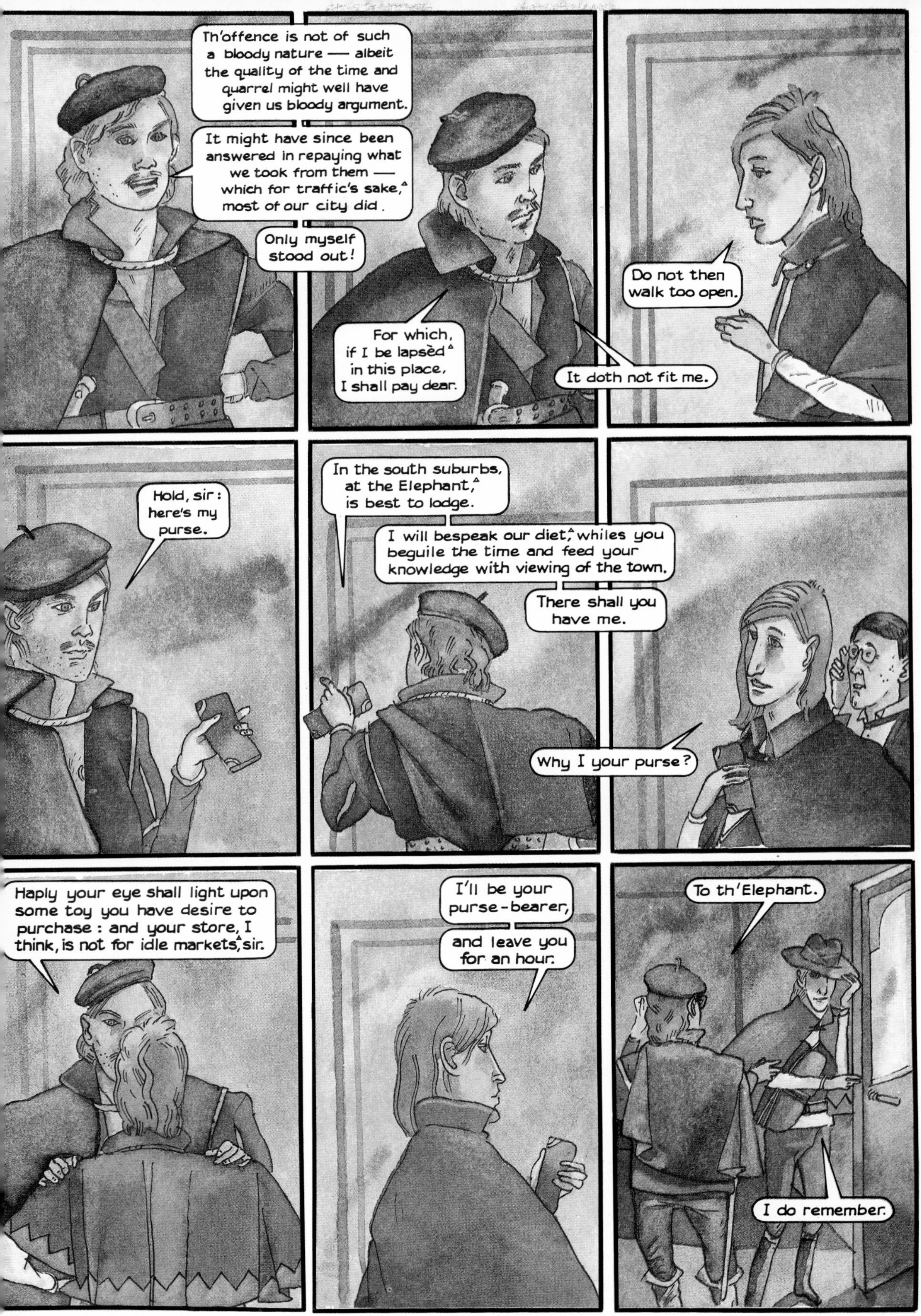
Th'offence is not of such a bloody nature — albeit the quality of the time and quarrel might well have given us bloody argument.
It might have since been answered in repaying what we took from them — which for traffic's sake, most of our city did.
Only myself stood out!
For which, if I be lapsèd in this place, I shall pay dear.
It doth not fit me.
Do not then walk too open.
Hold, sir: here's my purse.
In the south suburbs, at the Elephant, is best to lodge.
I will bespeak our diet, whiles you beguile the time and feed your knowledge with viewing of the town.
There shall you have me.
Why I your purse?
Haply your eye shall light upon some toy you have desire to purchase: and your store, I think, is not for idle markets, sir.
I'll be your purse-bearer,
and leave you for an hour.
To th'Elephant.
I do remember.

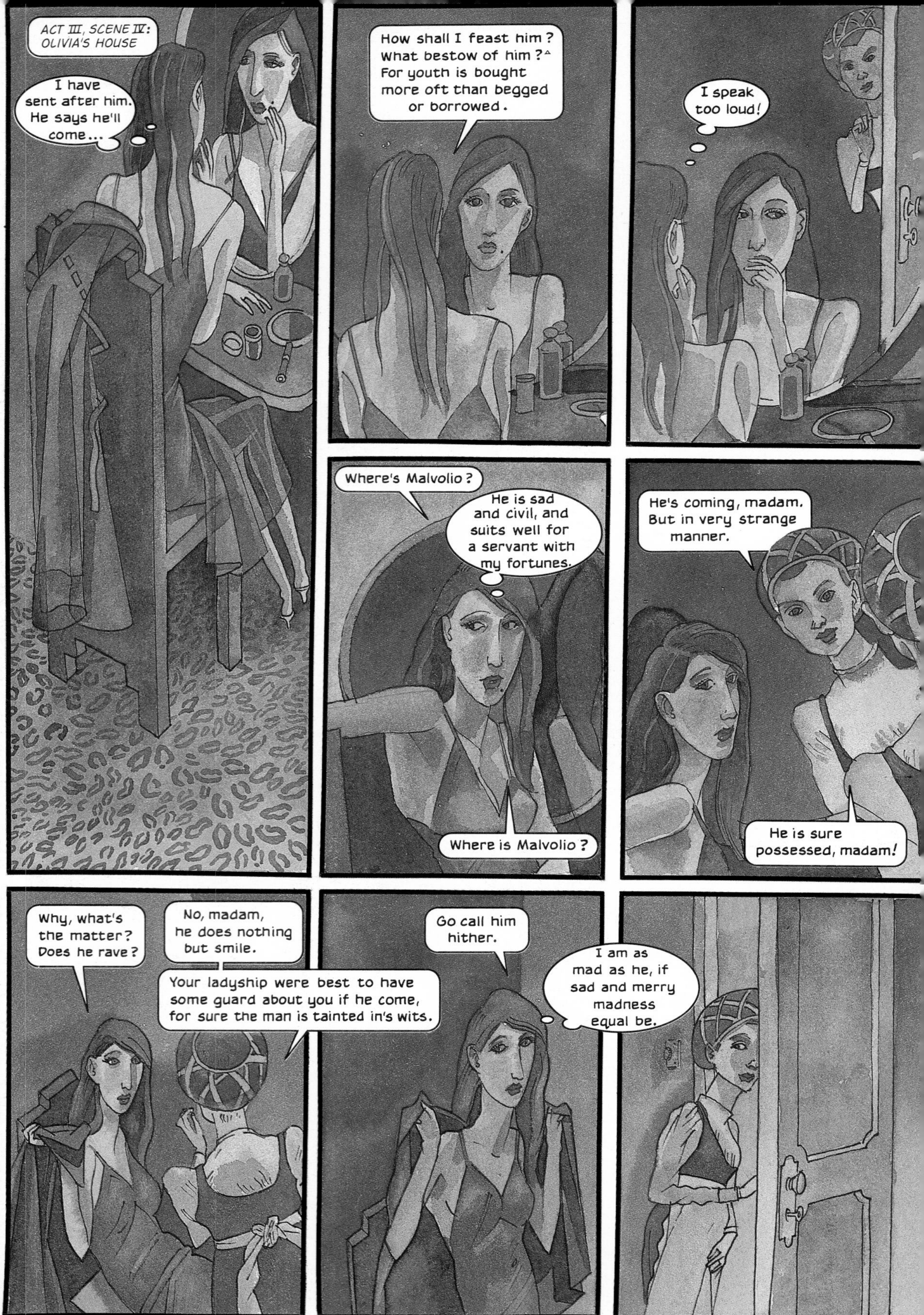

ACT III, SCENE IV: OLIVIA'S HOUSE
I have sent after him. He says he'll come...
How shall I feast him? What bestow of him?^ For youth is bought more oft than begged or borrowed.
I speak too loud!
Where's Malvolio?
He is sad and civil, and suits well for a servant with my fortunes.
Where is Malvolio?
He's coming, madam. But in very strange manner.
He is sure possessed, madam!
Why, what's the matter? Does he rave?
No, madam, he does nothing but smile.
Your ladyship were best to have some guard about you if he come, for sure the man is tainted in's wits.
Go call him hither.
I am as mad as he, if sad and merry madness equal be.

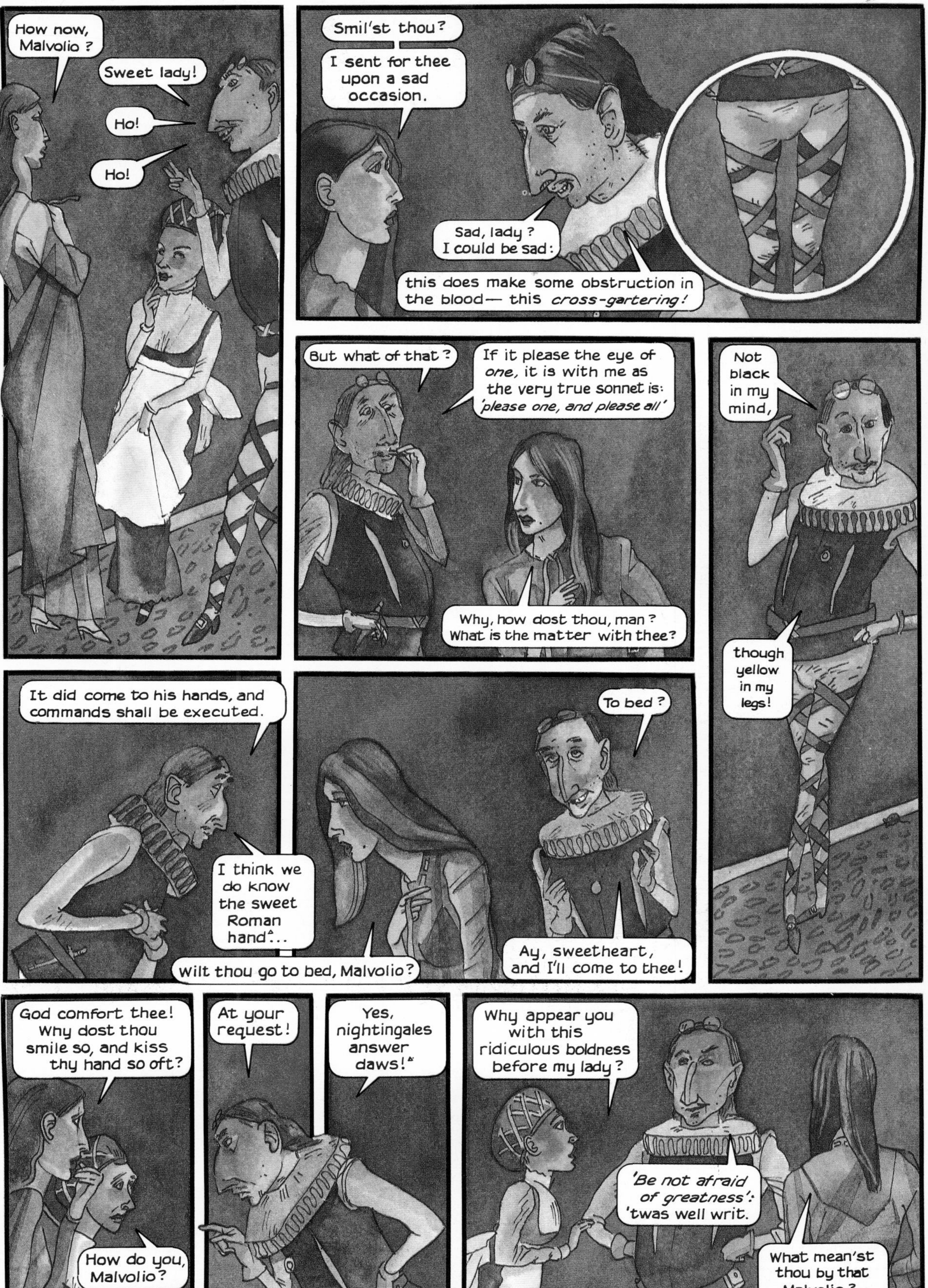
How now, Malvolio?
Sweet lady!
Ho!
Ho!
Smil'st thou?
I sent for thee upon a sad occasion.
Sad, lady? I could be sad:
this does make some obstruction in the blood— this *cross-gartering!*
But what of that?
If it please the eye of *one*, it is with me as the very true sonnet is: *'please one, and please all'*
Why, how dost thou, man? What is the matter with thee?
Not black in my mind,
though yellow in my legs!
It did come to his hands, and commands shall be executed.
I think we do know the sweet Roman hand*...
Wilt thou go to bed, Malvolio?
To bed?
Ay, sweetheart, and I'll come to thee!
God comfort thee! Why dost thou smile so, and kiss thy hand so oft?
How do you, Malvolio?
At your request!
Yes, nightingales answer daws!*
Why appear you with this ridiculous boldness before my lady?
'Be not afraid of greatness': 'twas well writ.
What mean'st thou by that Malvolio?

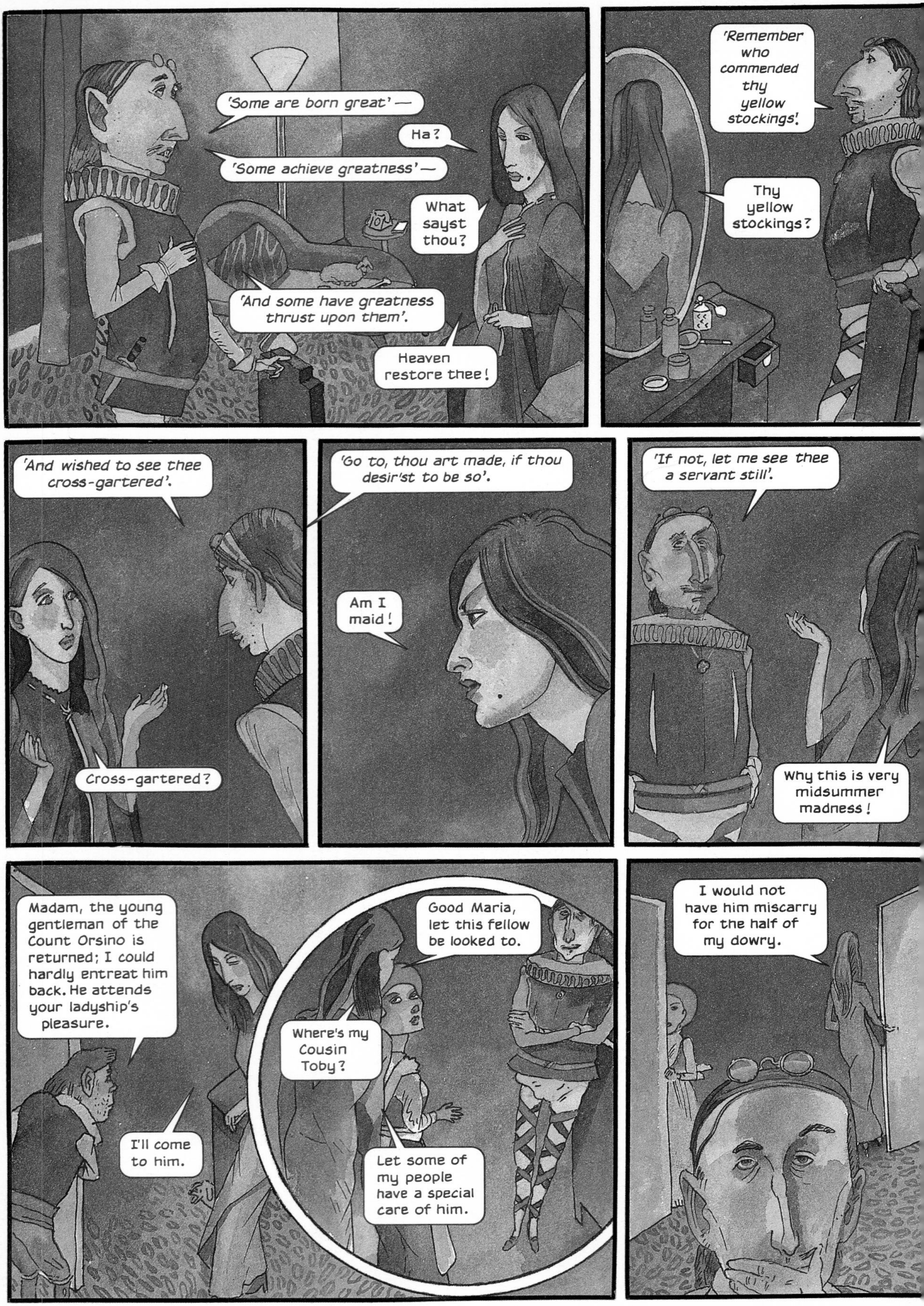
'Some are born great' —
Ha?
'Some achieve greatness' —
What sayst thou?
'And some have greatness thrust upon them'.
Heaven restore thee!
'Remember who commended thy yellow stockings'.
Thy yellow stockings?
'And wished to see thee cross-gartered'.
Cross-gartered?
'Go to, thou art made, if thou desir'st to be so'.
Am I maid!
'If not, let me see thee a servant still'.
Why this is very midsummer madness!
Madam, the young gentleman of the Count Orsino is returned; I could hardly entreat him back. He attends your ladyship's pleasure.
I'll come to him.
Good Maria, let this fellow be looked to.
Where's my Cousin Toby?
Let some of my people have a special care of him.
I would not have him miscarry for the half of my dowry.

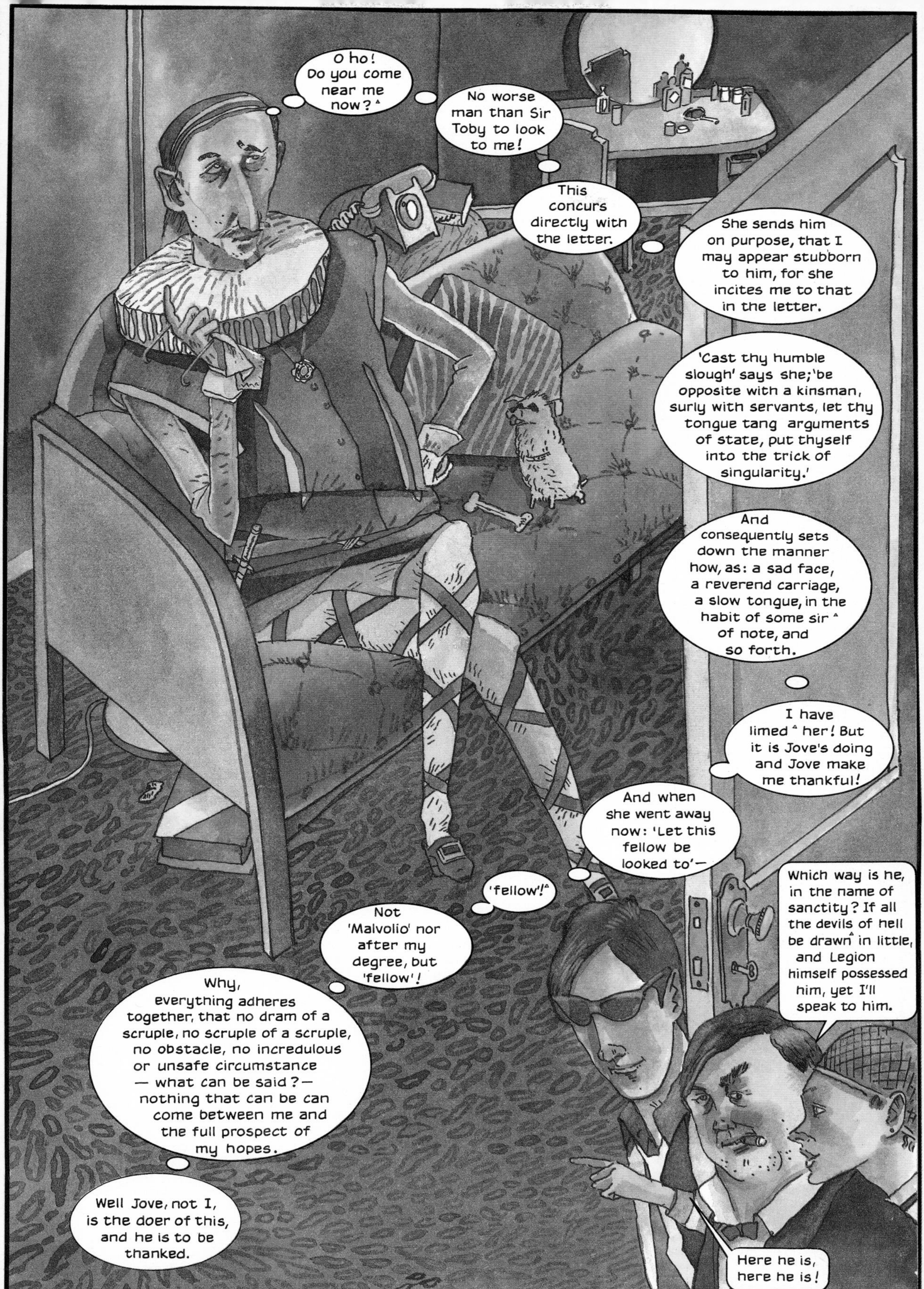
O ho! Do you come near me now?
No worse man than Sir Toby to look to me!
This concurs directly with the letter.
She sends him on purpose, that I may appear stubborn to him, for she incites me to that in the letter.
'Cast thy humble slough' says she; 'be opposite with a kinsman, surly with servants, let thy tongue tang arguments of state, put thyself into the trick of singularity.'
And consequently sets down the manner how, as: a sad face, a reverend carriage, a slow tongue, in the habit of some sir of note, and so forth.
I have limed her! But it is Jove's doing and Jove make me thankful!
And when she went away now: 'Let this fellow be looked to'—
'fellow'!
Not 'Malvolio' nor after my degree, but 'fellow'!
Why, everything adheres together, that no dram of a scruple, no scruple of a scruple, no obstacle, no incredulous or unsafe circumstance — what can be said? — nothing that can be can come between me and the full prospect of my hopes.
Well Jove, not I, is the doer of this, and he is to be thanked.
Which way is he, in the name of sanctity? If all the devils of hell be drawn in little, and Legion himself possessed him, yet I'll speak to him.
Here he is, here he is!

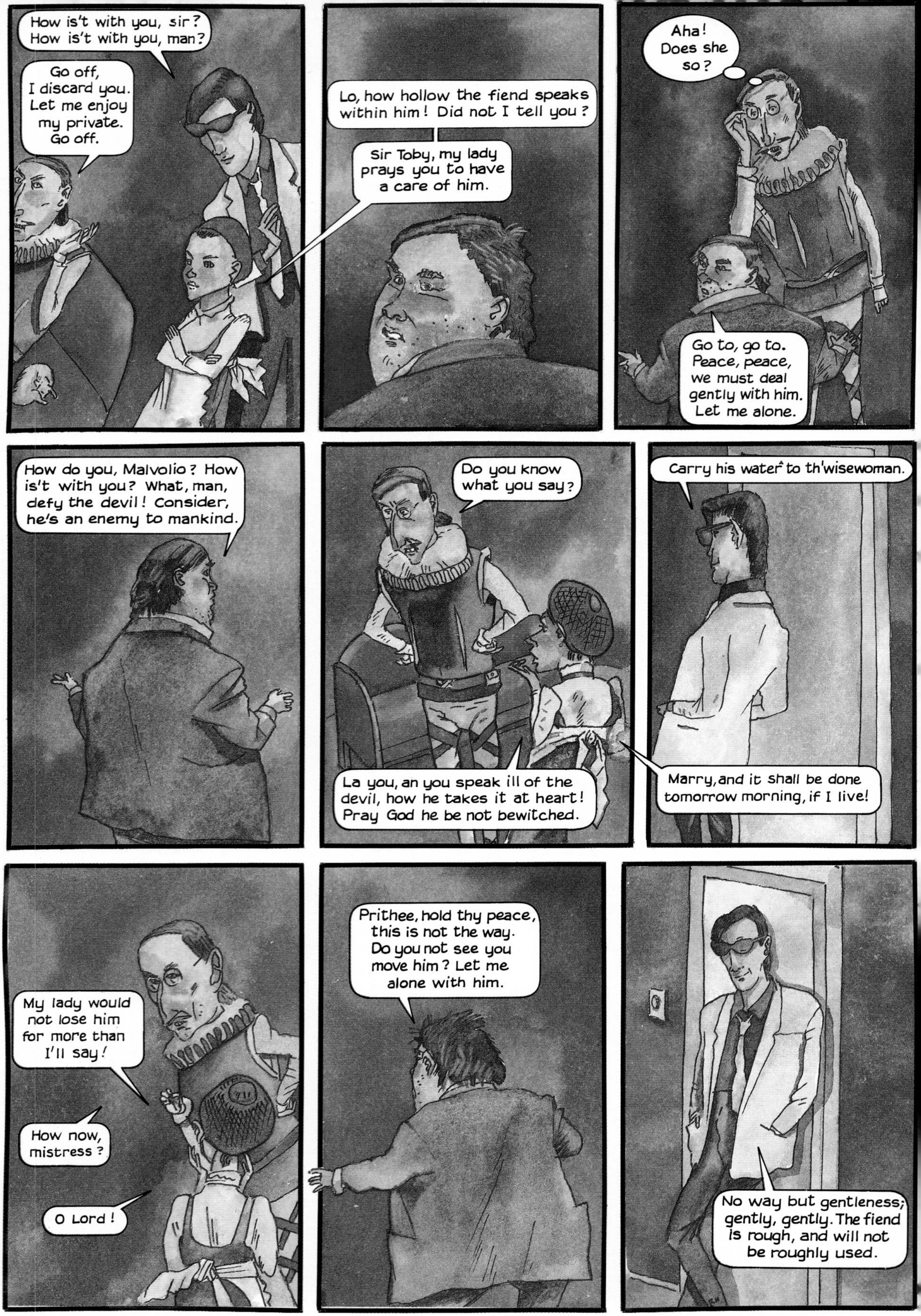
How is't with you, sir? How is't with you, man?
Go off, I discard you. Let me enjoy my private. Go off.
Lo, how hollow the fiend speaks within him! Did not I tell you?
Sir Toby, my lady prays you to have a care of him.
Aha! Does she so?
Go to, go to. Peace, peace, we must deal gently with him. Let me alone.
How do you, Malvolio? How is't with you? What, man, defy the devil! Consider, he's an enemy to mankind.
Do you know what you say?
La you, an you speak ill of the devil, how he takes it at heart! Pray God he be not bewitched.
Carry his water to th'wisewoman.
Marry, and it shall be done tomorrow morning, if I live!
My lady would not lose him for more than I'll say!
How now, mistress?
O Lord!
Prithee, hold thy peace, this is not the way. Do you not see you move him? Let me alone with him.
No way but gentleness; gently, gently. The fiend is rough, and will not be roughly used.

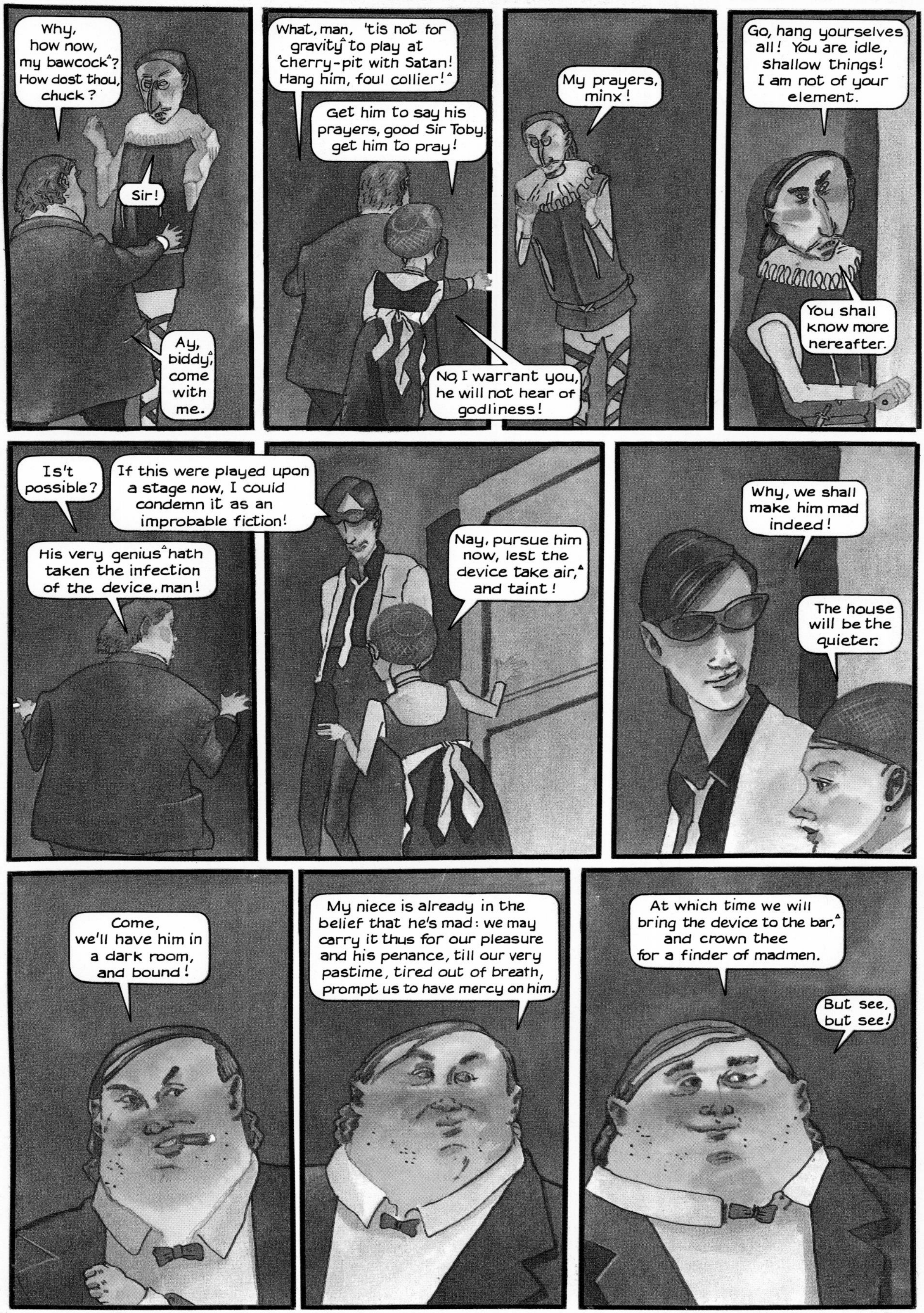

Why, how now, my bawcock? How dost thou, chuck?
Sir!
Ay, biddy, come with me.
What, man, 'tis not for gravity to play at cherry-pit with Satan! Hang him, foul collier!
Get him to say his prayers, good Sir Toby. get him to pray!
No, I warrant you, he will not hear of godliness!
My prayers, minx!
Go, hang yourselves all! You are idle, shallow things! I am not of your element.
You shall know more hereafter.
Is't possible?
If this were played upon a stage now, I could condemn it as an improbable fiction!
His very genius hath taken the infection of the device, man!
Nay, pursue him now, lest the device take air, and taint!
Why, we shall make him mad indeed!
The house will be the quieter.
Come, we'll have him in a dark room, and bound!
My niece is already in the belief that he's mad: we may carry it thus for our pleasure and his penance, till our very pastime, tired out of breath, prompt us to have mercy on him.
At which time we will bring the device to the bar, and crown thee for a finder of madmen.
But see, but see!

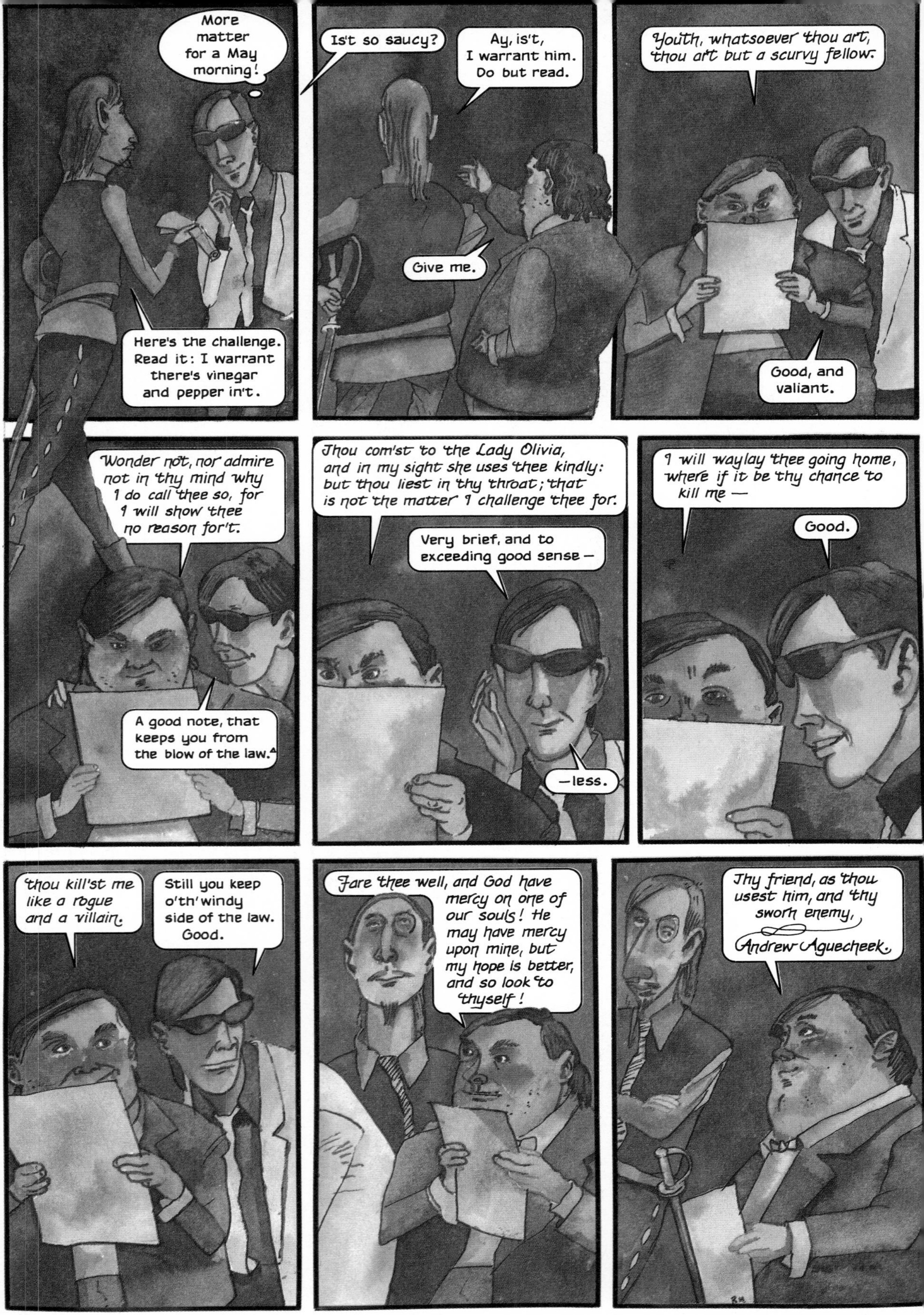
More matter for a May morning!
Here's the challenge. Read it: I warrant there's vinegar and pepper in't.
Is't so saucy?
Ay, is't, I warrant him. Do but read.
Give me.
Youth, whatsoever thou art, thou art but a scurvy fellow.
Good, and valiant.
Wonder not, nor admire not in thy mind why I do call thee so, for I will show thee no reason for't.
A good note, that keeps you from the blow of the law.
Thou com'st to the Lady Olivia, and in my sight she uses thee kindly: but thou liest in thy throat; that is not the matter I challenge thee for.
Very brief, and to exceeding good sense —
—less.
I will waylay thee going home, where if it be thy chance to kill me —
Good.
thou kill'st me like a rogue and a villain.
Still you keep o'th' windy side of the law. Good.
Fare thee well, and God have mercy on one of our souls! He may have mercy upon mine, but my hope is better, and so look to thyself!
Thy friend, as thou usest him, and thy sworn enemy,
Andrew Aguecheek.

If this letter move him not, his legs cannot. I'll give't him.

You may have very fit occasion for't: he is now in some commerce with my lady, and will by and by depart.

Go, Sir Andrew: scout me for him at the corner of the orchard, like a bum-baily.ᐟ

So soon as ever thou see'st him, draw, and as thou draw'st, swear horrible: for it comes to pass oft that a terrible oath, with a swaggering accent sharply twanged off, gives manhood more approbation than ever proof itself would have earned him.

Away!

Nay, let me alone for swearing.ᐟ

Now will not I deliver his letter, for the behaviour of the young gentleman gives him out to be of good capacity and breeding: his employment between his lord and my niece confirms no less.

Therefore, this letter, being so excellently ignorant, will breed no terror in the youth: he will find it comes from a clodpole.ᐟ

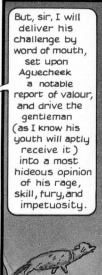

But, sir, I will deliver his challenge by word of mouth, set upon Aguecheek a notable report of valour, and drive the gentleman (as I know his youth will aptly receive it) into a most hideous opinion of his rage, skill, fury, and impetuosity.

This will so fright them both that they will kill one another by the look —

like cockatrices!ᐟ

Here he comes with your niece: give them way till he take leave, and presently after him.

I will meditate the while upon some horrid message for a challenge.

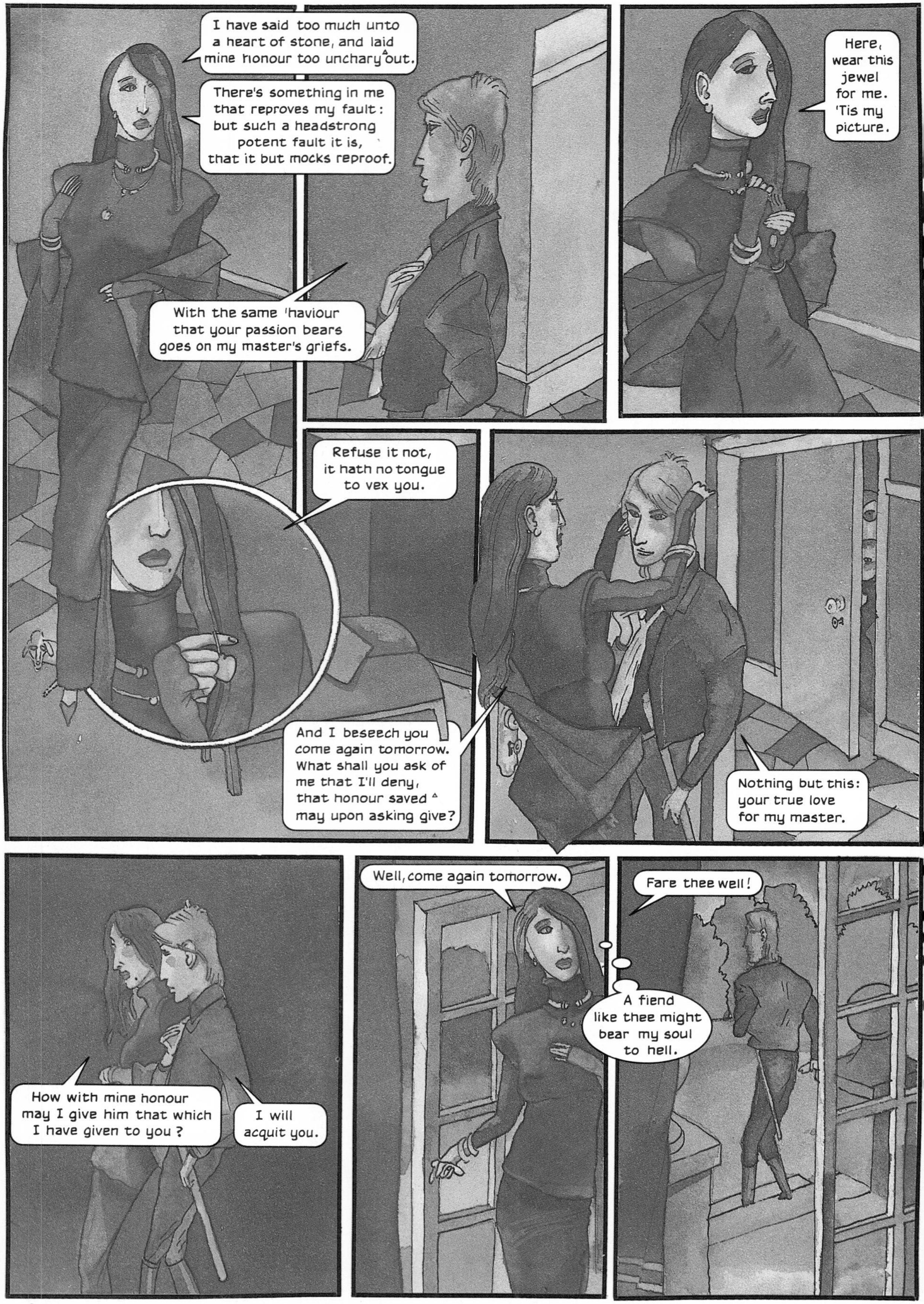
I have said too much unto a heart of stone, and laid mine honour too unchary out.
There's something in me that reproves my fault: but such a headstrong potent fault it is, that it but mocks reproof.
With the same 'haviour that your passion bears goes on my master's griefs.
Here, wear this jewel for me. 'Tis my picture.
Refuse it not, it hath no tongue to vex you.
And I beseech you come again tomorrow. What shall you ask of me that I'll deny, that honour saved may upon asking give?
Nothing but this: your true love for my master.
How with mine honour may I give him that which I have given to you?
I will acquit you.
Well, come again tomorrow.
Fare thee well!
A fiend like thee might bear my soul to hell.

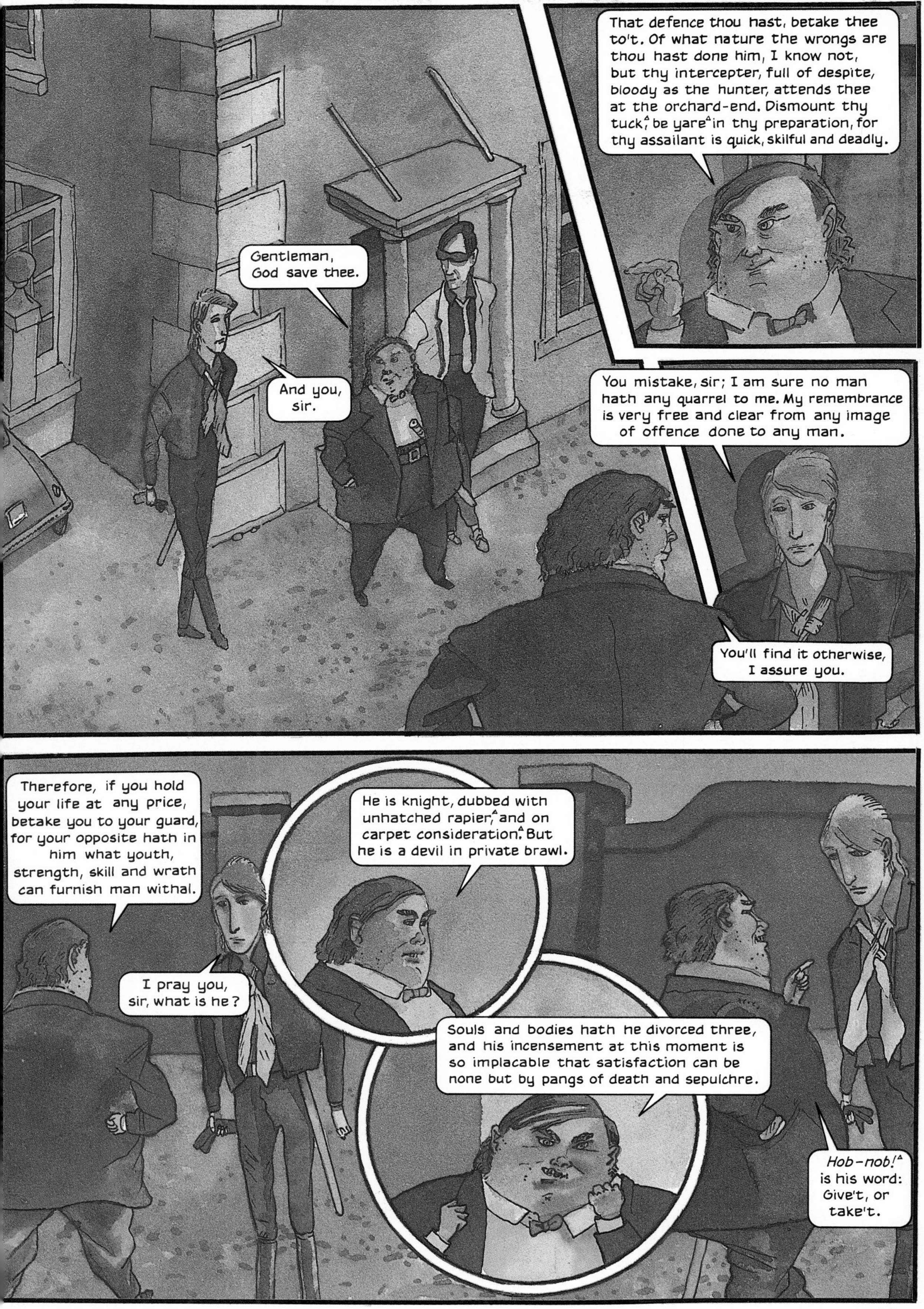
Gentleman, God save thee.
And you, sir.
That defence thou hast, betake thee to't. Of what nature the wrongs are thou hast done him, I know not, but thy intercepter, full of despite, bloody as the hunter, attends thee at the orchard-end. Dismount thy tuck,^ be yare^ in thy preparation, for thy assailant is quick, skilful and deadly.
You mistake, sir; I am sure no man hath any quarrel to me. My remembrance is very free and clear from any image of offence done to any man.
You'll find it otherwise, I assure you.
Therefore, if you hold your life at any price, betake you to your guard, for your opposite hath in him what youth, strength, skill and wrath can furnish man withal.
I pray you, sir, what is he?
He is knight, dubbed with unhatched rapier,^ and on carpet consideration.^ But he is a devil in private brawl.
Souls and bodies hath he divorced three, and his incensement at this moment is so implacable that satisfaction can be none but by pangs of death and sepulchre.
Hob-nob!^ is his word: Give't, or take't.

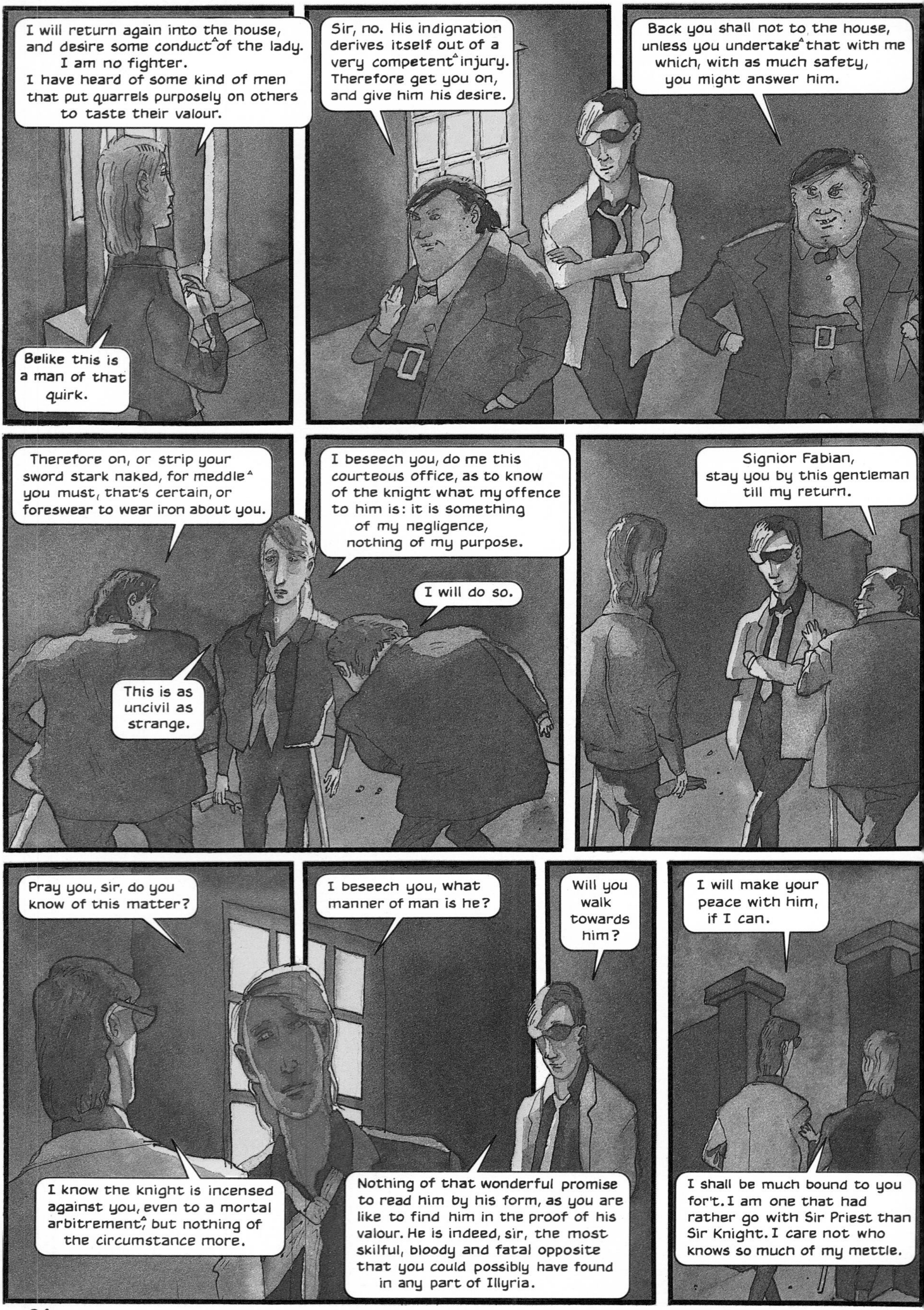
I will return again into the house, and desire some conduct of the lady. I am no fighter. I have heard of some kind of men that put quarrels purposely on others to taste their valour.
Belike this is a man of that quirk.
Sir, no. His indignation derives itself out of a very competent injury. Therefore get you on, and give him his desire.
Back you shall not to the house, unless you undertake that with me which, with as much safety, you might answer him.
Therefore on, or strip your sword stark naked, for meddle you must, that's certain, or foreswear to wear iron about you.
This is as uncivil as strange.
I beseech you, do me this courteous office, as to know of the knight what my offence to him is: it is something of my negligence, nothing of my purpose.
I will do so.
Signior Fabian, stay you by this gentleman till my return.
Pray you, sir, do you know of this matter?
I know the knight is incensed against you, even to a mortal arbitrement, but nothing of the circumstance more.
I beseech you, what manner of man is he?
Nothing of that wonderful promise to read him by his form, as you are like to find him in the proof of his valour. He is indeed, sir, the most skilful, bloody and fatal opposite that you could possibly have found in any part of Illyria.
Will you walk towards him?
I will make your peace with him, if I can.
I shall be much bound to you for't. I am one that had rather go with Sir Priest than Sir Knight. I care not who knows so much of my mettle.

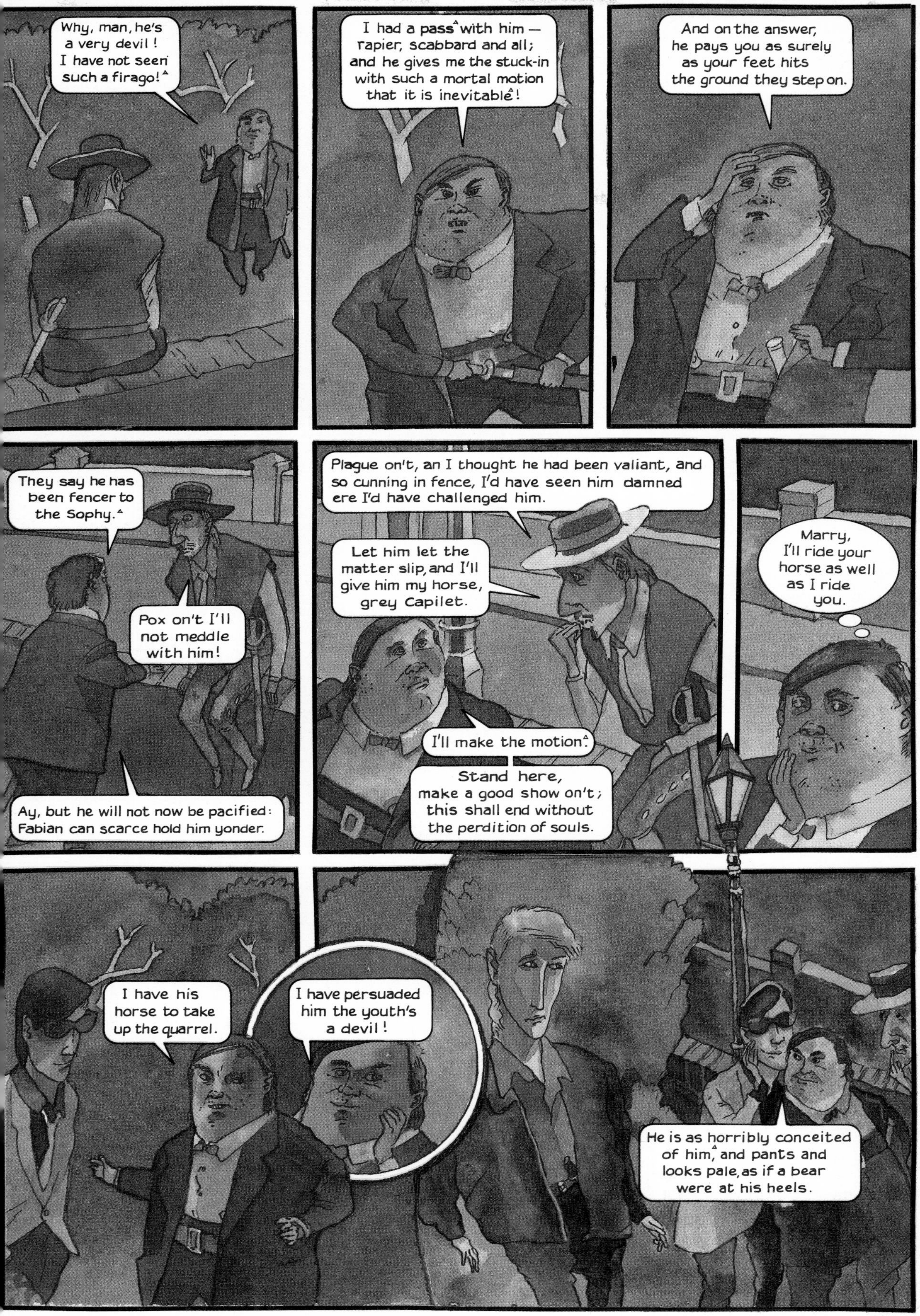

Why, man, he's a very devil! I have not seen such a firago!
I had a pass with him — rapier, scabbard and all; and he gives me the stuck-in with such a mortal motion that it is inevitable!
And on the answer, he pays you as surely as your feet hits the ground they step on.
They say he has been fencer to the Sophy.
Pox on't I'll not meddle with him!
Ay, but he will not now be pacified: Fabian can scarce hold him yonder.
Plague on't, an I thought he had been valiant, and so cunning in fence, I'd have seen him damned ere I'd have challenged him.
Let him let the matter slip, and I'll give him my horse, grey Capilet.
I'll make the motion.
Stand here, make a good show on't; this shall end without the perdition of souls.
Marry, I'll ride your horse as well as I ride you.
I have his horse to take up the quarrel.
I have persuaded him the youth's a devil!
He is as horribly conceited of him, and pants and looks pale, as if a bear were at his heels.

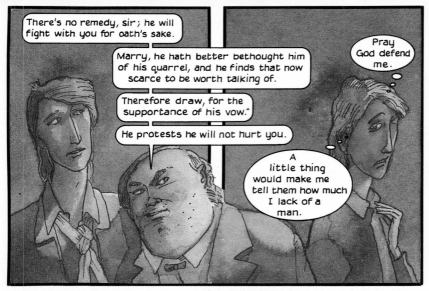

There's no remedy, sir; he will fight with you for oath's sake.

Marry, he hath better bethought him of his quarrel, and he finds that now scarce to be worth talking of.

Therefore draw, for the supportance of his vow.[a]

He protests he will not hurt you.

Pray God defend me.

A little thing would make me tell them how much I lack of a man.

Give ground if you see him furious.

Come, Sir Andrew, there's no remedy.

The gentleman will, for his honour's sake, have one bout with you. He cannot, by the *duello*[a] avoid it. But he has promised me, as he is a gentleman and a soldier, he will not hurt you.

Come on. To't!

Pray God he keep his oath!

Enter Antonio

I do assure you, 'tis against my will.

Put up your sword!

If this young gentleman have done offence, I take the fault on me. If you offend him, I for him defy you!

You, Sir? Why, what are you?

One, sir, that for his love dares yet do more than you have heard him brag to you he will.

86

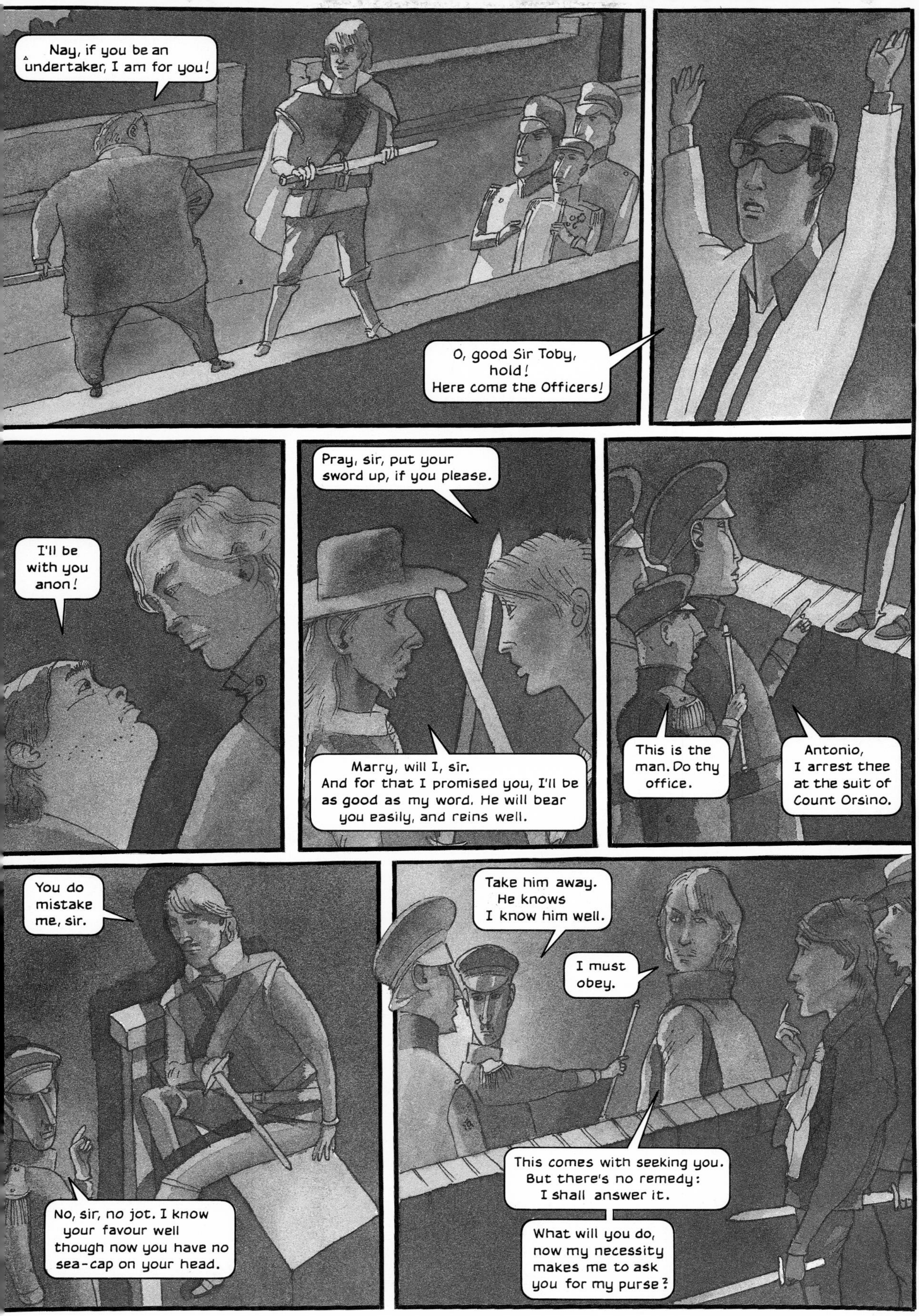
Nay, if you be an undertaker, I am for you!
O, good Sir Toby, hold! Here come the Officers!
I'll be with you anon!
Pray, sir, put your sword up, if you please.
Marry, will I, sir. And for that I promised you, I'll be as good as my word. He will bear you easily, and reins well.
This is the man. Do thy office.
Antonio, I arrest thee at the suit of Count Orsino.
You do mistake me, sir.
No, sir, no jot. I know your favour well though now you have no sea-cap on your head.
Take him away. He knows I know him well.
I must obey.
This comes with seeking you. But there's no remedy: I shall answer it.
What will you do, now my necessity makes me to ask you for my purse?

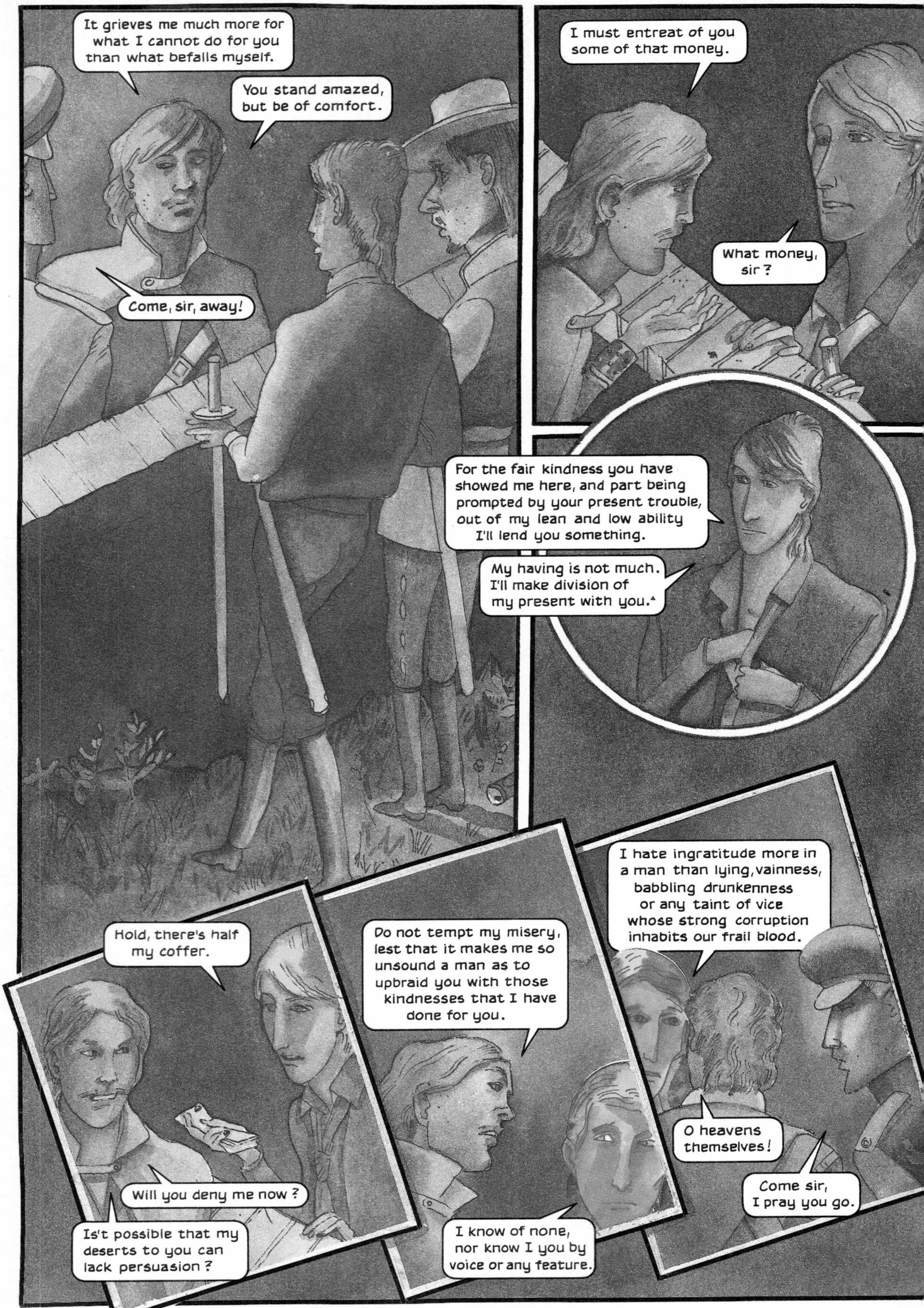
It grieves me much more for what I cannot do for you than what befalls myself.
You stand amazed, but be of comfort.
Come, sir, away!
I must entreat of you some of that money.
What money, sir?
For the fair kindness you have showed me here, and part being prompted by your present trouble, out of my lean and low ability I'll lend you something.
My having is not much. I'll make division of my present with you.
Hold, there's half my coffer.
Will you deny me now?
Is't possible that my deserts to you can lack persuasion?
Do not tempt my misery, lest that it makes me so unsound a man as to upbraid you with those kindnesses that I have done for you.
I know of none, nor know I you by voice or any feature.
I hate ingratitude more in a man than lying, vainness, babbling drunkenness or any taint of vice whose strong corruption inhabits our frail blood.
O heavens themselves!
Come sir, I pray you go.

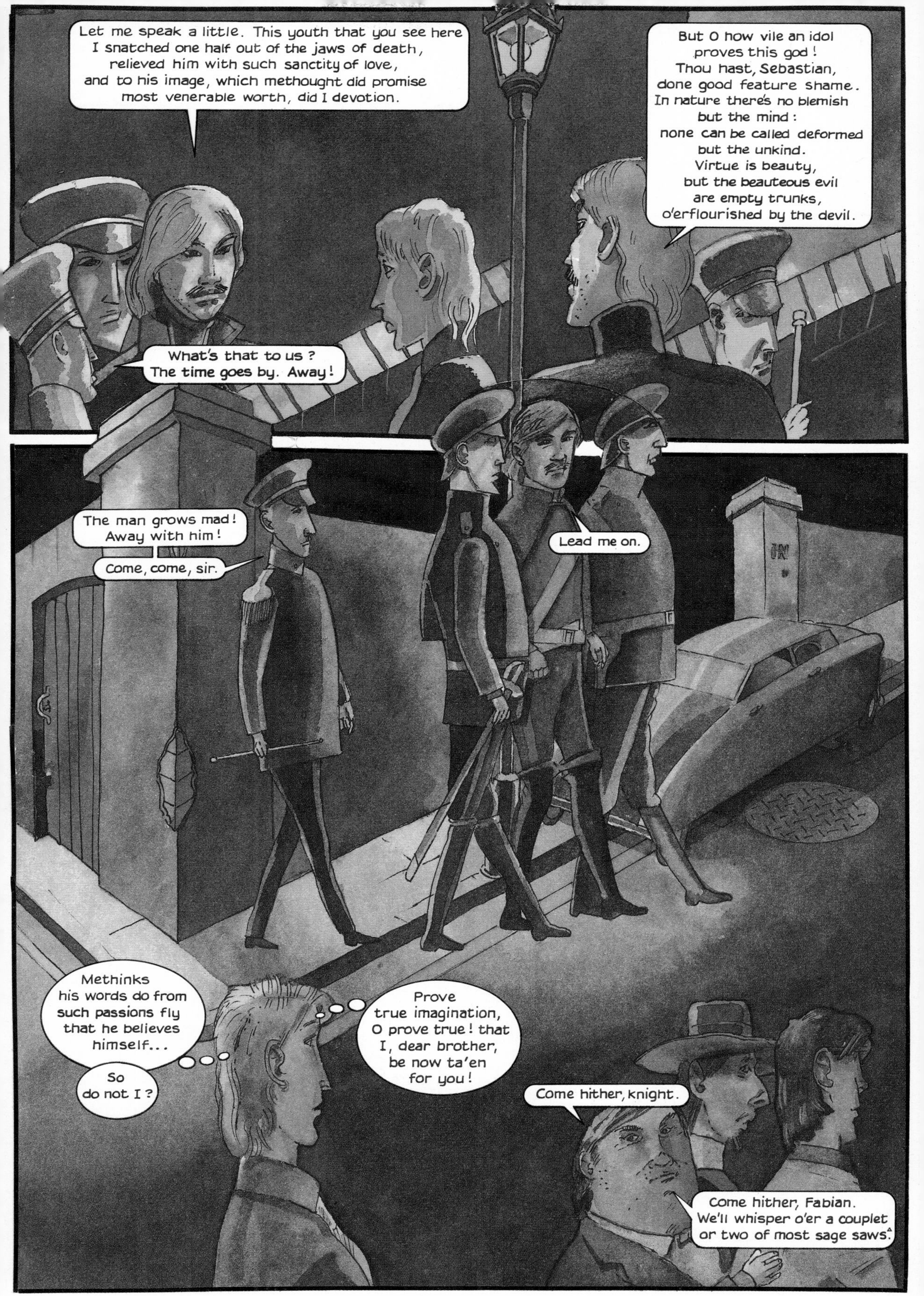

Let me speak a little. This youth that you see here I snatched one half out of the jaws of death, relieved him with such sanctity of love, and to his image, which methought did promise most venerable worth, did I devotion.
What's that to us ? The time goes by. Away !
But O how vile an idol proves this god ! Thou hast, Sebastian, done good feature shame. In nature there's no blemish but the mind : none can be called deformed but the unkind. Virtue is beauty, but the beauteous evil are empty trunks, o'erflourished by the devil.
The man grows mad ! Away with him !
Come, come, sir.
Lead me on.
Methinks his words do from such passions fly that he believes himself...
So do not I ?
Prove true imagination, O prove true ! that I, dear brother, be now ta'en for you !
Come hither, knight.
Come hither, Fabian. We'll whisper o'er a couplet or two of most sage saws.

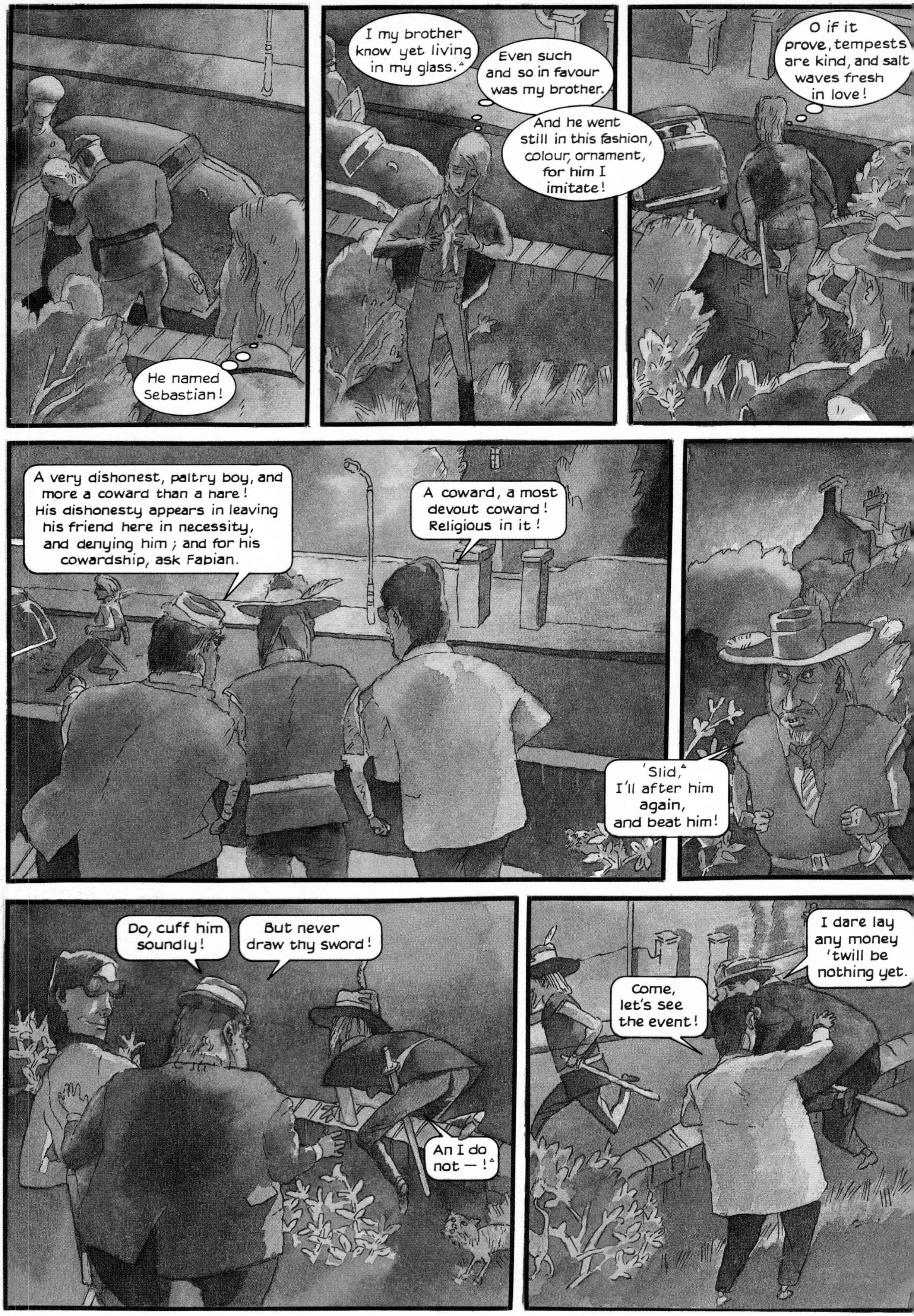
He named Sebastian!
I my brother know yet living in my glass.△
Even such and so in favour was my brother.
And he went still in this fashion, colour, ornament, for him I imitate!
O if it prove, tempests are kind, and salt waves fresh in love!
A very dishonest, paltry boy, and more a coward than a hare! His dishonesty appears in leaving his friend here in necessity, and denying him; and for his cowardship, ask Fabian.
A coward, a most devout coward! Religious in it!
'Slid,△ I'll after him again, and beat him!
Do, cuff him soundly!
But never draw thy sword!
An I do not —!△
Come, let's see the event!
I dare lay any money 'twill be nothing yet.

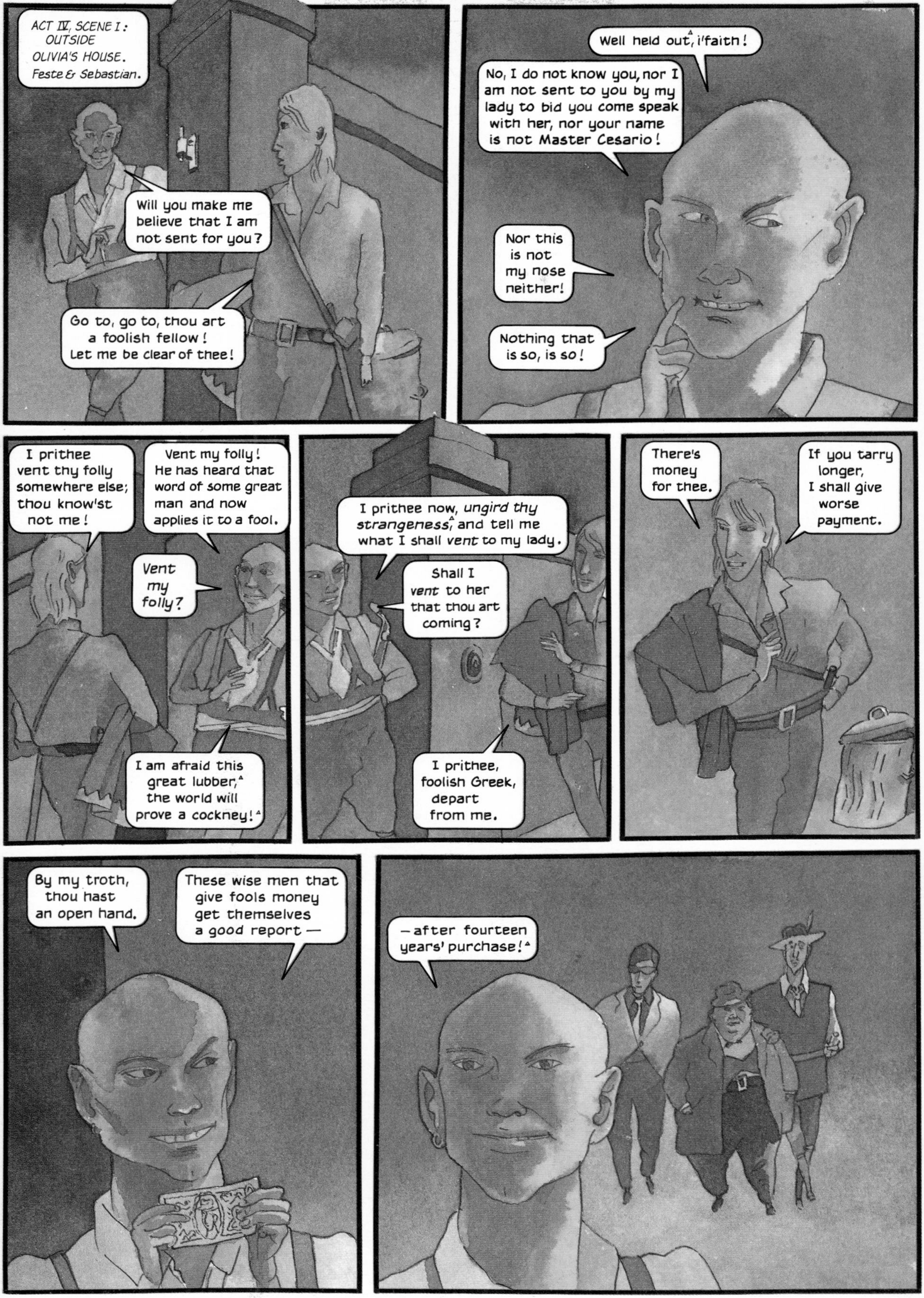
ACT IV, SCENE I: OUTSIDE OLIVIA'S HOUSE. Feste & Sebastian.
Will you make me believe that I am not sent for you?
Go to, go to, thou art a foolish fellow! Let me be clear of thee!
Well held out, i'faith!
No, I do not know you, nor I am not sent to you by my lady to bid you come speak with her, nor your name is not Master Cesario!
Nor this is not my nose neither!
Nothing that is so, is so!
I prithee vent thy folly somewhere else; thou know'st not me!
Vent my folly! He has heard that word of some great man and now applies it to a fool.
Vent my folly?
I am afraid this great lubber, the world will prove a cockney!
I prithee now, *ungird thy strangeness*, and tell me what I shall *vent* to my lady.
Shall I *vent* to her that thou art coming?
I prithee, foolish Greek, depart from me.
There's money for thee.
If you tarry longer, I shall give worse payment.
By my troth, thou hast an open hand.
These wise men that give fools money get themselves a good report —
— after fourteen years' purchase!

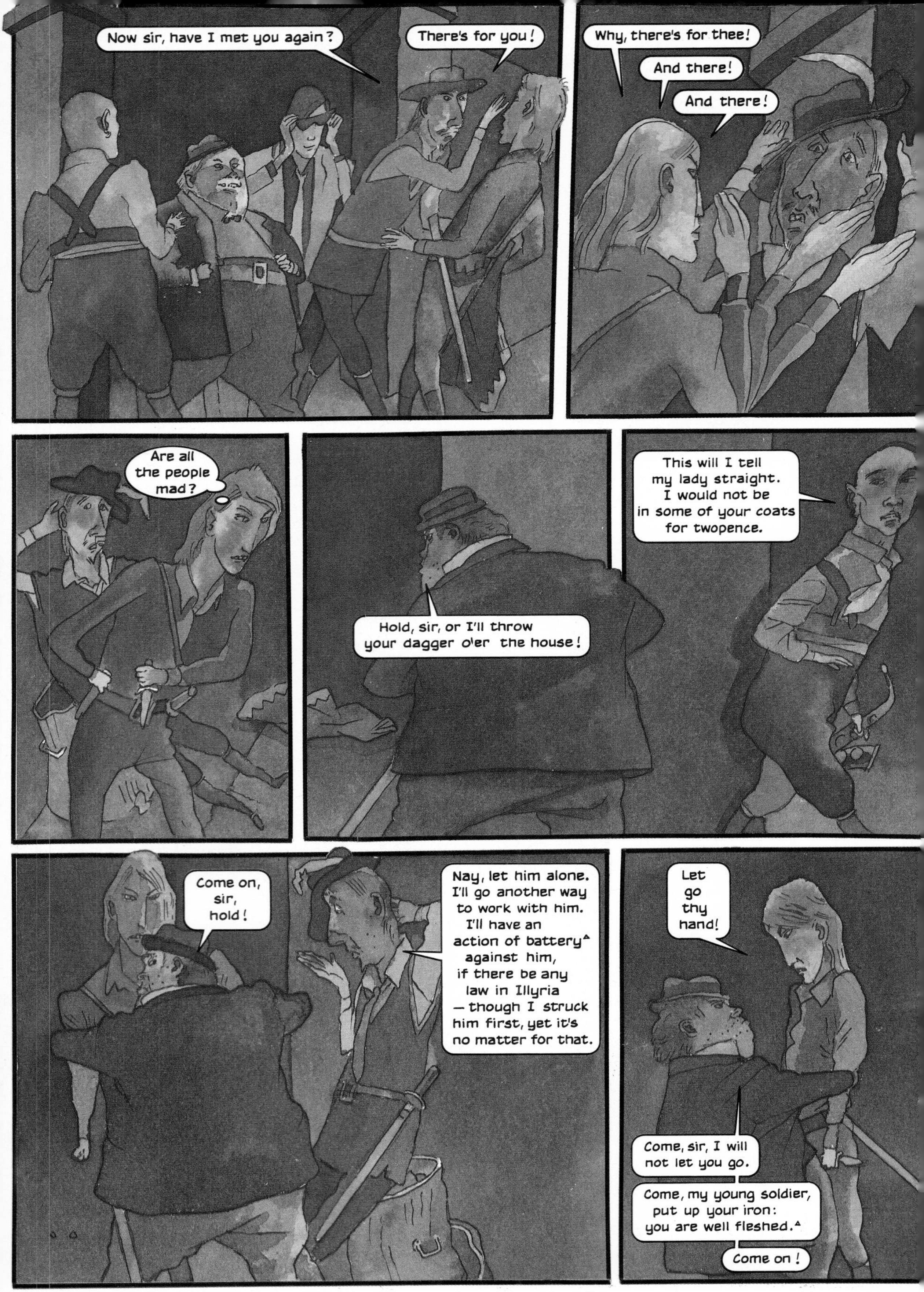

Now sir, have I met you again?
There's for you!
Why, there's for thee!
And there!
And there!
Are all the people mad?
Hold, sir, or I'll throw your dagger o'er the house!
This will I tell my lady straight. I would not be in some of your coats for twopence.
Come on, sir, hold!
Nay, let him alone. I'll go another way to work with him. I'll have an action of battery▲ against him, if there be any law in Illyria — though I struck him first, yet it's no matter for that.
Let go thy hand!
Come, sir, I will not let you go.
Come, my young soldier, put up your iron: you are well fleshed.▲
Come on!

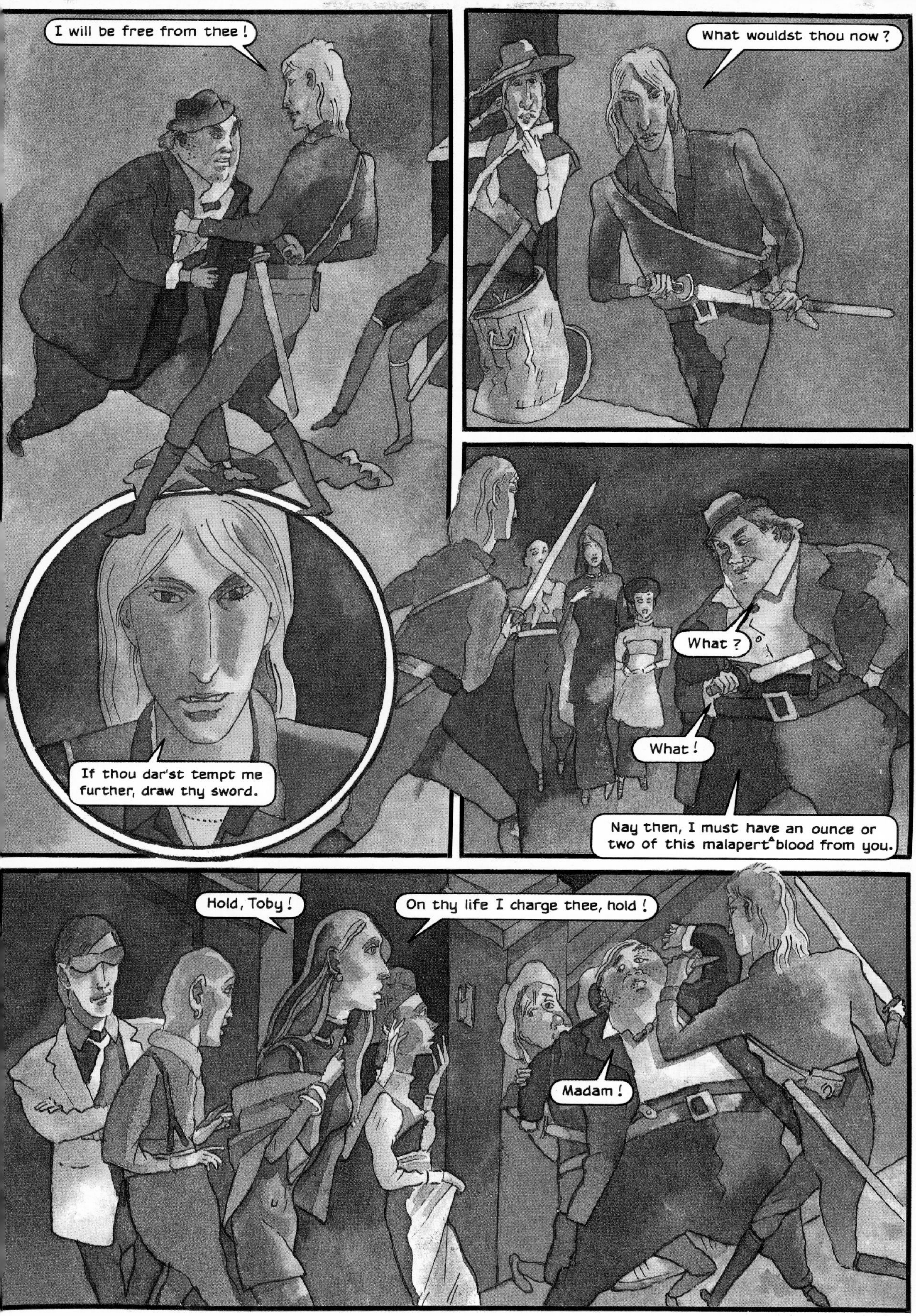
I will be free from thee!
What wouldst thou now?
If thou dar'st tempt me further, draw thy sword.
What?
What!
Nay then, I must have an ounce or two of this malapert blood from you.
Hold, Toby!
On thy life I charge thee, hold!
Madam!

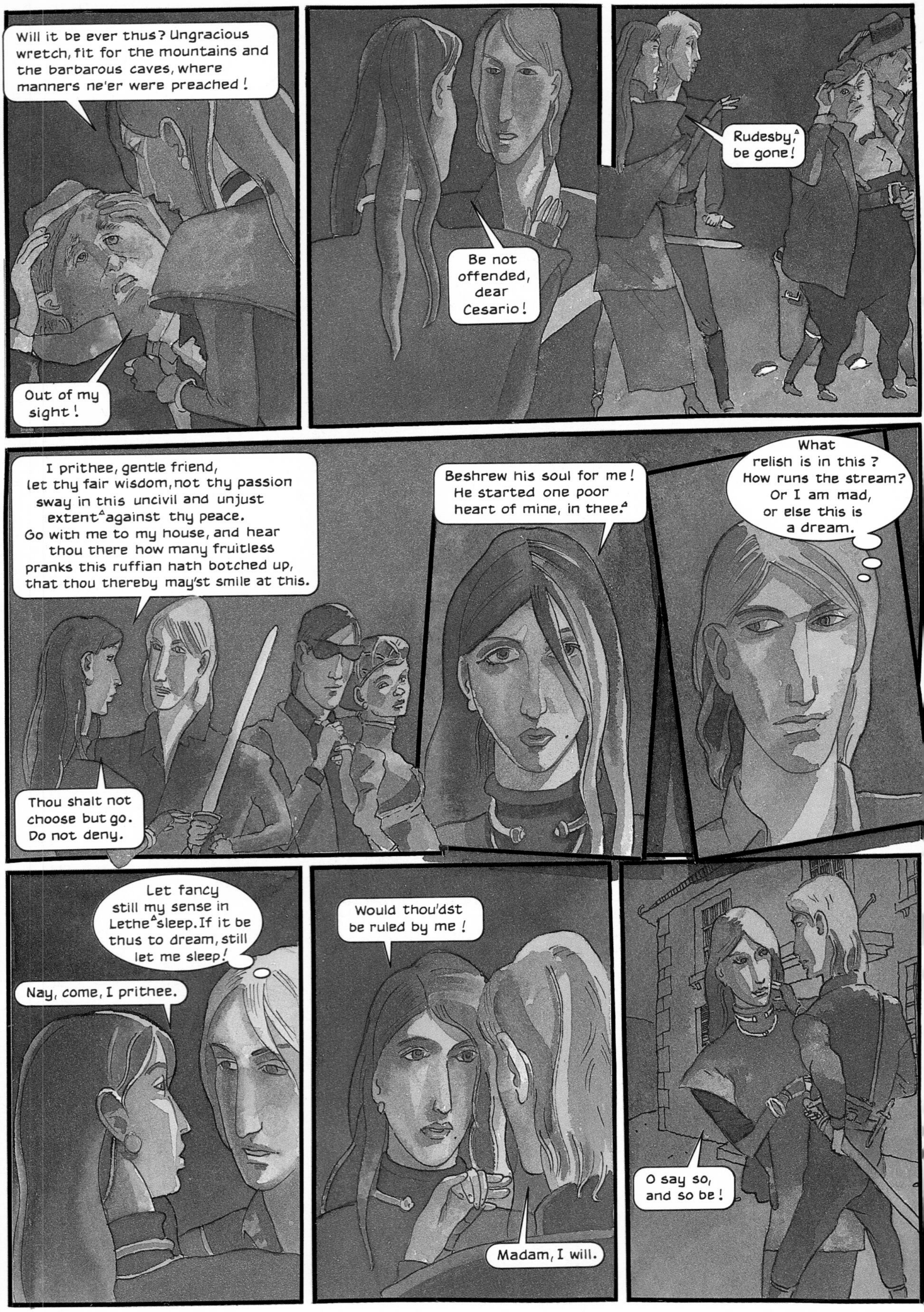
Will it be ever thus? Ungracious wretch, fit for the mountains and the barbarous caves, where manners ne'er were preached!
Out of my sight!
Be not offended, dear Cesario!
Rudesby, be gone!
I prithee, gentle friend, let thy fair wisdom, not thy passion sway in this uncivil and unjust extent against thy peace. Go with me to my house, and hear thou there how many fruitless pranks this ruffian hath botched up, that thou thereby may'st smile at this.
Thou shalt not choose but go. Do not deny.
Beshrew his soul for me! He started one poor heart of mine, in thee.
What relish is in this? How runs the stream? Or I am mad, or else this is a dream.
Let fancy still my sense in Lethe sleep. If it be thus to dream, still let me sleep!
Nay, come, I prithee.
Would thou'dst be ruled by me!
Madam, I will.
O say so, and so be!

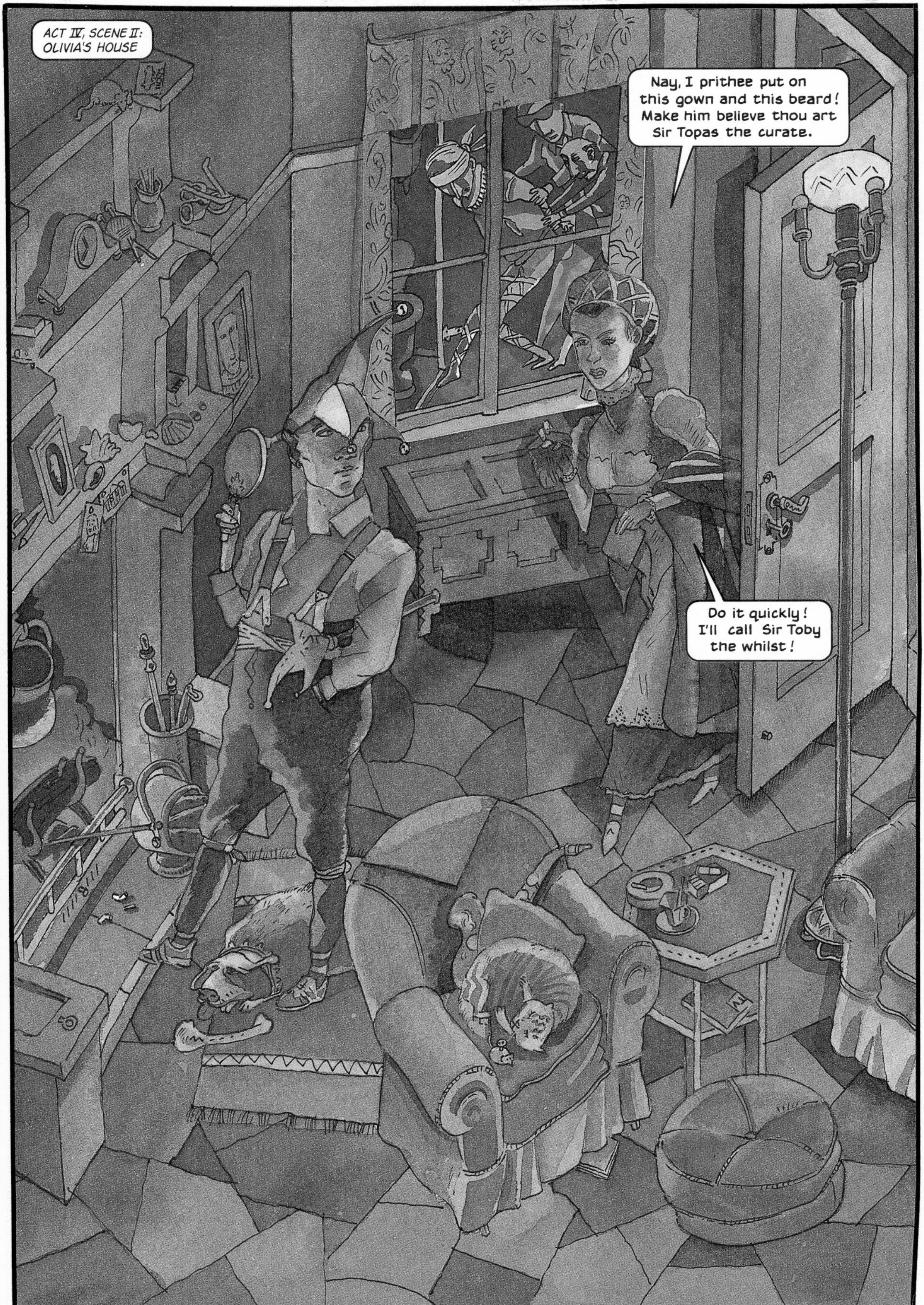
ACT IV, SCENE II:
OLIVIA'S HOUSE
Nay, I prithee put on this gown and this beard! Make him believe thou art Sir Topas the curate.
Do it quickly! I'll call Sir Toby the whilst!

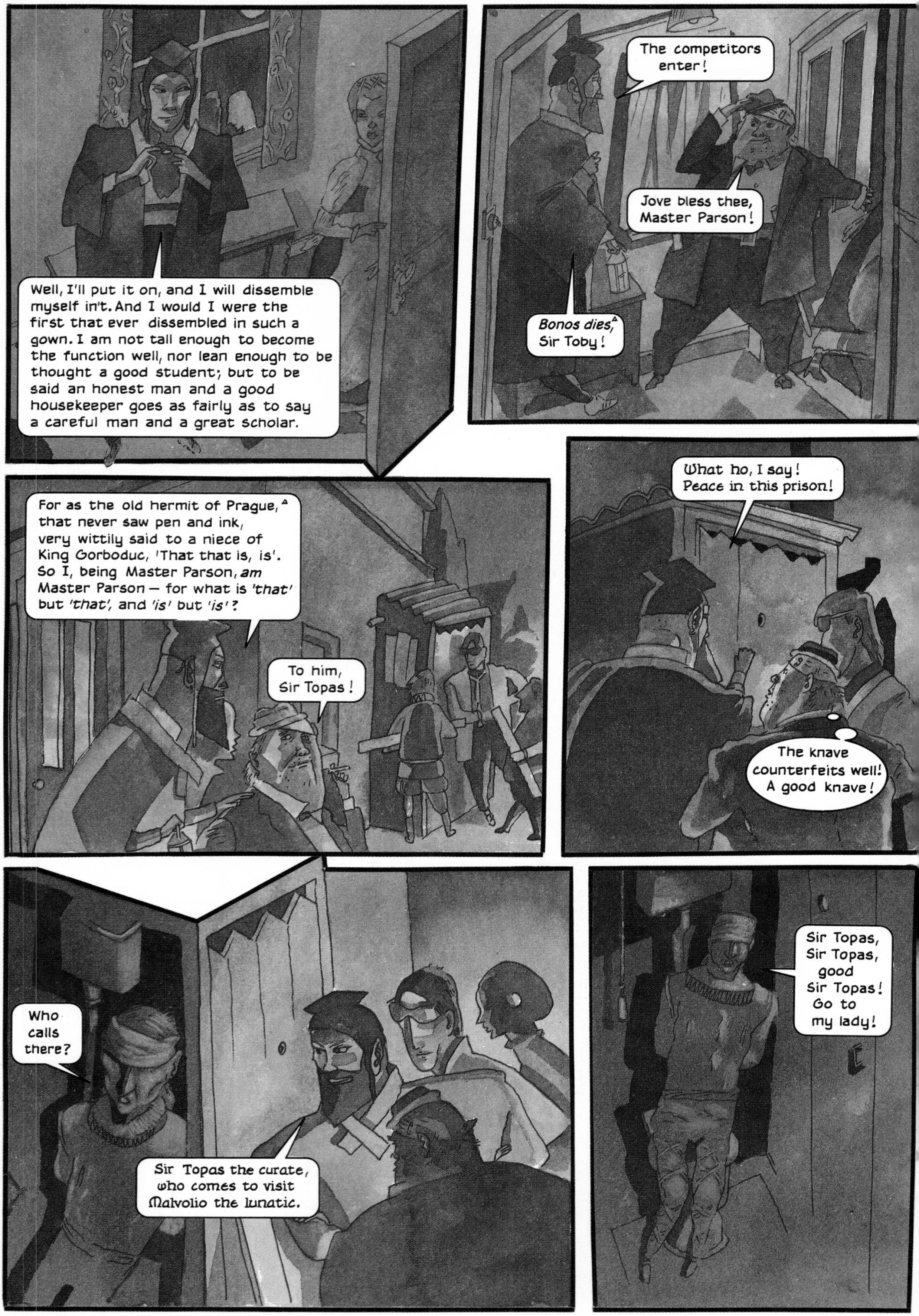
Well, I'll put it on, and I will dissemble myself in't. And I would I were the first that ever dissembled in such a gown. I am not tall enough to become the function well, nor lean enough to be thought a good student; but to be said an honest man and a good housekeeper goes as fairly as to say a careful man and a great scholar.
The competitors enter!
Jove bless thee, Master Parson!
Bonos dies, Sir Toby!
For as the old hermit of Prague, that never saw pen and ink, very wittily said to a niece of King Gorboduc, 'That that is, is'. So I, being Master Parson, *am* Master Parson — for what is *'that'* but *'that'*, and *'is'* but *'is'*?
To him, Sir Topas!
What ho, I say! Peace in this prison!
The knave counterfeits well! A good knave!
Who calls there?
Sir Topas the curate, who comes to visit Malvolio the lunatic.
Sir Topas, Sir Topas, good Sir Topas! Go to my lady!

Out, hyperbolical fiend! How vexest thou this man! Talk'st thou nothing but of ladies?

Well said, Master Parson.

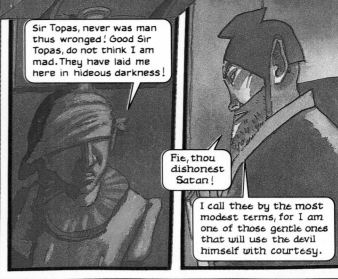

Sir Topas, never was man thus wronged! Good Sir Topas, do not think I am mad. They have laid me here in hideous darkness!

Fie, thou dishonest Satan!

I call thee by the most modest terms, for I am one of those gentle ones that will use the devil himself with courtesy.

Sayest thou that house is dark?

As hell, Sir Topas!

Why, it hath bay windows transparent as barricadoes,[A] and the clerestories[A] toward the south-north are as lustrous[A] as ebony!

And yet complainst thou of obstruction?

I am not mad, Sir Topas. I say to you, this house is dark.

Madman, thou errest!

I say there is no darkness but ignorance, in which thou art more puzzled than th'Egyptians in their fog.[A]

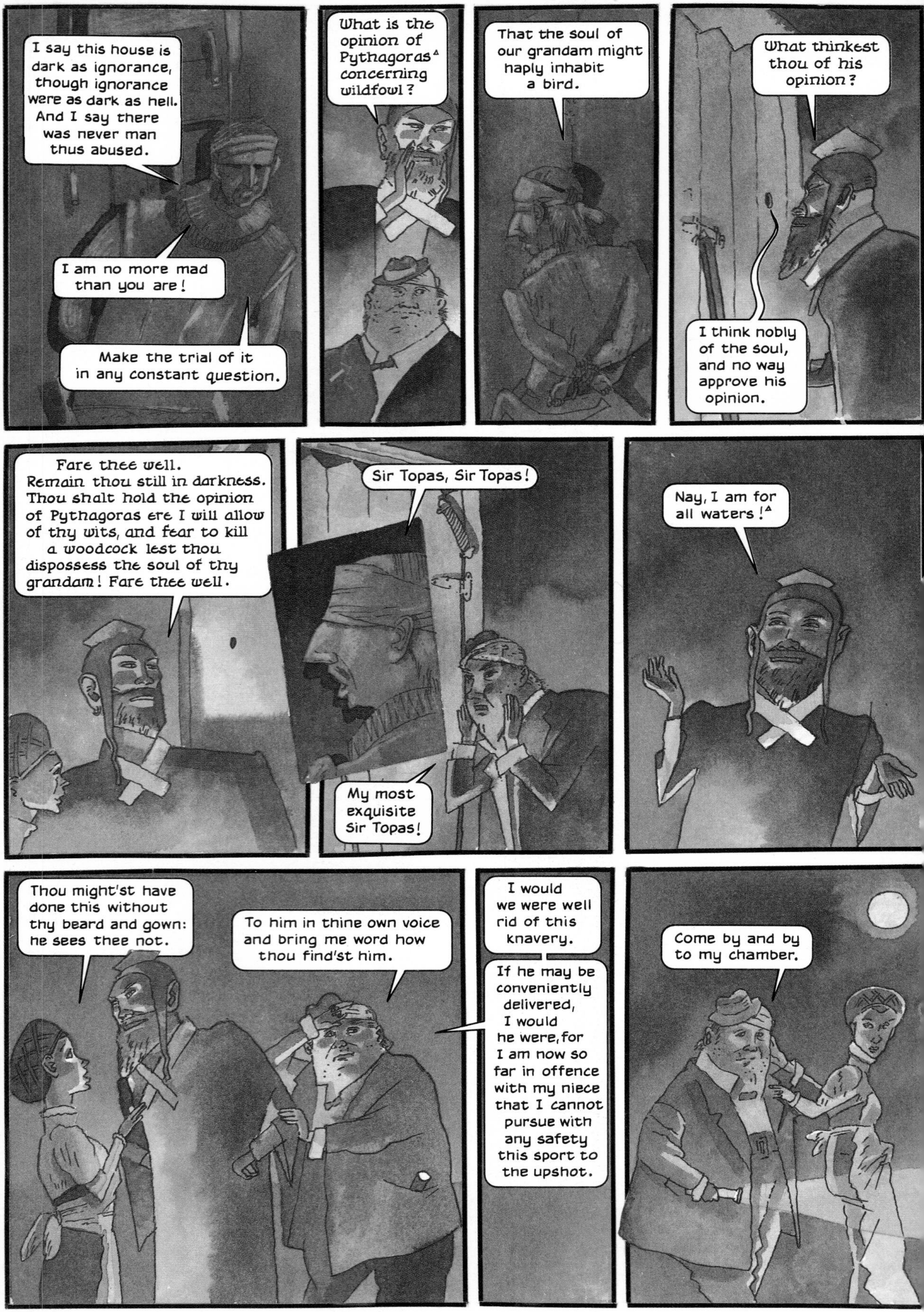
I say this house is dark as ignorance, though ignorance were as dark as hell. And I say there was never man thus abused.
I am no more mad than you are!
Make the trial of it in any constant question.
What is the opinion of Pythagoras^ concerning wildfowl?
That the soul of our grandam might haply inhabit a bird.
What thinkest thou of his opinion?
I think nobly of the soul, and no way approve his opinion.
Fare thee well. Remain thou still in darkness. Thou shalt hold the opinion of Pythagoras ere I will allow of thy wits, and fear to kill a woodcock lest thou dispossess the soul of thy grandam! Fare thee well.
Sir Topas, Sir Topas!
My most exquisite Sir Topas!
Nay, I am for all waters!^
Thou might'st have done this without thy beard and gown: he sees thee not.
To him in thine own voice and bring me word how thou find'st him.
I would we were well rid of this knavery.
If he may be conveniently delivered, I would he were, for I am now so far in offence with my niece that I cannot pursue with any safety this sport to the upshot.
Come by and by to my chamber.

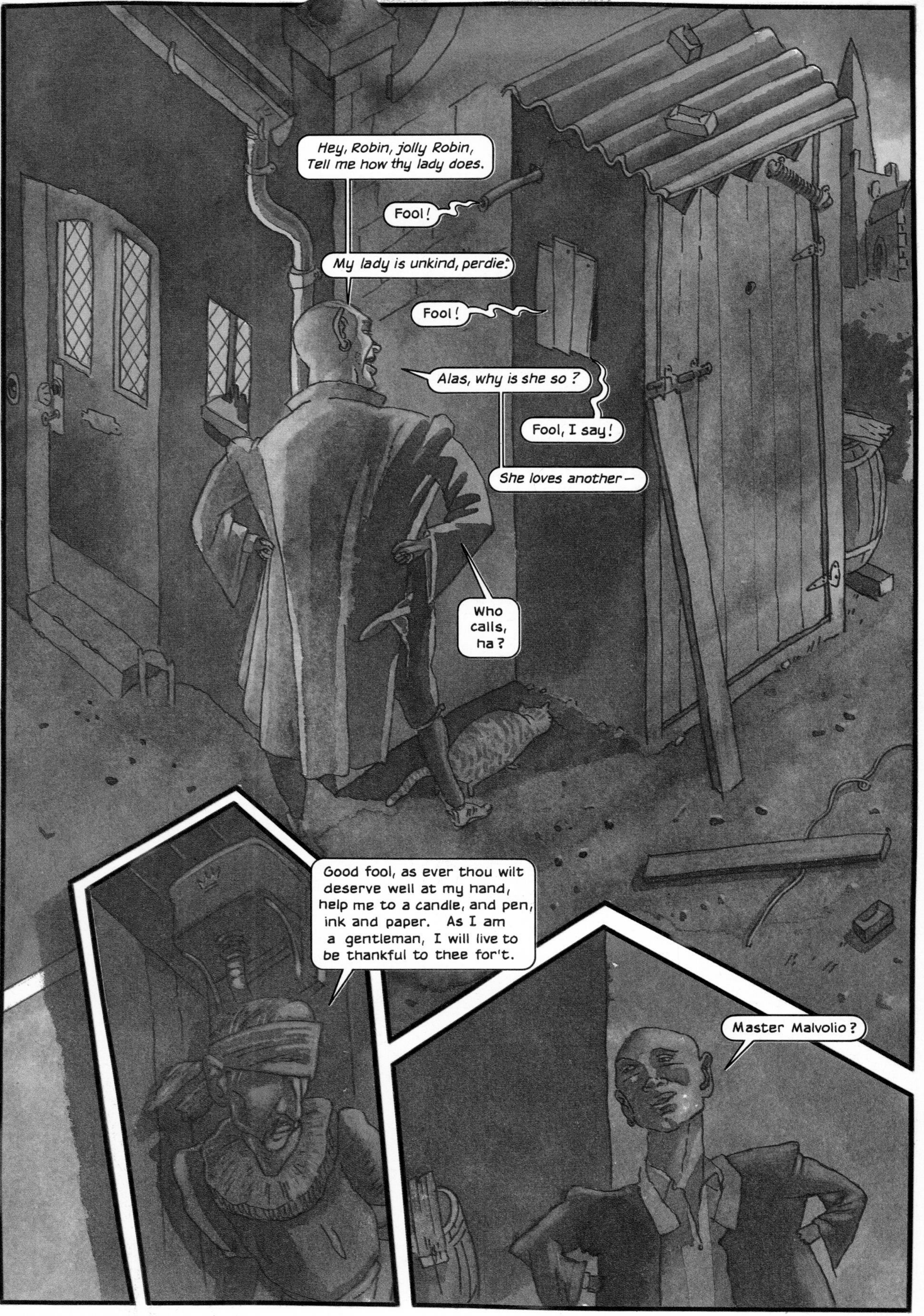
Hey, Robin, jolly Robin,
Tell me how thy lady does.
Fool!
My lady is unkind, perdie.
Fool!
Alas, why is she so?
Fool, I say!
She loves another—
Who calls, ha?
Good fool, as ever thou wilt deserve well at my hand, help me to a candle, and pen, ink and paper. As I am a gentleman, I will live to be thankful to thee for't.
Master Malvolio?

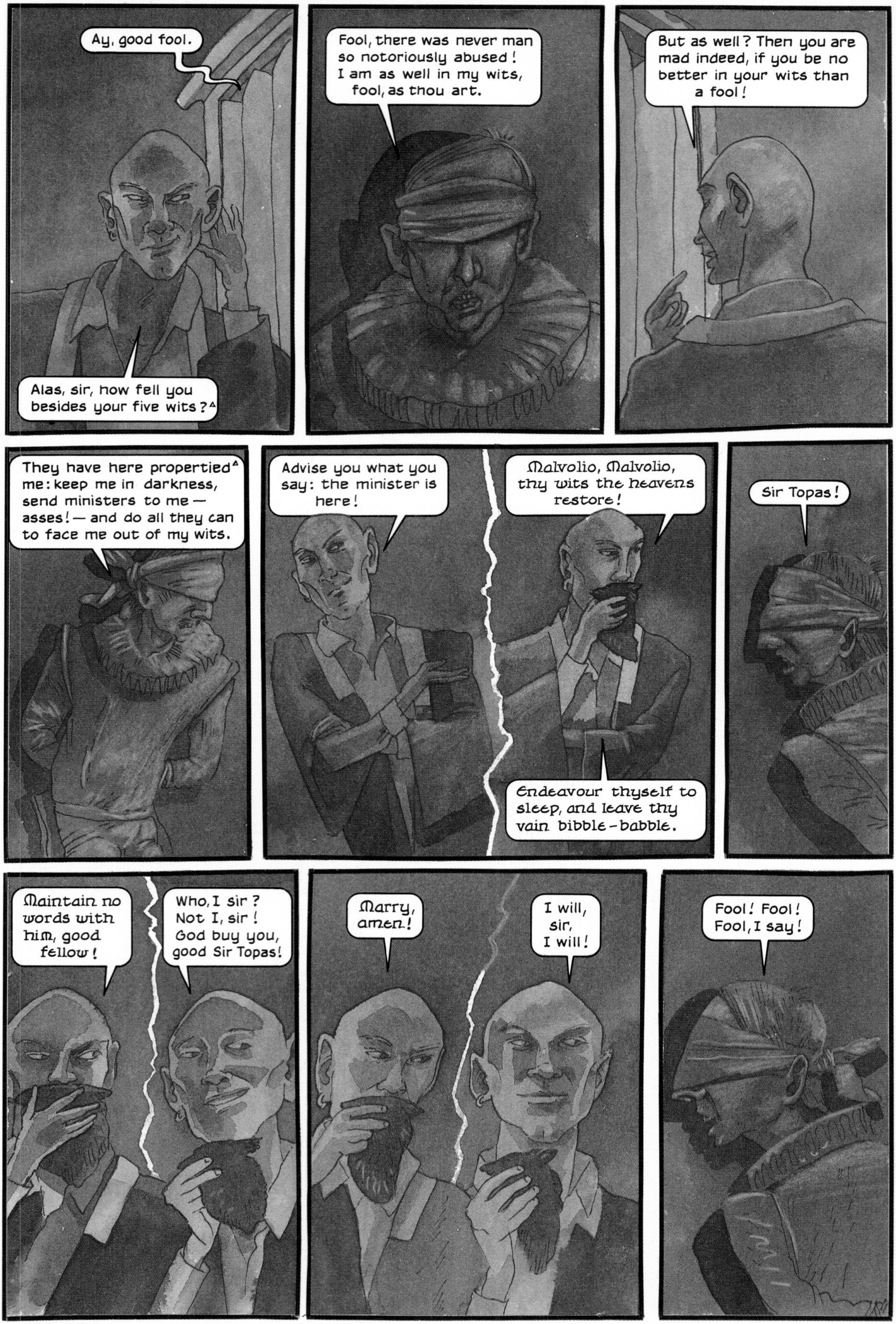
Ay, good fool.
Alas, sir, how fell you besides your five wits?^
Fool, there was never man so notoriously abused! I am as well in my wits, fool, as thou art.
But as well? Then you are mad indeed, if you be no better in your wits than a fool!
They have here propertied^ me: keep me in darkness, send ministers to me — asses! — and do all they can to face me out of my wits.
Advise you what you say: the minister is here!
Malvolio, Malvolio, thy wits the heavens restore!
Endeavour thyself to sleep, and leave thy vain bibble-babble.
Sir Topas!
Maintain no words with him, good fellow!
Who, I sir? Not I, sir! God buy you, good Sir Topas!
Marry, amen!
I will, sir, I will!
Fool! Fool! Fool, I say!

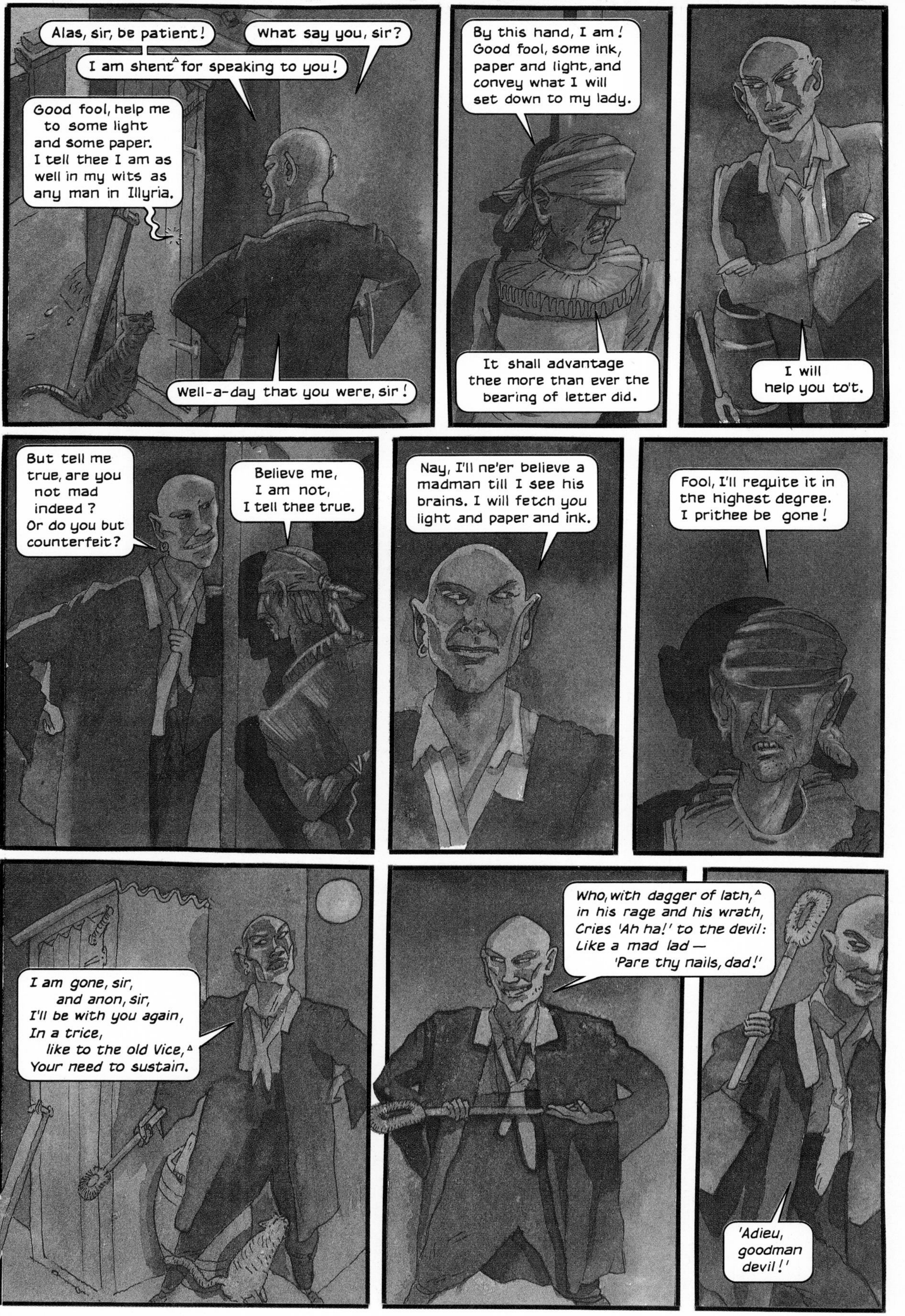
Alas, sir, be patient!
What say you, sir?
I am shent for speaking to you!
Good fool, help me to some light and some paper. I tell thee I am as well in my wits as any man in Illyria.
Well-a-day that you were, sir!
By this hand, I am! Good fool, some ink, paper and light, and convey what I will set down to my lady.
It shall advantage thee more than ever the bearing of letter did.
I will help you to't.
But tell me true, are you not mad indeed? Or do you but counterfeit?
Believe me, I am not, I tell thee true.
Nay, I'll ne'er believe a madman till I see his brains. I will fetch you light and paper and ink.
Fool, I'll requite it in the highest degree. I prithee be gone!
I am gone, sir, and anon, sir, I'll be with you again, In a trice, like to the old Vice, Your need to sustain.
Who, with dagger of lath, in his rage and his wrath, Cries 'Ah ha!' to the devil: Like a mad lad — 'Pare thy nails, dad!'
'Adieu, goodman devil!'

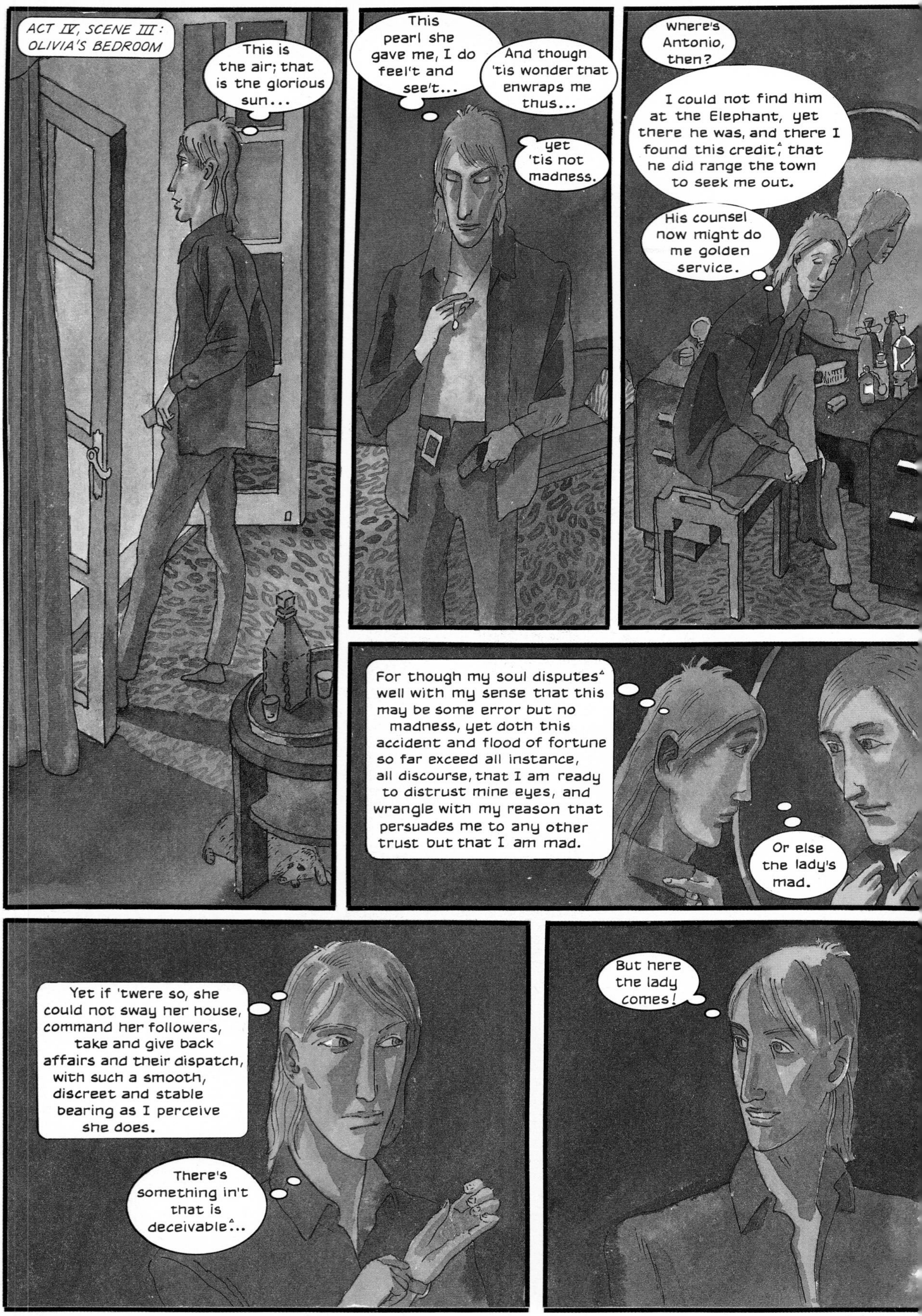

ACT IV, SCENE III: OLIVIA'S BEDROOM
This is the air; that is the glorious sun...
This pearl she gave me, I do feel't and see't...
And though 'tis wonder that enwraps me thus...
yet 'tis not madness.
Where's Antonio, then?
I could not find him at the Elephant, yet there he was, and there I found this credit, that he did range the town to seek me out.
His counsel now might do me golden service.
For though my soul disputes well with my sense that this may be some error but no madness, yet doth this accident and flood of fortune so far exceed all instance, all discourse, that I am ready to distrust mine eyes, and wrangle with my reason that persuades me to any other trust but that I am mad.
Or else the lady's mad.
Yet if 'twere so, she could not sway her house, command her followers, take and give back affairs and their dispatch, with such a smooth, discreet and stable bearing as I perceive she does.
There's something in't that is deceivable...
But here the lady comes!

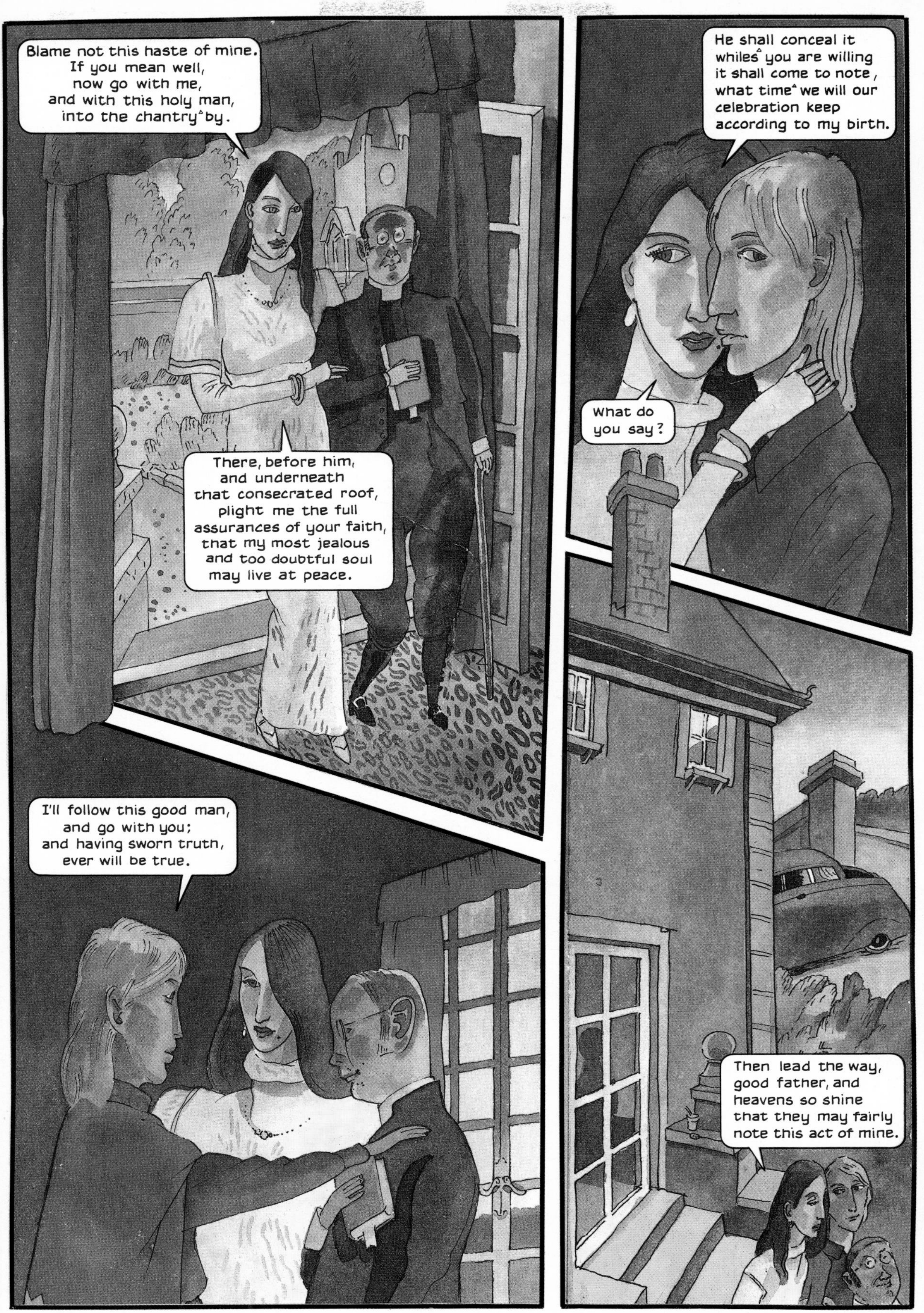
Blame not this haste of mine. If you mean well, now go with me, and with this holy man, into the chantry by.
There, before him, and underneath that consecrated roof, plight me the full assurances of your faith, that my most jealous and too doubtful soul may live at peace.
He shall conceal it whiles you are willing it shall come to note, what time we will our celebration keep according to my birth.
What do you say?
I'll follow this good man, and go with you; and having sworn truth, ever will be true.
Then lead the way, good father, and heavens so shine that they may fairly note this act of mine.

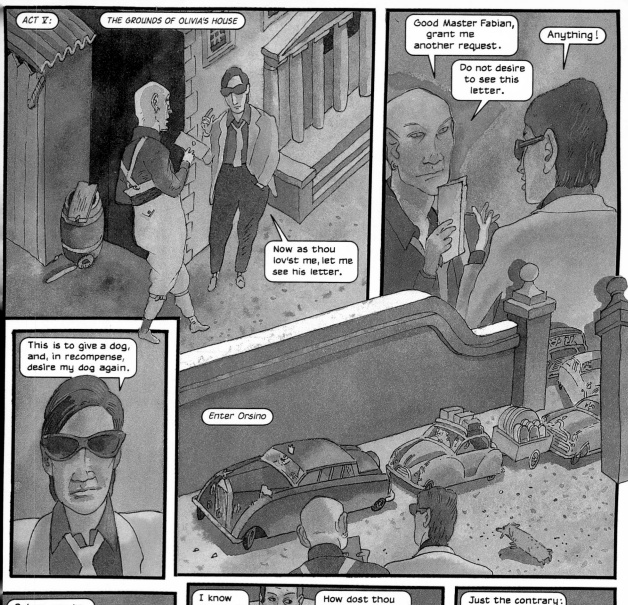

THE GROUNDS OF OLIVIA'S HOUSE

Good Master Fabian, grant me another request.

Anything!

Do not desire to see this letter.

Now as thou lov'st me, let me see his letter.

This is to give a dog, and, in recompense, desire my dog again.

Enter Orsino

Belong you to the Lady Olivia, friends?

Ay, sir, we are some of her trappings.

I know thee well.

How dost thou my good fellow?

Truly, sir, the better for my foes, and the worse for my friends.

Just the contrary: the better for thy friends.

No, sir: the worse.

How can that be?

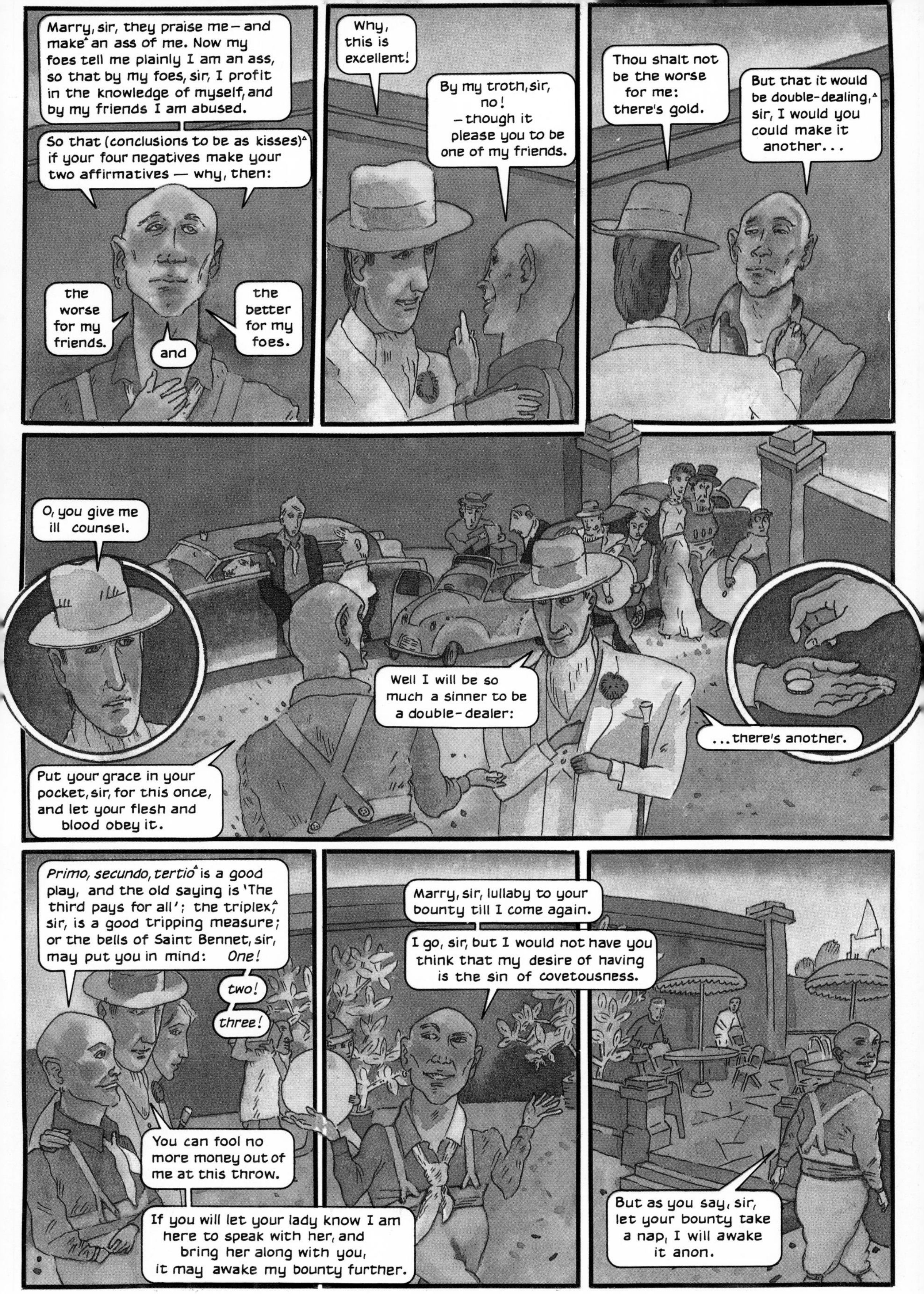

Marry, sir, they praise me – and make an ass of me. Now my foes tell me plainly I am an ass, so that by my foes, sir, I profit in the knowledge of myself, and by my friends I am abused.
So that (conclusions to be as kisses) if your four negatives make your two affirmatives — why, then:
the worse for my friends.
and
the better for my foes.
Why, this is excellent!
By my troth, sir, no! – though it please you to be one of my friends.
Thou shalt not be the worse for me: there's gold.
But that it would be double-dealing, sir, I would you could make it another...
O, you give me ill counsel.
Put your grace in your pocket, sir, for this once, and let your flesh and blood obey it.
Well I will be so much a sinner to be a double-dealer:
...there's another.
Primo, secundo, tertio is a good play, and the old saying is 'The third pays for all'; the triplex, sir, is a good tripping measure; or the bells of Saint Bennet, sir, may put you in mind: *One!*
two!
three!
You can fool no more money out of me at this throw.
If you will let your lady know I am here to speak with her, and bring her along with you, it may awake my bounty further.
Marry, sir, lullaby to your bounty till I come again.
I go, sir, but I would not have you think that my desire of having is the sin of covetousness.
But as you say, sir, let your bounty take a nap, I will awake it anon.

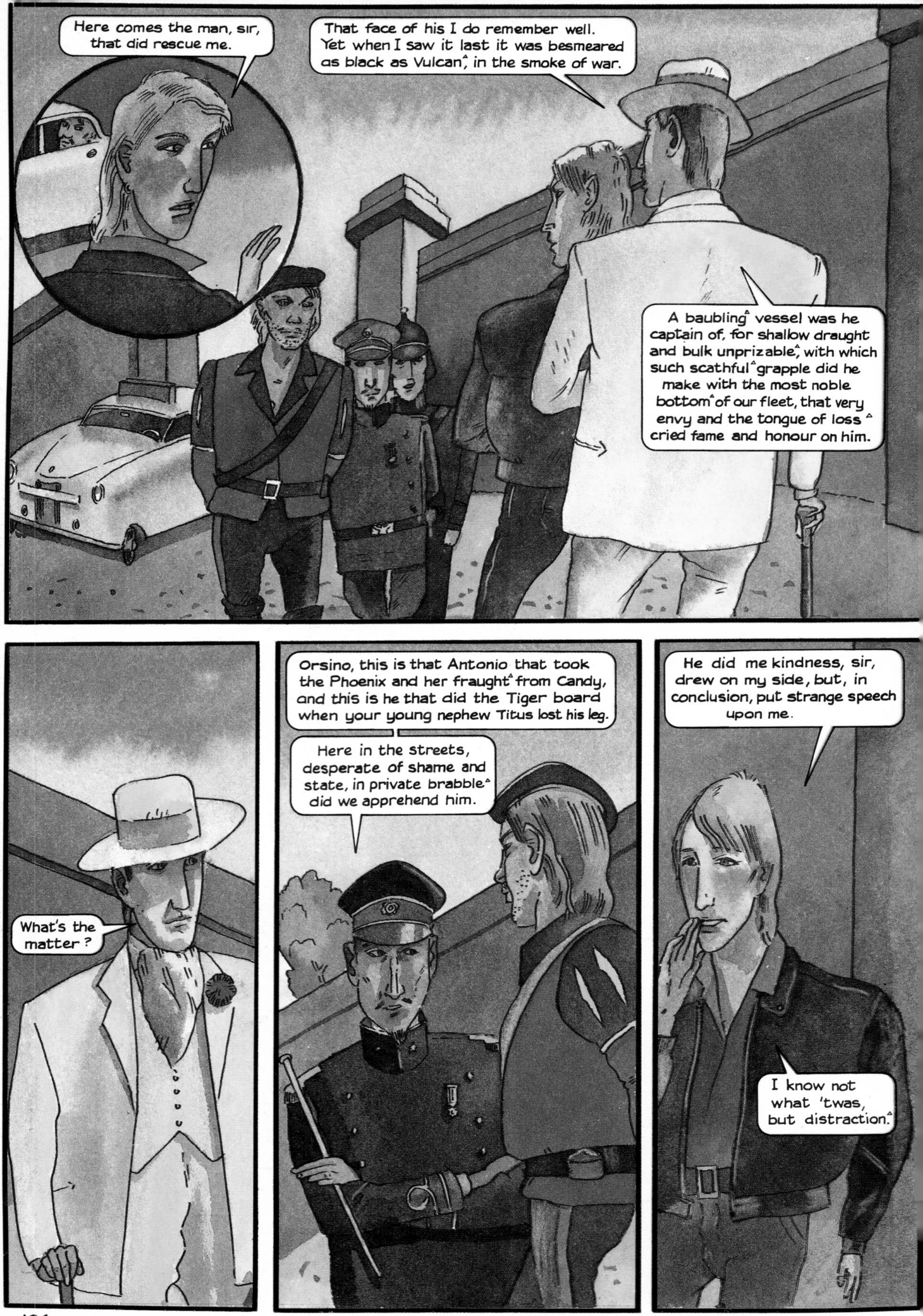
Here comes the man, sir, that did rescue me.
That face of his I do remember well. Yet when I saw it last it was besmeared as black as Vulcan, in the smoke of war.
A baubling vessel was he captain of, for shallow draught and bulk unprizable, with which such scathful grapple did he make with the most noble bottom of our fleet, that very envy and the tongue of loss cried fame and honour on him.
What's the matter?
Orsino, this is that Antonio that took the Phoenix and her fraught from Candy, and this is he that did the Tiger board when your young nephew Titus lost his leg.
Here in the streets, desperate of shame and state, in private brabble did we apprehend him.
He did me kindness, sir, drew on my side, but, in conclusion, put strange speech upon me.
I know not what 'twas, but distraction.

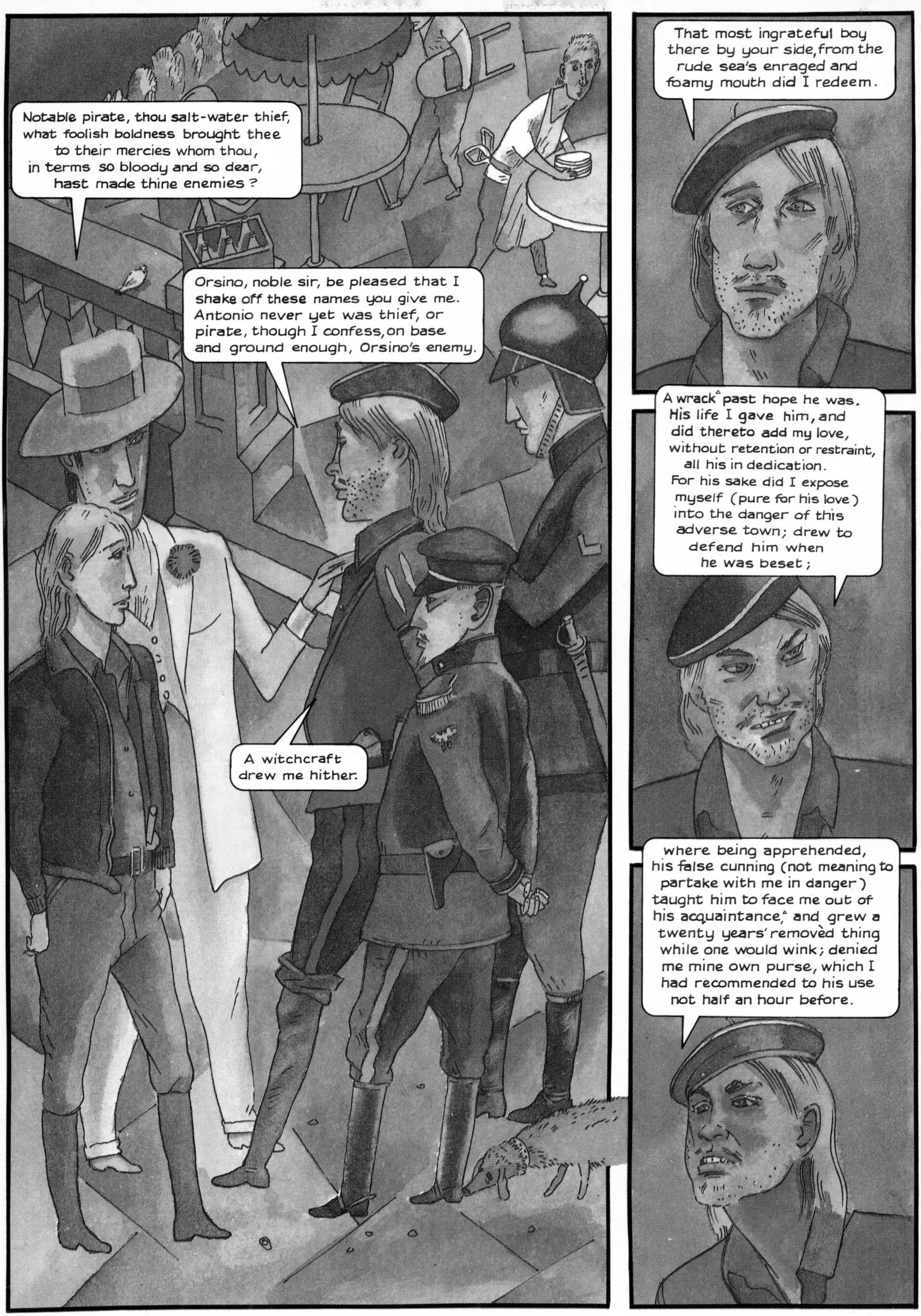
Notable pirate, thou salt-water thief, what foolish boldness brought thee to their mercies whom thou, in terms so bloody and so dear, hast made thine enemies ?
Orsino, noble sir, be pleased that I shake off these names you give me. Antonio never yet was thief, or pirate, though I confess, on base and ground enough, Orsino's enemy.
A witchcraft drew me hither.
That most ingrateful boy there by your side, from the rude sea's enraged and foamy mouth did I redeem.
A wrack^ past hope he was. His life I gave him, and did thereto add my love, without retention or restraint, all his in dedication. For his sake did I expose myself (pure for his love) into the danger of this adverse town; drew to defend him when he was beset;
where being apprehended, his false cunning (not meaning to partake with me in danger) taught him to face me out of his acquaintance,^ and grew a twenty years' removèd thing while one would wink; denied me mine own purse, which I had recommended to his use not half an hour before.

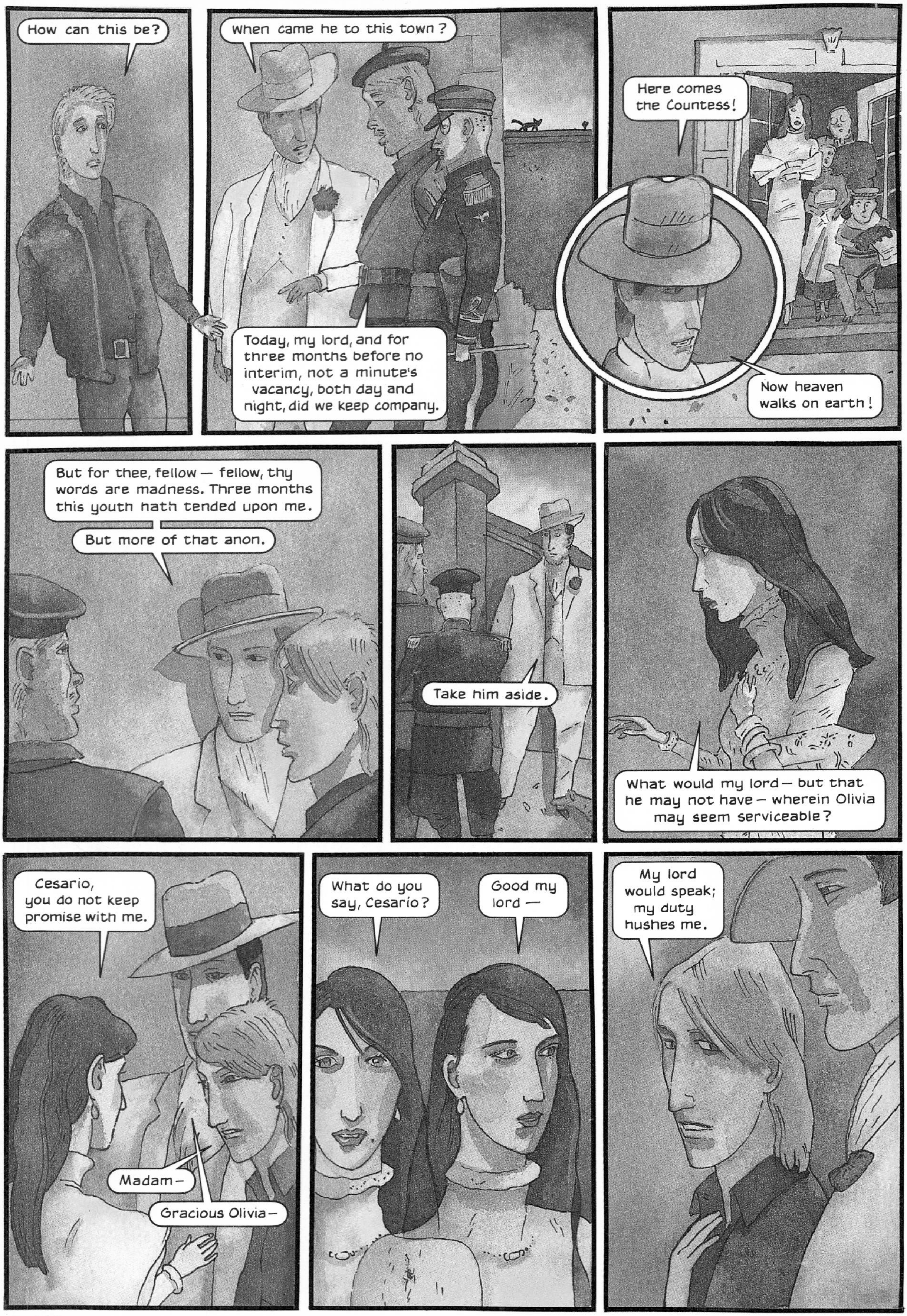
How can this be?
When came he to this town?
Today, my lord, and for three months before no interim, not a minute's vacancy, both day and night, did we keep company.
Here comes the Countess!
Now heaven walks on earth!
But for thee, fellow — fellow, thy words are madness. Three months this youth hath tended upon me.
But more of that anon.
Take him aside.
What would my lord — but that he may not have — wherein Olivia may seem serviceable?
Cesario, you do not keep promise with me.
Madam —
Gracious Olivia —
What do you say, Cesario?
Good my lord —
My lord would speak; my duty hushes me.

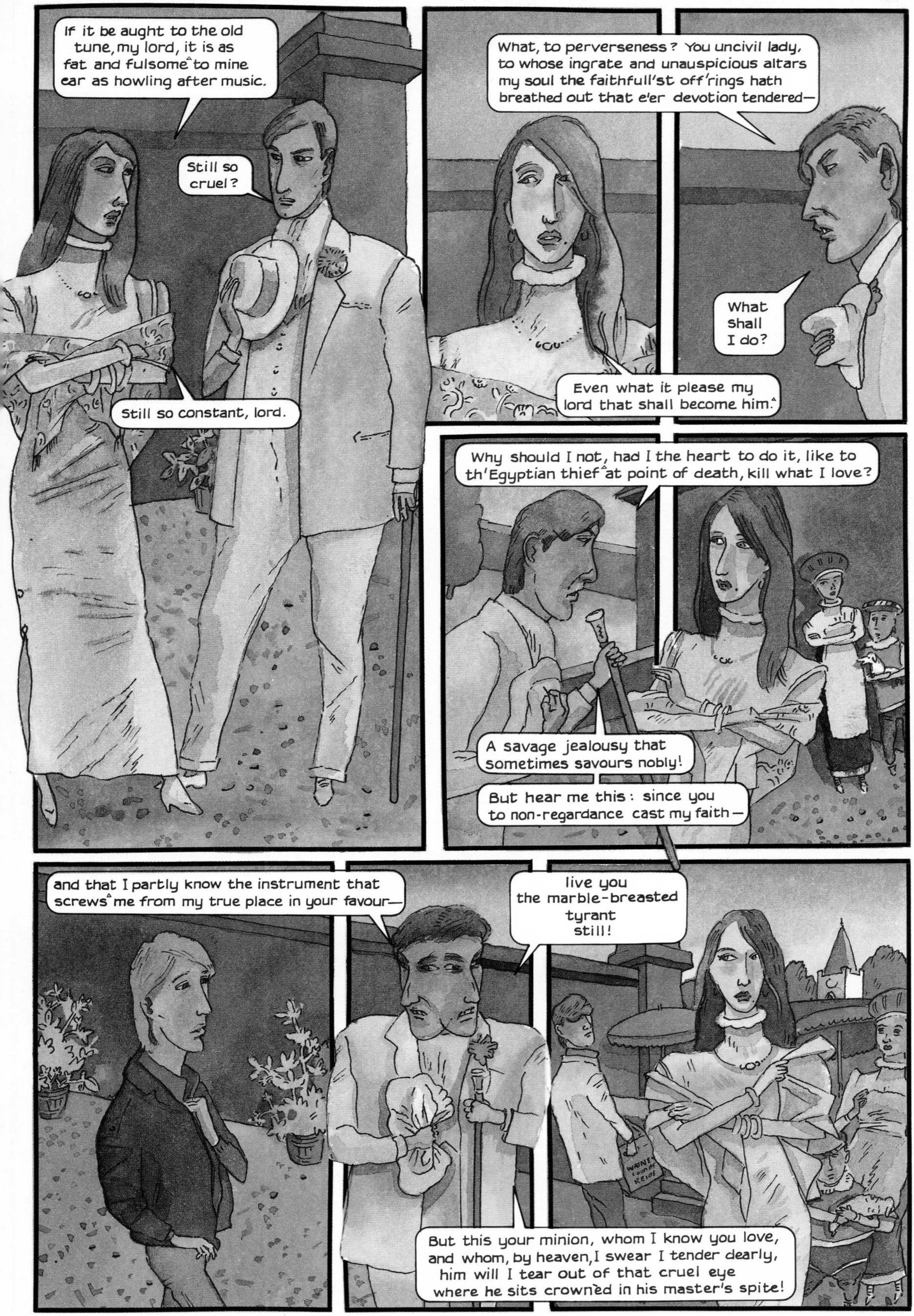

If it be aught to the old tune, my lord, it is as fat and fulsome to mine ear as howling after music.
Still so cruel?
Still so constant, lord.
What, to perverseness? You uncivil lady, to whose ingrate and unauspicious altars my soul the faithfull'st off'rings hath breathed out that e'er devotion tendered—
What shall I do?
Even what it please my lord that shall become him.
Why should I not, had I the heart to do it, like to th'Egyptian thief at point of death, kill what I love?
A savage jealousy that sometimes savours nobly!
But hear me this: since you to non-regardance cast my faith—
and that I partly know the instrument that screws me from my true place in your favour—
live you the marble-breasted tyrant still!
But this your minion, whom I know you love, and whom, by heaven, I swear I tender dearly, him will I tear out of that cruel eye where he sits crownèd in his master's spite!

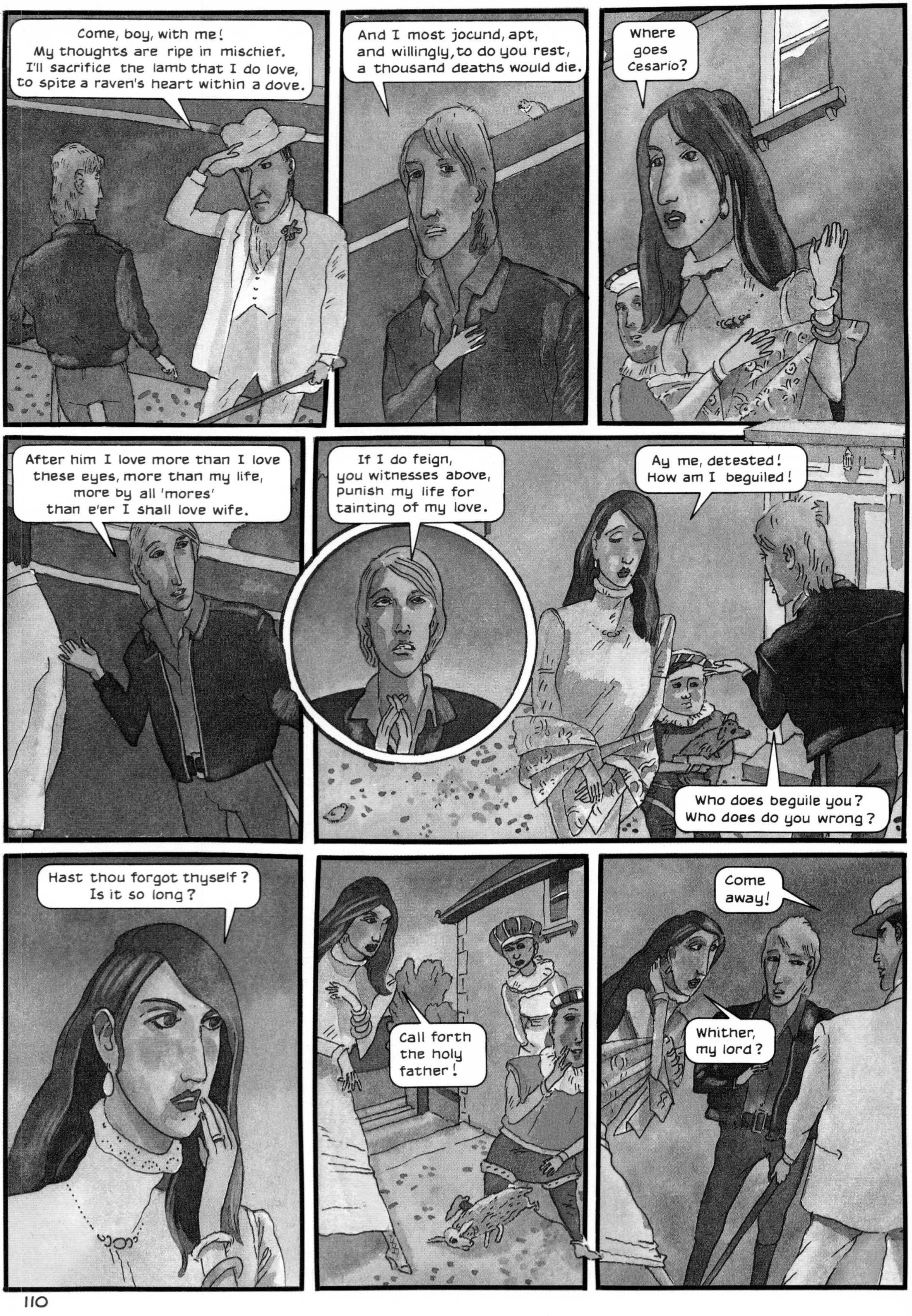
Come, boy, with me! My thoughts are ripe in mischief. I'll sacrifice the lamb that I do love, to spite a raven's heart within a dove.
And I most jocund, apt, and willingly, to do you rest, a thousand deaths would die.
Where goes Cesario?
After him I love more than I love these eyes, more than my life, more by all 'mores' than e'er I shall love wife.
If I do feign, you witnesses above, punish my life for tainting of my love.
Ay me, detested! How am I beguiled!
Who does beguile you? Who does do you wrong?
Hast thou forgot thyself? Is it so long?
Call forth the holy father!
Come away!
Whither, my lord?

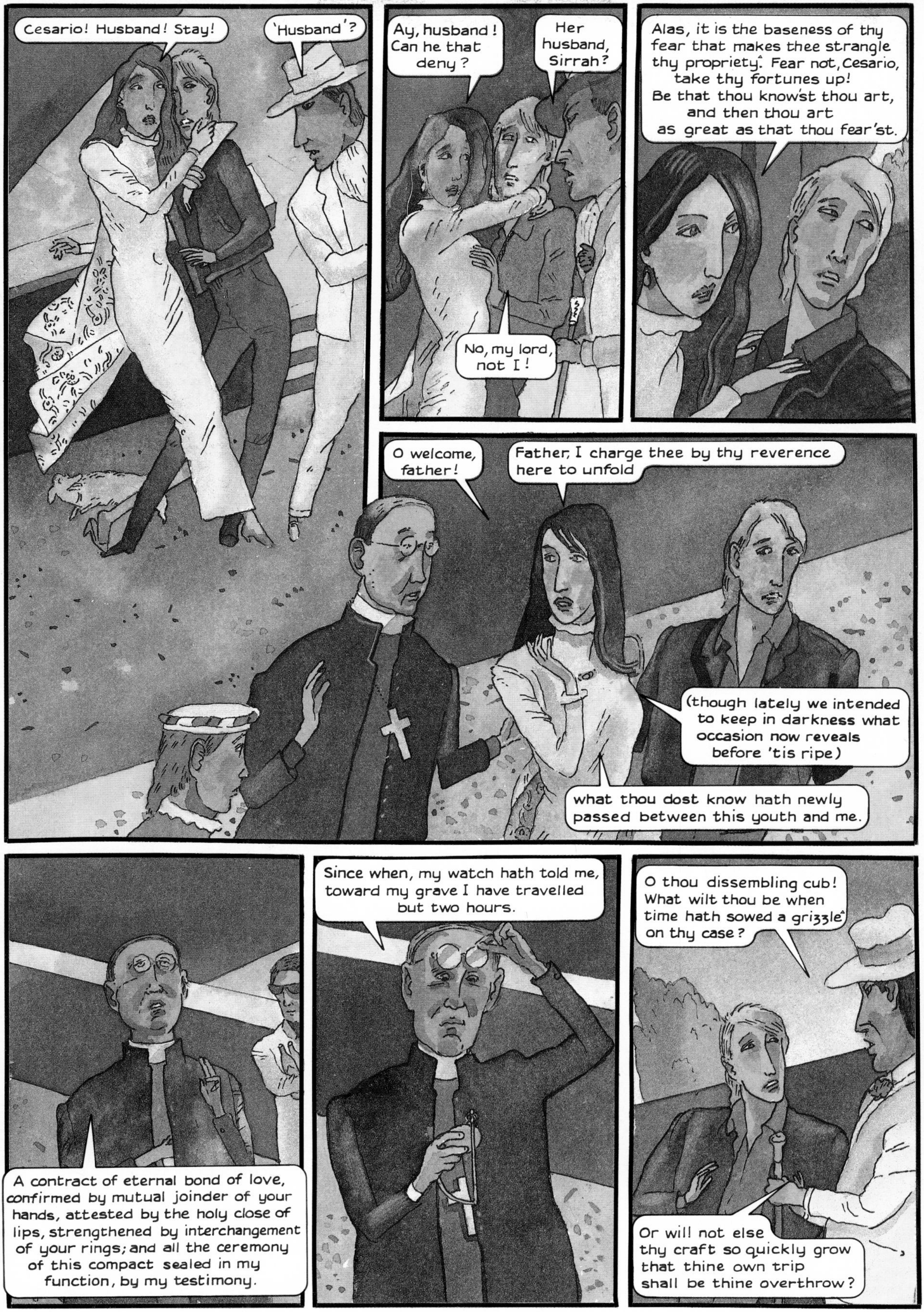
Cesario! Husband! Stay!
'Husband'?
Ay, husband! Can he that deny?
Her husband, Sirrah?
No, my lord, not I!
Alas, it is the baseness of thy fear that makes thee strangle thy propriety.^ Fear not, Cesario, take thy fortunes up! Be that thou know'st thou art, and then thou art as great as that thou fear'st.
O welcome, father!
Father, I charge thee by thy reverence here to unfold
(though lately we intended to keep in darkness what occasion now reveals before 'tis ripe)
what thou dost know hath newly passed between this youth and me.
A contract of eternal bond of love, confirmed by mutual joinder of your hands, attested by the holy close of lips, strengthened by interchangement of your rings; and all the ceremony of this compact sealed in my function, by my testimony.
Since when, my watch hath told me, toward my grave I have travelled but two hours.
O thou dissembling cub! What wilt thou be when time hath sowed a grizzle^ on thy case?
Or will not else thy craft so quickly grow that thine own trip shall be thine overthrow?

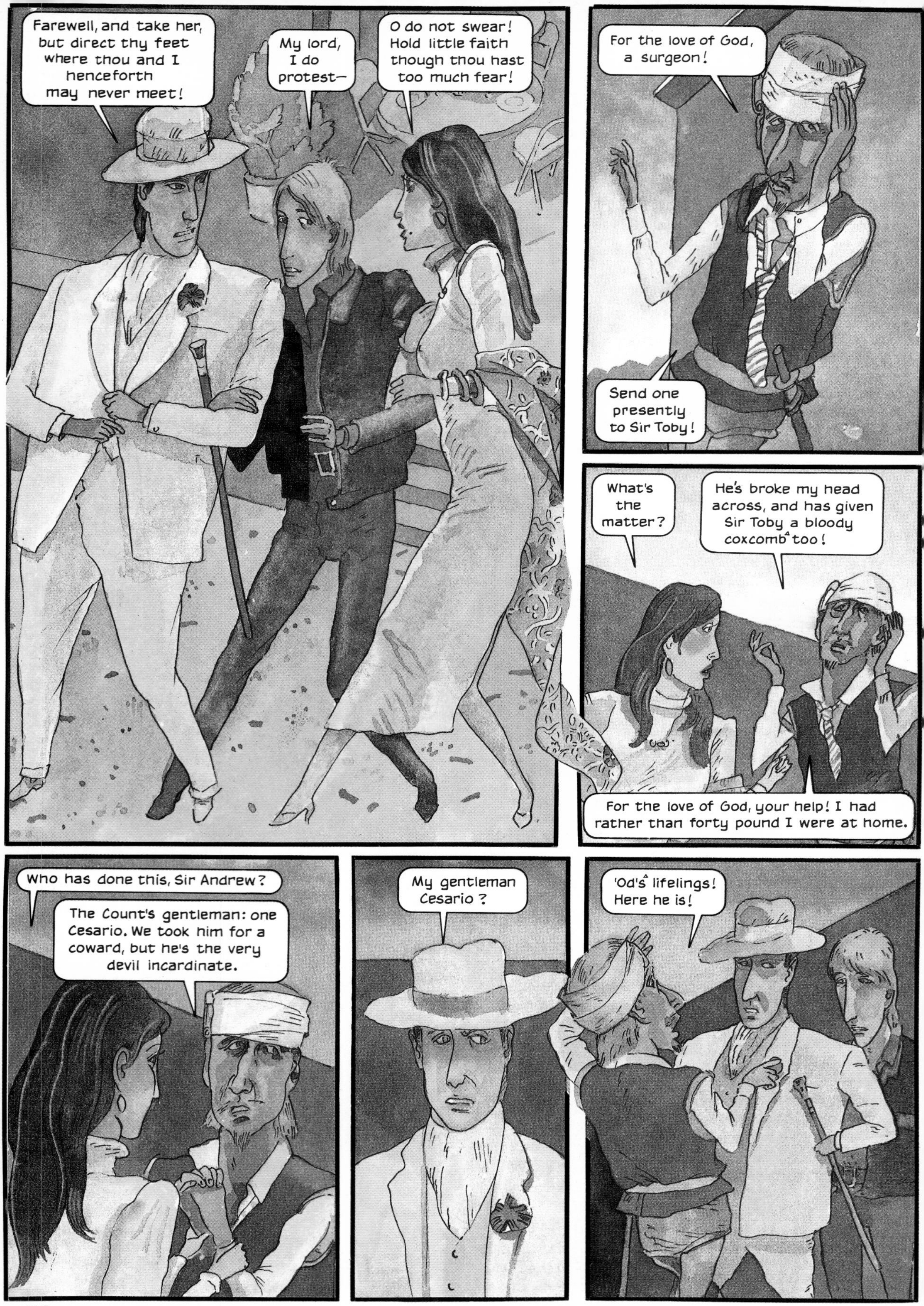
Farewell, and take her, but direct thy feet where thou and I henceforth may never meet!
My lord, I do protest—
O do not swear! Hold little faith though thou hast too much fear!
For the love of God, a surgeon!
Send one presently to Sir Toby!
What's the matter?
He's broke my head across, and has given Sir Toby a bloody coxcomb too!
For the love of God, your help! I had rather than forty pound I were at home.
Who has done this, Sir Andrew?
The Count's gentleman: one Cesario. We took him for a coward, but he's the very devil incardinate.
My gentleman Cesario?
'Od's lifelings! Here he is!

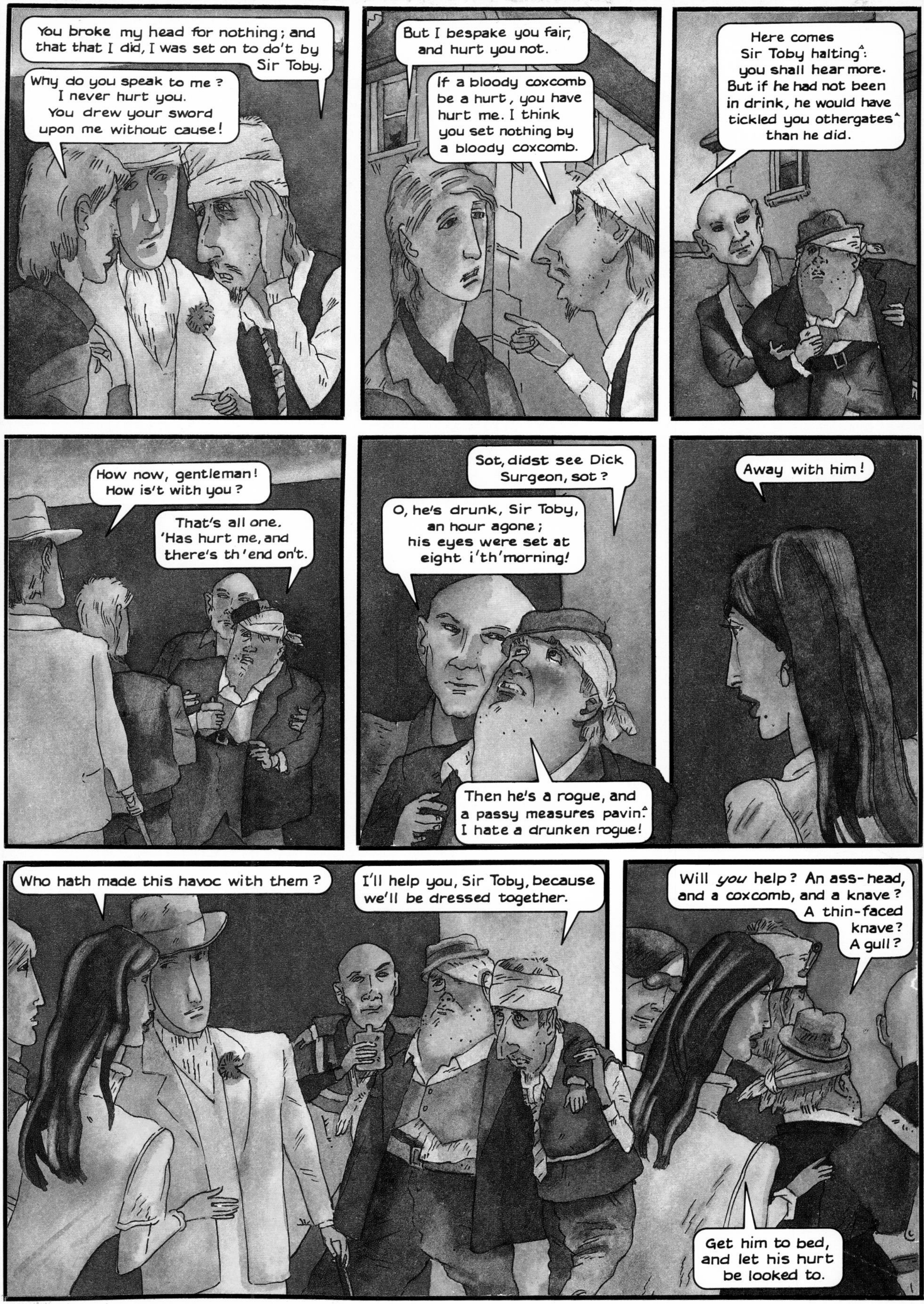

You broke my head for nothing; and that that I did, I was set on to do't by Sir Toby.
Why do you speak to me? I never hurt you. You drew your sword upon me without cause!
But I bespake you fair, and hurt you not.
If a bloody coxcomb be a hurt, you have hurt me. I think you set nothing by a bloody coxcomb.
Here comes Sir Toby halting^: you shall hear more. But if he had not been in drink, he would have tickled you othergates^ than he did.
How now, gentleman! How is't with you?
That's all one. 'Has hurt me, and there's th'end on't.
Sot, didst see Dick Surgeon, sot?
O, he's drunk, Sir Toby, an hour agone; his eyes were set at eight i'th'morning!
Then he's a rogue, and a passy measures pavin.^ I hate a drunken rogue!
Away with him!
Who hath made this havoc with them?
I'll help you, Sir Toby, because we'll be dressed together.
Will *you* help? An ass-head, and a coxcomb, and a knave? A thin-faced knave? A gull?
Get him to bed, and let his hurt be looked to.

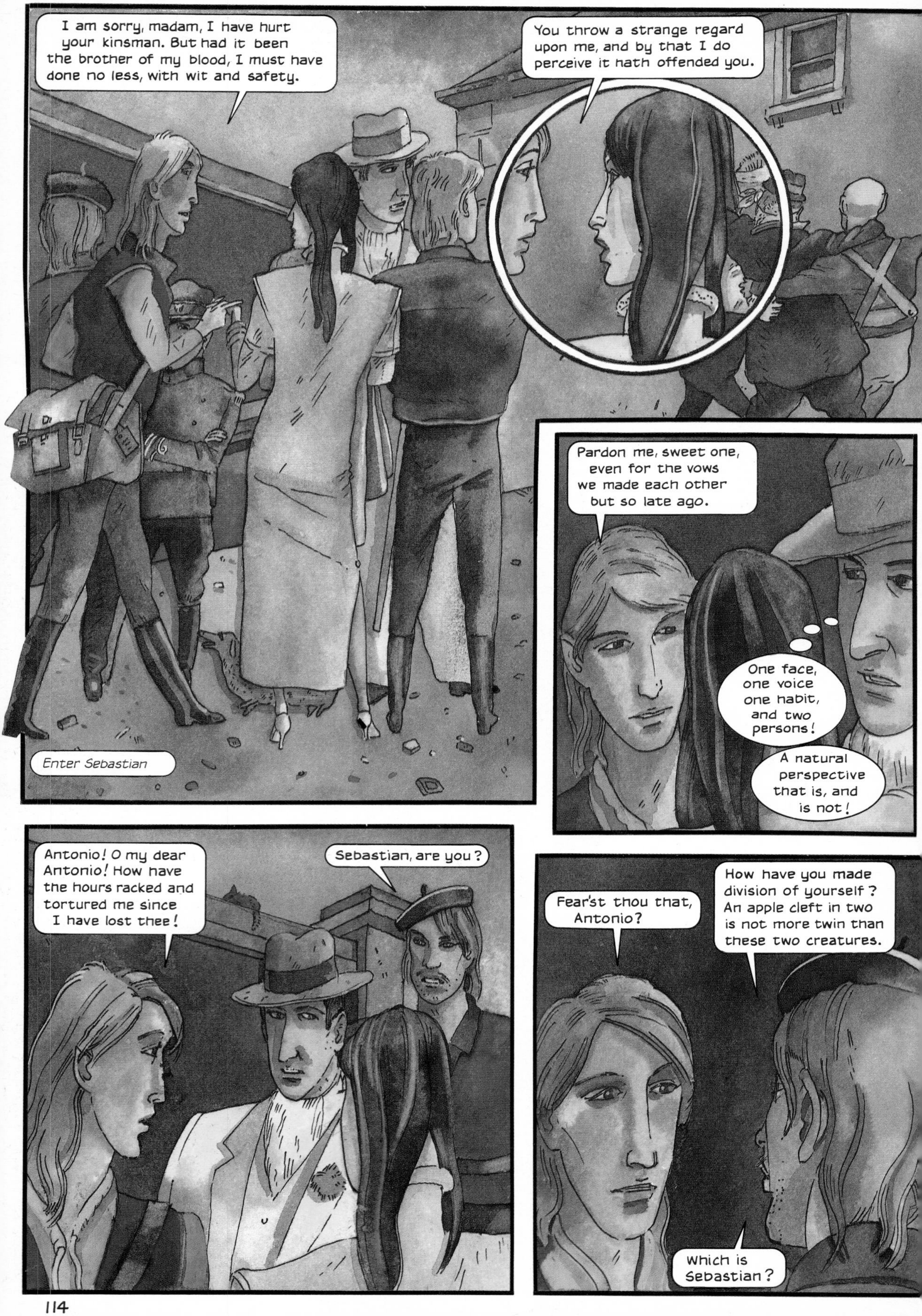
I am sorry, madam, I have hurt your kinsman. But had it been the brother of my blood, I must have done no less, with wit and safety.
You throw a strange regard upon me, and by that I do perceive it hath offended you.
Enter Sebastian
Pardon me, sweet one, even for the vows we made each other but so late ago.
One face, one voice one habit, and two persons!
A natural perspective that is, and is not!
Antonio! O my dear Antonio! How have the hours racked and tortured me since I have lost thee!
Sebastian, are you?
Fear'st thou that, Antonio?
How have you made division of yourself? An apple cleft in two is not more twin than these two creatures.
Which is Sebastian?

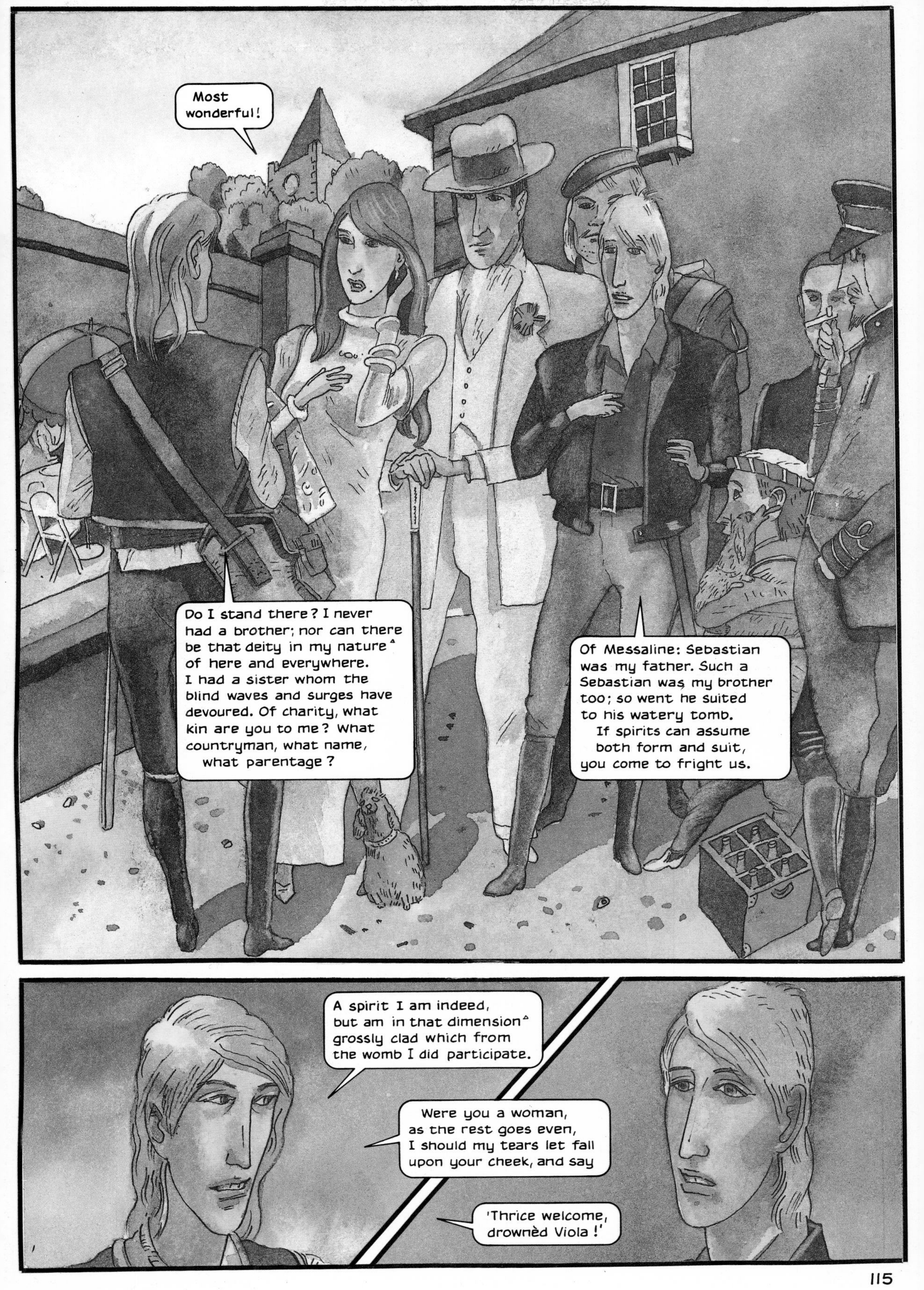
Most wonderful!
Do I stand there? I never had a brother; nor can there be that deity in my nature ^ of here and everywhere. I had a sister whom the blind waves and surges have devoured. Of charity, what kin are you to me? What countryman, what name, what parentage?
Of Messaline: Sebastian was my father. Such a Sebastian was my brother too; so went he suited to his watery tomb. If spirits can assume both form and suit, you come to fright us.
A spirit I am indeed, but am in that dimension ^ grossly clad which from the womb I did participate.
Were you a woman, as the rest goes even, I should my tears let fall upon your cheek, and say
'Thrice welcome, drownèd Viola!'

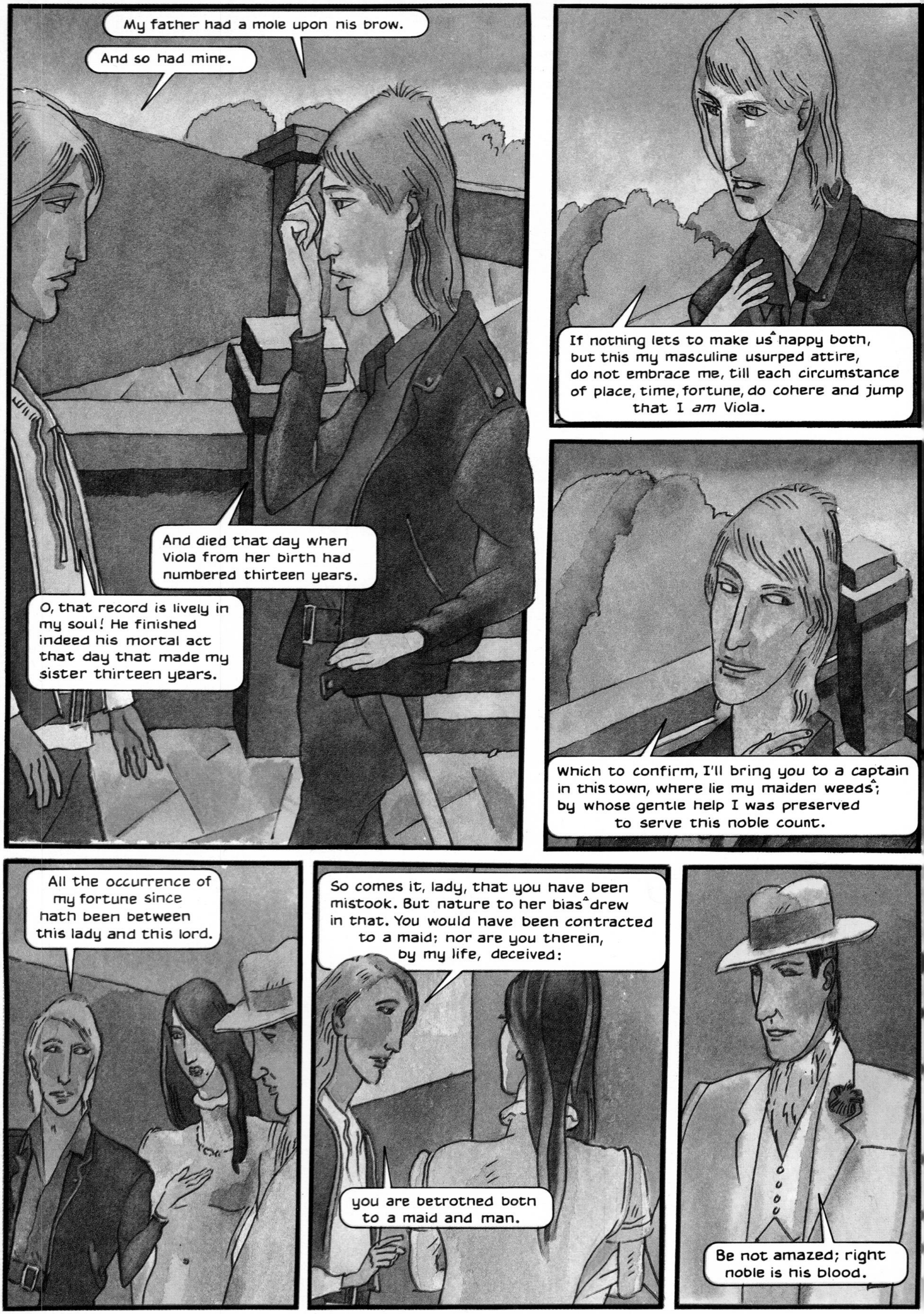
My father had a mole upon his brow.
And so had mine.
And died that day when Viola from her birth had numbered thirteen years.
O, that record is lively in my soul! He finished indeed his mortal act that day that made my sister thirteen years.
If nothing lets to make us happy both, but this my masculine usurped attire, do not embrace me, till each circumstance of place, time, fortune, do cohere and jump that I *am* Viola.
Which to confirm, I'll bring you to a captain in this town, where lie my maiden weeds; by whose gentle help I was preserved to serve this noble count.
All the occurrence of my fortune since hath been between this lady and this lord.
So comes it, lady, that you have been mistook. But nature to her bias drew in that. You would have been contracted to a maid; nor are you therein, by my life, deceived:
you are betrothed both to a maid and man.
Be not amazed; right noble is his blood.

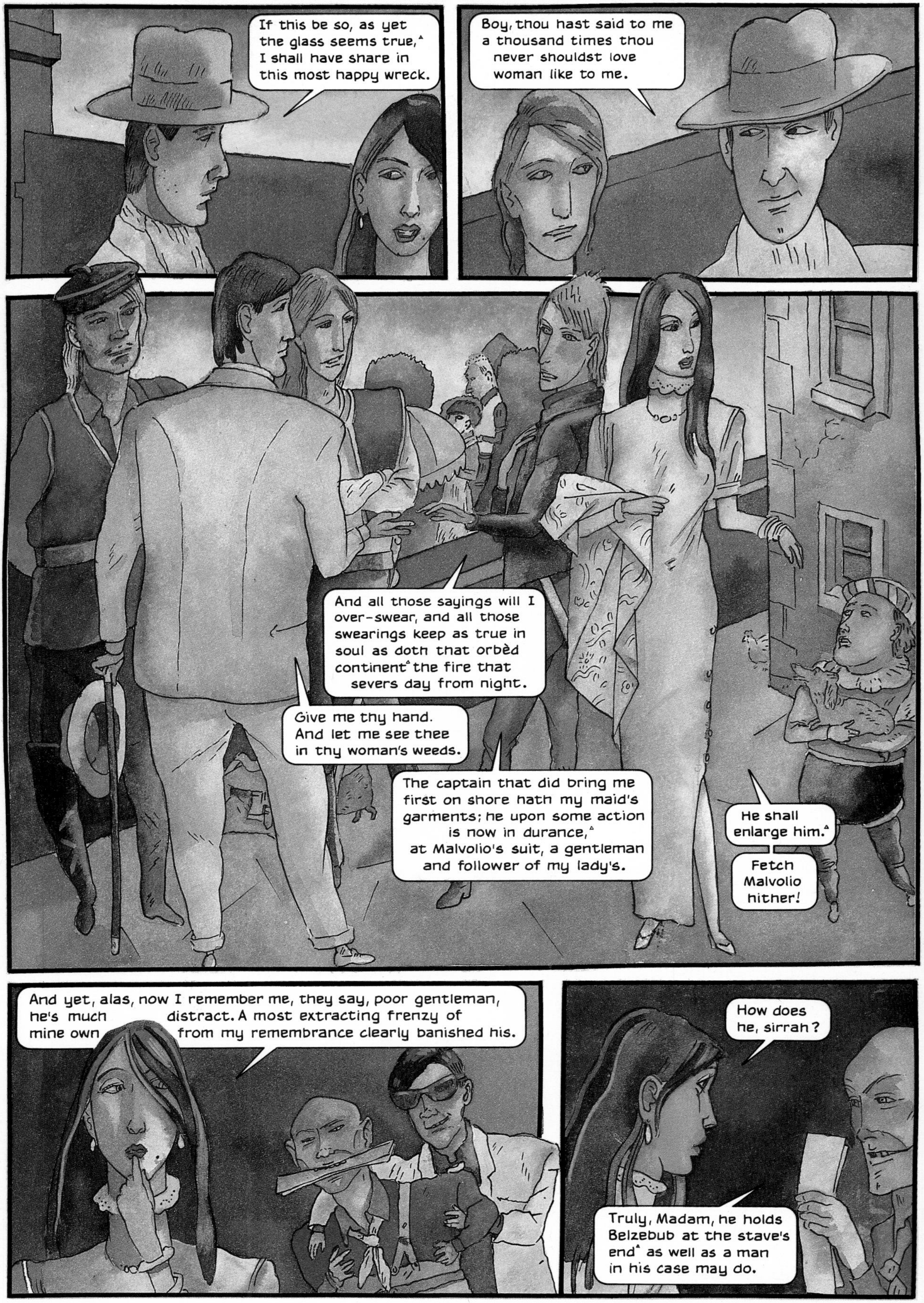

If this be so, as yet the glass seems true, I shall have share in this most happy wreck.
Boy, thou hast said to me a thousand times thou never shouldst love woman like to me.
And all those sayings will I over-swear, and all those swearings keep as true in soul as doth that orbèd continent the fire that severs day from night.
Give me thy hand. And let me see thee in thy woman's weeds.
The captain that did bring me first on shore hath my maid's garments; he upon some action is now in durance, at Malvolio's suit, a gentleman and follower of my lady's.
He shall enlarge him.
Fetch Malvolio hither!
And yet, alas, now I remember me, they say, poor gentleman, he's much distract. A most extracting frenzy of mine own from my remembrance clearly banished his.
How does he, sirrah?
Truly, Madam, he holds Belzebub at the stave's end as well as a man in his case may do.

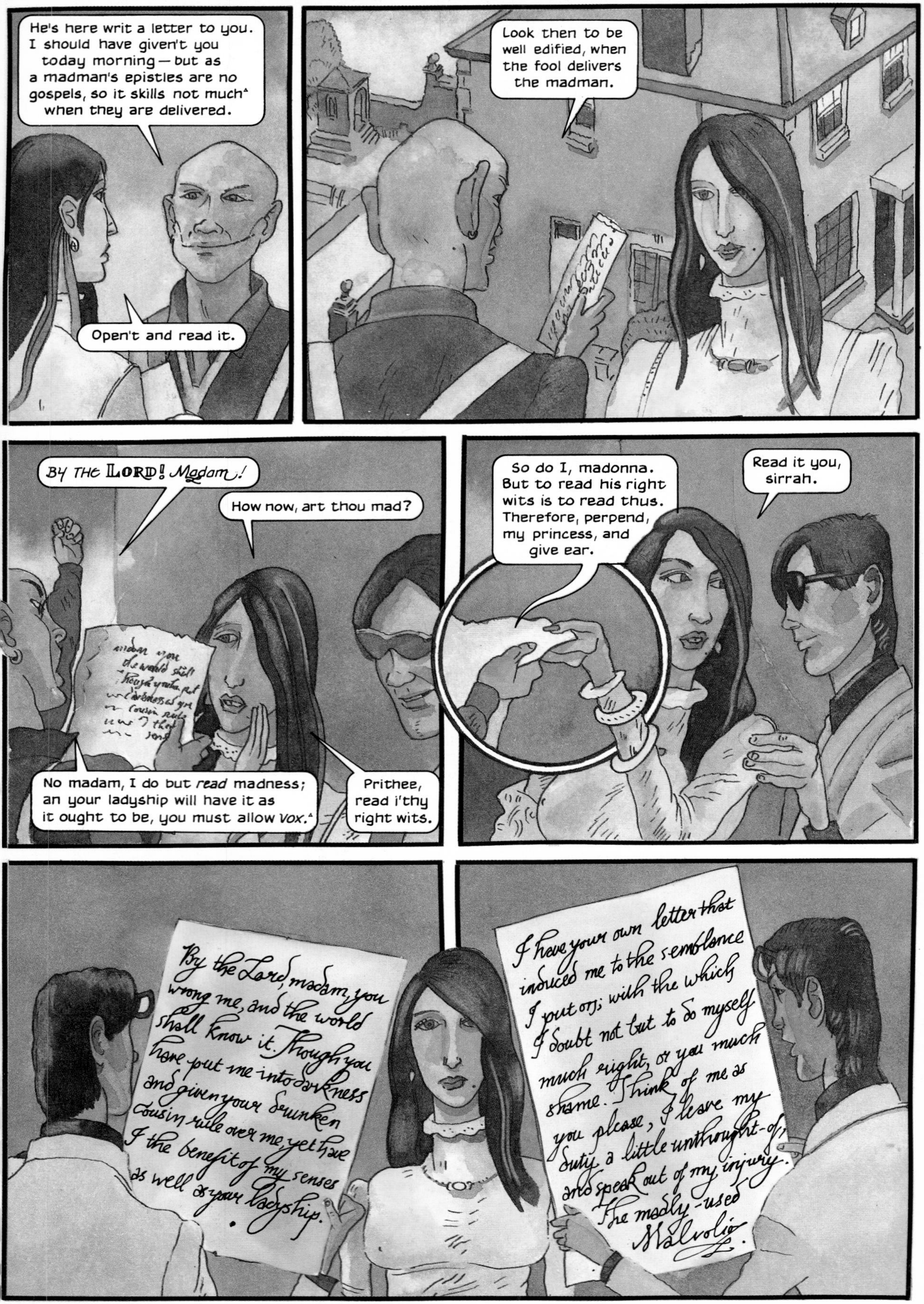
He's here writ a letter to you. I should have given't you today morning — but as a madman's epistles are no gospels, so it skills not much^ when they are delivered.
Open't and read it.
Look then to be well edified, when the fool delivers the madman.
BY THE LORD! Madam!
How now, art thou mad?
No madam, I do but *read* madness; an your ladyship will have it as it ought to be, you must allow *Vox*.^
Prithee, read i'thy right wits.
So do I, madonna. But to read his right wits is to read thus. Therefore, perpend, my princess, and give ear.
Read it you, sirrah.
By the Lord, madam, you wrong me, and the world shall know it. Though you have put me into darkness and given your drunken cousin rule over me, yet have I the benefit of my senses as well as your ladyship.
I have your own letter that induced me to the semblance I put on; with the which I doubt not but to do myself much right, or you much shame. Think of me as you please, I leave my duty a little unthought-of, and speak out of my injury.
The madly-used Malvolio.

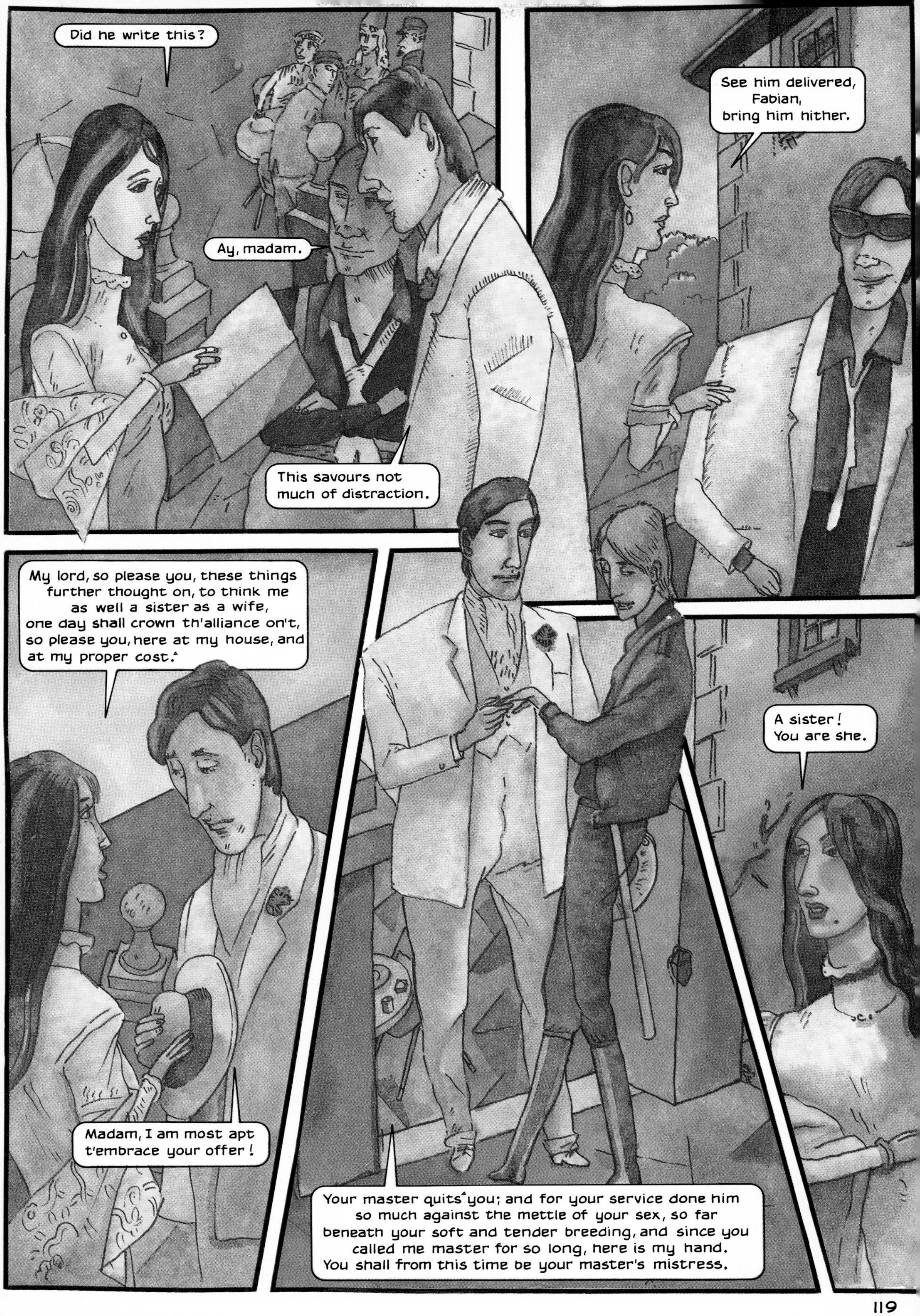

Did he write this?
Ay, madam.
This savours not much of distraction.
See him delivered, Fabian, bring him hither.
My lord, so please you, these things further thought on, to think me as well a sister as a wife, one day shall crown th'alliance on't, so please you, here at my house, and at my proper cost.
Madam, I am most apt t'embrace your offer!
Your master quits you; and for your service done him so much against the mettle of your sex, so far beneath your soft and tender breeding, and since you called me master for so long, here is my hand. You shall from this time be your master's mistress.
A sister! You are she.

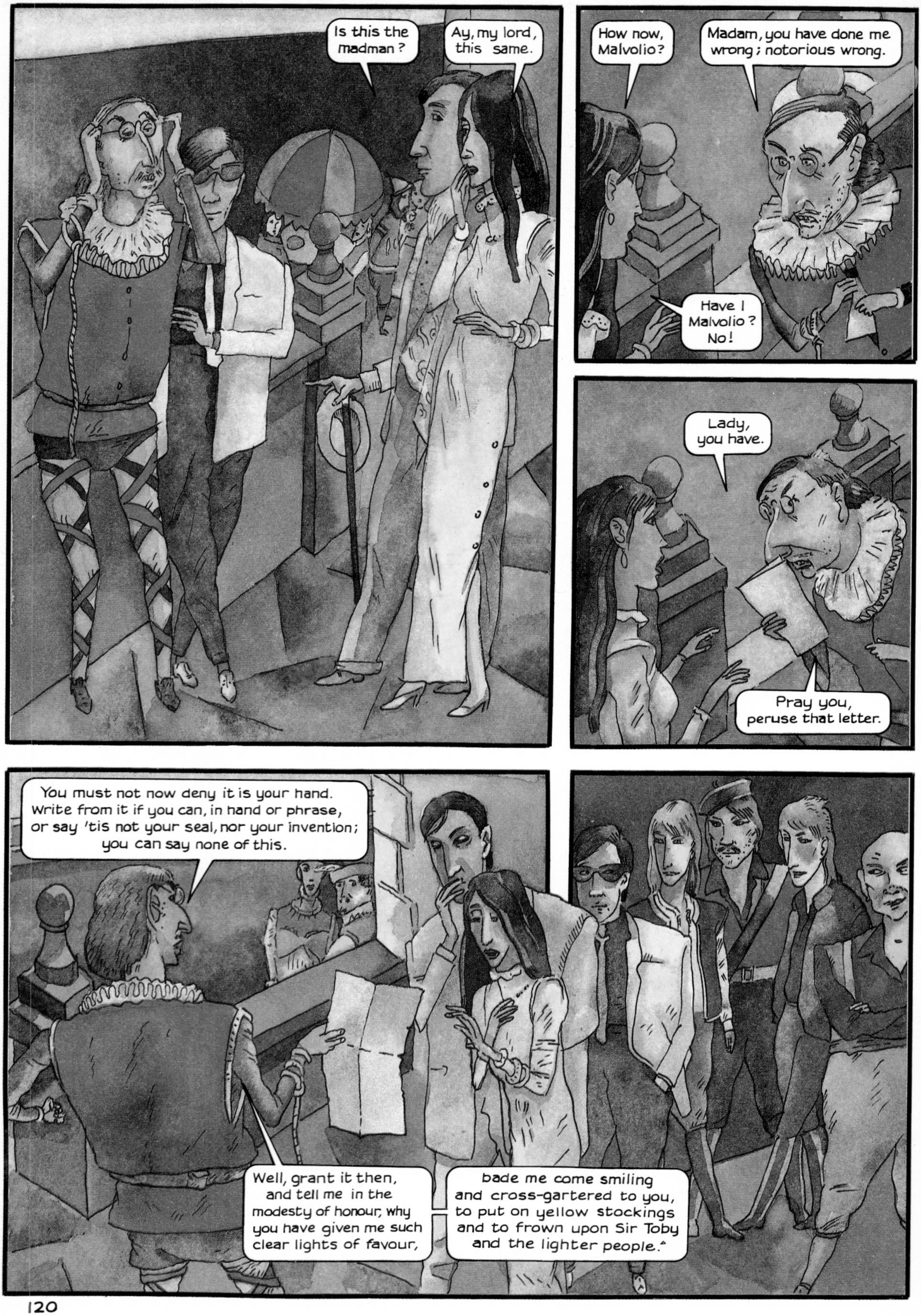
Is this the madman?
Ay, my lord, this same.
How now, Malvolio?
Madam, you have done me wrong; notorious wrong.
Have I Malvolio? No!
Lady, you have.
Pray you, peruse that letter.
You must not now deny it is your hand. Write from it if you can, in hand or phrase, or say 'tis not your seal, nor your invention; you can say none of this.
Well, grant it then, and tell me in the modesty of honour, why you have given me such clear lights of favour,
bade me come smiling and cross-gartered to you, to put on yellow stockings and to frown upon Sir Toby and the lighter people.*

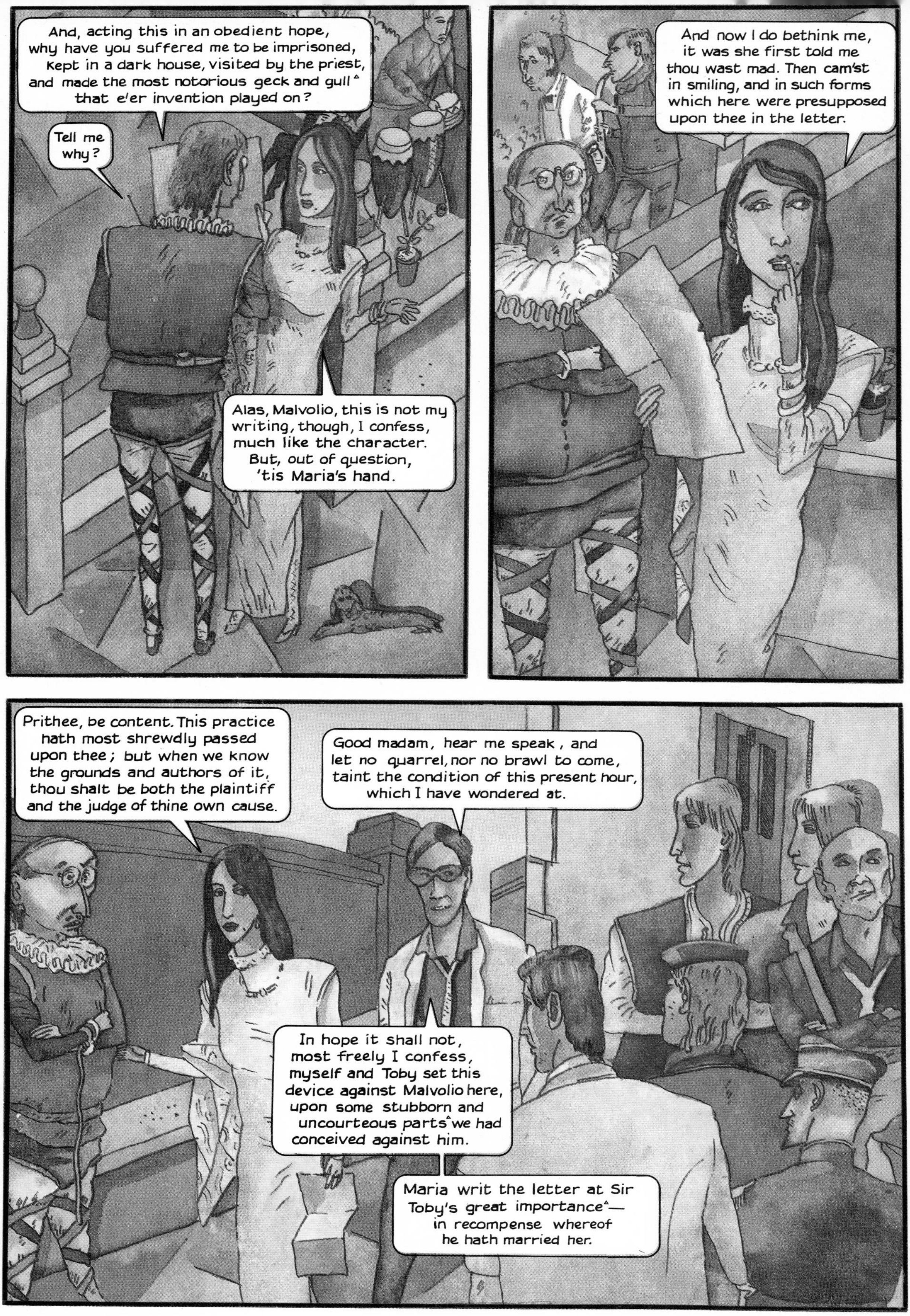

And, acting this in an obedient hope, why have you suffered me to be imprisoned, kept in a dark house, visited by the priest, and made the most notorious geck and gull that e'er invention played on?
Tell me why?
Alas, Malvolio, this is not my writing, though, I confess, much like the character. But, out of question, 'tis Maria's hand.
And now I do bethink me, it was she first told me thou wast mad. Then cam'st in smiling, and in such forms which here were presupposed upon thee in the letter.
Prithee, be content. This practice hath most shrewdly passed upon thee; but when we know the grounds and authors of it, thou shalt be both the plaintiff and the judge of thine own cause.
Good madam, hear me speak, and let no quarrel, nor no brawl to come, taint the condition of this present hour, which I have wondered at.
In hope it shall not, most freely I confess, myself and Toby set this device against Malvolio here, upon some stubborn and uncourteous parts we had conceived against him.
Maria writ the letter at Sir Toby's great importance— in recompense whereof he hath married her.

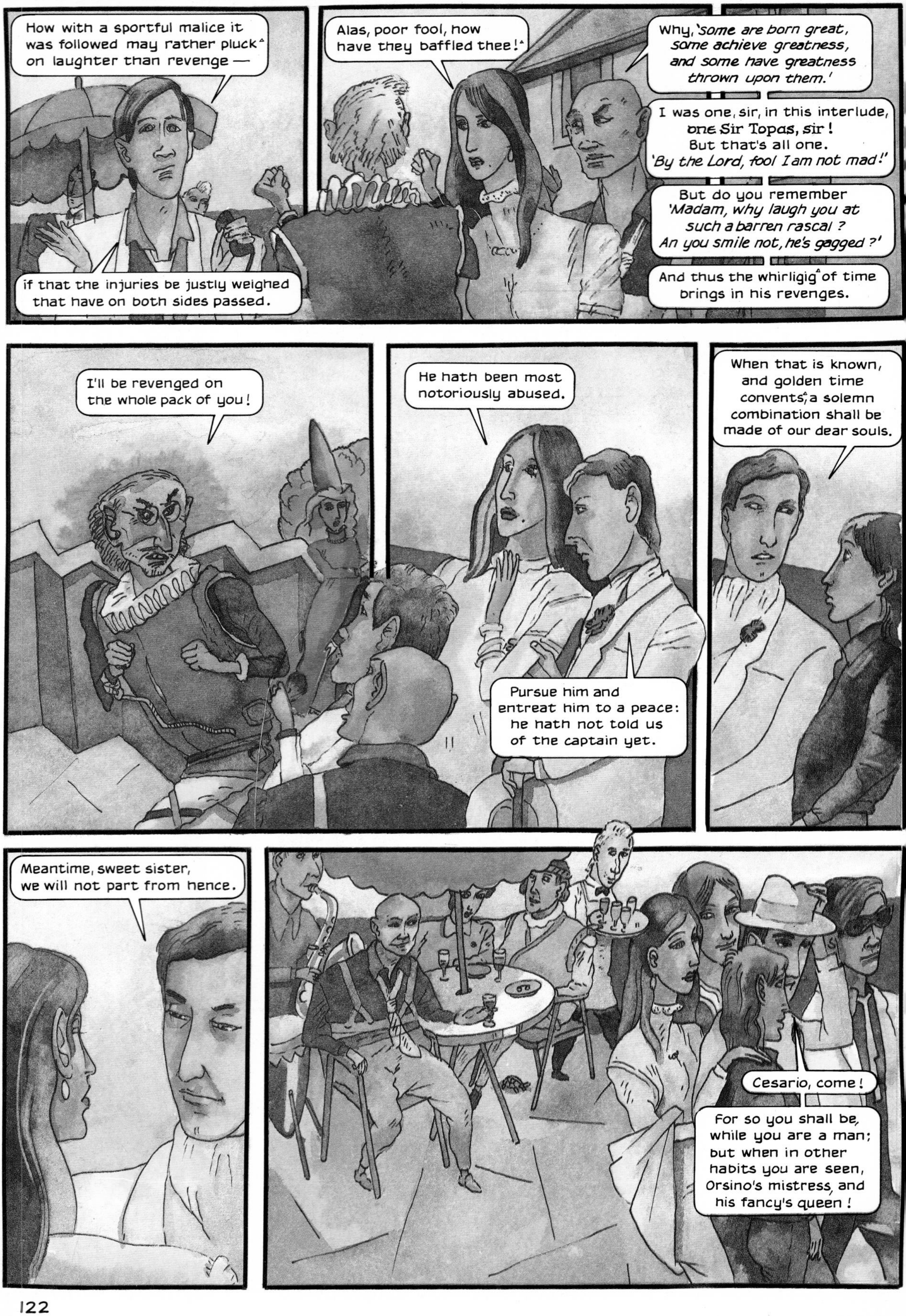

How with a sportful malice it was followed may rather pluck on laughter than revenge —
if that the injuries be justly weighed that have on both sides passed.
Alas, poor fool, how have they baffled thee!
Why, 'some are born great, some achieve greatness, and some have greatness thrown upon them.'
I was one, sir, in this interlude, one Sir Topas, sir! But that's all one. 'By the Lord, fool I am not mad!'
But do you remember 'Madam, why laugh you at such a barren rascal? An you smile not, he's gagged?'
And thus the whirligig of time brings in his revenges.
I'll be revenged on the whole pack of you!
He hath been most notoriously abused.
Pursue him and entreat him to a peace: he hath not told us of the captain yet.
When that is known, and golden time convents, a solemn combination shall be made of our dear souls.
Meantime, sweet sister, we will not part from hence.
Cesario, come!
For so you shall be, while you are a man; but when in other habits you are seen, Orsino's mistress, and his fancy's queen!

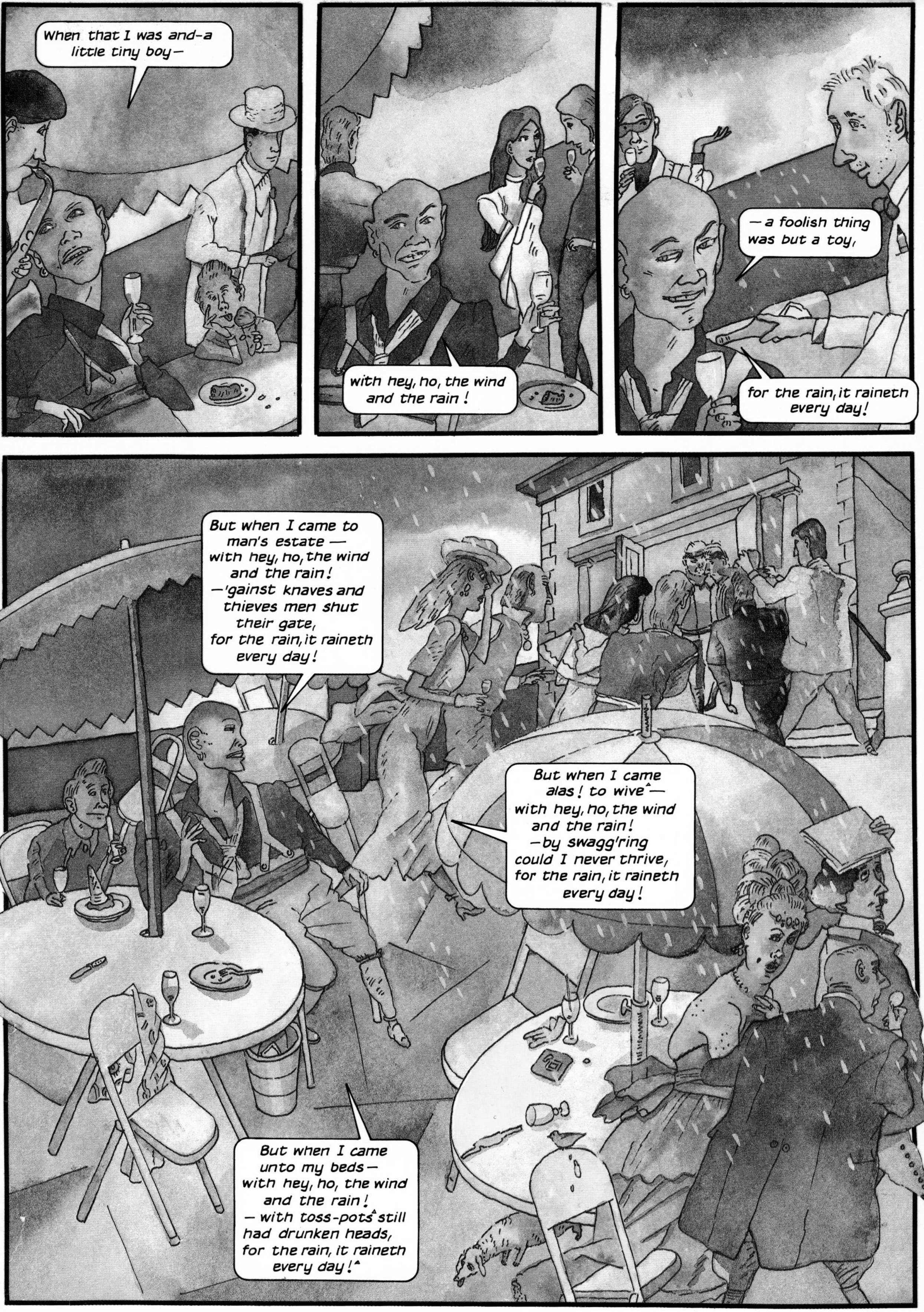
When that I was and-a little tiny boy—
with hey, ho, the wind and the rain!
—a foolish thing was but a toy,
for the rain, it raineth every day!
But when I came to man's estate — with hey, ho, the wind and the rain! —'gainst knaves and thieves men shut their gate, for the rain, it raineth every day!
But when I came alas! to wive— with hey, ho, the wind and the rain! —by swagg'ring could I never thrive, for the rain, it raineth every day!
But when I came unto my beds— with hey, ho, the wind and the rain! — with toss-pots still had drunken heads, for the rain, it raineth every day!

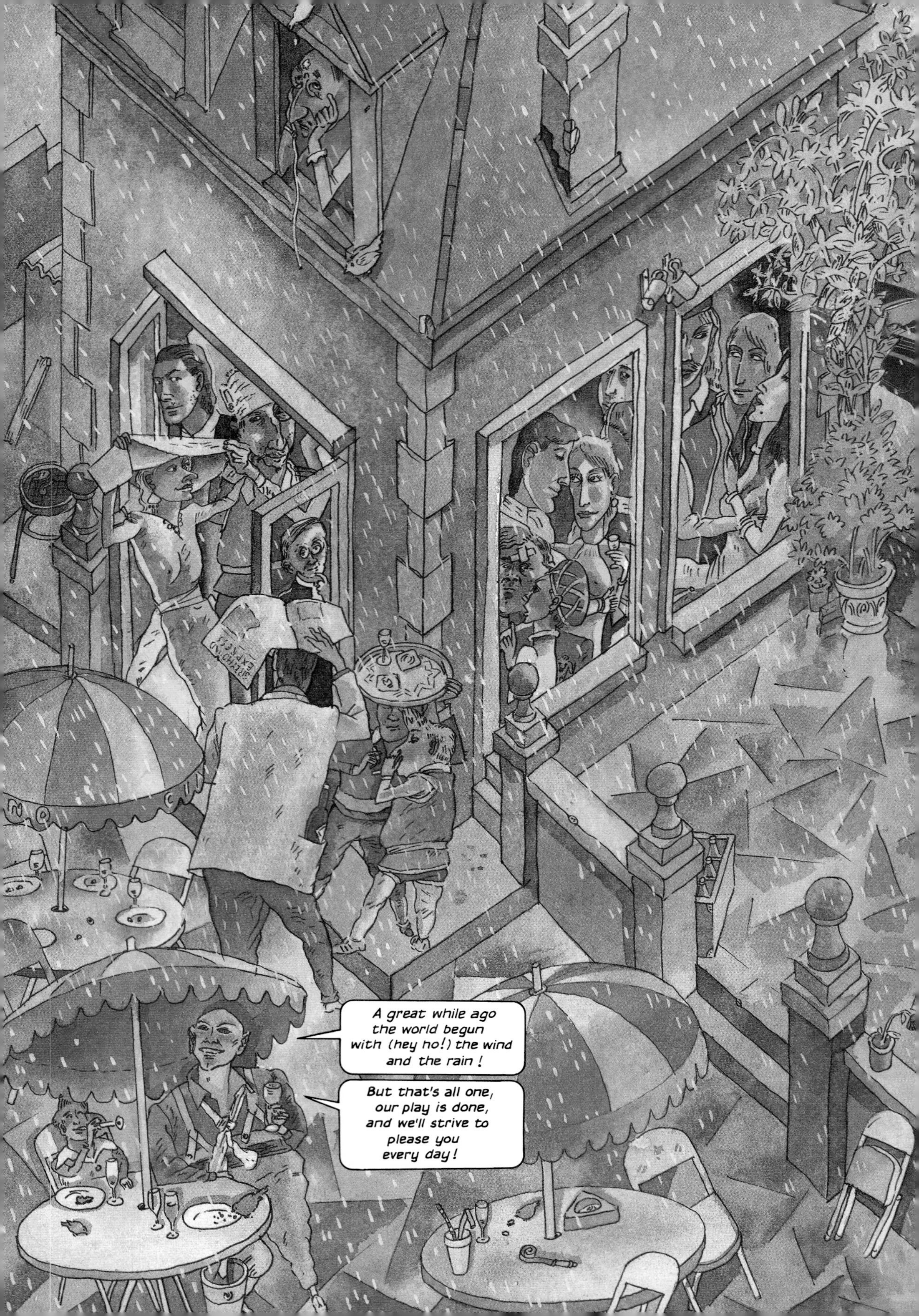
A great while ago the world begun with (hey ho!) the wind and the rain !
But that's all one, our play is done, and we'll strive to please you every day !

GLOSSARY
As shown in the text with a △

2
pitch – value

3
hart – stag
shaft – love's arrow
liver – passionate desires

4
Elysium – heaven

5
mine own escape . . . the like of him – my own escape
gives me hope that as you say, he's also escaped

7
let her except before-excepted – she's always put up
with it before

8
he'll have but a year – in a year he'll blow the lot
the viol de gamboys – a bass viol
natural – half-witted

9
a coistrel – a peasant
his brains turn o'the toe . . . top – he's as drunk as a
wobbling whipping top
Castiliano vulgo – put on a straight face

10
buttery bar – liquor shelf
it's dry – dried up, impotent
dry jest – stupid jest
barren – empty (of jests)

11
canary – sweet wine
in the tongues – in the study of languages
a huswife take thee between her legs and spin it off –
a. a housewife might use you as a distaff, (his hair
being the flax on it)
b. a whore give you VD so your hair falls out

12
kickshawses – antics (quelque chose)
an old man – an old hand
a galliard – a 5-step dance with a 'caper' before the fifth
cut a caper – do dance steps (capers were also used for
mutton sauce)
back trick – (a dance step, but the image implies he's
good in bed)
Mistress Mall – (a beautiful woman, fallen out of favour at
court)
a coranto – a fast dance
a sink-a-pace – (a dance step, but the image suggests
pissing in the sink)
formed under the star of a galliard – destined to dance
dun – brown
Taurus – (the 12 Zodiac signs were thought to govern
different parts of the body)

14
nuncio – ambassador
constellation – disposition
yet a barful strife! – what an obstacle course!

15
colours – enemies
a good lenten answer – an answer meagre enough for
Lent (a time of fasting)
let summer bear it out – it's not so bad being
unemployed in the summer
points – points (but also suspenders)
gaskins – wide trousers
if Sir Toby stopped drinking . . . Eve's flesh – if Sir Toby
stopped drinking so much he'd see you're as clever
and sexy a piece of womankind as any in Illyria

16
Quinapalus – (an imaginary philosopher)

17
let the botcher mend him – let the clothes-mender patch
him up
there is no true cuckold . . . – life's too short to lose your
good looks over old worries
misprision – misunderstanding
cucullus non facit monachum – there's more to a monk
than his habit (hood)
I wear not motley in my brain – I'm not such a fool as I
look

18
doth he not mend? – (Olivia means that Feste gets more
amusing; Malvolio interprets it as more foolish)
fox – back-stabber

19
zanies – stooges
birdbolts – arrows (i.e. mere banter)
Mercury – the god of cheating
endue thee with leasing – endow you with deception

20
pia mater – brain

21
above heat – above normal temperature
the crowner – the coroner
a sheriff's post – a wooden post outside the sheriff's
house, symbolising authority
a squash – an unripe pea pod (peascod)
a codling – an unripe apple
in standing water – (ie: as at the turn of the tide)

22
to con – to learn
comptible – sensitive

23
If I do not usurp myself – If I am not an imposter
usurp yourself – misuse your gifts
swabber – deck-washer
hull – float about
your giant (a pun on Maria's small size)

24

such a one I was this present – this is the real me

25

the nonpariel of beauty – unequalled in beauty
voices well divulged – well spoken of

26

cantons – songs
fee'd post – paid messenger

27

blazon – heraldic coat of arms (and therefore breeding)
mine eye too great . . . mind – I've fallen in love with just
  good looks

29

malignancy of my fate – evil influence
distemper – infect
my determinate voyage is mere . . . – I've no idea where
  I'll end up

31

put your lord into a desperate assurance – make it clear
  to your master he has no hope

32

pregnant enemy – Satan
proper false – good-looking
such we be – (i.e. weak)
fadge – turn out

33

diliculo surgere (i.e. Early to bed and early to rise, makes
  a man healthy, wealthy and wise.)

34

a catch – a song
Pigrogromitus . . . Vapians . . . Queubus – (scholarly
  sounding gobbledegook to impress)
leman – girlfriend
impeticos thy gratillity . . . bottle ale-houses – (more
  mock brilliance, but containing the ideas:
    a. I pocketed your tip
    b. who gives a toss for Malvolio?
    c. Olivia is a good sort
    d. we're real men who drink real ale, so to hell with it)
testril – sixpence

35

wise man's son – fool
contagious breath – bad breath
contagious – effective, moving
dulcet – sweet
welkin – sky
draw three souls out of one weaver – (weavers were
  noted for hot gospel singing)
dog at – good at
catch – grip

37

Cataian – Chinaman, promise-breaker
politians – shrewd operators
Peg-a-Ramsey – kill-joy
Tilly-Vally! – What nonsense!
natural – naturally (also, idiotic)

38

coziers – tinkers
Sneck up! – Hang you!
ginger – (used to spice ale)

39

gull him into a nayword – make a laughing-stock of him

40

cons state – learns etiquette
the best persuaded of himself – conceited
on a forgotten matter – when we can't remember which
  of us wrote it

41

Penthesilea – Queen of the Amazons
I am a foul way out – I'm up shit creek
call me cut – useless, castrated (i.e. 'no-balls')
burn some sack – mull sherry

42

antic – quaint
recollected terms – artificial phrase

43

favour – face

44

so wears she to him, so sways she . . . – so she grows
  naturally towards him, and he finds her power over
  him acceptable
hold the bent – stand the strain
bones – bone bobbins
it is silly sooth, and dallies with – it's the simple truth and
  dwells upon

45

cypress – cypress-wood coffin
my part of death, no one so true – I am the truest lover
  who ever died for love

46

opal – (gem symbolising inconstancy)

47

give place – go away
that mirace and queen of gems – (i.e. her beauty)
pranks – adorns
cloyment and revolt – sickness and revulsion

48

Patience on a monument (allegorical figure carved on a
  tomb)
our shows are more than will – we show out more than
  we really feel
bide no denay – endure no denial

50
metal of India – gold
contemplative – staring
close! – hide!

51
affect me – fancy me
jets – struts
advanced – puffed up
'Slight – God's light

52
the Lady of the Strachy (an aristocrat who married a
    commoner)
Jezebel – poseur
blows – swells
stone bow – catapult
branchèd – richly embroidered
demure travel of regard – cool look round

53
cars – carts (and horses)

54
gin – trap
spirit of humours – eccentricity
her very C's etc. – (C, U, T, spells 'cut': the slit through
    which a woman P's)
the impressure her Lucrece – (the image shows the
    Roman woman Lucretia, who stabbed herself to wipe
    out the dishonour of being raped)

55
numbers – verse-pattern
brock – badger, stinker
sway – rule
fustian – high-falutin'
dressed – served
the staniel checks at it – the kestrel turns in mid-flight to
    swoop at it
formal capacity – intelligence
Sowter will cry... – (Malvolio is compared to Sowter, a
    stupid hare-hound who follows cold scent – i.e. an old
    one – even though it's obviously the scent of a fox, not
    a hare, he follows an eccentric idea even though it will
    lead him to a wrong conclusion)
faults – breaks in the scent
suffers under probation – stands up to investigation

56
simulation – puzzle
crush – force
revolve – consider
cast thy humble slough – stop acting like a servant (as a
    snake casts its skin)
tang arguments of state – resound with socio-political
    wisdom and quotations
put thyself into the trick of singularity – adopt eccentric
    mannerisms (to distinguish yourself from the herd)
alter services – change roles
champain – open country

57
wash off gross acquaintance – get rid of common
    friendships
be point-device the very man – do exactly as she
    suggests
strange, stout – aloof, firm

58
Sophy – Shah of Persia
play my freedom at tray-trip – put my freedom on the
    throw of a dice
aqua-vitae – cheap liquor
midwife – (notorious for drunkenness)
Tatar – hell

59
tabor – drum

60
cheveril – soft leather
since bonds disgraced them – now that we can't take a
    man's word without putting it in writing

61
orb – the world
but the fool should be – if a fool were not
I think I saw your wisdom there – I can see you've had
    the same idea
an thou pass upon me – if you're going to start getting at
    me
commodity – consignment
I am almost sick ... – i.e. she's love-sick for Orsino)
I would play Lord Pandarus ... – if this coin were mated
    with another, I'd play the go-between to mate you with
    Olivia (as Pandarus did for Troilus and Cressida)
conster – announce
out of my welkin – beyond me

62
craves – demands
like the haggard – like a wild hawk, swoop at every
    opportunity
folly-fall'n – who try to be funny
the list – the point
prevented – anticipated

63
most pregnant and vouchsafèd – receptive
all ready – (i.e. to use myself)

64
lowly feigning – affected humility
give me leave – let me have my say
under your hard construction – under your adverse
    judgement
at the stake – (i.e. as in bear-baiting with dogs)
a cypress – thin gauze
a cypress ... hides my heart – gauze, not flesh covers
    my heart (therefore it's transparent how I feel)

65

a degree to – a stage of
not a grize – it doesn't get us any further
vulgar proof – simple fact of life

66

now I am your fool – (playing at double meanings, like a
    jester)
Love's night is noon – hidden love is now exposed
maugre – despite
do not extort . . . – don't let the fact that I'm courting you
    put you off responding to me
but rather reason . . . – but turn it round, and think how
    much better it is this way
deplore – report

67

'Slight! – God's light!
prove it legitimate – make good my case

68

balked – bungled
as lief be – as soon be
a Brownist – (follower of Browne, a church reformer)

69

curst – fierce
with the licence of ink – write more freely than you would
    speak
bed of Ware – (a famous oak bedstead, 10′ 9″ square)
gall – (oak-galls used in ink making, and 'bitterness')
goose-pen (goose-quill, and 'foolish pen')
cubiculo – cubby-hole

70

manikin to you – puppet for you
two thousand – (i.e. the money Toby has milked from
    Andrew)
hale – drag
the youngest wren of nine – (smallest in a nest of small
    birds; another pun on Maria's size)
the spleen – a good laugh
a pedant – an old-fashioned schoolmaster
the new map – (i.e. covered with new detail)

71

jealousy – concern

72

uncurrent – worthless
worth – wealth

73

for traffic's sake – merely for the sake of good relations
lapsèd – caught
the Elephant – (an inn of that name)
bespeak our diet – order our meals
your store . . . – you don't have enough to buy souvenirs

74

what bestow of him? – what shall I give him?

75

sweet Roman hand – pretty italic handwriting (and a
    reference to Lucrece)
yes, nightingales answer daws! – yes, I'm answering your
    call!

77

come near me now – do you now understand me?
sir of note – well-known gentleman
limed – caught
'fellow' – (he takes her to mean 'equal' or 'mate')
drawn in little – brought together

78

carry his water . . . – take his urine to be diagnosed (to
    see what's wrong with him)

79

bawcock – fine fellow (beau coq)
biddy – chicken
gravity – a dignity
cherry-pit – (children's game of throwing cherry stones
    into a hole)
foul collier – dirty coalman (i.e. one who gets as black as
    the devil)
his very genius – he's fallen for it totally
lest the device . . . – in case we're found out
bring the device to the bar – reveal all

80

the blow of the law – on the right side of the law

81

bum-baily – bailiff
let me alone for – I'm good at
clodpole – blockhead
cockatrices – (fabulous monsters that killed just by
    looking at their victim)

82

unchary – lavishly
that honour saved may upon asking give – that may be
    given on demand without loss of chastity

83

dismount thy tuck – draw your sword
yare – quick
unhatched rapier – ceremonial sword
on carpet consideration – at court
hob-nob! – death or glory!

84

conduct – safe conduct
computent – sufficient (for a challenge)
undertake that – (i.e. a duel)
meddle – get involved
to a mortal arbitrement – to the death

85

firago – warrior
a pass – a bout
inevitable – inescapable
the Sophy – the Shah of Persia
make the motion – put it to him
is as horribly conceited – has as terrifying a thought

86
for the supportance of his vow – so that his honour can
    be satisfied
duello – rules of duelling

87
an undertaker – a second

88
I'll make division of my present – share what I have on
    me

89
we'll whisper o'er . . . – we'll exchange a few flowery
    sentences ourselves

90
I my brother know . . . – I've kept alive my brother's image
    in my own appearance
'Slid – God's eyelid
An I do not – if I don't (cuff him)

91
well held out – well kept up (their wit match)
lubber – great lout
a cockney – a wet
ungird thy strangeness – stop pretending you don't know
    me
purchase – (i.e. hire purchase)

92
an action of battery – assault case
you are well fleshed – you've had your fight

93
malapert – insolent

94
Rudesby – ruffian
extent against – violation of
started one poor heart of mine in thee – he's made my
    heart miss a beat by making yours skip
Lethe – the river of forgetfulness

96
bonus dies – good day (bad latin)
the old hermit of Prague . . . – (scholarly sounding
    references, cobbled together)

97
barricadoes – (ramparts made of barrels)
clerestories – windows
lustrous – translucent
Egyptians in their fog – plague of darkness

98
Pythagoras – the Greek philospopher
for all waters – versatile

99
perdie – certainly

100
how fell you besides your five wits? – what's made you
    lose your senses
propertied me – treated me like a senseless object

101
shent – rebuked
the old Vice – (a character in morality plays who made
    sudden appearances, and pared his nails with a
    wooden lath or dagger)

102
credit – report
disputes well – agrees
deceivable – deceptive

103
chantry by – chapel nearby
whiles – until
what time – at which time

105
and make – and thus make
as kisses – (because they bring opposites together: four
    lips together, two mouths)
double-dealing – duplicity
primo, secundo, tertio – first, second, third
the triplex is a good time . . . – triple-time is good for
    dancing

106
Vulcan – (blacksmith of the gods)
baubling – insignificant
unprizeable – not worth capturing
scathful – damaging
bottom – ship
that very envy . . . – that even his victims admired him
fraught – cargo
brabble – brawl
distraction – madness

107
wrack – casualty
face me out . . . – deny that he knew me

109
fat and fulsome – gross and distasteful
even what it please my lord . . . – do what you like
Egyptian thief – (who was prepared to kill his lover rather
    than die alone)
screws me – wrenches

111
strange thy propriety – hide the fact that you're my
    husband
grizzle on thy case – grey in you hair

112
coxcomb – head
'Od's lifelings – God's little life

113
halting – limping
othergates – in another way
passy measures pavin – piss-artist

115
nor can there be that deity in my nature – I'm not a god,
    to be in two places at once
in that dimension . . . – still in my own body

116
lets to make us – stops us being
weeds – clothes
to her bias drew . . . – made everything happen as it
    should

117
the glass seems true – what seems to be illusions
    appears to be true
orbed continent – (the sun)
in durance – under arrest
enlarge him – release him
holds Belzebub at the stave's end – keeps the devil at
    bay

118
skills not much – matters little
allow vox – let me do the right voice

119
proper cost – own expense
quits you – releases you from his service

120
the lighter people – the light-weights

121
geck and gull – fool
parts we had conceived . . . – acts we held against him
importance – insistance

122
pluck on – call for
baffled thee – made a mockery of you
whirligig – spinning top
convents – calls us together

123
wive – marry
toss-pots – drunks
When that I was and-a little tiny boy . . . etc –
    When I was a child, I got away with murder, but when I
    grew up I was really up against it: I couldn't get one
    over on my wife, and all my floozies were drunks